Praise for *A History*

T0028383

"[Luke] Dumas's layered and atmospheric writing shines . . . engrossing."
—*The New York Times Book Review*

"[A] stellar debut, a complex whydunit . . . Admirers of Andrew Pyper's *The Demonologist* will be riveted."
—*Publishers Weekly* (starred review)

"Part thriller, part domestic fiction, and part horror, *A History of Fear* lives on the edges of genres as its protagonist also exists on the edges."
—*Bookreporter*

"Here are eight new horror novels to make you shiver with something other than cold this December!"
—Book Riot

"Psychological and possible supernatural elements mix in this thrilling horror novel about a murderer in Scotland who says the Devil made him do it, kills himself, and then leaves a manuscript telling his story. A smart, involving, and intriguingly enigmatic first novel getting some serious critical praise."
—*Locus* "New & Notable Books"

"*A History of Fear* is a chilling read for a dark winter night. It will leave the reader with questions and doubt, and will get under one's skin because of it."
—*The Library Ladies*

"A methodical story about evil—its mystery and its toll—takes its murderous narrator past the brink of sanity. . . . Lean and propulsive, this dissection of evil marches forward with a deadly logic and sleight of hand, with occasional gaps filled in by an enterprising journalist and a Scottish information commissioner. . . . It's a patient pursuit and a patient book, one that builds without the reader quite realizing it. It blurs the line between mental illness and something less definable, more supernatural, and sinister. A muscular, enigmatic, and devilishly smart read."

—*Kirkus Reviews* (starred review)

"A delicious walk along the razor's edge between the imagined and the supernatural, *A History of Fear* is candy for readers who like their thrills real and their horror a worrying whisper in their head."

—Andrew Pyper, author of
The Demonologist and *The Residence*

"*A History of Fear* presents itself as a disquieting cache of nightmares, a nested doll narrative that reads like a found-footage *Falling Angel* by William Hjortsberg. Readers, beware: this novel is not safe and will have you questioning what's real for many sleepless nights to come."

—Clay McLeod Chapman, author of
The Remaking, Whisper Down the Lane, and *Ghost Eaters*

"*A History of Fear* succeeds on so many levels—as a haunting tale of the supernatural, a harrowing story of suspense, and a stark warning about the power of our inner demons. I consumed this book breathlessly, and every time I think of its jaw-dropping ending, I feel a chill all over again."

—Megan Collins, author of
The Family Plot and *Thicker Than Water*

"*A History of Fear* is a disorienting, creepy, paranoia-inducing reimagining of the Devil-made-me-do-it tale. A clever, twisty novel, imbued with emotional and psychological insight. Luke's vision of Old Scratch left me thrilled and looking over my shoulder."

—Paul Tremblay, author of
The Cabin at the End of the World
and *The Pallbearers Club*

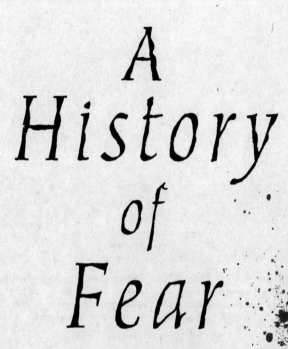

A
History
of
Fear

~ A NOVEL ~

LUKE DUMAS

ATRIA PAPERBACK

New York · London · Toronto · Sydney · New Delhi

ATRIA
PAPERBACK

An Imprint of Simon & Schuster, Inc.
1230 Avenue of the Americas
New York, NY 10020

First Atria paperback edition October 2023

ATRIA PAPERBACK and colophon are trademarks of Simon & Schuster, Inc.

For information about special discounts for bulk purchases, please contact Simon & Schuster Special Sales at 1-866-506-1949 or business@simonandschuster.com.

The Simon & Schuster Speakers Bureau can bring authors to your live event. For more information or to book an event, contact the Simon & Schuster Speakers Bureau at 1-866-248-3049 or visit our website at www.simonspeakers.com.

Interior design by Dana Sloan

Manufactured in the United States of America

1 3 5 7 9 10 8 6 4 2

Library of Congress Cataloging-in-Publication Data has been applied for.

ISBN 978-1-9821-9902-9
ISBN 978-1-9821-9903-6 (pbk)
ISBN 978-1-9821-9904-3 (ebook)

For Amy

Midway upon the journey of our life
I found myself within a forest dark,
For the straightforward pathway had been lost.

Ah me! how hard a thing it is to say
What was this forest savage, rough, and stern,
Which in the very thought renews the fear.

—*DANTE ALIGHIERI*,
　　TRANSLATION BY HENRY WADSWORTH LONGFELLOW

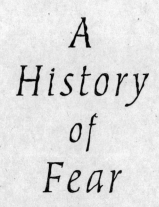

A
History
of
Fear

Editor's Foreword

The Devil is in Scotland.

Who among us did not experience a prickle of fear the first time they read those now infamous words? When Grayson Matthew Hale stepped foot on Scottish soil, few could have predicted that this ordinary young man, without a speck on his moral or criminal records, would soon be known throughout the country by a more sinister name, a name synonymous with cold-blooded murder and the dark side of American zealotry: the Devil's Advocate.

If you are reading this, you're likely already familiar with Hale and his precipitous rise to fame. You'll know that he made headlines in 2017, when, as a postgraduate student at the University of Edinburgh, he confessed to the slaughter of fellow student Liam Stewart and claimed the Devil himself as his master and accomplice. You'll know too that news of Hale's confession exploded across the nation with headlines such as KILLER CONFESSES, SAYS DEVIL MADE HIM DO IT, and AMERICAN KILLER CLAIMS SATAN IN SCOTLAND, propelling its subject to instant notoriety.

One might think that, as the journalist who broke the story of Hale's confession, I would be numb to the terror of those words by now, but their effect on me has scarcely dulled since they first appeared in my inbox.

I still remember that night. It was the second of March 2017 and I was burning the midnight oil at the offices of *The Scotsman*, where I freelanced as a news reporter focusing on petty crime in the capital. A major deadline loomed, and my flat was playing youth hostel to my boyfriend's rather exuberant kid sister and her friend. Seeking a bit of silence in which to work, I had set up camp at the desk of a stranger, liberally decorated with Disney figurines and photos of the owner's crusty-eyed bichon frise. Fueled by adrenaline and lashings of instant coffee, I had just crossed over into the wee small hours when came the unmistakable sound of a new email hitting my inbox.

I was used to getting messages at all hours, but this one made me pause. The address was anonymous, the subject brief and unsettling: *THE DEVIL'S BACK.*

Suspecting it was spam, I almost deleted the message unopened, but something, perhaps mere wanton curiosity, compelled me to explore further. Clicking through, I was met with a brief note from an unnamed writer informing me that an Edinburgh man named Grayson Hale had been charged with murder. I knew this name. Some months before, Hale had been trumpeted as a key suspect in the disappearance of Liam Stewart, whose case had garnered its own heap of press attention. This information, if it could be corroborated, was a lucky break.

But as I was about to find out, the real story lay in the untitled attachment: a full transcript, mysteriously acquired, of Hale's outlandish admission to police, which, in addition to sending a jolt of cold dread through my body, was about to change the course of my life.

Abandoning my existing project, I worked through the night to verify the document was authentic and scrape together five hundred words for the morning edition and its online equivalent. Little did I know, in the course of a single article I would become the author of the most-shared Scottish news story of the decade and inadvertently coin the moniker by which Hale is better known today.

Over the following weeks, I went on to appear on half a dozen news programs and podcasts, solidifying my reputation as the foremost expert on the crimes of Grayson Hale. Forced to enact a charade of journalistic neutrality when in reality the mere mention of Hale's name set my insides wriggling like a cavity of worms. It was not until I was assigned to report on his trial, however, that my fear reached a fever pitch.

Even more than the sensational nature of his claims, what disturbed me most of all was that those claims did not seem to tally with the person who spouted them from the witness box. Where I had expected a raving lunatic, Hale presented as exceedingly normal—a benign and intelligent if introverted young man, who fully acknowledged the absurdity of his tale and maneuvered the prosecution's mocking inquisition with such agility that anyone present would have been hard-pressed to doubt him. His was a story that became more unbelievable at every turn yet somehow more undeniable—a story not just of devils and fiends, but of the darkness that nests within the human soul like a seed awaiting rain.

For more than a year I believed that story had ended in the courtroom, when the jury delivered a guilty verdict condemning Hale to a life behind bars. It seemed a foregone conclusion that he would drift quietly into the obscurity of his sentence, his only legacy a harrowing and unresolved narrative that, like the legends of Thomas Weir and the Loch Ness Monster, promised to linger in the annals of Scottish history for years to come.

But as you are no doubt aware, he did no such thing. Just nineteen months into his sentence, Hale commanded the headlines once again when his body was discovered in a high-security cell at Her Majesty's Prison Edinburgh suspended by a bedsheet cinched around his neck. His government-issue jumpsuit was slashed and torn, the flesh beneath crisscrossed with bizarre lacerations. One prison officer reportedly described the wounds as being like "claw marks from a small, three-fingered animal."

No suicide note was found. There were no known witnesses to the event. According to a spokesperson for the Scottish Prison Service (SPS), Hale had been living in segregation, a.k.a. solitary confinement, for his own protection and the protection of others.

After a thorough investigation, the Prisons and Probation Ombudsman released a report declaring Hale's death self-inflicted. The marks on his person, which received only a few words' mention, were dismissed as "minor" and incidental to the hanging, which the autopsy recorded as the official cause of death. An inquiry into the possible cause of the wounds was inconclusive, although their shape and position reportedly made self-harm unlikely.

Naturally, speculation raged, each explanation more disturbing than the last. Some believed Hale had been murdered by a fellow prisoner, or even an officer, perhaps one with ties to the Stewart family. Others maintained a more ominous theory: that the marks on his body substantiated his well-publicized accounts of having been pursued by demonic spirits. What should have been a definitive end to his story left the nation—myself included—with still more questions about the Devil's Advocate and the demons, real or metaphorical, with which he had grappled in his final moments.

Like many, I didn't know what to think. Had Hale hanged himself as the report concluded? Was his suicide just the last in a long line of violent and psychotic acts? Or—there was no other way to put it—was it possible he had been telling the truth?

Soon the uncertainty became too much to bear. I found myself struggling to eat properly, or sleep. I lay awake at night, haunted by the questions I could not answer, questions that wore down my body to skin and bone and shredded my nerves to a throbbing pulp. My work suffered, my relationship on the rocks. Before long it became a matter of necessity: I *needed* to know what had happened in that cell. Needed to know the truth about the Devil's Advocate once and for all.

To my surprise, it seemed I just might.

Within days of the announcement of Hale's death, whispers began to circulate around the newsroom that prison officers had discovered, in his cell, a manuscript of more than two hundred A4 pages written in the deceased's own hand, presented on the desk like a last will and testament. Reportedly bearing the title *The Memoirs and Confessions of Grayson Hale*, the document was said to describe, in unflinching detail, Hale's account of his diabolical liaison and the months leading up to the murder of Liam Stewart. I privately rejoiced; this was it! At last we would hear it directly from him, the story he had been trying to tell us all along. At the very least we might catch a glimpse into the twisted mind of the country's most notorious killer and finally lay our fears of the Devil to rest.

However, despite the public thirst for answers, the SPS refused to release Hale's manuscript, stating there was no precedent for the publication of the private journals of prisoners living or deceased. They even denied my request for facsimiles of the document, citing section 34 of the Scottish Freedom of Information Act 2002, which exempts public authorities from having to divulge information related to the investigation of a person's death. Not even a media-fueled campaign of public outrage could dislodge the SPS from their pedestal of bureaucratic obstinance.

Still, I remained adamant that the nation had a right to answers— and I would not rest, literally or figuratively, until we had them. Thus, with the help of my friend Iain Crawford, a professor at Strathclyde Law School, I lodged an appeal with Scottish information commissioner Marjory Brown in May of last year. Upon reading her decision, my heart sank. Despite my best efforts, Commissioner Brown upheld the SPS's judgment, reiterating the exemption under section 34. I nearly tossed the letter aside, tears of frustration stinging my eyes.

But as with the mysterious email that had started it all, something told me to read on.

> *The public interest must nevertheless be taken into account. As the requestor clearly notes in her letter of appeal, Hale's manuscript represents far more than information held by a public authority. It rep-*

resents a document of extraordinary cultural significance, whose study, contemplation, and publication—as the requestor herself proposes to undertake, and for which she has demonstrated she is uniquely qualified—stands to contribute significantly to the nation's cultural and historical legacy. Therefore, I request that the SPS make available to the requestor, for the purposes of study, annotation, and dissemination, the manuscript of Grayson Hale and all related attachments.

And so, with the blessing of Commissioner Brown and the family of Liam Stewart, whom the sales of this book will benefit, I am pleased to present in the following pages Grayson Hale's full and unexpurgated manuscript—a document of a most singular nature.

You may be surprised to find, as I was, that much like its author, the manuscript confounds expectations and evades easy classification. *What is this strange memoir?* you might ask. An imaginative fiction of diablerie and death? An astonishing first-person account of one man's descent into madness? Or is it something even more ill-boding: a warning sent straight from the depths of hell?

In an attempt to answer this question, I've spent the last several months conducting extensive research into the man behind the manuscript, from his dark and complicated history to the events leading up to his arrest, unearthing much that Hale himself seemed keen to keep buried. To this end, I present this text with a series of supporting additions, including courtroom testimony, text messages, and interviews with Hale's relatives and acquaintances. Whether these inclusions go far enough toward revealing the true nature of Hale's memoir—well, I shall let you be the judge.

Daniella Barclay, MSc, NQJ
Edinburgh
13 March 2020

THE MEMOIRS AND CONFESSIONS OF GRAYSON HALE

BY HIMSELF

*With Intermittent Notes, and
Other Evidence, by the Editor*

BLACK WATCH BOOKS
Edinburgh | Glasgow

One

THE DEVIL FOUND me at the dodgy end of Leith Walk, having lured me by use of guile and the pretense of employment, the thing I needed more than anything.

It was night and a hatefully cold one for September. The wind ripped at my body like an ocean breeze turned inside out, its softness frozen over into a shrill and ragged edge. I shoved my fists in my pockets and pushed on toward my destination. I didn't know what it looked like, the pub where he had asked to meet. Only its name. My eyes flicked up to check the signage over every passing doorway. To my left, the wide four-lane street buzzed with a steady stream of cars and double-decker buses. The sidewalk was busy with carousers and tourists. A gaggle of teenagers in minidresses brayed in thick accents, unfazed by the chill on their bare skin.

I weaved between them, desperate to find the place—eager to escape more than just the night air. For at that moment I found myself gripped by a subtle anxiety, which quickened my pace to a hurried clip, and rained sweat down my forehead despite the cold: I was being followed.

It had begun a few blocks back, when the stranger emerged from a building on the opposite side of the street. I couldn't make him out in the darkness, but his eyes seemed to track me as I passed. Then, with a cold twist of discomfort as I glanced across my shoulder, I saw him crossing the road.

Surely it was a coincidence. Probably on his way to meet a friend for drinks, or to a movie at the Omni Centre. So then why did he follow in my wake, moving in and out of sight in the crowd as if trying not to be seen, closing the gap between us, then dropping back when I started to notice?

A feeling of panic burgeoned within me. I couldn't stop thinking about the man. All but forgetting my potential employer, I continued to throw casual glances over my shoulder, as if merely taking in my unusual surroundings.

I had been living in Scotland not quite two weeks and still couldn't wrap my head around its streets: the tiny cars, the flagstone sidewalks, the buildings joined in an endless repeat of weather-beaten sandstone, differentiated only by the variously colored shop fronts that made up the ground floor. A laundromat framed in royal blue. The gleaming black of an Indian restaurant. A bookshop draped in a hoary skin of hunter green. They blurred past me as I hurried ever faster through the night, panting under my breath, certain both that I was out of my mind and that my pursuer was gaining on me.

Then quickly the character of the street began to change. Where Leith Walk met Picardy Place, the bars blazed out pink and purple light, assaulting the street with throbbing music. Garrulous men stood under snapping rainbow flags, smoking and laughing and touching each other's arms. With my head down I barreled on, twisting my body so as not to touch or be touched. Not out of any sense of prejudice, you understand. I'd lived my whole life in California, after all. My aversion was simply to being touched, by anyone.

"Darlin', you look amazin'!" said a man swaggering toward me, his arms flung wide, a wedge of hairy chest exposed to the night. I leapt aside to avoid him, relieved when he threw his arms around someone else entirely.

As I moved past them I saw something that brought me up short: the sight of a man who was the mirror image of myself.

Indeed, for a moment I believed I was staring at my reflection in a pane of glass. A reflection whose movements seemed to operate independently from my own. It couldn't have been a reflection, then, but an identical stranger, for he resembled me in every way. My neglectful physique. My reluctant suntan. My ragtag outfit of hoodies heaped over sweaters and tees, because I still didn't own a decent coat. There was my double, slouched against the side of a club, dragging on a cigarette. I was unable to move, my mind reverberating with unintelligible sound, like a cavern in which a dozen people had shouted at once. His lips parted; smoke billowed and ran away on the wind.

The me who was smoking locked eyes with the me who was staring, and grinned.

Then someone crossed between us and, as my double passed back into view, he was a different person altogether. A person whose appearance was so dissimilar to my own that only a powerful delusion could have been responsible for such a mistake.

The stranger was taller by several inches. His clothes were black from head to toe. His dark hair gleamed violet in the radiance of the club. He was older than me, approaching thirty, yet there was a boyish quality about him. His lips set in a resting smirk. His eyes hooded and lingering.

"All right there?" His voice was low, shot through with a suggestion of amusement; I realized I was staring.

"Sorry, I—"

"Nae bother, mate. Look all ye like."

Mortified, I headed off, my eyes on the sidewalk.

The stranger called after me. "Grayson, is it?"

I twisted my head around. A glint of metal lettering over the entrance of the club caught my eye. But it couldn't be: SILVER STAG. The very place I was looking for.

"You're D.B.?"

A plume of smoke curled out of his open mouth.

"No' what you expected?"

Words evaded me. I couldn't easily say what I'd anticipated of my potential employer, but not this.

"We're the same, you and me." He dropped the butt of his cigarette and stepped on it.

I couldn't bring myself to ask what he meant.

"No' from here."

"O-oh?"

"S' just the accent. I tend to pick them up."

Now he mentioned it, I could detect the impurities in his brogue: plunging *u*'s that suggested time in the north of England, and something American, too, in his long *a*'s.

"So the job," I insisted.

He nodded, conceding. "I have a book that needs writing."

"A book? You mean, like a ghostwriter?"

This came as a welcome surprise. The online ad had been vague. *WRITING HELP NEEDED. Seeking a competent writer for part-time assistance. Postgrad in English lit/religious studies highly preferred.* I'd figured it was a tutoring gig. But writing a book . . . that had a ring to it. A good addition to the résumé. The kind of work my father would have done, if he'd had the chance. "What sort of—?"

"Come have a drink and I'll tell ye."

He motioned toward the entrance of the club. I spied the dance floor beyond, with its slicing purple light and so many bodies in motion. Most of them male, not that it mattered. The heat of the place poured out onto the sidewalk, inviting me in. Perhaps one drink.

But as D.B. held my gaze, something changed in his expression, or maybe it was my perception that changed. Like my eyes had finally adjusted to the dark and saw clearly what before had been cloaked in shadow. A shiver ran through me—not the kind that rattles the chest and shoulders but that emanates from deeper down, rumbling out of one's core. A shiver that had nothing at all to do with the climate.

I couldn't say what exactly, but there was something not right about this man.

"Sorry. I just remembered I—"

Someone pushed past me, shunting me forward. A random coincidence with the character of a threat, like whoever had pushed me was in league with the stranger. Like the whole street was conspiring to get me inside.

"Well?"

My feet were already working underneath me, carrying me backward. "I—I have to go."

Turning, I fled. A frightened animal bolting away from a threatening noise.

An effeminate voice jeered as I jostled through a crowd of pedestrians. "Well excuse me, Your Highness."

Keep going, just get away, I thought.

My would-be employer called after me. "Another time."

I pretended not to hear, pressing on at speed. Finding myself fleeing an unknown danger reminded me of the stranger from before, the one who had been following me. In the weirdness of meeting D.B., I'd completely forgotten him. Where had he gone? Was he following me now? Looking around, I ascertained my pursuer had gone. But something told me I had not seen the last of him.

Editor's Note
Exhibit A

Among the first of Hale's friends and acquaintances whom I interviewed as part of my investigation was Oliver "Ollie" Fillmore, Hale's Edinburgh flatmate from September 2016 to February 2017. We met at a swanky rum bar in Soho, London. He arrived nearly thirty minutes late, looking just as he had at Hale's trial: not tall but handsome and well-built, his designer clothes mismatched and wrinkled, as if hastily selected from a pile on the floor. His mop of light brown hair fell unwashed around his shoulders. He ran his hands through it as he dropped into the chair opposite me, drawing attention to the trace of a scar around his left eye. Here I present an excerpt of our interview, recorded 18 July 2019.

BARCLAY: Grayson writes in the manuscript about the night he went to Leith Walk, the night he claims to have met the Devil—

FILLMORE: Oh my god. That night was, like, the most horrific experience of my life, not even joking.

BARCLAY: You remember it?

FILLMORE: I'll literally never forget. I was having a drink at Teviot, right, and I had my phone in one hand, glass in the other. I go to take a sip and completely miss my mouth and literally spill cider all down my trousers. It looked like I'd actually pissed my pants. I had to walk all the way across Bristo Square with this huge wet stain down my leg to meet my Uber. I literally thought I was going to die of embarrassment.

BARCLAY: I'm confused. I thought you meant something happened with Grayson.

FILLMORE: Chill out, I was getting there.

BARCLAY: Oh—sorry.

FILLMORE: So I go back to the flat, and as soon as I get there I grab my iPad and FaceTime my sister—Victoria, she's a barrister in London. I was like, "Vic, you will not *believe* what just happened to me," and I told her what happened. She literally couldn't breathe, she was laughing so hard. Then Grayson comes in, and I'm like, *Here we go*, expecting him to be all hacked off—it always got his back up when I FaceTimed my family in the sitting room. But he was always hacked off about something, to be honest. One dish in the sink and he'd make some sarky comment and then literally storm around the flat like a black cloud for an hour. I used to call him Storm Grayson. That used to wind him up so bad.

BARCLAY: So you weren't good friends, then.

FILLMORE: He was literally a nightmare.

BARCLAY: How did you end up living together?

FILLMORE: Met online. I'd just transferred to Edinburgh from LSE for my third year. Pretty glad to be out of there, to be honest. Faculty were arseholes. I was by far the cleverest person in my year, but I didn't give a toss about excelling academically. I think my lecturers were intimidated by me, actually. Luckily, one of my father's best friends was a vice principal at Edinburgh. They thought I'd be a better fit there.

BARCLAY: He's an MP, isn't he, your father? Kensington and Chelsea, I believe?

FILLMORE: I don't get any special treatment because of it. Probably the opposite—everyone hates MPs, especially the Tory ones.

BARCLAY: Right.

FILLMORE: He doesn't know I'm sitting this interview. He thinks I've gone to see the polo. He ought to know I prefer cricket.

BARCLAY: So you transferred to Edinburgh . . .

FILLMORE: Father didn't want me living in halls, so he bought this flat—Victorian tenement, two-bed, nothing special, really. He said I needed to get a flatmate, a postgrad. Probably wanted someone older to keep an eye on me. So I posted on the uni student housing forum. Seeking laid-back guy flatmate. Straight, obviously. Grayson got in touch, and he seemed to fit the bill.

BARCLAY: I want to go back to that night. You said he came back from Leith Walk and he was hacked off?

FILLMORE: I expected him to be, but he seemed more nervous than any-thing. He came in all out of breath, and sweating, like he'd been running. I finished with my sister and found him standing at the window, looking out. When I asked why he was breathing like that, he jumped about a foot in the air. It was fucking hilarious. Said he'd just been to Leith Walk to meet some guy about a job. "A rim job, I'll bet," I said. He got all pissy and stormed off. "Oh *god*," I said. "Bundle up, everyone, Storm Grayson's rolling into town." It was literally the funniest thing I've ever seen.

BARCLAY: Did he say anything about the person he'd met on Leith Walk?

FILLMORE: Can't remember. But when I went to draw the curtains, I saw there was someone on the street down below. A man.

BARCLAY: What man?

FILLMORE: Dunno. Couldn't really see him. But he was staring up at the flat.

Two

THAT NIGHT, I dreamt my hands were on fire.

At first only a little—a small flame flickering at the center of my palm. It didn't hurt, but the surprise of it made me cry out. Instinctively I tried to brush it off, but doing so only caused my other hand to catch. Within seconds both hands were engulfed and there was nothing I could do to extinguish them. A pail of water appeared on the floor by my bed, but even after I plunged my hands in they continued to flame. I tried using my bedclothes to smother them but only set my bed alight.

The blaze traveled from the mattress, up the walls, and spread to the ceiling. From my room to the next, then flat to flat, floor to floor. The whole building crumbled around me as it went up in smoke. The fire spread out across the city, razing homes big and small, churches, schools, destroying lives. Continued on up to the clouds in the sky and the moon and the stars, until the world was nothing but a raging inferno. It swallowed me and flourished, for my body seemed to power it, to nourish it. The destruction, the terror: I held it in the palm of my hands.

And I liked it.

~

I woke with a start.

It was early, the first burst of daylight starting to spill across the bare white walls and heavy wooden furniture of my bedroom. Though I lay back, there was no hope of returning to sleep. I couldn't shake the familiar feeling of the dream. It swirled around my subconscious like an eel in dark water. I hadn't had that dream in years.

The events of the previous night came later, snapping back on my memory like a rubber band pulled taut. My faceless pursuer. My double. The man I knew only as D.B. I lay gazing up at the bedroom ceiling, not entirely sure of what, or who, had been real.

In the bathroom, I pulled off my shirt and regarded my body with the kind of numbness that follows years of daily shame. The soft, downy chest. The emasculating curve of my sides. The scars that stood out against the whiteness of my upper arm like tattoos. Three vertical lines, the middle one slightly longer than the others, the flesh pinkish red and rippled where the burns had healed over. Having almost managed to forget they were there, I perceived them with a tingle of discomfort, then slunk away from my reflection.

~

The main university library was a horizontal warehouse of sadness sandwiched between the verdure of George Square Gardens and the sprawling lawns of the Meadows. It contained more than two million books and some of the most important literary documents in Europe, yet a passerby might mistake it for a call center servicing a midsize life insurance outfit. Inside, the building was just as dull and gray, each floor a vast maze of metal bookcases, dust-colored carpet, and fluorescent lighting arranged around a central cluster of partitioned desks.

I had the third floor to myself that night. In a few weeks' time this place would be an ant farm, but in the preterm quiet it was ghostly and bereft, an atmosphere heightened by the lateness of the hour. I palmed a scrap of paper covered in numbers, reading the next on the list as I navigated the stacks. *RO581. The International Companion to Scottish Literature: 1400-1650.*

It took me a couple minutes to find the right section. Maneuvering through the row, I readjusted the books I was cradling as my arm began to ache. There were five or six of them, including a few my academic supervisor had rattled off in the final seconds of our afternoon meeting. It was the first helpful recommendation she'd made.

A moderately esteemed literary scholar specializing in the verse of the Scottish islands, though she herself was from Sussex, Dr. Fiona Wood was a disappointment as voluminous as the thick, oversized sweater that drooped over her rotund frame like a layer of burnt-orange blubber. Her research dealt largely with identity, place, and religion, which in theory should have qualified her to oversee my master's degree by research on the impact of Calvinism on Scottish identity in Enlightenment-era literature. However, she seemed to have barely looked at my proposal, more concerned that I was taking full advantage of the city's delights than getting started on my research.

"Have you done Arthur's Seat yet?" she said, elbow-deep in a rumpled tote bag. Her cell phone could be heard somewhere deep inside, emitting a swishy, tropical refrain. "It's a gorgeous climb if you're up for it."

"Not yet," I said.

"Oh, you must. You really must."

The chime of the marimba persisted as she continued to rummage.

"So about my research proposal—"

"You did send that over, didn't you?" She hoisted the bag up onto her lap. "You know, I wouldn't worry too much at this stage. You'll figure it out as you go. Let the research guide you. The important thing is to enjoy your time here. Twelve months, it'll fly by!"

I didn't mention that, but for the previous night's excursion to Leith Walk, I'd barely left my flat except to establish the most basic existence. Open a bank account, buy a SIM card for my phone, see what passed for

KFC on this side of the Atlantic. That, and the university's mandatory "international student check-in," which, if anything, had turned out to be more of a "check-out." After scanning my immigration documents and producing my student ID, the clerk presented me with an itemized bill for the remainder of nineteen thousand pounds in tuition and other fees—nearly triple what they were charging British students in the same program. This was my punishment for daring to be foreign in a place where hardly anyone seemed actually to be Scottish.

Still, there was no place for me but Edinburgh, the school and city both.

If I didn't know better, I would have said it was preordained, my coming here. Not by some woo-woo gravitational pull back to the motherland (I'd never been well-connected to my Scots heritage, which apparently ran deep in my otherwise scattered bloodline). Not even because I nurtured a particular passion for Enlightenment literature, though I did.

The real reason I was here was my father.

He too had attended the university, for a time. I didn't know all the details (though an accomplished orator on biblical subjects, he was rather ill-spoken where his personal history was concerned). All I knew was that in his twenties he had come to the university with ambitions of a career in academia before withdrawing a few months into his studies and returning home to enroll in Bible college in the backwoods of Indiana. There he met a charming blond Michigander named Vera Critchley, my mother, whose winsome smile belied a tortured history. A history about which I knew almost nothing except that it was dominated by poverty and abuse.

Shortly after graduation they married and departed the Midwest. Cyril Lagrand, the shyster millionaire who founded the Church of the Elected Heart, was encouraging members to move west to spread the true Word of God to the coasts and deserts. Fresno, Tucson, Eugene, and Spokane were a few of the two dozen cities designated as especially fertile ground for the Seeds of Righteousness. And so the couple settled

in the up-and-coming coastal community of San Diego, California, a
paradise of warm winters and white-sand beaches, and established their
own home-based ministry.

In the past several months I had pondered more about my father's
hasty transition from academic to minister than I had my entire life.
What had prompted so dramatic a change of course? And why had I not
asked him when I still had the chance?

Edmund Hale had been dead not quite a year when I moved over-
seas. They found his body, one overcast morning, prone on a strip of
rocky sand bed at the bottom of Sunset Cliffs, his limbs contorted, his
likeness having parted company with his face when his head smashed
a rock.

"Probably didn't feel a thing," one of the officers said.

The funeral, which was closed casket, drew a sizable audience. Believers new and long-forgotten piled in to pay their respects, more for
my mother's sake than their minister's. Vera had curried sympathy by
telling them my father's death was an accident. That Ed had been out
walking the trail like he did most mornings. Perhaps he'd leaned over
the rope to see the waves breaking at the base of the cliff, or had stumbled over a dip in the dirt and lost his balance. A tumble he couldn't
immediately correct. A scream no one was around to hear.

She didn't tell them about the note.

I discovered it in his study, scrawled by hand on a torn-out sheet of
paper, the same day they found his body. It was addressed to "My son,"
which could just as well have been my brother, Nathaniel, but some part
of me knew he had meant it for me.

*By the time you read this I'll have passed from
one plane of misery into the next. I've resisted the
urge for as long as I could bear—but as you'll one
day understand, one temptation or the other was always
bound to win. Son, listen to me, for nothing could be
more important: many years ago I was forced to make a*

choice—a choice that has never ceased to haunt me. It has followed me from the hills and glens of Scotland . . . stalked me to the very edge of my sanity. How I wish I could go back and unbind the shackles of my life—discover in that country the part of myself I didn't know existed, and not flee from it but welcome it like an old friend. It's too late for me—but there's time for you still.

I pray you enter by the narrow gate.

I had read the letter so many times that I could all but recite it from memory, yet it remained a mystery. The "narrow gate" I believed was a reference to the book of Matthew, but what was this choice he had been forced to make? What had transpired in those few months abroad to so drastically upend his self-view? Had it anything to do with his decision to abandon his studies, to throw away his future as an esteemed professor for a life of living room worship services and domestic imprisonment?

All I knew for sure was that, whatever decision he had made, it had killed him. Driven him to the edge of his sanity, he had written. Driven him, I had no doubt, to the edge of that cliff.

I might never know whether, if he had finished out his studies in Scotland, my father would still be alive today. But I was certain that, here and only here, I could live the life he couldn't. Only in Scotland could I become the man he never could.

I would stay here forever if they let me. Unfortunately that was looking more unlikely by the day. Before I could extend my visa, I'd first have to convince the UK government that I had sufficient funds to remain in the country without requiring public assistance. By July next year, I would need to have saved over twelve thousand pounds—no mean feat, given that the pay in this country borders on third world. As a start, I had secured a job as a teaching assistant for an undergraduate English course. If I could find another gig and be savvy with my student loans, I could just about sock away enough to keep me on Scottish soil another few years.

A lump of anxious guilt formed like a gallstone in my gut as I remembered the writing job—and the mess I had made of it.

So I'd had a bad feeling about D.B. What if I was wrong? What if my sudden departure the previous night had been nothing more than a momentary lapse in reason, a lizard-brained reaction to a fabricated menace? Now I'd have to take what I could get. Perhaps a job in a pub, or a shop. It was hard to imagine my father declining a potentially lucrative writing contract to stock shelves or pull pints.

My aching arms near breaking point, I crossed to a nearby table and dumped my books. Fishing out my phone, I tapped out a hasty email and hit send, realizing too late that the autocorrect had screwed me. *Sorry about last night* came out as *Sorry about lady night*, followed by *I'm still interested I the job, please can we meet?*

I cursed, hating myself. If there had been any chance of salvaging the gig, now I had well and truly fucked it; who'd want to hire a ghostwriter who couldn't write a single sentence without a mistake?

Then my phone dinged.

D.B. had replied, probably to tell me to get lost. Still, I opened the message.

Still want the job, meet me tomrw. The devils advocate 17.00

I couldn't believe it. He was giving me another chance!

I was getting ready to respond when, without warning, the overhead lights slammed off, plunging the entire floor into darkness.

"Hello?" I called out.

No one answered.

"I'm still in here," I tried again.

The quiet persisted, and yet my senses told me I wasn't alone. As I listened, I could hear sounds like whispered movement. Shapes formed in the dark as my eyes struggled to adjust, silhouettes etched against the blackness. I illuminated the flashlight on my phone, but its glow barely stretched a yard. There was something in the distance, beyond the reach of the light. A tall figure, almost human. Like a man. A man in black.

I staggered backward, my heart battering the walls of my chest—

And the lights stammered back on, reinstating the floor to its former buzzing grayness. My movement had tripped the motion sensors. The figure I'd perceived was a computer sitting on a high counter.

Confirming with relief that I was alone, I gathered up my books and left.

Editor's Note
Exhibit B

Whilst resident at HMP Edinburgh, Hale met regularly with Kathleen Prichard, a mental health counselor for the NHS. Though Ms. Prichard declined to provide comment on these interactions, her extensive case notes—to which I was granted access by Commissioner Brown's ruling—have proved invaluable to my research. Here I present the first of these illuminating extracts.

18 August 2017

After weeks without success patient is at last making progress—no longer avoiding eye contact and responding in short, superficial answers. This is thanks, I believe, to the removal of the supervising officer from our sessions. In this afternoon's session patient seemed at ease and even engaged in light small talk—he reports that he is sleeping well, eating, reading, and writing. Mental state seems stable. Unlike most, he appears to be thriving in segregation. Still, barring any change to patient's condition, I see no reason why he should not be able to join his peers.

5 September 2017

Though our conversations remain surface level, patient grows increasingly congenial week by week and appears to be adjusting well to life outside segregation. In today's session he spoke at length about the other inmates as well as several members of prison staff. His commentary, by turns sarcastic and scathing, suggests an unyielding personal standard—there was not one person he did not see fit to ridicule or criticize in some way. Critical nature likely a defense mechanism against his own self-criticism. After eagerly engaging in a brief writing exercise, patient refused to read what he had written or even hand over the assignment unless he first had "a chance to edit it." As he left he asked me to promise not to read it. My refusal to do so caused patient great consternation. However, a quick glance at the assignment revealed one of the most eloquent examples of prison writing I have yet encountered. Despite his guise of superiority, patient appears to bear an intense and unfounded fear of judgment which borders on phobia. The result of his public trial, I wonder, or does it go back further? Will seek to explore in future sessions.

Three

U P TO THAT point, I had put off exploring the Royal Mile. The unwavering enthusiasm people heaped on it had made me detest and distrust it; I imagined a street like a crusty outdoor museum of walking tours, religious monuments, and tarnished plaques. To my relief, the succession of cobbled streets snaking up toward Edinburgh Castle was as commercial and inauthentic as Disneyland, lined with overpriced whisky merchants, Americanized chain restaurants, and souvenir shops with twee names like Thistle Do Nicely hawking identical Nessie figurines and mass-produced tartan. A crowd gathered around a woman in a bonnet and puffy sleeves as she regaled them with a tale of haunting and murder. A man in full highland garb stood outside a Starbucks and suffused the air with the reedy cacophony of his bagpipes.

This was the heart of Edinburgh's Old Town.

The little bar to which I had been summoned was tucked away down a narrow alleyway off the Royal Mile. The entrance to the lane was so inconspicuous—a small rectangle of darkness pinned between a cigar shop and a newsagent's—that one almost had to be looking for it not to miss it. Like all the alleyways leading off the High Street, a thin, horizontal black sign clung to the wall over the opening. The words embossed in brass capitals read ADVOCATE'S CLOSE.

As I proceeded through the tunnel and down the narrow, stepped lane, the grizzled black spires of Scott Monument looming in the distance like an instrument of torture, I questioned my decision to reach back out to D.B. I'd been plagued all afternoon by vague misgivings and notions of danger, feelings I could not attach to reason. Perhaps it was just the unfortunate name of our meeting place. Even as a nonbeliever, the thought of the Devil's Advocate sent a cold tingle down my spine.

But I needed the money, especially if I was going to try for my PhD.

It was an ambition I had nurtured most of my life. A personal hardship at the close of my undergraduate studies had temporarily diverted me from that course, but that all changed after my father died. Suddenly my purpose became clear again, unfurling like a path laid before me. As Dr. Hale, esteemed professor of Scottish literature and the author of numerous award-winning books, I would finally find what I had been seeking all my life.

Halfway down the lane, the Devil's Advocate emerged from the shadows like a dark surprise. I had imagined a dusty little hole in the wall, but the bar was trendy and industrial, fronted by a wide arched window and black barn doors that led into a high-ceilinged room of beams and wood. The walls of exposed stone and brick reverberated the chatter of the mostly middle-aged patrons. A pair of young men commanded the steel-topped bar. Each was tall and robust, with a full beard. Tattoos grew out of their rolled-up shirtsleeves like tendrils, stretching down their hairy forearms to the nubs of their inked knuckles.

D.B. was nowhere to be seen.

At the top of a set of stairs, I discovered a busy mezzanine choked with rustic tables and mismatched chairs. My eyes scanned the room, spotting my prospective employer in a booth against the wall, sipping amber liquid from a stemless glass shaped like a tulip. He didn't notice me, his eyes fixed on a couple halfway across the room. There was no question why: their expressions and gestures indicated an argument was unfolding.

As I approached D.B. I could hear the woman hissing quietly under her breath. Without warning, her partner swept his arm across the table. Her dinner hit the floor with a crash at my feet.

There was silence as the whole room turned to look, conferring a share of the couple's embarrassment to me.

"You fucking joking?" the female diner half whispered, her voice frayed with humiliation. I leapt aside as she stormed past me and hurried down the stairs. Almost dazedly, as if coming round from some sort of trance, her date drained his lager and rose from his chair.

"They were fine till you showed up," murmured D.B. as I slid in across from him, still a bit shaken. "I blame you."

"Right." I laughed hollowly, unsure what to say.

He motioned to the waitress to bring another round of whisky.

Then he shifted his attention to me. "I guess you're no' afraid of me anymore."

"Afraid of you?" I could tell by his expression that there was no point denying it. "Oh. You mean the other night. Sorry, I—I shouldn't have taken off like that. I was feeling kind of—I thought someone might be following me."

A laugh. But it didn't belong to D.B. A few tables over, a boy of twelve or thirteen was having dinner with his father. He seemed to be staring at me—at us—caught in a look halfway between entertainment and disgust.

"Anyway." My eyes lingered on the boy as I turned back to D.B. "Thanks for giving me another shot. I'm eager to hear more about your book."

As he watched me I couldn't help noticing D.B.'s eyes: the dark gray irises were flecked with embers of gold. They shone in the low, warm light of the restaurant.

"Sorry," I said. "I never asked. Do you go by D.B., or should I call you—?"

"Call me what ye like."

I faltered. "Okay."

He chuckled, amused with himself. "Donald Blackburn. Donny."

Donny. The name didn't suit him. It was too plebeian, too familiar, the name of a game show host or a used-car salesman. Then again,
who's to say he wasn't?

"What is it you do, Donny?" I asked.

My interviewer was spared having to answer by the return of the
waitress with our drinks.

He raised his glass and held it there until I followed suit. *"Slàinte."*

"Sl-slanja." The liquid gilded my throat with golden fire.

Then something hit the side of my head.

As I looked around, the boy pawed a second fry off his plate and
chucked it in my direction. It missed me, bouncing off the wall behind D.B.

"What the—?" I had to stop myself cursing.

Several diners' eyes snapped in my direction. *Why gawk at* me? I
thought. The kid was the one causing a disturbance.

"If you want him to stop, make him stop."

I turned to D.B. "Sorry?"

"I said, make him stop."

Another fry bounced off the edge of the table and onto the floor.
The child now appeared to be filming us on his phone, while his father
sawed away at his venison, apparently unaware of the havoc his son was
wreaking.

I felt a flicker of annoyance.

"Excuse me," I called to the man, dodging another projectile. I was
on the edge of my seat now, adrenaline rushing through me. "Excuse
me—*sir.*"

Without a single indication he had heard me, he reached across the
table and snatched the phone away from his son. I thought he was going
to tell him off but, with the same dazed expression of the man who had
thrown his girlfriend's dinner to the floor, he dropped the phone and
smashed it under his boot.

For a second time the dining room went momentarily silent. The
boy gaped at his father, empty-eyed, and then shrank into his seat.

What is up with this place?

It was as if D.B. had heard me. "I told ye," he said. "It's you."

He signaled for the waitress as she came up the stairs. While he asked about the day's specials, I noticed the other diners were still peering in my direction, discomfort written on their faces. Why were they looking at me? The waitress left with our menus. D.B. had ordered for the both of us. Fine—I was eager to get this over with.

"What questions do you have for me?" I asked him.

They were more or less by the book to begin with. We talked first about my educational background: BA in English from UC San Diego ("Summa cum laude," I added. "That's the highest honor you can get"). Then my professional history: a little over a year helping foreign students write college admissions essays and a handful of freelance writing jobs, though no ghostwriting per se. Finally he tested my knowledge of Scots literature, and I passed the entire first course dissecting the roles of religion and gender in "Thrawn Janet" despite knowing he'd likely never heard of it. I wasn't above overwhelming him with my knowledge. Still, this dance of social niceties was getting old.

"So the book," I said.

"We'll get to the book."

Then he asked the question that would haunt me to this very day. "Tell me: What do you know about the Devil?"

An uncomfortable tightness gripped my sternum. "Well." I reached for my water and drank. "More than most, I guess."

The gold sparks in his eyes glowed bright; he was listening.

I explained that the Devil, or the Adversary as he was better known to me, had been a special interest of my father's. That before he died, Edmund Hale had been an accomplished theologian and a well-known reverend of the Church of the Elected Heart, the non-Trinitarian ministry to which my parents had committed their lives. That twice a week, for as long as I could remember, he had led a private worship service in the living room of our house—what was formally known in the church as fellowship.

Those lessons were perhaps the defining experience of my life, the foundation on which all else, good and bad, was built. Every Wednesday evening and Sunday morning, for an audience of twelve or fifteen, my father spoke with a power and eloquence to rival many working politicians'. His teachings were symphonic masterpieces of theological thought, underpinned by his original research and elevated by his evocative prose. Had he belonged to a more mainstream church there's no doubt he could have commanded one of the most illustrious pulpits in America. Instead he conducted his teachings from a creaky wingback chair at the front of the room, for my father's dedication to the Elected Heart was ironclad.

He refused to pander or compromise the church's message, which was, above all else, that all men were born with a sinful nature and justification could only be achieved by knowing one's fundamental evil and confessing it aloud. As he wrote in the preface to his third book, *The Divine Exemption: The Believer's Guide to Confession*: "The sin unspoken is man's greatest source of suffering and that which exempts him from salvation by grace. It is a sickness more devastating than any physical infirmity, poisoning the soul and befouling the carrier with its acrid, rotten smell, a smell known to the Adversary as the smell of blood is known to the shark."

The Adversary was named frequently in my father's oratory. Not merely as a character in the story of the Bible or a toothless metaphor for evil but also as a physical being with a material presence on earth, a shapeshifter who could take any form and speak any tongue. We were taught to fear him above all else, to remain vigilant against his deception. He circled in the shadows of my father's teachings like a wolf with a taste for sin. According to his teachings, the Adversary was not the root cause of man's wickedness but its loyal attendant. Where there was vanity, sexual depravity, greed, there he would appear and, by way of enticement and deceit, help guide one's temptation to action. For my father, wickedness was a precondition of humanity, a congenital disease of the heart that would smite down all but the most robustly constituted among us. Our condemnation, he foretold, was predetermined.

In accordance with the tenets of the Elected Heart, he believed that one's natural sin could be overcome through confession alone. That's why each fellowship, sometime after the singing of songs and before the night's teaching, we bowed our heads for the Sharing of Confession. Even among our faithful group, volunteers were thin on the ground. A silence would swell between us. If no one broke it willingly, he appointed a confessor—often me.

"Grayson. Tell us your sin."

Most of the time I went blank. My heart would hammer in my chest as I racked my brain for a confession. It had to be just right: sinful enough to be believed but nothing that would risk embarrassing my image-conscious mother. Why did he never call on my brother? Did he think I had more sins to divulge, or one in particular that he was trying to wrest from me?

"Dear Heavenly Father," I would answer, "I confess to having jealous thoughts about my friend's new bike," or "angry thoughts toward my brother. Please forgive me and grant me the strength to resist the temptation of sin. Amen."

"*Amen*," the group would echo, and my mother, at least, would be appeased.

But my father would cuff me with a look of blistering disappointment. The look that destroyed me like none other could. The rest of the week I'd eviscerate myself and devise a better, more compelling sin, one that illustrated both my integrity and my eloquence. A confession to make my father proud. Not that I ever succeeded.

Due to the intensity of his fellowship, turnover in the congregation was high. New faces disappeared as quickly as they came, leaving us with our core congregation of misfits and tortured souls, more commonly known in the church as believers.

There was Marlena, a soft-spoken former meth user with a gap-toothed smile and crepe-paper skin that drooped off her elbows in delicate flaps. Barry and Viv Purdue, a pair of bloated, red-faced Realtors, who confessed to every minor indiscretion without ever acknowledging their obvious alcoholism. And the Fernandezes, my parents' old Bible college friends. Beefy and mannish, Paola Fernandez resembled a grizzled bulldog with a mane of dyed-blond hair, constantly snarling at her dopey, doughy tree trunk of a husband, Esteban, whose wardrobe seemed to consist entirely of long-sleeved promotional tees, cargo shorts, and white tennis socks, which he wore scrunched down over his chunky ankles. Their boy, Carlos, was about the same age as me, and for a few months we were something like friends. We would play and do puzzles in my bedroom after fellowship, and pass lazy Saturday afternoons at each other's houses. Once, Paola even took us to the AMC at Fashion Valley for a matinee of *Beverly Hills Ninja*. I was electrified by the film's slapstick violence and crass humor, the likes of which I'd never seen before. It was as if, those few hours, I was living someone else's life.

Sadly, the friendship was short-lived, never recovering after the night Carlos slept over at my house while our parents were attending an out-of-town church conference. I can barely recall our minor disagreement, yet by seven o'clock he was crying to my brother, Nathaniel, about wanting to go home. While Carlos camped out in a sleeping bag on the couch, I lay awake in the fort I'd built for us on my bedroom floor, hoping one day to have a friend who would not hesitate to sleep next to me.

My mother said it was for the best; it was always her preference not to mix business with pleasure. After all, the believers were less our brothers and sisters in Christ than her clientele.

She called it the Joy of Abundant Sharing. It came after my father's teaching, before the parting prayer. The vessel: a wicker cornucopia basket purchased from the local arts-and-crafts store. It passed from hand to hand as my mother said the Prayer of Abundant Sharing, which was never quite the same, and yet never very different either.

"Dear Lord, today we honor and give thanks to You by sharing of our material abundance, as in the book of Acts the followers of Christ gave their every worldly possession so that He may spread His Gospel throughout the land. Lord, we give generously out of love and thankfulness for Your Word, knowing that our physical and spiritual needs will be supplied according to the riches, wealth, and abundance of Your glory."

By the time the cornucopia completed its circuit around the room, it was heavy with coins, spilling over with paper notes and checks.

This was my mother's ritual alone; although he dutifully bowed his head as she prayed, my father offered no supporting words but *amen.* He did not seem to approve of her salesmanship, but nor did he openly dissuade it. This was their tacit agreement, the reward my mother reaped for her exquisite performance in the role of loving wife and mother.

"So yes," I said to D.B. "I know quite a bit about the Devil."

There was a look on his face of having discovered a thing of great value. "You're just what I've been looking for. You're going to help me write my book."

I tried to look pleased, but something was bothering me. *What does knowing about the Devil have to do with anything?*

"What kind of book is this, exactly?"

"Text me your address," he said, ignoring my question. "I'll be posting a few things. A sample of my research to get ye started."

"But first can you tell me—?"

"Will twenty thousand be enough?"

I was certain I'd misheard. "Sorry, you said—?"

"Make it thirty, then. Ten at commencement, another ten for the first draft, and the remaining ten upon completion."

I hadn't misheard. *Thirty thousand pounds.* That was over forty thousand dollars. More than enough to keep me in the country. Probably enough to cover the first half of my PhD. I wouldn't even have to worry about funding.

"I'll advance ye a thousand pounds if we can make it official tonight."

"Official?"

From a bag at his side D.B. produced an agreement. Where I might have expected a document an inch thick, the contract before me was a single typewritten page.

CONTRACT AGREEMENT FOR WRITING SERVICES

This Contract Agreement for Writing Services ("Agreement") is effective as of 13 September 2016, and entered into by and between Grayson Hale ("G.H."), and Donald Blackburn ("D.B."), for the development and delivery of one original manuscript of literary nonfiction entitled—

"*A Scottish History of Fear?*"

"A working title only," he said, with a wave of his hand. "I'm sure you'll find something more appropriate."

I skimmed the document. As far as I could tell, it was all aboveboard. A simple contract for services. People signed pieces of paper like this all the time. So why did I have the dreadful feeling that I was about to pass a point of no return? What would my father have done, were this document laid before him?

D.B. proffered a fountain pen, the S curve of a serpent carved into the glossy black wood. As I reached for it, he moved his hand, an almost imperceptible jab. The razor-sharp nib pierced the tip of my index finger, causing me to wince.

"Shite. Terribly sorry."

"It's fine." Blood pooled at the tip of my finger. I searched for a napkin, but there wasn't one, and the waitress was nowhere to be seen.

D.B. was waiting. "If ye would."

With a sigh, I took the pen between my middle finger and thumb. My employer's signature was already on the contract, a spiky *D* interlocking a *B*. Holding my index finger out, I signed my name in a clumsy scrawl. The jerking movement caused a drop of crimson to thud onto the paper.

The nib caught it as it raced across the page, trailing inky blood in the shape of my name.

Four

A S I WALKED down the Royal Mile, a thousand pounds richer after my meeting with D.B., a man caught my eye from the side of the road. He was in his seventies and looked like he had dwelled outdoors for some time. His beard was overgrown, and there were holes in his gloves, with which he gripped a wooden stick upholding a poster. In cramped, black handwriting the man's sign bore a fragment of scripture, but not the warning of fire and brimstone I would have expected. In fact, it was not a warning at all.

MY SON, KEEP THY FATHER'S COMMAND AND FORSAKE NOT YOUR MOTHER'S TEACHING. BIND THEM ALWAYS UPON THINE HEART, AND TIE THEM ABOUT THY NECK.

—PROVERBS 6:20-21

On a different day I might have continued past such a man without much thought. But my conversation with D.B. had put me in a ruminative state of mind. Long after I left the man with a pound from my pocket, I was still thinking about his message.

Edmund Hale was not the commanding type. Serious and contemplative, he did not engage in idle chatter. He didn't "parent" my brother and me in the traditional fashion, by showing up to school functions or giving slaps on the back. He didn't even know who our friends were. Our banal, schoolboy lives were a world apart from his, as remote and irrelevant as those of the ants that burrowed in the dirt beneath our house. His work took priority, as it should for all who possess a God-given genius.

Although he earned his living teaching religious studies at the local divinity school, my father's true calling was as a theologian. He consumed books like breath mints, penned a new one seemingly every year, and published frequently in journals both scholarly and spiritual. His writing seemed to inhabit both worlds at once, smearing the lines between academia and religion until inquiry became an act of worship and confession a matter of intellectual discourse.

His work was all-consuming, and I saw very little of him. When he was home, he was shut away in the large, windowless study at the back of the house that could only be accessed by the backyard. Most nights he slept there too, bedding down on the threadbare couch pushed up against the wall. On the rare occasions he joined us for dinner, he never asked about our days or inserted himself into our conversations. The way he hung back from us and stared off with vague, glinting eyes, I could see that he was somewhere else, awash in an ocean of deep and impenetrable thoughts. Harrowing thoughts, I sometimes imagined, for there was a restless quality about him, something deeply unsettled behind his eyes, as if some nameless internal force never ceased to strain against him. It was as if in the hallowed cloisters of his study he had discovered things about the world the rest of us could never fully comprehend, a secret knowledge he endured as his own personal burden.

When I was young, I longed for his attention. It afflicted me like a terrible thirst. As a rule, he was not to be disturbed while he was working, but I would invent any excuse to barge in on him—to ask for help tying my shoe, or complain that Nathaniel had done something mean.

Rarely did my father look up from his work, his pen skating fast across the page as he scribbled critiques in the margins of his students' papers. I envied them, these fortunate strangers, for they seemed to command his attention in a way I never could.

He never begrudged me my intrusions or lost his temper; never once did he yell. But when he sensed they were becoming a pattern, he started to keep the door locked. For several years, until I was forced to as a teenager, I did not enter that room once.

I was left in the care of my mother, such as it was.

If Edmund Hale was an absent parent, then Vera was like two inhabiting the same body. The first of them, the one known to the world, was the most beautiful, the most perfect woman on earth. The ebullient hostess who presided over a party of homemade cookies and freshly squeezed lemonade in the dining room after fellowship. Who bore a steadfast aroma of rose oil and musk, scalloped hoop earrings dangling from her lobes like shells of gold. This woman was beloved by all who knew her. She never forgot that Esteban preferred his brownies without nuts or that Gerri's aunt had been unwell. Nothing was too much trouble, and no person left her company without having enjoyed a few glowing moments of her undivided attention.

If she had a fault, this woman, it was her tendency to gush over her sons—both of them. She would spot me in the crowd and call my name across the room. How alien it sounded, unlaced with acid. She would rest a hand on my shoulder as she rambled with pride over some small academic triumph. How strange to feel her bony digits through the fabric of my shirt.

After years I managed to train myself not to read into these gestures. Not to let myself hope that such tenderness would continue when everyone else went home.

For the other Vera Hale was altogether different, like a dour mirror image of her public persona. Her eyes, rather than sparkling with inner warmth, flashed with a keen and wasted intellect, poisoned with malice after decades of neglect. Voluble as she was in public, in the privacy of our home, my mother, like her husband, hardly spoke a word. She didn't call my name so much as eject it from her mouth. Did not touch me except to bathe or dress me, not minding if the water was too hot or if she pinched my skin between the snaps of my shirt. If I asked for help, she pretended not to hear. If I reached for her hand, she would snatch it away, as if by coincidence, and apply it to some needless task.

There was always a needless task. Ironing bedsheets. Raising the hem of a valance. Scouring gleaming white baseboards with a rag. Constantly the house echoed with the sounds of her industry; she was always toiling, always busy with nothing. Except for a few hours a week as a bookkeeper for a local consignment shop, she didn't work outside the home. Her career was the house and its contents, and her productivity was measured in its constant fluctuation. The decor seemed to change with each passing month: the departure of plastic sunflowers for rust-colored leaves marked the transition of September to October, the end of December heralded by the retreat of crimson-clad angels for a palette of snow and silver.

In the evenings she sat in her chair and read, exhausting half a dozen volumes a month. Woolf and O'Connor, Perry Mason and Poirot, endless manifestos on living in the light of the Lord. Once a week, she helped the Rescue Mission force homeless people to pray in return for food and shelter, and managed my father's business affairs, whoring him out for weddings and religious counseling as often as possible.

My mother's primary pastime, though, was my brother. Three years my senior, Nathaniel was the only thing Vera seemed truly to love. My earliest memories are of watching her heap attention upon him in all the ways she refused me and wondering what I had done to deserve her neglect. In my brother's presence, she could almost be mistaken for the other woman. She stroked his hair as he sat nestled into her on the couch, felt the suppleness of his arm with soft fingers as he passed by her armchair while she read. She had a way of fussing over him while barely uttering a word: circling like a buzzard, waiting for the slightest sign of distress so she could swoop in and make it right. She feasted on his long-winded diatribes about the classmates he didn't like and the petty injuries they had borne him. She beseeched him not to run or play too vigorously, lest he aggravate his congenitally weak heart.

I watched on, knowing even as a toddler it would do me no good to cry. Nathaniel must have known it too, because whenever Vera showed him any tenderness, he would find my eyes and fix me with a big, sneering grin. It didn't matter if she saw; she never told him off.

Forsake not your mother's teaching.

Each day my mother prepared a nightly lesson for Nathaniel. At a minimum this included a Bible story, a writing assignment, and a selection from the *Children's Workbook of Biblical Teaching*. I would watch from the hallway as they pored over books and worksheets at the coffee table in the den, as my mother read aloud in the voice of a dove. The story of Abraham and Sarah, or the Tower of Babel. At first I attempted to memorize every letter in the hope of later astounding her with my knowledge. But I soon learned that such feats of recall would only earn me a sharp reprimand for having eavesdropped on their lessons. She made sure to keep the door closed after that.

One night, however, when I was six or seven, that changed. I'm not sure why; perhaps my father had insisted she include me. Catching me dawdling outside the den, she ordered me in. For the first time I was to join them. I could have cried out in joy, but refrained to ensure she did not change her mind. And so began the happiest few months of my life.

My memories of our nightly lessons are vague, but as I recall, I was an attentive and obedient student. I learned the story of Noah's ark, and the baby Moses's journey down the Nile, and Daniel in the lions' den. More important, I learned that I was good at learning, and that even a grudging acknowledgment of my aptitude was ecstasy.

At fellowship, the believers complimented my biblical knowledge and reading skill, both of which eclipsed Nathaniel's by years. "My little whiz kid," my mother once said, beaming with artificial pride. "Grayson's going to be a writer one day, just like his father."

A feeling I'd never experienced before, and rarely since, bloomed inside of me like a flowering plant, its boughs draped in vivid and smiling blossoms.

But when I turned to my father, his expression was cold and faraway, lost in the ether of his thoughts. "Isn't he, Ed?" my mother said.

Seeming only now to realize where he was, he nodded curtly. "Excuse me," he said, and departed the room.

I wilted. Clearly reading well wasn't enough; it would take more to make my father see me. From that moment, I poured myself into my lessons, certain I could buy his esteem with biblical knowledge. But after a few months, they ended as abruptly as they'd started. One night, as I followed Nathaniel into the den, he slammed me back into the door.

"Mom says you're not allowed anymore."

"That's not true," I shouted, rubbing my head where it had smacked the knob.

Vera appeared in the doorway, her nostrils flared, the skin taut around the cords of her neck. She seemed to be caught halfway between rage and fear. *"Stay out."*

"What?" I cried. "But why? What did I do?"

"Your brother told me everything," she spat. "You darken this house with evil. You are a blight on this family. I know that now. *I know what you are.*"

As she pulled the door shut, the sharp corner grazed the top of my foot, inscribing a white line into my bare skin. I crumpled to the floor and wailed, clutching my bleeding extremity, though the pain of the wound was nothing compared to what I had lost. Most of all I was confused. What had I done? What had Nathaniel told her? My mind gnashed like rusty machinery, working to make sense of the words still clanging in my ear. *Dark . . . evil . . . I know what you are.*

Bind them always upon thine heart, and tie them about thy neck.

Editor's Note
Exhibit C

Further case notes prepared by Kathleen Prichard, mental health counselor at HMP Edinburgh.

7 September 2017

Received word that patient has been placed back in segregation after attacking another prisoner in the exercise yard. According to a report from the officer on duty, patient was seen approaching the prisoner before swinging his hand around, lodging in the prisoner's throat a sharp object which was later found to be a biro smuggled from his cell. Officers intervened and removed patient from the scene. The other prisoner survived his injuries but remains in critical care.

12 September 2017

First meeting with patient since the attack. Patient was out of sorts for much of the hour—uncommunicative, avoided eye contact, hands jittery—but denied his anxiety had anything to do with the incident in the exercise yard. When asked what was bothering him, patient stated I would think him insane if he told me.

"Then again," he added, "you probably already do."

I understood that patient was referencing his well-publicized demonic delusions, which until now we had not discussed. I impressed upon him that this was a safe space, that anything he told me—excepting any information which suggested an immediate threat to himself or others—would be kept in strictest confidence. Still patient did not speak. When I asked if it had anything to do with the Devil, patient suddenly

became extremely agitated and leapt from his chair,
demanding to know why I was asking that, what I knew
about the Devil. It was at this point the supervising
officer entered and took control of patient. Patient
resisted but was escorted from the room, shouting in
a tone that seemed more fearful than angry: "What did
he tell you? What did he say about me?"

19 September 2017

Patient appeared calm but unwell in this afternoon's
session. Wan, fidgety, rings around the eyes. He began
by apologizing for his outburst last week. Patient
expressed he has been under considerable stress as a
result of "the Devil" visiting his cell for the past
fortnight. When pressed for details about his visitor, patient described a lean, dark-haired man wearing
black—a description matching our own Resident Officer
McGilveray, all ROs being equipped with all-black uni-
forms. Before I could suggest such a connection, however, patient asserted his visitor was not an RO. Then
he backtracked and said the Devil has visited him but
not in human form. He stated it was due to the "Devil's" influence that he attacked the other prisoner in
the exercise yard. CCTV shows no evidence of a visit
to his cell other than by uniformed staff. Likely suffering hallucinations induced by psychosis. Patient
evaded questioning but implied that his fear of the
Devil goes back to childhood. Refused to say anything
more after that, apparently afraid that to do so would
cause the Devil to appear in the room.

Five

THE ENVELOPE WAS large and yellow and stuffed so fat it barely fit through the letter box, where I discovered it crammed along with a smattering of bills and junk mail. After a couple stiff yanks it slid free and hit the carpet with a slap. As I went to pick it up, I was shocked by the weight of it. The parcel may as well have been filled with sand.

There was no return address on the front or back. Still, my stomach turned with the knowledge of who had sent it. For a reason not yet clear to me I'd been dreading this moment.

"What's that?" my flatmate said from the adjoining kitchen, depressing the contents of the trash can to make room for his lunch waste. A spoiled undergrad majoring in international relations, Ollie was two years my junior and hadn't yet mastered the finer points of sanitation and, far less, personal responsibility. Given that his rich parents had bought him our shared, two-bedroom flat as a present for flunking out of his last university, this wasn't altogether surprising.

"Nothing," I said. "It's—from my mom."

I didn't want Ollie to know about D.B. Perhaps it was the exorbitant fee I was being paid. Perhaps it was D.B. himself and that there was something about him that still made me uneasy. Whatever the reason, it felt illicit, our deal. Something that needed to be kept secret, free from scrutiny.

Back in my bedroom, I tore the parcel open, accidentally ripping it down the middle in my impatience. Paper spilled onto the floor like the viscera of a gutted pig. I scraped it into a pile and spread it out across the desk. What I found baffled me.

A collection of seemingly random documents lay before me. Photocopies of academic articles, newspaper clippings, amateur blog posts printed out from the internet, pages cut out of books—each document decorated with largely indecipherable marks and notes, in the same spiky handwriting that had addressed the envelope.

A printout of a website called the Devil's Dominion drew my attention, bearing a crude drawing of what looked like a demon surrounded by text that struck me as funny rather than serious. *A known metamorph, he can take a myriad of human and animal forms—traditionally red in hue and half man/half goat in shape, but more recently he has been spotted in various locales disguised as a fly, a monitor lizard, and even a speckled grouse.*

There too was an extract from a book called *Ancient Criminal Trials in Scotland Vol. III Part II (1615-1624)* concerning the confession of one Isobel Gowdie. I was well-read in Scots by this point, but even I struggled to make sense of it.

First, as I wes goeing betwixt the townis of Drumdewin and the Headis, THE DIVELL met with me, and thair I convenanted with him. He wes a meikle blak roch man, werie cold. He stood with an blak book in his hand; quhair I cam befor him, and renuncet JESUS CHRIST. He re-baptised me, and marked me in the shoulder, and with his mouth sucked out my blood at the place, and spowted it in his hand, and sprinkling it wpon my head and face, he said, 'I baptise ye to my selff, in my own nam!' And within few dayes he cam to me, in the New Wardis of Inshock, and ther haid carnall cowpulatioun with me—

There was a *bang bang bang* on my bedroom door. I jumped.

"The bloody Wi-Fi's gone down again," Ollie shouted.

"Well fix it, then," I hollered back.

"I tried. It's completely fucked!"

"Just restart the router."

I heard a groan, then silence.

As I returned to the documents, I realized my heart rate was up. Ollie's outburst had startled me. But more than that, the documents had me feeling uneasy. The sensation worsened as I proceeded to sift through them. An old newspaper clipping, as thin and delicate as skin, describing how a herd of highland cattle had been slaughtered in a suspected satanic ritual. A bound, coffee-ringed film script titled *The Elect*. A Wikipedia article on Boleskine House, the Inverness-shire home of Aleister Crowley.

And finally, a strange document printed out from the internet. I initially mistook it for a Twitter feed, before I clocked the Yahoo! logo above.

Why has everyone forgot the Devil?

0 Following 6 Answers

Answers

Rachael Well I know I haven't 😊

Answer King It's probably because of like the different gods who have been created by men, Devil doesn't exit.. Simple!

Joj19 The Devil represents the government... the deep state... the Illuminati... which is controlled by aliens... their mind control make you forget what you have seen....

Greg C Exchange the word Devil drop the D you get Evil, evil does exist in the minds of man somtimes minds can be changed but there is no devil one person it is an act not a person!!

1WithTheUniverse The Devil is the ego-mind, a demonstration of man's innermost conceptions about himself based on his upbringing, experiences, the society he grew up in, etc. Forget the Devil, all you need's a good therapist.

db Because he wanted you to... but now he will make you remember.

My eyes lingered on the last line, the nape of my neck prickling as if icy pins danced upon it. That answer in particular didn't sit right with me. And those initials—*db*—could that be a coincidence?

The second *bang bang bang* made me jump. "It's still not working!"

"*I'll be out in a minute!*"

"Fuck sake," Ollie said. "I don't have all day."

My flatmate could wait. First I needed to understand this, needed to know what D.B. meant for me to do with these documents. They seemed less like literary research than the raw materials for a lunatic's scrapbook.

Clearly he intended for me to write a book about the Devil. But a second glance at the documents revealed an additional commonality. References to Scotland appeared again and again, often circled multiple times and attended by a flurry of handwritten notes. I remembered the title he'd named in our contract, the one he'd dismissed as a placeholder. *A Scottish History of Fear.* Is that what his book was about—the Devil's dominion over my new country of residence?

I experienced a cold inward tremor, but was I surprised? I should have known, from his strange questions, that this was no ordinary book.

Perhaps I hadn't wanted to believe it, knowing I would never have signed the contract otherwise. As good as the money was, to be ghostwriting a book about the Adversary given my personal history on the subject—only part of which I had revealed to my employer—I could not escape the feeling that I was playing with fire.

Six

THE ANXIETY CAME in waves and a multitude of forms over the following days. Each time my phone buzzed, I experienced a wave of dread, imagining it might be my employer following up on the materials he'd sent. I had the same feeling when I opened Gmail to find an unread message at the top, but it was only a terse email from my mother requesting photos. I knew the kind she meant: pictures of me smiling in front of Edinburgh Castle, or feasting on haggis, neeps, and tatties with a gang of jolly foreigners. Images she could post to Facebook to maintain the illusion of our closeness. *Missing my brilliant boy while he has a blast in Scotland!! Thank goodness for Skype!!!*

Then my employer began to appear in my dreams. In one of them, I was in a derelict factory, something like a woolen mill deep in the highlands. The building was empty except for a writing desk on the factory floor, where I sat scratching out a draft of the book while D.B. stood over me. He snatched the paper out from under my pen.

"What's this?" he bellowed. "No, no, this is all wrong! Have ye never met the Devil before?"

I looked up at him, unsure of the answer.

When I was thirteen, I developed an intense case of satanophobia, a condition that caused me to not just fear the Devil but to believe that at any moment he would appear and force me to do unspeakable things against my will. Although it was several years delayed, I credit the affliction to my brother, Nathaniel: it was he who had planted the seed of fear in my mind.

Nathaniel and I were far from friends. Just as my mother gloried in the cultivation of his righteousness, so he thrilled in my daily suffering. It seemed, in a way, to buoy him. To add purpose to a life that, due to concerns for his health, was otherwise largely ornamental. Nathaniel had longed to be an athlete; forbidden by our mother from joining Little League or the flag football team, he took me as his sport. But far beyond the injuries he inflicted on my body, it was his words that left the deepest mark.

Years before the mention of Satan's name sent me into a spiral of terror so bad that I passed out cold on the living room floor, Nathaniel convinced me the scars on my arm had been left by the Devil. When no one was around, he would whisper to me about the night it happened. The details of it remain vivid in my memory, though it's hard to recall now which were Nathaniel's and which my mind invented to fill in the gaps.

In any case, the lasting image is of a night like a military assault on the earth: rain hammering the house like machine-gun spray, thunder exploding like falling bombs. A younger Nathaniel—four or five, I imagine—lies quivering beneath his race car bedspread as the storm rages above, the roof keening and moaning as if any moment the wind might rip it clean off its rafters.

Suddenly Nathaniel shoots up in bed as he hears another sound: breaking glass, followed by a slam. It sounds as if it has come from the nursery. His infant brother begins to scream.

Slowly, Nathaniel creeps out into the hallway and follows the sound of my wailing. It is dark, but he can make out something on the floor. Black shapes darkening the floorboards, which moan with every step.

"Hello?" he calls out. A flash of lightning illuminates the hall, and for a second he can see them: a trail of black, cloven hoofprints scorched into the wooden boards, leading down the hall through the open door of the smallest bedroom.

Were any of this true, no doubt he would have turned back or run screaming into my parents' room. But as he told it, he continues to inch along the hallway, terrified yet spurred on by the baby's cries.

As he stops in the doorway, my brother's blood runs cold.

Silhouetted in the moonlight streaming in through the shattered window, a monstrous form hovers over the crib. It's gargantuan, the size of two or three men at least, with skin the color of tar. Its legs end in glossy hooves, and great twisting ram's horns protrude from its head.

Barely twelve months old, I lie in the crib, continuing to wail as the Beast leans over me, drooling on my stomach as its maw gapes open. Rigid with shock and terror, Nathaniel watches on helplessly, as out of the Beast's mouth snakes a tongue as long as a T-ball bat. It is luminous orange, as if constituted of burning embers, and forked. Not two prongs like a snake's, but three. Lowering its head to my body, the Beast drags the glowing appendage up my arm, causing me to erupt in a piercing shriek of pain, accompanied by the sizzle of burning flesh. Nathaniel too screams, the sound of it drawing the Beast's scarlet eyes with a snap.

Then instantly the creature explodes into a cloud of wings and claws, its enormity divided into a dozen black fiends, which gnash and screech and flee through the open window. Upon hearing Nathaniel's cries of terror, my mother rushes in, and he explains to her what he saw, barely able to form the words. Peering into the crib, she perceives the damage to my arm: three vertical burn marks, the center one slightly longer than its brothers.

In my head the look on her face is not of terror or shock but disgust. She clasps a hand over her mouth, suppressing the urge to vomit. Was that Nathaniel's detail or mine?

Staggering back from the crib, Vera snatches Nathaniel up and whisks him back to his bedroom, where, having ensconced him securely beneath his covers, she kneels beside the bed.

With trembling lips and tears in her eyes, she entreats God to shield him from the Adversary, to seal this bedroom against His enemy's accursed trespass. Rocking back and forth, her head bowed over the mattress, she prays that the Adversary takes the other from this house as his prize and never troubles Nathaniel for as long as he lives.

"She wouldn't!" I used to cry. "She wouldn't say that!"

But my words rang hollow even to me. There was nothing my mother prized more than her firstborn's righteousness. There is no life she would not sacrifice, least of all mine, to preserve his ascendancy to the Kingdom of God.

True or not, mine or his, the ending remains the one part of the story I've never questioned.

Although it's easy enough now to dismiss Nathaniel's tale as a cruel fiction—not to mention one riddled with inconsistencies; for example, if the Devil entered my room through the shattered window, why did the hallway floorboards bear his hoofprints?—as a young child I accepted every word. For months I lay awake at night, fearing the Adversary's return like other children fear the threat of monsters under the bed. Although in general I tried not to aggrieve my mother by asking questions, this time I could not help it.

"You've always had those scars," she said.

"But how did I—?"

"You were born with them. Don't mention them again." Her face was colorless, her eyes glinting through the windshield of the car as she drove. It was like she knew. Like she knew and was trying to hide the truth.

With medication I was able to start sleeping again, but I was besieged by outlandish and frightening dreams, not all of them featuring great horned devils. In fact, there were surprisingly few of those. Mostly the threats were existential. I had visions of being visited by a secret fraternity of murderers and criminals who insisted on inducting me into their ranks despite my protests that I was good. Visions of my hands engulfed in flame, ending always in destruction and death. Again and again, my dreams gave voice to the anxiety that had been fermenting inside me for months, the only one that seemed to explain why the Adversary had singled me out: that inside of me resided an evil so dark that the Devil himself, sensing one of his kind, had come to mark me as his own.

Was that why my mother had thrown me out of Bible study lessons with Nathaniel? *You darken this house with evil. You are a blight on this family. I know that now. I know what you are.* Was that why my father never wanted to talk to me? Was I the last person in this house to learn the truth of what I was?

Fortunately, these concerns were only temporary. Certainly the Adversary remained an ambient threat, as he did to all raised in the church, but at least for a while I stopped dreading his physical reappearance. By the time I entered the third grade I was convinced Nathaniel had been lying, well acquainted, by now, with his proclivity for storytelling and the pleasure he derived from my distress.

Still, the fear he'd sown did not abandon me completely. As I would later discover, it merely stalked me from a distance, lurking in the tall grass of my mind like a panther waiting to strike.

Editor's Note
Exhibit D

Prior to the publication of my report detailing Hale's confession and his claims of having murdered Liam Stewart under the influence of the Devil, no one could have predicted what a phenomenon he would become. He dominated the news cycle for weeks, driving an insatiable hunger for information. Like many on the crime beat, I was asked to make Hale my full-time priority, do whatever it took to give the readers the sordid details they craved—the more gruesome and chilling, the better. Hardly a day went by without the emergence of "shocking new details" in Hale's case, many of them clearly exaggerated, if not downright overblown. Others so disturbing, one had to wonder if they could really be true.

Here I present one such article, published in the morning edition of the Edinburgh Daily News, and replicated in online format, 10 April 2017.

BROTHER OF DEVIL'S ADVOCATE BREAKS SILENCE ON SIBLING'S DARK PAST

The brother of an American man accused of murdering his Edinburgh University classmate says of his younger sibling: "I always knew there was something wrong with him."

Grayson Hale, 25, from San Diego, California, was arrested on 28 February on suspicion of murder of his university classmate Liam Stewart, 23, from Kirkcaldy. Hale's reported insistence that the Devil influenced him to commit the crime, and remains living in Scotland, has since earned Hale the nickname "the Devil's Advocate."

In an exclusive interview with *Edinburgh Daily News*, his brother, Nathaniel Hale, 28, said of his younger sibling: "Even when he was a kid, there was something kind of 'off' about him. You could tell he was different than the other boys.

"We had this painting of Jesus on the cross. It was

pretty disturbing, you know—He was being tortured, blood dripping down His wrists—and Grayson would just sit there staring at it. Like, for hours. It was like he enjoyed seeing Jesus suffer. Like he got off on it or something."

Hale says he wasn't the only member of the family who found young Grayson frightening.

"My mother was scared s—less of him too. If she so much as hugged me, he'd fly into a rage, try to force us apart. Even attack us.

"And the things he'd say. Normally he was a quiet kid, like weirdly quiet. But when he spoke, he'd say things you'd never imagine coming out of a kid that young. He'd look you right in the eye and say, 'You should die.' He'd look at you and say, 'I'm gonna kill you.'

"There were times I was pretty sure he meant it."

The accused murderer's brother expressed sympathy for Liam Stewart's family: "I've been keeping them in my prayers." Still, when asked whether he believed his brother was guilty, the older Hale reserved comment.

"I don't know anything about what happened. But if you're asking me if Grayson's capable of murder? Yeah. I'd be willing to bet he is."

Grayson Hale remains remanded in custody, where he awaits trial, which is scheduled to commence on 20 June.

Seven

ALTHOUGH I SUSPECTED the onus was on me to contact D.B. re-garding next steps for our project, I avoided the task for a few days on the pretense of needing to acclimate to my new schedule of school and work.

I'd been assigned to TA English Literature I, an introductory un-dergraduate module focused on fundamental texts. The class consisted of thrice-weekly lectures taught by a rotation of professors and weekly tutorial sessions led by the assistants, each of us responsible for our own group of a dozen or so students. Unlike in the States, where such a class would have been compulsory for students of all disciplines (many of them barely literate), my tutorial was filled with students who had been specializing in English studies since the age of fourteen. With just a bachelor's degree, I was barely more educated in the subject than they were, a fact that caused me no small amount of unease; were I in their shoes, I could not imagine being anything less than ruthless.

Sitting at the head of the classroom in that first tutorial, I felt phys-ically ill, an invisible hand clenching my gut, my mind ringing with the criticisms I read in my students' eyes. *Who's this American? What's he wearing? God, they are fat, aren't they?* Befuddled by self-doubt, I fumbled my own introduction and elicited several titters during the roll call by forgetting the *ck* in Cockburn was meant to be silent. What would my father have thought of his son's bumbling ineptitude in front of the classroom? His son, who was meant to be carrying on his legacy, laying waste to it with every stammered word and lost train of thought?

Surely his eyes would have reflected their own message, that his doubts about my academic future had been confirmed.

In addition to my TA work I had my own studies to contend with, a combination of independent research and taught classes.

The former was slow going. Having finally received Fiona's blessing on my research proposal, I'd made only halting progress so far. Sir Walter Scott's *The Heart of Midlothian*, which I'd selected as the focus of my research, proved a more wearisome read than I remembered, having read and adored it years before. Still, the lowlight of my week was easily my Research Skills and Methods course. Mandatory for all postgraduate researchers in English literature, it was designed to equip students with "vital scholarly skills," such as how to type words into a library catalog and assemble a bibliography—the very thing we'd had to provide to gain entry to the program in the first place.

The class was every bit as tedious as its course description suggested, but it was the instructor I detested most of all. A scruffy man with a receding hairline and thick-framed glasses, Dr. Porter held an unyielding view of student participation, which he expressed with a rancor at odds with the meekness implied by his forearm crutches. It was his apparent belief that any pupil who didn't actively contribute to group discussion was either disengaged, mentally deficient, or suffering from a delusion of superiority, a viewpoint he made clear by the barbs of sarcastic poison he tossed out languorously around the long table.

"Perhaps we could hear from some of the mute students in the room," he would say.

"Sign if you must," he'd add, his gaze sweeping across me like a slashing knife.

In a test of pen and paper I had no doubt I was unmatched among my peers, perhaps even Porter himself (I'd read a few chapters of his book on contemporary American fiction and found the prose to be as dry and joyless as its author). Forced to speak on the spot, however, my mind went as thick and gummy as cold syrup. I couldn't seem to access my own thoughts, and instead of focusing on the discussion, I would retreat into myself to devise a worthy contribution. Something I felt certain would impress, or at least not embarrass me. After several minutes spent honing and polishing it, I would then pass the next ten failing to find a break in the conversation, overpowered by the room's more dominant voices, who inevitably carried the conversation in a different direction.

But there was one person who clearly didn't struggle to make himself heard.

Perhaps you have already guessed who.

Like most of my classmates, Liam Stewart was a year or two younger than I was. The ink barely dried on his bachelor's degree—twenty-two, maybe—with a well-defined jaw, eyes the color of a California sky, and the casual athleticism of a backyard footballer. His strawberry-blond hair was cropped short at the sides, his clothing stylish but approachable. I couldn't help noticing he wore the same watch every day. Brushed silver and expensive-looking, the wide, glistening face bursting with dials and hands. His one nod to extravagance, I imagined. A graduation gift from his father, perhaps.

He was one of the few actual Scots among us, and the first time he spoke, introducing himself as we went around the room the first day of class, he caught me off guard with his rich, full-throated brogue, with its soft extended vowels and rolled r's, the sound melodic yet underpinned by something hard and jagged, like clear water flowing over a bed of pointed rocks. Even the other Scot in the class, a chirpy blonde who happened to be from the same seaside town, couldn't match the wonder of his speech.

But apart from his voice, I can't say I took an immediate liking to him. Liam was the sort of person who generally annoyed me for being my superior in all the ways that mattered to the world. He was tall and handsome and likable. He held the door for strangers, asking how they were even if he didn't know them. He lacked any semblance of insecurity or egoism, commanding the kind of friendly intelligence that dazzled in the classroom. He never shied away from offering his opinion on the topic at hand, and, most vexing of all, it was usually a thoughtful one—unlike most of our classmates, who merely regurgitated the course text in a desperate show of having read a few pages of it. Right away I knew he was something of a golden boy.

Little did I realize, our paths would soon converge.

It all began one day in October. Hungry after missing lunch, I stopped for a bite at the Blind Poet after class, a dingy pub a few steps from campus, the kind of place that billed itself as cozy and authentic but was actually just a bit depressing with student-priced drinks. Halfway through my burger and fries, a group of five or six students entered the pub at great volume: Liam and a few others from Research Methods, plus a couple I didn't recognize. They pushed tables together and ordered drinks at the bar. One of them caught me looking: the blond girl. What was her name again? She seemed to recognize me.

I returned to my burger, pretending not to have seen her, but it was futile.

"Grayson?" she said, coming over. "I'm Sophie. From your Research Methods module?"

"Hi," I said, forcing myself to make eye contact.

"Hello. Em, a few of us are having drinks. You're welcome to join us."

"Thanks," I said, reaching for an excuse, thwarted as usual by my inability to think on my feet. Her enthusiasm was coercive, her smile impervious to my discomfort. The decision was out of my hands.

"Right. Okay."

She beamed.

Food in hand and bag on my shoulder, I followed Sophie through the bar, my feet heavy with dread. She didn't stop talking except to introduce me to the group as we reached the table.

"Most of you know Grayson." She added, for those with blank looks on their faces, "From Research Methods?"

Liam smiled in my direction and offered up his chair. "I'll grab another."

Of course you will, I thought.

I had never felt more like an outsider than I did that afternoon. As they sat around the cluster of round tables pushed together, they gabbed with ease about everything and nothing—classes, TV shows, books—as if they had been friends for years. Set back slightly from the others, I hovered at the edge of their conversation, watching as it splintered off into little side discussions, then smashed back together with a cry of "Oh my god, *Fleabag* is incredible!"

A couple times I opened my mouth to speak and closed it again, crippled by the fear of sounding stupid or dull—then fearing I looked both stupid and dull for having not yet uttered a word. I felt vulnerable, exposed. An object of derision and contempt, even though no one had said a thing to or about me.

My eyes were drawn to Liam and Sophie, who seemed to know each other even better than the rest. Every so often they pulled back from the main conversation to consult each other in low voices. "How's it going?" or "Do you want another drink?" And yet their intimacy felt oddly sexless, more like siblings than lovers. Sophie didn't so much as bat an eye when Liam struck up a conversation with Jenna, the group's second American, whom I had noticed from afar.

A bad girl with a fashionable edge, she wore a black choker with a cross pendant, her hair hoisted up in two dark buns. She spoke with her hands, which were thin and delicate, with long nails painted eggplant. Apparently she was from Bethesda, and ribbed Liam about the way he pronounced her home state.

"It's not 'merry land,' " she said. "You make it sound like the North Pole." She was funny. Sexy, too. The kind of girl I would have liked to date.

But it was Sophie who kept glancing in my direction, Sophie who tried to bring me into the conversation before one of the others cut across her and she let the question die on her lips. Cute, not quite beautiful, with her square jaw and wide-set eyes. Sweet, though. Kind.

I drained my glass just to give myself an excuse to step away. Crossing to the bar, I ordered another Diet Coke, spending down the thousand-pound advance I should have been saving. It would be the last payment I'd receive from D.B. if I didn't touch base with him soon. I had planned to do so all week, managing each day to find a reason to postpone it.

My procrastination had little to do with school or work; the longer I put off reaching out, the longer I could fool myself into thinking that I had it wrong, that it wasn't a book about the Devil he wanted me to write. But I was starting to look unprofessional. I had to bite the bullet. I would email him that night.

Someone stepped up beside me. Turning, I saw it was Liam. A wave of animus rose inside of me. Still, I returned his polite smile as we waited for the bartender, who was busy pouring my soda at the end of the bar.

"All right?" Liam said.

"Good, thanks."

"Noticed you've been quiet."

My cheeks burned with embarrassment; was my awkwardness that obvious? "Sorry."

"Sophie twist your arm into coming over?"

I glanced at him, gauging his expression. His smile told me I could speak freely.

"A little bit."

"She's a sweet girl, but she tends to see what she wants to see in people. I just mean," Liam added, rephrasing, "she's not good at reading signals."

"You know her well?"

"We go way back." He looked around. Then dropping his head, he said more quietly, "If you want to slip out, I'll cover for you. Tell them you had an emergency and had to run."

I hesitated. Tempting as it was, I couldn't tell what he meant by the offer. Was he genuinely trying to help, or would he laugh about it with the others the moment I'd left?

The bartender returned with my soda. "Two pound ten."

"I'll get this," Liam said, already reaching in his pocket. "You go."

"But why?" The question was too blunt, almost rude, but Liam didn't seem to mind.

"Sophie's just gone to the loo. Now's your chance."

He was right.

"Thanks," I said.

Liam winked. It caught me off guard, in a pleasant way; I nodded. Then I crossed back to the table, stopping just long enough to grab my bag before anyone noticed.

As I reached the door of the bar, I found myself hesitating, hanging back to spy Liam returning to the table with my dripping soda in hand.

"That a Coke?" said one of his friends.

"Aye, just fancied it."

"Lightweight."

Liam didn't acknowledge the comment. "Grayson had to run. Some kind of emergency."

"Good. Bit of a weirdo, wasn't he?"

"Not compared to you, mate."

I retreated toward the door, suppressing a grin.

Editor's Note
Exhibit E

Following the Prisons and Probation Ombudsman's inconclusive inquiry into the wounds found on Hale's body, I sat down with Dr. Irene Murray, assistant professor of animal biology at Edinburgh Napier University. The resulting article ran in Scotland on Sunday, *3 February 2019. Here I present an excerpt of our recorded interview.*

BARCLAY: The prison officer who found Hale's body said the marks looked like they'd come from a small, three-fingered animal. Do you agree this was an animal attack?

MURRAY: I would, at first glance, looking at the photos. The marks are quite interesting. You see they're relatively straight? Short but deep. Like raptor talons. My father was a handler of large birds. Owls and hawks. These look like the scratches he used to get on his arms.

BARCLAY: So you think it was a bird?

MURRAY: Ah. Well, no, actually. These marks, you see they're grouped in threes. Most avian species have four toes. We call that tetradactyl. I can only think of a few tridactyl birds native to Scotland. Quail, and a few varieties of grouse. But whatever did this was bigger than that.

BARCLAY: How big?

MURRAY: Forty, fifty centimeters. Something like that. But at any size, a bird attack would leave feathers. I don't believe any were found at the scene?

BARCLAY: Not as far as we know.

MURRAY: Because that would be quite telling. Not many birds could lodge such a vicious attack and not leave anything behind.

BARCLAY: Any guess what it was, then?

MURRAY: It's hard to say. There are remarkably few vertebrates in the animal kingdom with three fingers, especially in the forelimbs.

BARCLAY: There must be a few.

MURRAY: The three-toed sloth? Seems unlikely, doesn't it?

BARCLAY: Hard to imagine a sloth scarpering off unseen.

MURRAY: If I'm being honest, it's hard to imagine any animal of this size getting away unnoticed. Especially when you consider there may have been more than one.

BARCLAY: More than one?

MURRAY: Two or three, I would think, given the distribution of the claw marks.

BARCLAY: And you have no idea what they could have been?

MURRAY: Your guess is as good as mine. [Laughs] A bat out of hell, perhaps?

Eight

THE RADIATOR SEEMED to do nothing, as it ticked away in the corner of the bedroom, but inject the air with the stench of burning metal. I sat huddled before my computer in the thick gray puffer coat I'd recently acquired from H&M—another hit to my thousand-pound advance—the room so cold I could see my breath. Even through the curtains drawn over the window behind the desk, the night air seeped in, sliding its slippery fingers around my neck as I tried out different words in my head.

I had two so far: *Hi D.B.*

The cursor blinked impatiently.

In the hallway, floorboards creaked as Ollie passed by. I braced myself for an intrusion.

My flatmate had become something of a parasite of late. Like me, he had made few friends in the city. But while I wore my solitude like a blanket, he bore his like a rash, one he seemed intent to spread to me. It was expected now that, as I cooked dinner, his bedroom door would open and he would emerge, grasping at straws to make it appear a coincidence.

"Have you seen my headphones anywhere?" he'd say, checking under the pillows on the couch, or "I need a drink," pulling a can of Carlsberg from the fridge.

He would mill around until I finished cooking, then pull out a chair, making some overblown pronouncement as he sat. "I have had *the most horrific* day of my life." Or "Today I encountered the *stupidest* person on the planet."

It didn't matter how or even if I answered. Ollie didn't crave conversation so much as a sounding board for his blathering. If I was lucky, I would finish eating and retreat to my room before he helped himself to leftovers, for once he started making a plate I was stuck.

Fortunately he had recently joined the university water polo team, a move I hoped presaged a change in his availability. Over spaghetti Bolognese the previous week, he'd told me about the initiation ceremony, which saw him and his fellow new recruits led on an all-night pub crawl wearing nothing but Speedos and sneakers. Required to down a pint at every stop, he'd barely made it out of pub number four when he spilled his guts in the street and was forced to do four shots at the next one to make up for it. "Ended up passed out on my mate's floor. Woke up in a pool of my own sick. It was fucking mental."

Eager to abandon the thought, I wrestled some words onto the screen.

Hi D.B.,

Thanks again for the opportunity to work on your book. I'm excited to

I hit backspace until they were gone.

The problem, it occurred to me, was that I wasn't sure what I wanted to communicate: readiness to move forward, or a desire to step back.

My eyes wandered to the strange photocopies and printouts he'd sent me as research for the book. Their mere presence at the corner of my desk left me with a greasy, unclean feeling, which didn't bode well. Thirty thousand pounds was a lot of money, enough to ensure the future I desired. But was it even worth it? It had taken me years to overcome my satanophobia. Writing a book about the Devil seemed akin to injecting the affliction directly into my veins.

Perhaps I was overthinking it. As good as the money was, it seemed foolish to make any decisions until I knew more about the manuscript I was expected to produce.

I sat forward, my fingers moving assuredly across the keyboard.

Hi D.B.,

Sorry for the delay in reaching out. Things have been hectic with the start of the semester, new job, etc. I had a chance to look at the materials you sent over. Not what I expected.

I deleted the last line.

Interesting stuff! I'm looking forward to learning more about what you have in mind for the book. Would you be available for a call or video chat sometime next week so I can get a better sense of what you're looking for?

    Thanks,

    Grayson

The satisfaction I felt upon hitting send was immediately cut short. There was a sound coming from outside.

A low, incomprehensible gibbering, like a man speaking fast under his breath, underlain with something utterly inhuman, a hum like the buzz of a wasp.

It felt as if a ball of ice had exploded within me, spraying my insides with frozen needles. The sound was unmistakable. I had heard it hundreds of times before—but no. It couldn't be that. I had not seen them in years. Anyway, hadn't I decided they never really existed? That they were nothing more than figments of a tortured imagination?

Still, I rose to my feet, trembling slightly. Throwing the curtains wide, I scanned the dark garden below. Nothing could be seen moving but shirts and trousers swaying from the clothesline. I opened the window and stuck out my head. Never mind the cold and the buffeting wind; I needed to be sure the gibbering was nothing. A human voice, or the burbling of someone's television. I needed to be certain they weren't back.

There was silence. Whatever the source of the gibbering, it was gone now. I thumped the sill angrily and reeled my head back in.

The moment I shut the window, a horrible, birdlike shriek rent the night. Then *SLAM!* I jumped back. Something had collided with the glass, a winged creature the size of a house cat. The only part of it I could see clearly were its talons, three of them on each hand, grappled around the pigeon it had smashed against the windowpane. The bird was clearly dead, its beak open in a frozen cry, intestines spilling out of a diagonal slash across its belly like a burst seam. They left a crimson smear across the glass as the bird's attacker retreated from the window, flapping away with its prize.

My hands shook violently as they fumbled to lock the window. My mind raced. *What was that? What the fuck was that?* I was still acting like I didn't know, though in the darkest place of my heart I had been dreading this for days.

Had been dreading the creatures' return since the day I opened D.B.'s parcel and sensed, as one might register the relapse of a deadly cancer, the encroaching return of my fear.

A dinging sound drew my eyes back to the laptop. D.B. had responded to my email.

Meet me at the witchery tmrw, 18.00. Ive been looking forward to this

Nine

SATANOPHOBIA IS NOT a clinical term. You won't find it in any psychology handbooks. No encyclopedia of mental ailments contains it. It is a term known primarily to those who bear the affliction. A word we use to classify and validate a pattern of fear that others, perhaps rightly, would call insanity.

Some disagree. They say we're not sick at all.

They say, *The one you fear is real—and he's coming.*

～

It arrived unannounced on my thirteenth birthday, the strangest of my life to date.

Other than the store-bought sheet cake my mother might serve after fellowship, the seventh of February tended to come and go without fanfare. There were no parties full of children, no bouncy castles in the backyard. Gifts were practical: a shirt or two, some underwear, a backpack to replace the one coming apart at the seams.

For my thirteenth, we celebrated with a home-cooked dinner of chicken thighs, rice, and canned green beans, a meal my mother prepared at least three times a month. The only special treat to be found around the table was my father. He hadn't joined us for dinner in weeks. It was nice to imagine my first day of adolescence meant that much to him.

We ate our thighs and sipped our water, speaking hardly a word. I had already opened my gift from Vera: a pair of scuffed leather shoes from the Rescue Mission thrift store. I lingered at the table, wondering if my father might offer some acknowledgment of my special day, but when he pushed back from the table and departed without a word, I retired to my bedroom.

I was on the bed reading a chapter out of my social studies textbook when there came a knock at the door. I expected it to open right away—my mother delivering a stack of clean laundry, perhaps. When it didn't, I turned with curiosity.

"Come in," I called out.

The door opened. The sight of my father startled me off the mattress.

"What are you doing in here?" I regretted these words, which made it sound as if he weren't welcome. But I was merely surprised; he never came inside my room.

He had something in his hand. He held it out for me to take: a slim, rectangular object, wrapped in childish paper patterned with balloons.

As I accepted the gift, I could feel immediately it was a book. A very small one, about the size of a postcard.

Eagerly I removed the wrapping. One tear revealed a cover bound in grayish-blue cloth. I fingered the supple gold lettering across the front. Old-fashioned in style yet clearly brand-new, as if he had commissioned it specially. *Jack and the Devil's Horn* by Ned Duhamel.

I thanked him. "I've been wanting to read this," I added, not wanting him to know I was unfamiliar with the title.

He paused, his eyes narrowing under thick brows. "Well. It's time you did, in any case."

Why now? I wondered. The book appeared to be a story for children. He seemed to notice my confusion, pausing as he retreated to the door.

"You're a young man now. Soon you'll face new temptations. Or old temptations, strengthened by the changes to your physiology. You'll have questions," he said. "The answers are in that book."

Answers I could not find in the Bible? The thought was strangely unsettling.

"I should hope you understand it," my father said. He closed the door behind him as he left the room.

For several moments I remained rooted to the spot, my emotions a jumble. On one hand, here was the most precious gift I'd ever received, for no other reason than my father had given it. Somewhere behind that mask of aloof genius, Edmund Hale had thought of me—and me only. Nathaniel had never received a special gift from him; if he had, he would have been sure to wave it in my face until I cried. The book signified that he saw me as different than my brother, perhaps more worthy of teaching. I was elated—but at the same time, concerned.

I should hope you understand it. Was there a chance I might not? Was the book difficult to read, like Chaucer? Like *Animal Farm*, did it hold some deeper meaning that might elude me? It was this thought especially that filled me with dread. What if I didn't comprehend its hidden message? Would he think I was stupid, a blockhead like my brother?

Determined to prove his doubts unfounded, I carried the book to my desk and sat. It didn't take long to get through. The story was only thirty or so pages, even with generously proportioned typesetting and several illustrations, like nineteenth-century wood engravings.

But it was not the fear of disappointing my father that kept me glued to my seat; by the time I turned the final page, an entirely different kind of anxiety possessed me.

The book represented a single story written in the tradition of a Scottish folktale. In this tale, a young traveler named Jack is walking through the forest when he encounters a stranger cloaked in black. Famished from his travels, Jack strikes a bargain with the stranger, promising to take his horn into the village and blow it so that all should hear, and in return he shall receive a feast beyond imagining.

But when he reaches the edge of the village, Jack loses his nerve, not wanting to anger the villagers with the call of the horn. And so, upon returning to the forest, he lies to the stranger, saying he has blown the horn when he has not. Apparently none the wiser, the stranger presents Jack with his promised meal and goes off. All seems well until Jack realizes his ill-begotten feast has been cursed. Enslaved by its power, he finds himself unable to control his most savage impulses, becoming, without realizing it, an instrument of the Devil.

The book left me in a dreadful state, my flesh chilled and raised in hard bumps. It had been years since I feared the coming of the Devil, but in the reading of the book, the thought forcefully rebounded.

After all, he had come for me once before. Long-forgotten images flooded back to my mind: the storm battering the house, the great horned Beast looming over my crib, the glowing orange tongue slithering toward me, searing his mark into my arm. For years I had managed to block Nathaniel's story from my memory. Now it came slingshotting back, bringing with it the sickening fear that I played host to a rank and inborn evil. That it had drawn the Devil to me, and he had marked me as his own. That one day, perhaps one day soon, he would return to collect what was rightfully his.

And from that small germ, a great sickness was born.

⁓

As is typical in cases of satanophobia, my symptoms were subtle to begin with.

The first occurrence was during third-period English, seventh grade. The class was taught by Mrs. Aguilar, an obese woman with a large mole on her chin, her long black ponytail shot through with strands of silver. Mrs. Aguilar was strict, but she liked me because my essays were generally pristine and if I wasn't sure something was right, I would stay after class and ask. Most of the time my assignments earned A's, but one day not long after my thirteenth birthday, she handed back an essay on *Lord of the Flies* marked with a B+. *Good but a few too many errors. The devil's in the details!*

I couldn't explain it: reading those words, I felt a slight twist of shock behind my sternum, as when a disgusting image is thrust under one's nose without warning. It made no sense. I'd heard that saying a thousand times. If anything, it was the grade that should have concerned me, but compared to the note I hardly noticed it. Not sure what else to do, I stuffed the essay in my backpack and tried to forget it.

I couldn't. As I went about my day, my mind kept scuttling back to that scribbled note, that *word*. I was hyperconscious of its presence in my bag, and that I didn't want it there. At lunch I crumpled up the essay and threw it in the dumpster outside the cafeteria, relieved, if perplexed, to be rid of it at last.

The feeling was short-lived. I had never thought of *devil* as a common word, but it seemed to crop up everywhere in the days that followed—a Dirt Devil vacuum commercial, a pack of deviled eggs at the grocery store, a filler track of my once beloved Five for Fighting album—that little twist of discomfort growing more pronounced each time it did.

Demonic imagery was even worse. Be it a William Blake painting or an episode of *Family Guy*, one look and I'd be dizzy with fear. Soon my aversion expanded to depictions of hellfire, pentagrams, the number 666—especially the number, which dogged me without rest. I'd grab a burrito from my neighborhood taco shop, and the total would ring up $6.66. I'd place an order on Amazon and, a minute later, that same succession of sixes would appear in my inbox, buried in a seventeen-digit order number. Before I even knew what I was scared of, I would scramble to erase it: supplement my burrito with a bag of tortilla chips, or cancel my online order, deleting not just the email but the entire contents of my inbox, which were contaminated with the presence of his number. Like Mrs. Aguilar's note, these manifestations of the Adversary felt dangerous somehow. More than just symbolize him, they seemed to portend his arrival, each one the conduit through which he might finally strike. As if that cartoon Satan on *Family Guy* might compel him to appear and regard his image. As if to receive an email containing the number 666 was to send *him* a message: *Come, Master.*

Within weeks, life itself had become a minefield of anxiety, for any-thing that could be regarded as sinful seemed likely to induce his ar-rival. Eating too much at dinner. Having impure thoughts. Losing focus during fellowship. Each illicit act like a beacon to the Devil. Just the thought of it would make my hands shudder and my temples stream cold sweat. I would experience a physical sensation of fear like I'd never known before: a sudden feeling of emptiness in my chest, as if the bot-tom had fallen out of my body; of tendrils climbing the walls of my torso and choking my heart.

Sometimes, when I really lost control—when Nathaniel tormented me so badly that I lashed out against him, when I found my desires too much to control—my head would spin and I would wobble on my feet and it would get so hot it was like the world was engulfed in flames. Like he'd already got me and dragged me down to hell.

But no matter how bad things got, I never went to my parents. In the church, mental illness was often thought to signal the presence of de-monic spirits in the body. I could only imagine what my parents would do if they found out. Confine me to my bedroom, perhaps, or send me away to be exorcised by men in white robes. My mother would insist on it, I had no doubt.

Fortunately, she remained as inattentive to my well-being as ever. It was as if she were actively ignoring the signs. One year on Halloween, Feliciano Montoya showed up to homeroom costumed in red face paint, plastic horns from Party City, and a Sun Devils jersey, and even this crude representation was enough to leave me shaky and short of breath. The school nurse sent me home early, telling my mother I'd had a panic attack. Although she made a scene of acting shocked and concerned in the office, in private she did not even acknowledge I'd been ill.

Moving into my sophomore year, I still hadn't told a soul about my condition, and the secret was taking its toll. Internet forums on satano-phobia became my only outlet, and they were hardly reassuring, rife with stories of people who had been living with the condition for de-cades and others it had driven to suicide. I began to despair that this sickness would never pass, that I would be stuck this way forever: living in fear of my fear, humiliated each time it struck.

I didn't think it could get much worse.

I was wrong.

In the Point Loma neighborhood of San Diego, it was hard to sleep past six in the morning. The trees were inhabited by a species of Mexican parrot, small and lime green with a splotch of red above the beak, that screeched and squawked a terrible morning song. It wasn't known exactly when they had come to reside in the area, but they were daily visitors to the branches of the carob tree outside my parents' house, lighting up the sky with their shrill conversation. Walking out the front door each morning I was greeted by their racket.

But one morning that changed. The night before had been a rough one; my father had referenced the Adversary twice in his teaching about the sin of venality, leaving me tossing and turning all night. As I trudged out of the house, exhausted, to catch the morning bus, there was no screeching or squawking to be heard—only a sound I could not place. A low sort of gibbering.

I turned my gaze up to the carob tree and perceived a silhouette perched on a high branch. It was a foot and a half tall, not feathered but smooth-skinned, large wings folded behind its back. Whatever it was, it seemed to be watching me.

Some minutes later I boarded the school bus at the end of the road. As I laid my head against the window to catch a few minutes' extra sleep, I thought of that strange shape in the tree. A new species of bird? It looked more like a bat, but weren't they nocturnal?

At that moment a dark shadow dove past the window, jolting me upright. Peering through the dirty glass, I glimpsed a black winged body flapping away over the traffic, its squidgy face peering back at me, revealing hundreds of needlelike teeth.

Shaken by the sighting, I kept my guard up all day, checking for winged shadows as I walked from building to building. The only wings I saw were on a seagull during lunch period, waddling across the sidewalk to peck at a stale french fry; I convinced myself I had imagined the whole thing.

My error was corrected when I arrived home to find a dozen sets of yellow eyes peering down at me from the carob tree, my ears ringing with a chorus of gibbers.

After that day, these creatures—these fiends, as I began to think of them—started following me around town. Mostly after intense bouts of satanophobia, but sometimes heralding one to come. They tore open a box of cereal at the grocery store. Scratched at my bedroom window as I undressed. Circled me like buzzards as I walked home from the library.

Only I could see them or the destruction they wrought. Once, I caught them playing tug-of-war with a neighborhood cat. They ripped it limb from limb while the old lady who owned it stood outside watering her begonias. "Beautiful day, isn't it?" she called out to me as I passed, the poor tabby audibly screaming in the background.

Meanwhile, the condition was getting harder to hide. After I missed three fellowships in a row—one because I was "ill," two others to attend to falsified extracurricular commitments—Vera called an end to my truancy.

I didn't often argue, but that night I raised hell. My shouts could likely be heard down the street, and I was glad, knowing there was little that could upset my mother more. She put an end to my remonstrations by taking the underside of my arm between her fingers and twisting the flesh until I gasped.

"Raise your voice to me again," she murmured close to my ear, "and I will show you the full wrath of the Lord."

That night, believers were still trickling in as I forced myself into the living room, my arm bruised and purple where no one could see, my heart thumping at the thought of my father's teaching.

Fellowship started at seven thirty sharp. Seated on the couch, I obediently joined the believers in prayer and confessed to having disrespected my mother. She responded with a polite, forgiving nod.

When the Sharing of Confession was over, my father confirmed the worst by asking us to turn to John 8:44. I knew what was coming before I even opened my Bible; I'd had the verse memorized by the time I was five.

"Grayson, please read aloud."

I shook my head, my Bible closed in silent protest. I didn't care that the believers were turning to look. That my mother was seething behind her smile, and Nathaniel grinning with callous amusement. My eyes were on my father, his usually impassive expression clouded with confusion.

It seemed he was about to do the reading himself, but before he could begin, my mother intervened.

"Don't be shy, Gray. You're a wonderful reader." Her sunny tone concealed a hint of steel.

My eyes flicked to my father, who gave me nothing.

The Bible remained closed on my lap as I began.

"'You belong to your father, the d-devil, and your will is to do your father's desires.'"

My lips were shaking. I had that familiar sensation of emptiness in my chest, of something crawling the interior walls of my body and strangling my heart. The Adversary was on the move, I could feel it.

"'He was a murderer from the beginning, and abode n-not in the truth—'"

The room began to spin, my mind engulfed in sounds that only I could hear. Talons scratching at the window. A chorus of gibbering screams.

"'Because there is—there is no truth in him—'"

"Is he okay?" one of the believers was saying.

"He hasn't been feeling well," trilled my mother, bustling over to me. "Come on, G, let's get you to bed."

The fiends grew louder, shaking the glass as they assaulted the window-pane. I pushed on, for the moment I gave up would be the moment they broke through, the moment they got me and took me away.

"'When he speaketh a lie, he sp—when he speaketh a lie—'"

"Come on, darling." Vera was tugging me up to my feet. The Bible slid off my lap and onto the floor.

"'When he speaketh a lie, he speaketh in his native tongue,'" I said, staggering forward. "'For he is a liar—and the father of lies—'"

My knees buckled, and then everything went dark.

At the hospital later that night, the doctor told my parents I had suffered a panic attack. My mother was getting used to hearing this.

"Why would he have a panic attack?" she snapped, a rare break in her public persona.

"Perhaps you should ask your son," the doctor said, and left the three of us alone.

It was quiet but for the beeping of machines and the ambient noise of nurses treating patients. My mother regarded me contemptuously.

"Well?"

I didn't know what to say. I looked at my father, who merely held my gaze. There was something knowing in it, but what?

The time had come to tell them the truth.

Once I started, it was impossible to stop. Everything came out: the return of my childhood fear, the arrival of the fiends, even the weird feeling of emptiness in my chest when the Adversary was near. The only thing I omitted was that it was my father's birthday gift that had caused my affliction, not wanting him to think this was somehow his fault.

As I had guessed she would, my mother treated my phobia less as a mental illness than a miscarriage of faith. She subjected me not to a battery of psychological evaluations and drugs but to a mandatory program of spiritual fortification led by my father.

We met nightly in his study for a period of months. More than instructive, these sessions were interrogatory, an hour spent questioning me about the events of my day: any episodes or hallucinations I had experienced, any impure thoughts I'd acted upon before or after. Most of all, he wanted to know whom I had met. What they had said to me, what they were wearing, if I had seen them again. It was of the utmost importance that I describe every detail.

"The eyes, what color were they?" he might say.

"I don't know," I'd answer, and my father would slam his fist on the desk.

After years of hungering for his attention, our meetings were an acrid treat. Most nights I left Edmund's study more unnerved than I had entered, and yet routinely I embellished the day's events to prolong my time in his company. I hated his seeing me this way, all haunted and defective, wincing every time he spoke the Adversary's name. Still, I could not deny the pleasure of at last being seen.

My mother was predictably cruel. She instructed Nathaniel to maintain a physical distance of at least six feet, as if I were contagious, and forbade me from breathing a word of my condition to anyone, especially the believers. She had convinced them my fainting spell was the result of low blood sugar. No doubt she knew the truth would be bad for business. After all, who would pay to receive spiritual guidance from a man whose own son was beset with visions of the Devil?

Somehow, Vera blamed my father for my condition. Once I heard her berating him, her loud whisper carrying through the closed door of their bedroom. "We could lose the whole ministry because of this. Everything I've worked for is hanging by a thread, thanks to you. Did you really think it would never catch up with you?"

What had he done? My condition had nothing to do with him.

"Did you think you'd be able to lead a normal life after all that?" she continued. "I always knew he would be the same. His father's son."

I leapt back as my father burst out of the room, pausing momentarily at the sight of me. The embarrassment on his face speared me with guilt.

Determined to prove my mother wrong about me, about both of us, I doubled down on fighting my phobia. And yet everything I did just seemed to make it worse. Instructed by my father to cleanse my soul through righteous acts, I started reading the Bible again. An hour a day at least, sometimes two or three, using Wite-Out to obscure any verses likely to aggravate my condition. Upon seeing how I had desecrated my Bible, my father castigated me and made me beg the Lord's forgiveness. That night, I heard gibbering under my bed as I tried to sleep.

Meanwhile, my mother got me a weekend volunteer slot at the Rescue Mission, a brutal 6:00 a.m. shift serving breakfast to the homeless. Due to my worsening insomnia, I routinely overslept it, missing so many Saturdays that the organization eventually removed my name from the roster, putting me in a more precarious moral position than when I had started.

The only thing I seemed to be able to do without exacerbating my condition was pray. Three times a day, seven on the Sabbath, I entreated the Lord. But it turned out the more frequently and fervently I begged for His protection, the more I transgressed. Every day the fiends grew in number, circled ever nearer. Any moment now I would feel their hands pull me up by the collar of my shirt. Any moment they would take me to their master.

It was too much to bear. Suicide crossed my mind often. I just wanted the pain to end. But of course it wouldn't—not with death. To end one's life was its own sin, one of the Adversary's most prized. There was perhaps no faster way to realize my fear.

All I knew was that something had to happen. I could not go on like this much longer.

~

The end came swiftly. Too swiftly to be fully believed or trusted, and yet in a way I had been building to it for years, ever since Drew Bowden, a boy who lived in my neighborhood, told me his family didn't believe in God.

It was the first I had encountered such open disbelief. I was shocked, and angry too, when he said my whole family was stupid for believing in God.

"We're not stupid," I said, digging my heels into the sand of the neighborhood playground. I was six. "God's real."

"Oh yeah?" he said, sliding off of the swing. "Then why can't we see him?"

I stammered, unable to answer.

Drew threw his arms wide and shouted to the sky. "God, if You're real, hit me with lightning right now!"

As he held his pose, waiting, I peered up into the sky. An expanse of gentle blue, not even a cloud. *Please, God*, I pleaded, my fingers laced. *Please, show him You exist.*

Finally Drew dropped his hands to his sides, a smug grin on his face. "See?"

My belief was rattled, and so I sought to undergird it. I went to Reyna, one of the regulars at fellowship. A petite, round-faced woman who had immigrated from the Philippines by way of Canada, she was kind and complimented my reading, always in her charming acquired English that saw prefixes swapped freely and words substituted with their almost-right counterparts.

"You are very comprehending," she would say approvingly, after I'd read aloud or shown her a bit of my schoolwork. "One day you will be a scholar like your daddy."

Though very serious about the Lord, she had a playful side too, and as we waited in the living room for fellowship to start, she would joke with me and tickle my neck until I collapsed on the floor in a puddle of laughs.

A couple times a year my parents put on a big potluck at Mission Bay Park, and believers came from all over the county to pray in public and eat free food. My mother would don a vibrant dress and go person to person, drumming up business. It was during one of these potlucks that I pulled Reyna aside and asked her the questions I could not ask my parents. *Why can't we see God? Why doesn't He prove He's real when I ask Him? Why don't I hear Him in my head when I pray?*

She looked surprised but understanding. Smiling, she crouched down before me and said, "God is unvisible as a test of our faith. It would be easy to believe something you can see with your eyes and touch with your hands, but they call us believers because we believe even when it's demanding."

It was a compelling enough explanation to my six-year-old mind, and in the short term it came as a great relief. I could feel the joists and girders of my belief beginning to steady. But Drew Bowden had put cracks in the foundation, and those cracks would grow with every passing year. By the time I entered high school, not even Reyna could fully satisfy my doubts.

As my satanophobia reached its peak in my teenage years, I stopped confiding in her altogether. A receptionist at a mental health and rehab clinic, she probably dealt with crazy people all day. No doubt she would recognize my condition for the sickness it was—perhaps even tell my parents. It seemed safest to put some distance between us. No more after-fellowship powwows. No hugs. No contact at all. I shut her out, holding firm even as she sobbed at my bedroom door, demanding to know what she had done to warrant my disdain, before my mother finally came and spirited her away, murmuring, "No need to make a scene. I'm sure it's just a misunderstanding."

I did not relent even when she stopped attending fellowship altogether.

Then one day, I experienced an awakening. I was sitting in fellowship as my father lectured about the Resurrection of Christ, how on the third day He rose from the grave, and I found myself wanting to roll my eyes. *Jesus rose from the grave?* I thought dubiously, as if hearing it for the first time. *He just got up and staggered out of that tomb like a zombie? And I'm just supposed to believe that?*

The harshness of my skepticism surprised even me. It was as if I'd been so focused on managing my condition, I hadn't noticed the doubt silently accumulating under the foundations of my faith, building up pressure and threatening to blow them apart, sending my entire belief system crashing down around me.

Several days later, my newfound skepticism met my condition head-on. I was riding the express trolley downtown, on my way to meet my fellow Key Club members to serve lunch to some old folks at the senior center, the kind of forced servitude people said was good for college admissions, when I found myself besieged by fiends. My mother had dropped me at Old Town station, and on the way we had passed a billboard for the movie *Drag Me to Hell*, depicting a screaming woman surrounded by flames, monstrous hands grasping possessively at her body. Since then, the loathsome creatures had been steadily gathering—rooting through the trash cans at the station, then following the trolley as it pulled away from the platform.

As the scarlet train bore me south through the city, they appeared in the window opposite my seat. By the time we reached Washington Street, two had become ten. Come Little Italy, they crowded every window and door, darkening the car as they blocked out the sun, clawing ferociously at the glass as if trying to get at me.

As their number continued to grow, I sat forward clutching my head in my hands, my whole body shaking. I'd never seen so many at once— fifty now. A hundred. They rocked the trolley off its tracks as they threw themselves against it, moments away from breaking through the glass and snatching me away. The terror built up inside of me like steam, a violent, scalding tension. I couldn't take it much longer; the scream was rising in my throat when someone said—

"Grayson? Is that you?"

My eyes snapped open. A young man stood before me, stubbly and tall. Someone I both recognized and didn't.

"Drew Bowden, remember? From across the street?"

I blinked. So it was. I hadn't seen my old neighbor in over a decade. His family had moved away not long after that day at the playground.

"You okay, man?" he said, when I failed to answer.

"Sorry. Yeah."

I stood, unsteady on my feet. I held out my hand to him, and taking it, he pulled me in for a black-slapping hug. Yellow eyes watched menac-

ingly from the window, the fiends screaming and champing and slamming against the wide pane. I felt dizzy.

"You good? How're your parents?"

"They're good . . . all fine."

The sound of breaking glass drew my eyes to the sliding door to my
left; the fiends were beginning to punch their way through.

"Still doing that fellow-thing?"

"Huh? Oh, fellowship. Yeah."

They clawed at the jagged edges of the glass, opening it wider. Then
another crash, this one behind Drew. And a third, somewhere to my
right.

"You don't still believe in that stuff, do you?"

"What? No. No. I mean—" I broke off. Distracted by the fiends'
advance, I'd spoken without thinking, giving voice to a fact I hadn't
known, until that moment, to be true. "No. I guess I don't."

"Finally wised up, huh? Realized that shit was all in your head?"

All around us fiends were reaching into the train with long-fingered
talons, superheating the atmosphere with their rank, gibbering breath.

"Shit, you were *so* scared of the Devil." He laughed. "Do you remember that?"

"It was all in my head . . ."

"Your brother had you believing in demons."

"But I don't anymore. I don't believe."

It was as if I had unknowingly uttered a spell; in an instant the trolley
car went silent. The window in front of me, like all of them, was whole
again, its view out to North Harbor Drive and the bay unobstructed.

The fiends had disappeared.

And with them, so had Drew. I turned my head left and right, searching the trolley for him. Like my tormentors, it was as if he'd never been
there at all.

Part of me struggled to believe it. Drew couldn't have vanished like
that. I must have nodded off in the heat of the train, must have dreamt
him up. The fiends too. They weren't there any longer, but it was only a

matter of time. They'd be waiting for me at my destination (they weren't). I'd walk in to find them swiping the seniors' lunches and dumping them over their heads (I didn't). I'd hear them under my bed as I lay down to sleep that night (I couldn't).

Little though I could believe it, my satanophobia had gone into re-mission. From that day, the name of the Adversary no longer sent me into paroxysms of fear. How could it, when I could no longer fool myself that he was real? The fiends too were a thing of the past; no matter how I sinned, they did not reappear.

If I continued to avoid depictions of the Devil after that day, that was because I was less frightened of them than of reawakening my condi-tion. The only thing I feared now was its recurrence.

Finding myself reading the Devil's intent into a random coincidence. Thinking, once again, that he was after me.

Sitting in my bedroom on a cold dark night and hearing, outside my window, the sound of his coming, on the wings of a fiend.

Editor's Note
Exhibit F

Further case notes prepared by Kathleen Prichard, mental health counselor at HMP Edinburgh.

17 October 2017

Today patient disclosed past mental health struggles, namely a three-year bout of what he calls "satano-phobia," i.e., extreme fear of the Devil coupled with persecutory delusions that the Devil is "after him," visual hallucinations of winged creatures ("fiends"), feelings of hopelessness, and suicidal ideations. Multiple times patient mentioned having felt, at the onset of and throughout his condition, that there lay inside of him a kind of darkness, or evil, that attracted the Devil like a magnet. Patient could not describe this "darkness" further. Unclear what it could represent. Possible manifestation of some form of unconscious repression, perhaps as the result of patient's religious upbringing? Will continue to explore in future sessions but will need to tread carefully.

Ten

THE SUN WAS falling fast toward the sea, casting shadows of gold and purple over the Royal Mile. I found the Witchery sequestered off a dark courtyard of potted plants just feet from the castle esplanade, the great fortress of Edinburgh Castle looming like a monolith in the distance.

The downstairs dining room was sepulchral and Gothic in style, the walls and ceiling paneled in dark, carved oak, the seating upholstered in oxblood leather. It would have been a cave except for the gilt candelabras and ornate brass candlesticks casting a glow over the white table linens. It seemed an appropriate venue to deliver bad news.

D.B. wouldn't like my decision, but my mind was set.

Once again he was already seated when I entered the dining room.

"Sorry I'm late," I said, slinging my bag over the back of the chair and peeling off my jacket.

Was I imagining it or was there something different about my employer? His features appeared somehow reapportioned. The jaw a little squarer, the nose just slightly bent. Still recognizable as himself but different enough to make me question the image I had held in my mind. I sat. There were a few other parties scattered around the room. Like D.B. they were finely attired. The menu before me confirmed the restaurant's pedigree. After a few pleasantries I ordered a Diet Coke.

"And for your main, sir?"

Feeling under pressure, I panicked, and spoke the first recognizable words I saw on the menu. "The pot roast, please."

"Pot roast pigeon. Excellent choice."

I managed a smile as the waiter left with the menus. I couldn't help thinking of the previous night. The mirth tugging at the corner of D.B.'s mouth gave the impression that somehow he knew.

"Ye look unsettled," he said.

"I'm fine."

"Ye read what I sent ye?"

"Yes."

"All of it?"

"Yeah. Yes. Of course." This wasn't true. Not by half. Even knowing what I needed to do, the lie discomfited me. "That's what I wanted—"

"Fascinating stuff, no? Perhaps no' all academically significant— I trust your judgment there. But enough to get started."

Get started on what?

But the question was irrelevant now. I unbuttoned my shirt cuffs and rolled them up to the elbow. The restaurant was like a sauna.

"Donny—"

The waiter returned with drinks. Meanwhile a man and woman took seats at the next table. He was in his twenties, luxuriantly rugged. The woman, quite a bit older, shrugged off a fur coat to reveal a slinky dress of red velvet underneath, low-cut to show off her enhanced breasts. The young man took her spotty ringed hand in his, gazing across the table with a roguish gleam in his eye.

"Donny, I've given it a lot of thought," I said when the waiter departed. "Unfortunately I don't think I can write your book."

He paused as he swirled his glass of whisky. "I thought we had an agreement."

"We did."

He put the glass down. "If this is about money—"

"It's not." Already I felt my resolve waning. Felt myself wanting to take it back, yell *gotcha*, anything to make this excruciating awkwardness end. "I just don't think—"

"What is it?"

Say it. Just say it: your book terrifies me.

"I just don't feel right taking this on, knowing how much is already on my plate. I thought I could do it, but between my research and student teaching, I just won't have time. Not enough to give it the attention it deserves."

D.B. was impassive. For a moment I thought he might say something nasty, at least chide me for wasting his time. But he didn't. "Your mind's made up, then?"

"It is."

"Well then." At last he raised the glass to his mouth and drank. "No point trying to convince ye otherwise."

I breathed out for what felt like the first time in minutes. "Thanks for understanding." I reached for my soda and swilled it. "About the advance, I'm going to the bank tomorrow. I should be able to—"

"Don't bother about that. We'll square up when you're ready. You'll at least stay for dinner?"

"Of course."

We made small talk until the food came, the atmosphere—to my relief—amiable and relaxed. It felt as if a great weight had been lifted from my shoulders. Still, I balked when the waiter set a whole pigeon before me, flat on its back with its wings akimbo. I pushed the meat around the plate.

"You don't have to answer this," I said, eager to think of anything but the previous night, the bird's cold orange eyes and fleshy innards pressed flat against the glass, "but I'm still curious about your book. What you intend for it. I thought it was a history of Scotland—you know, one of those touristy local-history books with the sepia covers."

D.B. let out a barking laugh.

"But the documents you sent me, they're all about—"

"The Devil?" He cracked open a red shellfish with his hands. "Well, aye. What could be more Scottish?"

I stopped nodding when I realized I didn't know what he meant.

"Are you afraid of the Devil, Grayson?"

"I'm an atheist, so—"

"That's no' what I asked."

"I mean . . ." I attempted to coax a pea onto my fork. It was really very hot in there. "Isn't everyone?"

"Good answer." His eyes gleamed approvingly. "Very good. But no. Not Scotland."

"Not Scotland?"

"They've forgotten him."

I shook my head, still not understanding.

"You'll know this because of your research: the Devil was like royalty here once. The second king of Scotland, ye could say. He ruled over the Scots, their innermost thoughts. Their darkest fears. In the sixteenth century, every man, woman, and child north of Berwick grew up knowing the 'Deil' lived among them. They lived in constant fear of him. In fear of themselves."

"Okay," I said, wishing now that I hadn't asked.

"Today the Scots haven't got a clue. They indulge their vices like there's no consequence. Like they're *in control* of their sin. They don't realize he never left. They don't realize *the Devil still lives in Scotland*."

A chill ran through me, in defiance of the elevated temperature of the room. "Metaphorically, you mean."

"Metaphorically. Always with the fucking metaphors, aye. Maybe you're a metaphor. A metaphor for 'take the advance and piss off.'"

"Sorry. I didn't mean to—you're really passionate about this."

D.B. allowed a grin. "Ye could say that."

As he flagged down the waiter for another round, my eyes strayed to the woman in the red dress. She had gotten up to visit another table, an adult family she seemed to know. Left to his own devices, her young lover eyed the silver clutch hanging off the back of her chair. Certain his date couldn't see him, he unhooked the strap from the corner of the chair, extracted a handful of paper notes from the bag, and secreted the cash in his jacket pocket. Swiftly restored to its former position, the bag looked as if it hadn't been touched.

"Ye see it now," D.B. said, as the woman resumed her seat unawares.

The man grasped her hand again, and covered it in open-mouthed kisses.

"The Devil . . . he's here."

After we finished eating, D.B. paid the bill and we walked together down the Royal Mile, both of us headed in that direction anyway. It was dark now and seemed to have rained. The cobblestones shone in the night like the scales of a black mamba as we passed the Tolbooth Kirk, towering over the street with its black gothic spires and belfry, a scarlet door crouched under its central arch.

Tall metal lamps illuminated the front courtyard, decked with clashing jewel-tone banners reading words like TICKETS, EVENTS, CAFÉ. The church now existed as a community art space, yet another venue for the annual festivals. Even for an atheist there was something sad about it, like a piece of history melted down to make souvenirs.

"Your father would be ashamed," remarked D.B., following my sightline.

I turned to him in surprise, then remembered I had told him about my minister father at the Devil's Advocate.

"No?" he said.

"I-I'm sure he would."

Now I was thinking about my father, I couldn't help imagining him as a student, walking down the same street. Dwarfed by the same historic buildings. Feeling the unevenness of the cobbles through the soles of his shoes. Had he carried on past the church like I did, or had he stood before it, already feeling himself being pulled toward a life of devotion?

"He's no longer with us," I added. A poor choice of words. I'd never liked that phrase. It felt overly precious, too resonant with the lies of the Gospel.

"Sorry to hear that."

"He was a student here too, back in the day."

"And now you're carrying on the family legacy."

"Sort of."

A black taxi pulled up to the side of the road and disgorged its fares.

"He withdrew from the university early. Always regretted it."

"How d'ye know?"

There was something strange about D.B.'s interest, as if he were personally involved. We split apart as a lone pedestrian passed between us. When we reunited, I could see my companion was still waiting for a response.

"He left a note," I said.

"What did it say?"

This line of questioning was starting to make me uncomfortable, but there was an intensity about D.B.'s question that was hard to refuse. "Not much. Just that he wanted more for me . . . that he prayed I 'enter by the narrow gate.'"

"The narrow gate?"

"Matthew 7:13. 'Enter by the narrow gate. For the gate is wide and the way is easy that leads to destruction . . .'"

"'And those who enter by it are many.'"

I wasn't sure whether to be impressed or disconcerted.

"That's the difference between Americans and Scots," said D.B. bitterly.

"What is?"

"Americans, like your father. They fear their sin."

This was true, at least of Edmund Hale. I'd never met a man more concerned for the sanctity of his soul, or that of his congregation.

"Why should they no'," D.B. continued, "when every morning they wake up to news of another school shooting or shopping-center massacre? They know better than anyone what evil man's capable of. That's why they arm themselves with guns. Why they're constantly enacting legislation against their own freedoms. Gay marriage, abortion, a man's right to piss in the women's toilets. They're scared of what they might be tempted to do, given the choice."

I was meant to turn at George IV Bridge to get home, but curious, I stayed with him. "And the Scots?"

"Just look at them." He nodded to a pub across the street. Although it was not yet seven, the place was so full that people were starting to spill out onto the street, cradling cigarettes between their fingertips as, with the same hands, they raised full glasses to their lips. Their hacking laughter carried all the way across the road. "Indulging vice has become the foundation of Scottish society, its cultural identity. Even its political agenda: sin dressed up as progressive social values. They used to fear the Devil. Now it's like they never heard of him."

"What changed?"

"The two structures that govern all fear. I'll bet ye can guess."

I shrugged. "Religion? Politics?"

"Clever lad." He smiled. A feeling of warmth flooded my chest.

"So is that what your book's about? Not the Devil as a supernatural entity, but, how would you put it? The way changing sociopolitical structures have informed Scottish attitudes about, and belief in, the Devil?"

"Beautifully worded," he said admiringly. "Shame you're not available. You're just the kind of writer I need. The very person to make Scotland remember the Devil."

It was pathetic how much his approval buoyed me, working against my natural skepticism. I could already feel my defenses weakening.

"Why don't you just write it?" I said. "You seem to know so much."

"Never been much of a writer myself, and I haven't time to do all the research that's required, not that I'd even know what I was looking at."

The words *I could help* were already on my tongue as I sealed my mouth against them. *Don't let him suck you in.*

Was he, though, or was there something genuinely intriguing about the project? Certainly the subject matter was less frightening than I'd assumed, not to mention well aligned with my research interests. Religion, Scottish identity—it was all there. If the book was a success, just imagine the doors it could open. Universities, PhD funding, a tenure-track position. It could be exactly what I needed to jump-start my career, the whole thing tailor-made to fit my ambitions. Of course, the book would have D.B.'s name on it, not mine—but perhaps a partial writing credit could be negotiated down the line.

Crossing traffic on North Bridge, we started down the lower half of the Royal Mile, toward the palace and Holyrood Park. I was getting farther and farther from home with every step, but curiosity had overtaken my better instincts. Before long I found myself interrogating D.B. for details—his timeline, his publishing ambitions, the source materials on which the book's arguments would hinge. I wasn't shy about expressing my opinion that blog posts and internet forums were not the foundation for serious discourse.

"I'd really want to focus on published writings with cultural significance. Popular fictions, memoirs, newspaper articles, theological texts."

"Starting to come round to the idea, then?"

"No, I—I just meant as a reader," I said. "That's the kind of material I'd want the book to engage with."

I could tell by his smirk that he didn't believe me.

"How much work have you done on it," I asked, "out of curiosity?"

"No' a lot. Just the introduction, or most of it, anyway. I was hoping to send it to ye, see if there's anything worth salvaging."

D.B. stopped on the sidewalk, prompting me to do the same. I realized we had walked as far as Abbeyhill. A white modern terrace with beige brickwork stood before us, separated from the sidewalk by a lawn of half-dead grass.

"Is this where you live?"

The building was shabbier than I'd have expected, the gutters slightly corroded, with brown stains trailing under the window ledges.

D.B. didn't answer. Merely reached a hand inside his jacket and removed a plain envelope. It hovered between us like an unexpected guest, generously padded around the middle.

"The remainder of your commencement," he said. "If ye want it."

The truth was, I did. And why shouldn't I? I'd already signed the contract. Already accepted—and spent—the signing advance. It was getting harder to find reasons to refuse.

A grin spread D.B.'s face. "Excellent."

I stared, confused.

Then my gaze fell to my hand, and I saw that I was already holding the envelope.

Eleven

TWO DAYS LATER I visited the university administration office, this time not as a condition of my enrollment but to satisfy a new-found curiosity.

Ever since that night at the Witchery, when I found myself strolling down the Royal Mile wondering if my father had once done the same, I had struggled to shake the image of young Edmund from my mind. Everywhere I went I was met with questions. While leaving home in the morning, I wondered where in the city he had resided. As I grabbed a latte from the café around the corner, I wondered which had been his favorite haunts. Wondered if at some point he had occupied the very same spot, breathing the same air I did then.

My father had rarely spoken about his time in Edinburgh. I knew nothing of what his life had been like, who his friends were, even what he had studied. But surely the university would have some record of his time here—perhaps not the specifics of his personal life, but what classes he had taken, maybe even where he'd lived.

The university administration office, to which I had previously re-ported for international check-in, was located in what was called the

Old College, one of the most ancient parts of campus. Situated on the busy, two-lane thoroughfare of South Bridge, the eastern facade loomed over the street with grand austerity and neoclassical style, its Grecian-inspired columns pointing up toward a frieze carved alternately with medallions and the heads of horned animals like goats, to a steepled dome so high one had to crane one's neck to see it.

Beyond the arched entrance was a long quadrangle, which, in addition to student administration, housed the Law School and a contemporary art gallery. The rectangle of grass at the center of the courtyard was a shock of color against the mottled gray walls that encircled it. A second large dome and cupola at the end of the quad upheld the Figure of Youth, a statue of a naked man raising a torch into the air—not proudly, I thought, but reticently, his empty fist clenched in apparent discomfort.

Hurrying up the wide staircase, for it was beginning to rain, I entered the office. A number of clerks manned the long counter. After a short wait in line, one of them turned to me with a friendly nod.

She was different than the woman who had served me before. Slender and not yet forty, she had ebony skin and smiling, almond-shaped eyes. When she asked how she could be of assistance, I was surprised by her refined Scottish accent, which embarrassed me. What had I been expecting?

"Hi. I, uh—" I struggled to withdraw my student ID from my wallet, flustered in the way I always was when required to engage with a stranger. "I'm a student at the university, and I was wondering—the thing is, my dad used to go here—I'm not sure what kind of information you might be able to give me, but maybe an address, or an academic record—?"

"Sorry . . ." She looked confused.

I huffed internally, irritated with myself.

"My father was a student here back in the seventies," I said. "I don't know much about his time here and I was hoping the university might have some record of it. Like where he lived, what classes he took? Maybe even some old coursework."

"In the seventies, you said?"

I nodded.

"Our digital records only go back to the nineties, unfortunately."

"What about paper files?"

She sweetened her sigh with a smile. "The university has a duty of confidentiality. We can't give out student information, even to family—not without your father's written permission."

"Well, good luck with that. He's dead." The words came out more forcefully than I had intended.

She stared.

"Sorry," I said. "I'm just trying to—I just thought the university could help."

The woman considered me, her expression pitying. She glanced quickly to her right.

"What was your father's name?"

"Hale. Edmund Hale." I spelled it for her, and she penned it in the margins of a notepad. She glanced around again, and this time I followed her gaze to a woman with a long silver braid, who was helping a student at the end of the counter.

"I can take a look in the archives," she said quietly, "but no promises I'll find anything. Come back tomorrow. One p.m. That's when she takes her lunch."

After my afternoon Research Methods class, I returned home and shut myself in my bedroom. There I would remain for the rest of the evening—all but four minutes spent microwaving my frozen dinner—answering student emails and typing up my lecture notes, before turning my grudging attention to *Midlothian*.

My goal was to read fifty pages a day, but I might've settled for twenty that night; my mind kept drifting back to the Old College, and the rabbit's warren of dusty archives I imagined ran underneath it, endless cabinets filled with musty student records. What if the clerk couldn't find anything? What if she discovered there was nothing to find, because my father hadn't been a student at the university after all, and I had come all this way for nothing? The more far-fetched the scenarios became, the more they troubled me.

I didn't often struggle to keep my mind on work. It was a point of pride that, even as a kid, I approached my studies with the same rigor and focus my father had applied to his research. While my mother invested hours into helping Nathaniel achieve academic mediocrity, I surpassed him with no help at all.

School came naturally to me—but as the brainless memorization of grade school gave way to the rigors of trigonometry and AP Spanish, it demanded more of me than God-given intelligence. Come junior year, I was studying for hours every night, breaking only for fellowship and extracurricular activities. Partly, I was attempting to make up for my freshman and sophomore years, which, while impressive by most people's standards, were less than perfect as a result of my satanophobia. With the condition behind me, I doubled down on my studies and became neurotic about my GPA, flying into a panic if any one of my grades dropped below an A-. Math and science were particularly troublesome, and I often stayed after school for tutoring, never too proud to be seen with the slow kids and slackers if it ensured my report card remained pristine.

This was essential. For while my peers dreamt of glittering futures as reality TV stars and basketball players, I envisioned a life as Grayson Hale, Stanford graduate and doctoral candidate. Or better yet, Dr. Grayson Hale, endowed chair of something or other at Harvard or Yale.

Then not even my father could overlook me.

For no matter what accolades I earned at school, he hardly seemed to notice. One straight-A report card after another. Induction into the National Honor Society. My high school's award for outstanding achievement in English. He acknowledged these accomplishments, when I told him about them, with the same empty nod he gave the believers when they raved about what a brilliant young man I'd become, when they clapped him on the back and said things like, "You and Vera must be so proud." Not a smile. Not a murmur of agreement. Just a nod, communicating nothing more than that he had heard.

Gradually, a wall of stone rose inside my heart: a great dam, erected over years, holding back an ocean of pain and resentment. Each time my father withheld his approval, another crack appeared in the stonework, bringing me one step closer to crumbling. But still I toiled away, convinced that this was my issue, not his. It was natural, after all, that a genius like him would not be wowed by such minor accomplishments as mine. I told myself that if I wanted his respect, he needed to see me not as a son, but an equal. And how could he not when I was a world-renowned academic. The author of many books. The first PhD in the family.

When it came time to select my undergraduate college, I had planned to apply to multiple universities. But to my great surprise given my spotty record, I got in early to Stanford, my first choice, and I abandoned all my other applications. The only other acceptance I received was to UC San Diego, my backup school. They offered me a full scholarship, but still I accepted Stanford's offer straightaway. I didn't care that it would cost six figures more; shockingly, at seventeen, enormous decades-long debt was not a concept I fully grasped.

But my plans changed in the second half of my senior year, when my father's health rapidly declined.

After years without so much as a cold, Edmund suffered three ministrokes in the span of two months. The worst one was at home during Easter lunch. Nathaniel, then a junior at California State University, Fullerton, was home for the holiday weekend. He was telling my mother about the "pray-in" he was organizing for the university's InterVarsity Christian Fellowship, when he was interrupted by a sudden clatter.

My father had been taking a drink of iced tea when his left arm went numb, releasing his glass. It came down against his plate, inundating the tablecloth with brown liquid. Half his face drooped downward. Realizing something was wrong, Vera and I hurried to his side. We grabbed his arms as he attempted to stand, but his legs were as limp as the asparagus on his plate. The dishes on the table rattled as his body hit the floor.

Although the incident left no lasting damage, the neurologist was adamant the worst was yet to come. "Three TIAs in two months?" I heard him say to my mother in hushed tones. He had explained earlier the technical term for mini-stroke was *transient ischemic attack.* "I'm afraid your husband's staring down the barrel of a full-blown stroke."

My mother produced a gasp of horror, in character as the tragic wife. "You're sure?"

"I'd say it's a near-certainty." Still, he could not put a date on it. "Could be next week, could be next year."

Though I refrained from erupting in tears like my mother, the thought of it filled me with a dread I hadn't felt since the departure of the fiends. What if I was away at Stanford when it happened? How would I feel if he died and I didn't have the chance to say goodbye—or worse, hear him say to me what he otherwise might have, knowing it was his last chance? *I love you, Grayson . . . I'm proud of you, son . . .*

The thought of going away to college should have made me dizzy with excitement, but in the weeks that followed, the prospect of moving upstate in a few months' time was unbearable. The school counselor advised against my plan, reminding me that Stanford had been my dream for years, but what did she know? She didn't understand Dad's and my relationship. She didn't understand that Stanford didn't matter if he wasn't around to see it.

Not long after, I found my father in his study, bringing with me his dinner of salmon, steamed broccoli, and brown rice; the doctor had him on a strict low-cholesterol diet, along with a cocktail of pills, which I delivered with the meal. When I entered, he was answering emails. He'd refused to take time off even after his third attack, returning to work the same evening he was released from the hospital. He barely looked up as I put the tray on the desk. He downed the pills without water and kept typing.

The analog clock on the wall ticked over as I stood there, waiting for his acknowledgment. Absently, I scanned the bookshelves along the wall. They contained hundreds of books, bound manuscripts, and boxes of paper; my father was fanatic about keeping all his old writing. I cleared my throat, about to interject, but lost my nerve and bent down to retie my shoe. I felt like I was six years old again, dancing around his desk or tattling on Nathaniel—whatever it took to get a few seconds of my father's attention.

"What is it?" he said.

I stood. Now the moment had come, the words stuck in my throat.

"I wanted to tell you something."

He didn't speak.

"I just wanted to tell you, I-I've withdrawn my acceptance at Stanford. I've decided to live at home and go to UCSD."

It was as if the words had possessed a physical weight. I felt lighter having spoken them; the truth was out now.

I don't know what reaction I'd been expecting. None, I suppose—just the same disinterested nod he always gave. But to my immediate discomfort, I perceived something was different about this news. There was silence as his fingers paused in midair over the keyboard. He swiveled his head, narrowing his eyes. *"Why?"*

The bottom dropped out of my stomach.

"You're not well," I said, hearing the defensiveness in my voice as if it were somebody else's. "I thought I should stay close, in—in case something happened."

He regarded me like an animal at the zoo. Curious. A species apart.

He returned to his typing.

Another crack in the dam. The biggest one yet. Emotion spouted through the fracture, filling me up.

"You never even congratulated me on getting in." I was angry now, yet on the edge of tears. "Now you're disappointed I'm not going?"

"You can't disappoint me," he muttered.

I scoffed. "Well, I can't fucking make you happy, either!"

The words came out as a shout. I'd never raised my voice to my father like this before, and it frightened me, not knowing how he'd react. Before I could find out, I bolted from the room.

The dam quaking but not yet broken. For a little longer, it remained intact.

—

It was cold and gray but not raining when I left the flat the following day. By the time it started to come down, I was too far from home to turn back for my hooded jacket. I pressed on at my fastest walk.

By the time I reached the Old College, my puffer coat was soaked through, my hair slick and dripping. I squelched with every step, barely able to feel my feet.

Separate from the discomfort of the wet and cold, a jittery, crawling feeling lodged in my chest like a plague of locusts. What had the clerk dug up? I wondered anxiously, as I ascended the stone steps up to the quad. Again I considered the possibility she hadn't found anything. Perhaps she had started the job but lost her nerve, or been caught and forced to halt her investigation.

I had arrived fifteen minutes early. Reluctant to cause her any more trouble than I already might have, I passed the time under the archway, pretending to be engrossed in my phone. A couple minutes before 1:00 p.m., a woman walked past holding an umbrella aloft. It was the one with a silver braid I had seen the day before, whom I assumed was the clerk's supervisor. Feeling it was probably safe to go in, I ventured out into the quad, my head bent down against the driving rain. The warmth of the office engulfed me the moment I stepped inside. There was no line this time. The clerk regarded me as I approached. Her smile was thin.

"Hi," I said. "Were you able to find—?"

"Will you please keep your voice down?"

I didn't speak. She turned away from me, rifling in a lower drawer for a moment before setting a folder on the counter before me. "Your tuition statement, as requested."

Stepping forward, I lifted the flap. Inside was not my tuition statement at all but a photocopy of what appeared to be some kind of contact form. The left side of the page contained a column of typewritten
student names, many of them foreign, each followed by a handwritten
address, phone number, and signature. Was this what students filled out
at international check-in in the 1970s? My eyes followed down the left
column, stopping at the line reading *Hale, Edmund*.

To the right of the name was an address: *70B Ratcliffe Terrace, Edin.,
EH9 1ST*.

"It's all I could find," the clerk said.

"Where is this?"

She took a second look at the address. "Ratcliffe Terrace? That's
down by King's. The south campus," she explained. "That's where the
College of Science and Engineering is. Did you father study science?"

"No." I didn't know this for sure, but it seemed unlikely. My father
was a man of letters. A writer, like me.

"Is there anything else I can help with?" her voice rang out, as her
coworker seemed to notice our murmuring.

"That's all. Thank you." I slipped the papers into my bag. "You've
been very helpful."

Twelve

THERE WAS SOMEONE at the door.

I was in the shower, my hair frothy with pound-shop shampoo when I heard the doorbell start to go, the muffled *ring ring ring* insistent over the drum of water against the floor of the stall.

"Ollie, can you get that?" I shouted, and received no answer. "OLLIE?"

After several more fruitless attempts to get my flatmate's attention, I cut the water, threw a towel around my waist, and padded, dripping and furious, to the entry, which continued to resound with the ringing of the bell.

"Yes?" I said as I snatched open the door, my bare torso half hidden behind it. Instantly I regretted my tone, having to adjust my gaze upward to match the height of the man who towered above me, copper-haired and massively proportioned.

His green eyes looked past me, slightly glazed. "Ollie here?"

"Come in," I said, a little relieved.

As I stepped aside, Ollie at last sauntered out of his bedroom looking rudely awoken from a nap. He greeted his friend with a broey handshake, apparently unsurprised to have company, though I had not been warned.

Burying my ire for the present moment, I closed the door and spotted, on the small entry table, a pile of mail that Ollie had left for me to sort out. Among the usual junk and bills was an envelope addressed to me. I recognized the handwriting immediately.

As Ollie and his friend disappeared into the sitting room, I retrieved my clothes from the bathroom floor and headed to my room to finish dressing. There, sliding my finger under the paper flap, I opened the envelope and extracted what appeared to be a handful of torn-out notebook pages, jagged-edged and scrawled over in spiky handwriting.

There was no note except for the title scrawled across the top page: *Intro.*

I hadn't expected much from my employer's writing. Still, I was unprepared for what I was about to read. D.B.'s first draft of the introductory chapter was like the work of a deranged child, a cram of broken nonsense prose filled with bizarre shorthand I could barely decipher.

> Evryl nos the Devil. Hes the evilst l n makes
> them do bad things but sumtimes ppl forget.
> Scotland used to know him . . . now all memry has . . .
> becuz poltics has made scots be afraid of god
> not the Devil scots don't know wut they do is
> bad . . .

More than anything I was confused. Surely I'd seen proof he could write better than this. Or had the few texts and emails we'd exchanged been similarly riddled with errors, and I had simply excused them as internet language, texter's shorthand? What about the job posting? The contract I'd signed? Had he gotten someone to draft those for him?

Even if he had, it seemed unthinkable that a person as articulate and presumably successful as D.B. (not that he had ever told me what he did for a living) could flirt as audaciously with illiteracy as the author of this document clearly did.

It went on for most of three pages, including the frequent strike-throughs and parenthetical notes to self, ending in a series of sentences that cut into my memory like a cold kitchen knife.

> the Devils n scotlad the devils n Scotland the devils n scot but u forgot him, he does no likeit ... He wants u to remmber and we rite ths book make u remmber—Scotld must nvr agen forget the Devil

The chill that twisted through me was quickly extinguished by a weird noise coming from the sitting room. A low grunting, coming from Ollie and his friend.

What are they doing? I thought with discomfort.

Blocking them out, I took a seat at the desk and spent some time trying to translate D.B.'s gibberish into English, and secondly into something resembling an acceptable introduction. It soon became clear there was no point. If this book was going to be a book at all and not just a three-hundred-page Reddit thread, I would have to start again from scratch.

But in principle the thought of doing so didn't trouble me. Being able to compartmentalize the project as an academic manuscript—a sort of second dissertation, as harrowing as that sounded—had transformed my outlook on the book, dulling the anxiety it had previously engendered and replacing it with the same dutiful resignation I brought to my TA work. Even now, I felt myself sinking into a productive rhythm, hacking back D.B.'s prose and sculpting it anew like a woodworker with a log—interrupted only by the grunting that had progressed now to low groans.

"Oh fuck," Ollie's friend yelled out.

I experienced a pang of discomfort behind my navel. Pushing the ridiculous thought from my mind, I opened Spotify and clicked on a random station. The sinister, psychedelic beat of a Twenty One Pilots song flooded my room.

> *All my friends are heathens take it slow.*
> *Wait for them to ask you who you know.*

I clicked the volume up until I could barely hear my own thoughts, let alone what was happening in the next room. My nerves settled, but what was I going to do about this introduction?

Bringing up Gmail, I tapped out a new message.

Hi D.B.,

Received your intro draft. Thanks, that's a helpful guidepost of where you see the book going. I'm thinking I might save the intro for last, when we have a better sense of our main arguments. Before diving into writing, I want to spend some time immersing myself in the research and putting together a chapter outline. Maybe 4-6 weeks, with everything else on my plate. That okay?

Grayson

The reply came back within seconds.

Yes good

At least I had some time to figure this mess out.

Glancing across the desk, I spotted the yellow Post-it that lay there. I'd found it in the envelope with D.B.'s introduction, floating between two pages like an accident. I had meant to ask him about it in my email. After all, the note contained just a few words, in the same spiky handwriting as the introduction.

dbismyname
DevInScot2016

The second part looked uncomfortably like a password—probably to his Gmail, whose handle was dbismyname. Reluctant to send a second message, I reminded myself to ask him about it later, and filed the note away with the rest of the papers in the deep bottom drawer of my desk.

And now I could not ignore it any longer: the outcry coming from the next room had become outrageous, so loud they could be heard easily over the music. They were screaming, unrestrained.

"Fuck me!" Ollie shouted. "Fuck me!"

"Take it!" his friend was hollering over the final lines of the song. "Fucking bitch."

I exploded out of my room. "What the fuck is going—?"

Ollie and his buddy sat apart on the couch, hammering the buttons on their PlayStation controllers as a computer-animated soccer game raged on the television.

"FUCK ME! FUCK ME! FUCK—!" Ollie hurled his controller at the carpet. It bounced away, clattering against the TV stand. "God damn it! Fucking Madrid!"

The other one slumped back and exhaled, savoring his win. "Bitch!"

Only then did they turn to face me.

Ollie's eyes flashed. *"What?"*

"I—I was just saying," I stuttered out, "keep it down, I'm . . . trying to work."

Editor's Note
Exhibit G

In a lengthy earlier chapter of his manuscript, Hale narrates the destructive advance of his satanophobia as it progressed, over the course of years, from a subtle aversion to demonic language to a nightmarish virtual reality plagued by fiends. The night I first read that chapter I slept fitfully, keeping the man I was seeing awake as I cried out in my sleep, kicking violently as if to fend off a descending threat. So great was the disturbance that my sleeping partner retreated to the sitting room sofa—the first of many nights he would be forced to do so.

Though there was much in that chapter that disturbed me, there was one thing, too, which brought me solace: Hale's relationship with Reyna Moya-White, the Filipina regular at the Hales' home worship service, to whom young Grayson spoke about his crisis of faith. It reassured me that there was at least one person in his life in whom Hale felt he could confide.

Eager to learn more about their special connection, I contacted Mrs. Moya-White in July of last year, requesting a virtual interview. Here I present the first part of the exchange that followed, published with Mrs. Moya-White's permission.

Sent: 4 August 2019
From: Reyna Moya-White
To: Daniella Barclay
Subject: Re: Interview Request

Hi, Ms. Barclay,

   Apologies for delay in getting back to you, I have given your request good thought and even though I approve your mission to spread the TRUTH about Grayson against the lies told by the UK tabloid snakes, unfortunately I must rebuff your interview request. I feel it would be too painful to endure because of how things went with him and me and then learning of his death earlier this year, it is a very painful subject and I hope you can understand, however if you want to send questions I will try to answer as best as I can by email. Would that be opportune?

Faithfully,

Reyna Moya-White

Sent: 4 August 2019

From: Daniella Barclay

To: Reyna Moya-White

Subject: Re: Interview Request

Hello Reyna,

I understand your position completely, and thank you for your generous offer to provide written answers to my questions. That would be very much appreciated.

I had a number of questions prepared, but out of respect for your time I have attached just a few. Some are about things that happened several years ago, but as much detail as you can provide would be immensely helpful and appreciated. Please let me know if you have any questions or concerns in the meantime.

Warmest regards,

Daniella

Sent: 25 August 2019

From: Reyna Moya-White

To: Daniella Barclay

Subject: Re: Interview Request

Hi, Daniella,

Sorry once again for the delay in responding, thinking about your questions brought up many difficult memories for me but I wanted to get back to you so here are my answers below.

I would describe young Grayson as kind and clever, respectful, and very shy. I thought for one year that he did not like me because he did not want to talk to me after fellowship or before and would pull back when I came near but this changed when he started to come and talk to me, he was just shy at first as many people told me he was.

Once he lost his shyness I learned that he was a very smart little boy, not only could he read very excellently for his age but he knew the Bible very well in fact better than many of the grown-up believers. He was inquiring about the stories his father taught at fellowship but was shy about asking his father questions so sometimes he asked me. He wanted to know the reason for things in the Bible like why God said this or why someone did that. I tried my best to answer, but sometimes he didn't like my answers and he would decide his own.

Like for an example he asked me why in the Book of Kings the weeping woman ate her baby [2 Kings 6:28-29: *And the king said unto her, "What aileth thee?" And she answered, "This woman said unto me, 'Give thy son so that we may eat him today, and we will eat my son tomorrow.' So we boiled my son and ate him." The next day I said to her, "Give up your son so we may eat him," but she had hidden him*.]. Well, I explained that there was a famine in the kingdom and the woman was so hungry she was forced to devour her child to survive but Grayson didn't think so, he believed she ate the baby because it was evil but she wept in front of the king's feet so he would give her jewels and treasure.

The relationship I had between Grayson and myself was a special one. I cannot say we were friends because of course he was only a little boy and I was almost forty years of age. The truth was that Grayson had only one friend I knew of, Carlos Fernandez. He and Grayson were very entwined at least for a while but that is a different story I think.

But what I can say is that I adored Grayson very much. Each

time I saw him was a light spot in my week and I sometimes came
early to fellowship so that I could visit with him for a few minutes. He
would beg for tickles and sit in my lap and tell me about what he was
learning in school and show me the artwork he made in class, he was
very happy when I said it was good. I wondered why he didn't show
his mother, after all she seemed to be excited when I took his art proj-
ects to show her. "Why didn't I get to see this?" she would say. "Why
does Reyna get all the good stuff, you silly goose?"

It was odd that Grayson confided in me instead of his family but
I did not discourage him even when I should have. I think the reason
is because I always wanted children of my own and the way Grayson
came to me for attention and even advice gave me the feeling of
being a mother, a feeling I never had before and that unfortunately I
became addicted to.

You asked what happened to cause me to leave fellowship. Well,
it was a slow progress but it started when Grayson got to be in his
teenage years. Like all kids that age stop needing their mothers he
stopped coming to me so much and when we talked he would answer
me in one-word answers. "Yes . . . no . . . I don't know . . ." I thought
he was just being a normal juvenile but eventually I could not deny my
feeling that something was not all right with him. He seemed anxious
and distracted much of the time and he looked rather sick. I married
my husband around this timeframe and went away to Costa Rica
for my honeymoon and when I got back I heard from my good friend
Marlena that Grayson fainted while reading from the Book of John
in fellowship, she said he fell over and soiled himself on the carpet.
Vera assured me that everything was fine but I was still very nervous.
Grayson needed help and though I wasn't his real mom I still felt like I
had the responsibility in this situation.

After the next fellowship I took Grayson out back and said,
"Grayson, what is wrong? Is everything okay with you, I hear you
have been fainting, what is going on?"

And he said, "Nothing is going on, stop it, Reyna"—very annoyed with me. But I couldn't help it and continued to ask him and he got angrier and angrier and finally he shouted into my face, "SHUT UP!" The outburst was so loud that some believers inside turned to look at us through the door, which was made of glass, I couldn't believe it. He had never talked to me like this and I admit that in that moment I was even a little scared. Grayson was a gentle boy but he looked so angry I thought he might hit me. But he just stormed off to his bedroom, and I left in tears on the side of the house. I didn't want anyone to see me or ask what happened, it was my own fault for playing *nanay*.

The next time I saw him I tried to apologize even though I was still scared that something was wrong but Grayson was not talking to me, he would not even look in my eye. For a long time he continued to ignore me even while he continued to look sicker and more not like himself and Vera just kept saying, "It's fine I've got it handled," but nothing was changing in Grayson's activity. I began to wonder if Vera was not to be trusted like the woman in the Book of Kings who was only pretending to weep for the baby she boiled.

It was a very painful time. I was like Grayson's second mother for more than ten years and now he did not want anything to do with me. My husband said, "You can't keep going there, Reyna, it's destroying your spirit," and I had to say to myself that he was right. So that's why I stopped going to fellowship because it was too hard seeing Grayson there and being reminded every day that I had lost him as the son I never possessed.

Sorry I cannot think of anything more to answer your questions, I hope this is enough. It has not been easy but I feel God has called me to testify to this truth, may He bless you for doing His work of clearing Grayson's name so he may rest in peace.

Faithfully,

Reyna

Sent: 26 August 2019
From: Daniella Barclay
To: Reyna Moya-White
Subject: Re: Interview Request

Dear Reyna,

Thank you so much for your thorough and heartfelt response. It is much appreciated and will be a huge help. Thank you, too, for your kind blessings.

I hate to ask any more of you after all you've done already, but I was intrigued by your reference to Grayson's friendship with Carlos Fernandez. You mentioned there's a story there. I know this has been very difficult for you, but if you can find the strength to share a little more, I would be much obliged.

Warmest regards,

Daniella

Sent: 30 August 2019
From: Reyna Moya-White
To: Daniella Barclay
Subject: Re: Interview Request

Hello again, Daniella,

I don't know if there is too much to tell about Grayson and Carlos, they were like any other boys that age, very active and imaginary, they liked to play pretend. As I said there was a time when they were latched together at the hip, it was when Grayson and Carlos were around the age of seven. They spent every moment together whispering and giggling and they would disappear after fellowship and lock themselves in Grayson's room at least until Vera put a stop to that. She was anxious about Grayson playing with the door closed. When I asked why, she said she did not want them

playing anything too violent like make-believe police and bad guys
with guns.

One time he closed the door to play after fellowship and the
next time I saw Grayson he had a bruise on his arm. This was normal
because he was a very clumsy boy, he always had bruises that he got
from falling down on the playground or banging his arm, Vera would
tell me. Anyway after that she said the boys were not allowed to play
in his room anymore only the den.

There was one time she and Ed went to a ministry conference in
Riverside and Paola and Esteban went too and I babysat the boys at
the Hales' house. Nathaniel was there also but Vera told me to keep
an eye on the younger boys especially. We were coloring Bible stories
in the den and I got up to go to the bathroom and when I returned the
boys were not there. I checked Grayson's bedroom but it was empty
also and Nathaniel had not witnessed them anywhere. I became very
neurotic, I thought somehow they were kidnapped or ran away and I
searched all over the house even went out in the backyard.

As I went down the steps to the bottom of the yard I was happy
because I could hear the boys behind the garden shed. Grayson was
saying, "Now you go. Show me it."

"We'll get in trouble," Carlos said.

"You have to," Grayson said.

When I came around the corner I saw them huddled close together on top of some old sticks of timber behind the shed, they were
looking down at something and when they saw me they jumped up
like a frightful cat. I said, "What are you doing?"

Grayson answered very fast, "Nothing."

I asked Carlos, "What have you got, what did you put in your
shorts?" Because I had seen him put something down there.

"It was just pretend," Grayson said.

Carlos looked scared. I took one step forward and suddenly
Grayson pulled his hand out of his waistband and it was making the
shape of a gun.

"We were playing police and bad guys," he said.

Carlos looked nervous I think because he knew that they were not supposed to play those violent games and now he would get in trouble. Grayson asked if I would tell his mom and I told to him, "Don't worry I won't tell just come inside now." I just was so alleviated that they were safe I did not even think about notifying Vera.

Carlos was very quiet that night and after that weekend I did not see him and Grayson play together again. I asked Grayson why they did not be friends anymore, he looked angry and sad a little bit and with a shrug he said, "Carlos doesn't like how I play."

Thirteen

HOLYROOD PARK WAS not like a park at all but an expanse of rugged wilderness excised from the northern highlands and transplanted to its new home at the center of the capital. Monolithic hills stood like mountains against a silver sky, their pelt of overgrown grass and yellow gorse dancing in the pulsing wind. To the west, the basalt cliffs of Salisbury Crags cut up at a slant, its scabrous ridge turned up to the heavens like the nose of a dolphin breaching the surf. A little farther still, the dark waters of St. Margaret's Loch took no heed of their manmade origins, supporting their own ecosystem of wild fauna as if they had existed there for centuries.

Enveloped in the park's vast, emerald hug, I felt as insignificant as a speck of sand—and guilty. Instead of there, I should have been on Ratcliffe Terrace visiting my dad's old flat. After returning home from the Old College the previous week and entering the address into Google Maps, I'd been relieved to learn the place was just over a mile from my flat. And yet for some reason I still hadn't ventured down there—an oversight I blamed on my hectic schedule but which I sensed deep down was something else, a hesitation my body could not square with my mind.

"There you are," a voice called out, startling me slightly. I'd been so deep in thought, I hadn't noticed my classmate jogging toward me.

"Oh. Hey."

"All right?"

A little awkwardly I accepted the hand Liam held out for me to shake and withered at the sight of his sneakers and windbreaker.

"Looks like it's just the two of us. All set?"

"I think so," I said, gazing ashamedly at my dirty footwear, the dark blue canvas coming away from the rubber bottom. "They're all I had."

"You'll be all right, long as the rain holds out. Well, better get started."

As he headed off up the sidewalk, I had another realization—namely, that I couldn't remember agreeing to this outing.

I'd been scrolling idly through Facebook when I came across his post. I had added him as a friend after that day at the Blind Poet, when he'd covered for me so that I could sneak away. *Hiking Arthur's Seat this afternoon, anyone want to join me?* There had followed half a dozen comments, all of them regrets but one, some girl who asked when and where she could meet him. *2pm at the Queen's Drive roundabout,* he'd written, and the girl bemoaned that she was in class until half past.

I remembered having been tempted to respond. But we hardly knew each other. It would be weird, surely. And yet I must have written something, for here I was, following him up a broad dirt path toward Arthur's Seat, the tallest of Holyrood Park's great hills. It dominated the skyline with its famed dual peaks—one taller and pointed, the other broad and sweeping—its body of craggy, volcanic rock bursting through a delicate skin of green.

Falling into line behind two dozen others, from serious-looking joggers to camera-wielding families jabbering in Italian, I was already starting to regret it. The path leading up Arthur's Seat was no gentle ramble, but a zigzag of earthen steps etched into the steepest part of the hillside.

Before I could so much as gulp, Liam pressed ahead, leaving me no choice but to follow.

We'd barely been walking two minutes when I started to lag behind.

"Maybe I should turn back," I called after him, working to conceal the heaviness of my breathing, which only put me further out of breath. "I don't want to hold you up."

"You're doing fine. Come on."

Pausing to allow me to catch up, Liam slapped me approvingly on the shoulder as, a moment later, I closed the gap between us.

At this I had to suppress a smirk, unaccustomed to the carefree bodily contact that was normal among athletes. At least I assumed Liam was an athlete—a swimmer, or maybe a soccer player. Though he didn't make a show of it, his lean, muscled physique was evident through his clothing, and the path, even as it progressed from a manageable incline to a steeper set of stairs made of wide, jutting rocks, appeared to give him no trouble; he reopened the gap between us without even seeming to try. Soon it had grown so long that half a dozen hikers moved forward to fill the open space.

"Come on, you can do this," he called out from above, waving me up the hill as he rounded a switchback.

And yet each time I got near him his pace seemed to increase, as if, despite his encouragement, he were trying to put distance between us.

As I ground my muscles into action, a drop of water splashed my forehead.

It was starting, the gentle *pit-pat* of rain.

Over the next quarter hour my trepidation curdled into cold, visceral fear. As I forced my body up the hill, openly panting, my feet slipped and slid underneath me. The rain had turned the path to mud, the wind buffeted me at gale-force speeds, and there were no guardrails or ropes, nothing to hold on to but the occasional branch of a gorse bush overhanging the path. I contemplated turning back, but how could I? The slope was too steep, the ground too slick; I'd never get down that way without falling. I had to keep going, even though my breathing was ragged, my thighs and calves screaming. I quickened my pace, desperate to reach the top and be done with it already.

As I stepped forward, my foot slid out from underneath me, pitching my body forward. My hands smacked the mud, struggling for purchase as I slid backward, out of control. A man let out a yell as I nearly took him out by the ankles.

"Christ," he said. "You'll do someone an injury, wearing shoes like that."

Humiliated, yet grateful for the rock that had curtailed my descent, I remained on the ground until he and his partner had passed.

Finally, with a fistful of foliage as leverage, I pulled myself into a standing position, holding fiercely to the branch as my feet continued to skate on the greasy earth. At least Liam wasn't around to bear witness to my shame. Peering up the path, I just managed to spot him. Judging by the way he kept glancing over his shoulder, he seemed to be looking for me too.

Finally he saw me, and for a second we regarded each other.

Then his eyes snapped away, and he continued up the hill, if anything, even faster than before.

～

Half an hour later I gazed into the misty horizon, balancing on the pitted mound of rock at the top of Arthur's Seat as the wind spattered my face with sharp pinpricks of rain. My ears were numb, my socks heavy and sodden. But there was something about it, the way the breeze pushed my hair back over my head, the way the world stood back and opened its arms to me, that gave me a feeling both triumphant and familiar.

I was reminded of Sunset Cliffs, the stretch of brown striated rock overlooking the Pacific Ocean not far from where I grew up. When I was young, my father went there often to look at the surf. He preferred to go alone, but I would plead with him, and cry. "Please, I want to go with you. *Please.*" And so, for a while, he allowed me to accompany him.

I knew to remain buckled as he parked and got out of the car. It wasn't safe for me, he would say, out on the cliffs. Especially where he went, proceeding past the end of the road along the wild dirt path heading south. I sometimes wondered why he needed to walk so far when the waves were perfectly visible where we were parked. I sometimes wondered why he cared about the surf at all, when his longboard had not seen the light of day in years; why even after he gave the thing away, he continued to stop on this road and vanish.

I never bothered asking, for these visits were a special treat, especially when I was a little older and he allowed me to get out and stretch my legs. Instructed to stay by the car, I would stand behind the rope guardrail that ran along the edge of the cliff and peer out into the two-tiered expanse of blue, the yawning softness of the sky over a calm sea with arms as wide as infinity. Glorying in the salty breeze, which enveloped me and made me feel like a king.

There was one day though, when I was seven or eight, that my father was gone too long and I grew restless. I thought it would be okay if I took a walk, provided I didn't wander too far.

At the corner of the street, where Sunset Cliffs Boulevard curved away from the sea and became Ladera, there was a staircase of concrete steps with metal handrails. It zigzagged down, landing on a strip of rock at the foot of the cliff. At high tide the waves rushed right up to it, filling the tidepools and splashing up on the rocks.

I only descended halfway, hanging on to the railing and admiring the water. The waves were much closer from this height, spraying my cheeks as they battered the rocks below. As I scanned the distant, curling swells for the shadow of a shark or the leaping outline of a bottlenose dolphin, my eyes alighted on a surfer paddling in. He was easy to spot against the dark tide, his shortboard a deep, lurid red.

At the base of the cliff, he hauled his board out of the water. I watched as he released his hair from its bun and wrung it out, as he unzipped his wetsuit and peeled it off down to the waist, leaving the top half dangling off him like a second skin.

I lost sight of him as he navigated the strip of rock. A moment later he reappeared, heading up the staircase with the board under his arm. I looked away, staring out at the ocean. He passed behind me, swinging the board up over my head, sending a jolt of electricity through my body.

As the surfer departed, I examined him from behind. His back showed a sprawling tattoo depicting a writhing creature with seven heads, like the Beast from the book of Revelation. It had a preternatural hold on me. As the surfer padded away, I found myself drawn to the image of the Beast. It compelled me to follow him up the steps, follow him as he turned right at the top of the staircase and proceeded, barefoot, down the forbidden dirt path. I hesitated only momentarily. I would not travel far. Just as far as it took to gaze upon the Beast, the trio of scars smarting beneath my shirtsleeve. I could not control my feet. They moved fast underneath me, delivering me to the creature. Its heads were just coming into focus when suddenly a hand grabbed me roughly by the arm.

"What are you doing here?" my father spat.

"I—I wasn't—"

Looking around, he spotted the image on the surfer's wet back. As the color drained from his face, my blood ran cold. He understood perfectly. He could see it as clearly as if it were daubed on my forehead, the terrifying secret I'd kept buried for so long, the one that had drawn me to the image of the Beast like a moth to the flame: I was one of the Devil's kind. His mark tethered us together, him to me and me to him—an unbreakable chain, wrenching me into the darkness.

A sudden burst of wind brought me back to Arthur's Seat and destabilized me. I stumbled forward, my arms windmilling for balance. A curse escaped my mouth as I collapsed. My palms, as I turned them over, were red and indented with the texture of the rock, my knee bleeding through a cut in my jeans.

Onlookers openly watched me struggle to my feet. I burned with embarrassment as a teenage girl covered her mouth to hide her smile.

The only person who didn't seem to be watching was Liam; he was nowhere to be seen, long gone by the time I had reached the peak. After my performance on the hill, he probably hadn't wanted to be seen with me.

Having had enough of the place, I began the long descent down Arthur's Seat.

The path around the backside of the hill was gentle and muddy. I took it in short, careful steps, eager to avoid another fall. To the right of the path, an immense glen plunged down and out toward the city, the light-colored hills peppered with dark bushes. Ancient walking paths inscribed the tall grass.

A stone structure passed into view. From a distance it had the ghostly, weathered look of standing stones. But as I approached, it became something different: the ruin of a small, rudimentary building, cobbled together from rocks of various sizes and colors. ST. ANTHONY'S CHAPEL, read an informational plaque. A corner of the building was all that remained, rough-edged and wearied by the elements over centuries. This high up in the hills, with nothing around but grass and sky, there was something eerie, almost out-of-place about it. Like something that was not supposed to be found.

I started to head off, then paused at the unmistakable sound of gibbering.

The source of the disturbance stood in the open arch of the ruin, a foot and a half tall, leering at me with reptilian yellow eyes. A trio of long talons dangled from its tiny hands, which, like the rest of its body, were tinted a slick, oily black. The grin spreading its scrunched face revealed hundreds of needlelike teeth.

The sight of the creature, for the first time in nearly a decade, filled me with numb disbelief. Only when it leapt off the arch, its leathery wings exploding outward behind it, did the adrenaline finally hit.

As the fiend descended on me, I staggered back with a scream, throwing up my arms against the rush of gibbering sound.

Then nothing.

I spied the ruin through the gap between my arms. The fiend, if it had been there at all, was gone now. In its place, a crow perched in the same open arch, preening the feathers under its wing.

Fourteen

I HADN'T SEEN WHAT I thought I had. The thing in the arch was a
bird, a common crow. I had gotten it wrong, mixed it up in my head
with a darker, more terrible thing because I was physically exhausted
and hanging by a thread. A malfunction of the senses—it had to be. If
I had encountered the thing I feared was there, I would have seen or at
least heard it again by now. More important, it would mean my condition was back, and that was not a possibility I was willing to allow.

This is what I told myself in the weeks after the incident on Arthur's
Seat; it was easy enough to accept given everything else on my plate.

Nearly halfway into the semester, I found myself busier than I had
been in recent memory. Drowning in assignments to grade for English
Literature I, I also had my own coursework to think about (a pair of five-
thousand-word essays due in a week's time) and, delusional as I was, I
wanted to have *something* to show to Fiona for our next one-on-one. The
night before our meeting, I worked into the small hours crafting an
extensive précis on my research to date—a formless hodgepodge of re-
flections on class and Cameronian radicalism in *The Heart of Midlothian*.
The effort was in vain. Come our scheduled meeting, Fiona greeted me

like a friend she hadn't been expecting. It was clear by the abstractness of her feedback that she hadn't even looked at my write-up, evidently more interested in my take on the upcoming US presidential election and hearing "what the young people are up to these days."

What the fuck do I know? I wanted to say.

"Going to the pub?" I supposed.

"Ah yes." A dreamy glow of nostalgia wafted over her. "Pubs . . ."

It was true, at least, that I had seen my fair share of them. Despite my awkward experience at the Blind Poet, Sophie had managed to convince me to join her and her friends for further outings—once to the Pear Tree and a couple times to the bar at Teviot Row House, the century-old student union like a baronial manor, its mullioned windows and stepped gables flanked by turrets. What ever had compelled me to agree? Perhaps it was the raw animal magnetism Jenna exuded every time she brought her bottle of wild-berry cider to her lips.

Liam was there too, which proved slightly uncomfortable. Neither of us had yet acknowledged how he'd abandoned me on Arthur's Seat, but the way he kept glancing at me from across the table gave me the distinct impression he hadn't forgotten either. Intent to clear the air, I drained my Diet Coke, then followed him as he headed off to grab another round. He was waiting to be served when I stepped up beside him.

"Hey," I said, when he didn't immediately notice me.

"Oh. Hey." His gaze dropped to the floor, then crossed back toward the others.

"I, uh—just wanted to say sorry about Arthur's Seat. You know, lagging behind like that. I get why you went on ahead."

"Yeah. Sorry." He scratched at his jawline. "You should have said—"

"Just embarrassed. Probably shouldn't have come at all."

The admission seemed to counteract his discomfort. He paused and pressed a smile between his lips. "No worries."

Although a whiff of awkwardness still hung between us, it did not linger. By degrees Liam seemed to warm to me, and by the time we left the bar, he and I were conversing as easily as we had at the base of Arthur's Seat.

To my surprise, he even texted me that evening. He must have pulled my number off the student directory. I don't recall the details of his message, something about the reading for Research Methods. A clarification of terms, nothing particularly memorable. But still it must have meant something that he'd chosen me to ask the question. Me of all the people in our class—even Sophie, with whom he was so close. It suggested an intimacy between us. Perhaps even an acknowledgment of my superior knowledge. It was oddly exhilarating. Made me feel, for a moment, like I had a friend.

It was a feeling I would experience again and again over the following weeks, each time more strongly than the last. For although our face-to-face interactions were barely more than small talk, Liam began to make a habit of sending me private messages—while I was studying in the library, in the middle of class, even as he sat across from me at the pub, his attention appearing to be focused elsewhere. Funny little things. Snide comments about Dr. Porter's invective. Exasperated emojis when a long-winded classmate rambled on. Winking acknowledgments that eventually became in-jokes. Through our phones we entered our own private world of scorn and sarcasm—a delicious break from the wholesome, goody-two-shoes persona Liam presented to the world. It turned out the golden boy was a bit of a devil after all.

Such was our rapport that, one day during Research Methods, I even let slip to Liam my attraction to Jenna. She had arrived late to class, peeling off her faux-fur coat to reveal a small crop top underneath, her cleavage barely suppressed by the garment's lattice of crisscrossing straps. My phone instantly buzzed with Liam's bulging-eye emoji.

Dibs, I texted back. A stupid thing to say. He knew as well as I did that I didn't have the balls to ask her out. Still, I waited nervously as a series of bubbles appeared on the screen, anticipating his response. Then three words.

U fancy her?

I left it for a while, unsure if I could trust him with the information. As if we weren't in the middle of a text conversation at all, he raised his hand into the air and delivered a devastatingly cogent response to Dr. Porter's question. When he finished, Liam caught my eye, a question burning in his own. *Well?* he seemed to say.

Finally I answered, returning an emoji of a hand pinching the air.

He responded with a series of faces that were laughing so hard they cried, along with the words *Crack on mate, she's yours.*

I could not contain my grin.

I'd had friendships before, of course, but there was something different about Liam. I could feel in my gut that he was special: the rare person whom I not only liked but also respected, who not only accepted my dark and captious nature but admired it especially. In response to a particularly brutal burn, he once wrote, *You are a savage and a scholar sir*—a silly and offhand comment that nevertheless made me feel seen in a way I never had before. Not by Carlos Fernandez, who had abandoned me after a few short months, or the mother and brother who had valued me as little more than an emotional punching bag. Certainly not by my father.

No, there was something unique about Liam and me. Something about the way we fit together, how our outward personalities were so dissimilar yet our intellect and humor so unexplainably congruous, that put a warm, buzzy feeling in my stomach every time my phone vibrated with a new message.

Between work, school, and my newfound partner in banter, it was easy to forget that I had to deliver the outline for D.B.'s book in just a few weeks, a fact of which I was frequently reminded by the arrival of the morning mail.

I had thought D.B. and I were on the same page about the direction of the book. Abandoning the strangeness of his early mailings and his hack job of an introduction, we had agreed *A Scottish History of Fear* would chart the evolution of the Devil as a religious, literary, and even political figure throughout the history of post-Reformation Scotland.

This evolution was well reflected in my half-completed outline. The book would start with a chapter on the rise of Calvinism in the sixteenth century, a branch of Reformed Protestantism based on the writings of French theologian John Calvin, known partly for its high-handed views on sin and predestination.

Despite its belief in the fundamental wickedness of man, Calvinism taught that a select group of souls, known as the elect, were permitted entry into heaven, not because they were morally superior or free from sin but simply because God willed it. In the lottery of Calvinist predestination, people were marked at birth, placed in one of two camps: some selected for salvation and others for eternal damnation, a determination made by God with no consideration given to a person's actions or beliefs. Once decided, there was nothing one could do, good or bad, to alter their fate.

If I could find the right primary sources, chapter two would explore how Reformed theology seeped into the consciousness of the Scottish people, who increasingly came to view the Devil as a tool by which God inflicted the punishment of evil on the unjust—a material being conspiring always to corrupt them. Chapter three would tell the story of how rising paranoia about the Devil's physical presence in Scotland fueled the witch hunts of the 1590s, leading to the deaths of more than two thousand people, mostly women. That was not even the worst part. The little research I'd done so far showed that many of the accused, like Isobel Gowdie, had refused to reject their demonic association, confessing they had met and fornicated with the Devil, even renounced their baptisms. (This section would require more research and thought; I still couldn't understand why anyone would make such a reprehensible claim if it wasn't true, and the fact that hundreds had, all over the country, left me feeling dreadfully uneasy.)

Reassuringly, as I would go on to explain over the next several chapters, by the eighteenth century Satan's supremacy over the country had waned. He was reduced to little more than a metaphor as a new supreme evil took his place: the English oppressors, hell-bent on drowning the flame of Scottish nationalism in a sea of Caledonian blood. After authorizing the Massacre of Glencoe, which saw thirty members of Clan MacDonald slaughtered for refusing to pledge allegiance to the new English monarchs, the British government had passed the Act of Proscription in 1746, crushing the clan system in order to destroy their ability to revolt. The act even outlawed the wearing of traditional Highland dress, including the kilt and one's own clan tartan—a crime punishable by no less than six months' imprisonment. Truly, who needed the Devil when they had politicians like that?

And that did not even get us to the nineteenth century.

Although I was still developing the central argument of the book, its tone and academic focus were clear—and yet the yellow envelopes that continued to clog my letter box were just as weird and unsettling as the first.

Their contents comprised a scattered assortment of papers, clippings, and articles, all connected by a thin, diabolical thread. A photo of a stone circle shaped like a pentagram. A Facebook post from a woman who ran a guesthouse in Ardnagrask, claiming she'd housed a lodger with hooves for feet. A photocopied chapter from a book called *Legends of Auld Reekie: A Dark History*, which described a sixteenth-century soldier and local icon of Presbyterian values, Major Thomas Weir, who from his sickbed had shocked the whole of Edinburgh by confessing to a secret life of deplorable crime including witchcraft, incest, and bestiality.

> *Believing Weir had gone mad, officials approached his spinster sister, Grizel. Rather than reassure them of her brother's righteousness, however, she confirmed all her brother had claimed and more.*
>
> *She said that Satan had come to them, in the form of a man with dark hair, wearing a fine black jacket and breeches. Avowing that she and her brother had made a pact with him, she described being transported to a distant town and back again in a flaming, horse-drawn coach. According to Grizel, Thomas even fornicated with the Devil himself.*

At those words, my head spun away in disgust. Between the graphic description of Weir being strangled and burned at the stake, and Grizel ripping the clothes off her body as she plunged to her death at the gallows, I could barely make it to the end of the chapter.

Preposterous though most of them were, I felt these documents chipping away at my soundness of mind. Even if my affliction hadn't returned yet, that was no reason to bait it, and I'd already made it clear to D.B. that there was no place for this kind of sensational material in the book. It appeared we would need to have a frank chat.

Before we could do so, however, I found myself distracted by yet another threat to my mental well-being. For the first time in years, I had a date.

It happened as I was leaving Teviot after drinks. Liam had been texting me about Jenna under the table practically nonstop: *You should talk to her. Her bottle's empty, offer to get her another.* As usual I had been gun-shy, convinced she would greet my overtures with laughter, if not outright repugnance. Eventually we dispersed, and as I shuffled off, cursing my cowardice, a feminine figure appeared at my side.

Blond and shorter than Jenna by nearly a foot, Sophie walked alongside me as we exited through the double doors into the chill gloom of the afternoon.

"How are you?" I said, to mask my disappointment that it was she, not Jenna, who had hurried to catch me up.

"Good, aye." She took an ungainly pause before adding, "I'm so glad you've been coming out with us. It's been really great getting to know you."

How could that be possible? Since that day at the Blind Poet, we'd barely exchanged a few sentences.

"Maybe sometime we could, I don't know," she said, her voice high and tinkly, "do something just the two of us?"

I went quiet, not quite sure what I was hearing—or how I felt about it. Was she asking me out? I'd never viewed Sophie as girlfriend material. Still, I couldn't help being flattered.

In the intervening silence, she'd gone fidgety, hands rifling distractedly through her bag as if to give her a reason to look away.

"I would like to—" I began.

"You would?"

Shit. I had been about to add that, now that Liam and I were friends, our dating might prove awkward. Thwarted in my attempt to let her down easily, I was forced to agree.

She looked positively delighted.

Glancing at Liam as he emerged from the building with one of the guys from our group, I swapped numbers with Sophie, agreeing when she suggested we meet for drinks the following night.

Once she had scampered off like a giddy schoolgirl, throwing me an embarrassed wave as she went, I wheeled around, searching for Liam. I was hoping to catch him and explain what had happened before he heard it elsewhere, perhaps even enlist his help in getting me out of it. But he was gone. I planned to text him when I got home—but once again, my date was too fast for me. Before I even reached my flat, my phone buzzed with Liam's message.

Heard you're going out with Sophie??

The emoji that followed expressed shock more than anything else. I didn't know what to make of it. Was he angry? Should I tell him I hadn't really meant to agree to it, or would that just enrage him further?

Yeah, looking forward to it. That okay?

You kidding? Of course, mate! ☺

At least our friendship wasn't in jeopardy.

Though it pained me I added, *Guess that means Jenna's all yours.*

His reply was swift and reassuring.

Don't worry, I still won't go there, a promise is a promise.☺

It felt as if a great weight had been lifted. An imaginary one, for I was more likely to spontaneously combust than make a pass at the most attractive girl in Research Methods.

Still, a part of me wondered if dating Sophie might help my chances. It pleased me to imagine Jenna might see us together and feel a hard knot of jealousy tying itself around her heart.

⁓

I texted Sophie the next day, suggesting we meet at the Pear Tree, the only pub I knew that had grown-up chairs and didn't offer one-pound shots of sambuca on Thursdays.

Though we had agreed on eight, we both arrived early. At 7:50 I found her already sipping a vodka cranberry at a small table, looking as pretty as I had ever seen her. Although we got off to an awkward start, botching the initial hug and then talking over each other in our nervousness, the date was not a complete shambles. Sophie possessed a natural facility for filling uncomfortable silences, often with questions I wouldn't have thought to ask in a million years. They seemed to flow from some deep infinite source, like whatever the opposite of a black hole was: a never-ending stream of apparently genuine curiosity.

As she quizzed me about my favorite childhood books and their film adaptations, I drifted into an agreeable stupor. For her faults, she made a pleasant companion, and I felt more comfortable in her presence than I could have anticipated. It wasn't hard to imagine being married to her, even. The easy, bourgeois life we would lead. Fundamentally passionless, but a more companionable union than most couples enjoyed. Borrowing Sophie's knack for prematurity, I imagined what the wedding might look like: the extravagant loch-side venue; the front-row chair reserved in memory of my father; Liam standing beside me as my best man, a white rose in his buttonhole and a cheeky glint in his eye.

At some point between rounds two and three he texted me to ask how it was going. When Sophie went to the restroom, I returned his message with a photo of the empty glasses piling up on our table and a wink.

You cheeky monkey, he wrote back, *glad it's going well.*

But had he meant it? After all, Liam's outlook seemed rather different a few days later, when I accompanied Sophie to a Halloween party hosted by a mutual acquaintance. Not having understood the memo of "fancy dress," I showed up in a blazer and slacks to find everyone else costumed as witches and topical references. When I claimed to be impersonating Dr. Porter, someone foisted upon me a broomstick and mop to use as crutches. I set them aside the moment he'd gone, merely grateful no one had come as Beelzebub.

Jenna, as a matter of course, put all the other girls to shame dressed in kitten ears and a body-hugging black leotard. Liam, a soccer player, caught me stealing glances at her, and didn't look overly happy to see my eyes wandering from Sophie. I felt nervous when he came over to talk to me. He'd gone uncharacteristically quiet on me the last couple days. In fact, I hadn't heard from him since my date with Sophie. What had she told him? If I'd done anything too egregious, surely she wouldn't have been so adamant about my accompanying her to the party.

"So, you and Sophie," he said into his Heineken, turning to stand beside me. His blue jersey bore his own name, the white lettering pulled taut across his chest and cracked from multiple washes. "How's it going?"

"Good. Yeah. Really good."

"You like her?"

I could feel him examining me out of the corner of his eye, sizing me up.

I sipped my beer. "She's a great girl. Really sweet."

"Too sweet, maybe."

He noticed my inquiring look and hesitated.

"She has a history of, sort of, not picking the best blokes. Blokes who don't care much about her. The last guy she was with—kind of a loser—she did everything for him and the whole time he was shagging some other lass. Not saying you're like that. Just, you know . . ."

"Just looking out for her."

"I'd do anything for her."

I nodded.

It was all very friendly, but we both knew that when he said "anything," he meant it.

The conversation left me in a state of mild anxiety, convinced Liam had lost faith in Sophie's and my pairing, that our friendship was already on the decline. Why had I ever said yes? I hadn't even wanted to go out with her in the first place.

I soothed my anxiety with alcohol. A couple beers led to a couple shots, then several glasses of a soupy green-brown concoction labeled "Witch's Brew," which tasted like a mixture of melted-down Skittles and rubbing alcohol. Fortunately Liam was drinking too, helping to clear the strange atmosphere that had settled between us. The looser we got, the harder it became to remember why I had felt anxious, our previous conversation like a dream I could barely remember upon waking—like most of that night would end up being.

By the end we were both, as the locals say, "rat-arsed," the last hour of the party a blur of laughter and people dancing on the couch and a sound that reminded me dully of gibbering. A hazy smear of winged shadows crashed around the drinks table, smashing bottles on the walls and upending a bowl of candy over their heads. In my inebriated state, it was all too easy to look the other way.

The last thing I remembered when I woke the next day, feeling as though my skull had been split open, was Liam inviting me back to his flat for another round, then standing out on St. Leonard's Street, hugging myself against the cold while he jabbed at a keyhole with his key. I reached for my phone and recoiled from its light. It was already after three in the afternoon. I had slept through my morning elective.

A dull pain throbbed at the back of my head. Although the idea of food made me nauseous I'd heard somewhere that vitamin C was good for a hangover.

Slightly woozy, I fumbled out of bed, threw on a jacket, and walked to the Sainsbury's Local down the road. The people on the sidewalk seemed to come at me too fast, each screech of brakes from the passing cars driving a spike into my skull. Ten minutes later I was on my way home with my meal deal—OJ, apple slices, and a prepackaged breakfast sandwich.

It was only when I returned home and stopped at the top of the stairwell that I saw the yellow envelope wedged in my letter box.

I let out a grunt of frustration, mostly with myself. I'd been meaning all week to give D.B. a call; now I was too late. The last thing I needed in my delicate state was to have to carefully catalog the online ramblings of psychopaths and illustrations of Satan sodomizing farm animals. Deciding to leave it until the following day, I took the package inside and tossed it unopened on the desk.

It nagged at me like a scab begging to be picked, and after a couple hours, I submitted.

Among the expected smattering of bizarre documents, I discovered something else. Enclosed in the envelope were several Polaroids. They each showed D.B. in a different part of the country: standing before a mushroom-shaped rock alongside a brook (*Devil's Pulpit, Glasgow*, read the note at the bottom of the photo), hiking a dirt path through a valley of rugged green mountains (*Devil's Staircase, Glencoe*), and a rather puzzling one labeled only *Edinburgh*.

Alongside my employer, there was a man I didn't recognize. He was slightly younger, perhaps midtwenties with untamed brown hair. They seemed to be friends, standing side by side at the top of a hill that, between the vivid grass and the hazy sprawl of cityscape behind them, I would have bet anything was Arthur's Seat. It left me puzzled; there was something weirdly familiar about the stranger. But I wrote it off as a symptom of my brain fog, which wasn't helped by the continued pounding in my head. My brain felt too big for my skull, as if it had swollen in the night.

Setting the photos aside, I discovered a final document, containing an urgent note in D.B.'s handwriting: MUST READ

It was a manuscript of some sort, committed to musty, yellowish paper by typewriter. My father used to have a black Royal from the fifties that produced print like that. I glanced at the title at the top and, at the sight of the words inked upon the sallow page, my body went still, the room silent but for the drumbeat of my pulse pounding against my eardrums.

Hastily my eyes scanned the first lines of the manuscript. I needed to be sure it wasn't true, that this was something else—of the same name, perhaps, but different.

My body shrank away from the words even as my eyes remained fixed on them.

```
A long time ago, long before your time or your
father's, there lived a young man named Jack
who was traveling across the hills and glens
of Scotland. It is not known where or for what
purpose young Jack was traveling, only that,
each day, he walked miles and miles, along a
solitary path leading straight.
```

With an involuntary motion I flung the story to the floor; I did not need to read another word to know that this was no fluke, no frightening coincidence.

The damnable folktale, the one that had started it all, had found me again.

Just reading those few opening lines struck a chord so low down in me that it shook my entire body. I could actually hear it, my dread, pressing in on me from all sides. Filtering in through the closed hangings over the window, through the crack under my door. It grew, morphed. A rising buzz that suddenly, viciously, I recognized as something else. Something scratching at the windowpane with razor-sharp talons, rattling the door off its hinges.

Shoving *Jack and the Devil's Horn* in the bottom drawer of my desk, I crumpled on the floor with my back pressed against it, blocking my ears against their gibbering, my lips pleading noiselessly against the din of their barrage.

"No, no, please no, *please!*"

There was no denying it any longer: they were back.

Editor's Note
Exhibit H

Sophia Grant, whose romantic relationship with Hale began in October 2016 and continued for several weeks, understandably declined my invitation to participate in this book, stating she felt it would "only further sensationalize what, for me, has been a deeply personal tragedy, one I'm still dealing with each and every day." And yet her testimony in the trial of HM Advocate v. Hale [2017], in which she stood as a witness for the Crown, was among the most sensational of any given during ten days of proceedings. In the course of a single interview, Grant singlehandedly threw the reliability of Hale's story, including this manuscript, into serious doubt.

With all due respect to Ms. Grant's wishes, here I provide an excerpt of the aforementioned testimony, given under oath at Edinburgh High Court, 21 June 2017.

HIGH COURT OF JUSTICIARY
Transcript of Proceedings

ADVOCATE DEPUTE: How would you describe your relationship with Liam Stewart? Friends? Confidants?

GRANT: Friends. Close friends.

ADVOCATE DEPUTE: And when he disappeared, for how long had you known him?

GRANT: Seventeen years.

ADVOCATE DEPUTE: That long?

GRANT: We went to school together. We lived next door to each other for years.

ADVOCATE DEPUTE: I'm sorry for your loss. This must all be very difficult for you.

GRANT: Thank you.

ADVOCATE DEPUTE: Did Mr. Stewart know the accused?

GRANT: He did.

ADVOCATE DEPUTE: And what was their relationship?

GRANT: They were classmates. Acquaintances really.

ADVOCATE DEPUTE: Not friends?

GRANT: No.

ADVOCATE DEPUTE: You're quite definite in that.

GRANT: Em . . . Liam didn't care for Grayson.

ADVOCATE DEPUTE: He told you this?

GRANT: Sometimes.

ADVOCATE DEPUTE: And did he give a reason for this dislike?

GRANT: He said he found Grayson quite . . . unusual.

ADVOCATE DEPUTE: Unusual how?

GRANT: He said . . . He said Grayson was obsessed with him.

ADVOCATE DEPUTE: That was the word he used? "Obsessed"?

GRANT: It was.

ADVOCATE DEPUTE: Did he explain why he held this view?

GRANT: Not at first. But I noticed he was quite uncomfortable around
Grayson. Avoided speaking to him, that sort of thing. When I asked
him why, he said Grayson was overly interested in him. That he was
constantly looking at him. Trying to catch his eye, when we were
out for drinks, or in class.

ADVOCATE DEPUTE: Had you observed this behavior too?

GRANT: No. But I did notice that when Grayson spoke to Liam, often it
was like he was coming into the conversation halfway through, as if
they'd been talking for hours when really they hadn't spoken a word.

ADVOCATE DEPUTE: As if they had a secret relationship.

GRANT: Or . . .

ADVOCATE DEPUTE: Go on.

GRANT: An imaginary one.

ADVOCATE DEPUTE: But isn't it true that Mr. Stewart and the accused
saw each other separate from your social group?

JUDGE: Please rephrase, Advocate Depute.

ADVOCATE DEPUTE: Apologies. Ms. Grant, did Mr. Stewart mention having been followed by the accused on any occasion?

GRANT: He said that one time he put on Facebook that he was going to hike up Arthur's Seat, and when he got there he found Grayson hanging around, watching him from a distance. He said they sort of noticed each other but didn't speak. Then Grayson started following him, and Liam, well, he was quite unsettled. He had to hurry to get away.

ADVOCATE DEPUTE: Was the accused known to have ever followed Mr. Stewart home?

GRANT: Yes.

ADVOCATE DEPUTE: The night of Halloween?

GRANT: That was the first time.

ADVOCATE DEPUTE: The first time, you said.

Fifteen

THE RETURN OF my satanophobia should have been the death knell of my contract with D.B. The document was cursed. I ought to have known it the moment D.B.'s pen sliced my fingertip and spilled my blood onto the page. What had I been thinking, agreeing to ghostwrite a book about the Adversary when my fear of him had made my life unbearable for years? How had I allowed myself to fall for D.B.'s flattery, to become besotted with visions of academic grandeur, knowing the price I would later have to pay?

It was easy to condemn the agreement as a disastrous mistake, a mistake needing urgently to be corrected. And yet for the same reason I had signed the contract then, I struggled to bring myself to cancel it now. Something held me back—a ghostly shape darkening my mind, the eyes lit with cold, empty appraisal.

Though my father was gone, it felt as if he were studying my every move, measuring my every choice against his own. Would he agree with my decision to cancel the contract, or would I have found yet another way to disappoint him?

I wished I could talk to him—receive his counsel like I had all those years ago, locked in his study night after night, laying my fears out on the desk like pieces on a chessboard and allowing him to instruct me which moves to play. He would tell me what to do about the book.

At the very least I needed to feel close to him. Needed to be reminded of why I had traveled to this godforsaken country in the first place.

By afternoon, all but two of the fiends had abandoned the outer boundaries of my bedroom. The remaining pair stood sentinel at the window, watching me as I lay curled on the mattress like a desiccated insect, trying to block out their menacing susurrations.

But I knew what I needed to do. I pulled open the drawer of my nightstand and dug out the paper that lay folded at the bottom. As the fiends gibbered more animatedly, approving, my eyes shifted from the window to the address in my hand.

It was time.

Sixteen

THE DOOR WAS concealed among the aging, mom-and-pop shop fronts that lined the block, its coat of chipped red paint clashing with the pale yellow bakery to the left and the peeling green chiropodist's office to the right. Above the shops were three rows of flats, hardly more refined than the businesses below. The sandstone was weathered and stained, affixed with ugly electrical boxes spewing ropes of bundled black wires. I gazed up at the building from the opposite side of the road, covetous of its hidden knowledge.

This was where my father had lived. In one of those rooms, behind one of those windows, he had made a decision that would change the course of his life. A decision that would follow him over land and sea, from decade to decade. Marriage, the birth of his sons, a dozen books to his name—still it haunted him.

Maybe even killed him.

Whatever had happened, it all started here.

That was as close as I had planned to get. But now I was there I felt myself wanting to move nearer, even find a way in. Get as close as possible to the place my father had called home, as if its mysteries were merely a function of proximity; as if the nearer I got, the closer I'd be to knowing the truth.

Dodging traffic down Ratcliffe Terrace, I crossed the street. The door was locked, the buzzer out of order. I tried knocking, but no one answered.

I took a step back and peered up. There was a sign in one of the windows—TO LET—and the number of a leasing agent. With only a vague notion of a plan, I took out my phone and dialed. It rang twice before a man's voice answered.

"Lets4U, Asif speaking."

The realization of what I was about to do throttled me.

"Hi, yes. I'm outside, uh"—I snatched the paper from my pocket and quickly unfolded it, even though I knew the address by heart—"I'm outside Seventy Ratcliffe Terrace, and I see there's a flat available."

Traffic roared down the road behind me, drowning my words.

"Say again? I can't hear a thing."

"I see there's a flat available at Seventy Ratcliffe Terrace," I said, half shouting. "Would it be possible to view it today?"

"Ratcliffe Terrace, you said? Which unit is it you're wanting to see?"

I hadn't realized there was more than one.

"Unit F is occupied," the man said, "so we'd need to arrange with the tenants. But there's another unit—B, I think it is. I could show you that now."

The paper shivered in the wind as I held it before me, the address upon it almost incandescent, burning the digits into my retinas: *70B.* The available unit was the same one my father had lived in.

"That would—that would be great," I stammered.

"Sure, fine. I'll just need to run back to the office for the key. I can be there in twenty."

"Okay. Thanks—"

The line went dead. Not sure what to do with the nervous energy racing through my body, I hunkered down in the neighboring bakery. I sipped at a mug of burnt coffee, feeling as if my insides were crawling with ants.

Finally a gleaming black SUV pulled up outside and a tall, brown-skinned man got out. He was sharply dressed in a gray suit. I left my cup and went out to the street.

"Asif?" I called, and the man turned. He was in his midthirties. The top two buttons of his white shirt were undone, revealing a chest sprinkled with dark hair. I shook his hand. "Grayson. We spoke on the phone."

"I only have a few minutes, we'll need to be quick."

As Asif unlocked the door, he rattled off the specs of the flat perfunctorily. These details glanced off me, leaving hardly a dent. All I could think about was getting inside. After nearly forty years, there was unlikely to be any trace of Edmund left in the building. Any neighbors who had known him would be gone or dead now; any physical possessions he might have left, long since cleared away. Still, I felt as if our reunion were imminent. As if I would enter the flat to find him, sixty-three years old, seated in his favorite wingback chair preparing to deliver the weekly teaching.

"Unit's on the first floor," Asif said, leading me up the gloomy stairwell, "which I personally prefer. Means you don't have to lug your shopping up three flights of stairs. It's just here." He indicated a door displaying a tarnished silver *B*.

My heart pounded as he fit the key in the lock.

When at last the door creaked open, I experienced a sudden urge to pull the man back, to prevent him from crossing the threshold. The flat was like hallowed ground, his intrusion a desecration.

"Like I said," he went on, "it's a one-bed, partly furnished—"

He broke off as his phone began to ring. He glanced down at it, and cursed. "I need to take this. You go in, have a look around."

He turned away, raising the phone to his ear. I could hear a woman yelling on the other end of the line.

"Mum—Mum, stop shouting. I told you, Oma's lying. *She's lying*—"

I left him on the landing in the hallway as I entered the flat, relieved he was occupied. All my life I had yearned to feel close to my father, to feel bonded to him by more than just blood. I needed this time with him, alone.

It wasn't difficult to imagine the flat as it might have looked when he lived there; just three tiny rooms off a central hallway, the place appeared not to have been updated in decades. The shoebox kitchen was old and dirty, with grungy white appliances and chintzy floral tiles. A narrow sitting room contained a lumpy sofa and a blocked fireplace. The wooden floors creaked underneath me as I entered the bedroom, which was so small that the full-size bed left hardly any room for the nightstand and chest of drawers. The en suite shower room reeked of mold, and if my father had been taller than six feet, his knees would have touched the shower door when he sat on the toilet.

Still, I understood this place. Small, and a bit far from campus, but he'd had it all to himself. Had I gone to Stanford instead of staying local, I'd have lived alone too.

Just thinking about it caused me physical discomfort. What had I been thinking, withdrawing my acceptance from one of the best schools in the world? Enrolling at UCSD on the off chance that—what? My father died of a stroke? Or survived a stroke, only to be rendered incapable of coherent speech? What difference would it have made whether I was five feet away or five hundred miles? What did I think I might achieve by staying?

It was a moot point anyway. The neurologist was wrong: my father never did suffer a full-blown stroke. The doctor put this down to his new diet and exercise regimen—a thirty-minute walk every other morning, which eventually became a daily jog. Its benefits were manifold. My father lost weight. Color returned to his skin. A few years on, he looked better than ever.

Meanwhile I was still living at home, rounding out my senior year at UCSD. I could have transferred to Stanford, but I hadn't seen the point. I'd been excelling in my classes, thriving off the positive feedback of my instructors, and if I maintained my 4.0 GPA, I'd have every chance of getting into a top-rated graduate program. According to my adviser, that's when it really mattered what school you went to, far more than where you received your bachelor's. I cycled these thoughts through my head almost daily, lifting away the doubt and insecurity that had collected in the crevices. It looked like I might even graduate with Latin honors, an accomplishment—I deluded myself—that even my father could not deny.

~

The morning of commencement I woke to my alarm, congested and weak. The cold I'd been battling for days had hardly improved with sleep; my body, mutinous, demanded ten more minutes. I hit what I believed to be the snooze button. But when I jolted awake a second time, this time to the screeching of parrots outside, I knew immediately I had overslept.

As I tumbled out into the living room five minutes later, pulling my graduation gown over my clothes, I found my mother seated on the sofa fully dressed and waiting. She slid a bookmark between the pages of her paperback and stood, looking almost disappointed I hadn't slept straight through.

"You didn't wake me?" I said as I forced a pair of Oxfords onto my feet.

"Summa cum laude. Would've thought you were smart enough to set an alarm."

My father wasn't there. Out somewhere, she said. This shouldn't have surprised me. He'd been disappearing a lot lately, sometimes for hours at a time. His car would be gone, and no one would know where he was. Then he'd show up out of nowhere, his shoes dusted with dirt. I assumed he was going to Sunset Cliffs again; why, I didn't know.

But he couldn't, not today. It didn't matter that Nathaniel had blown off my graduation, or that my mother insisted on going just to spite me. Dad was the only one I cared about. Even if it meant nothing to him, he had to see me walk across that stage. Had to hear my name called out to thousands of spectators, trailing honors behind it like a garland of gold.

But we couldn't wait. He'd have to meet us there.

It started to rain as we drove north to La Jolla, squeezing traffic along the I-5. When we finally arrived at the campus, the gridlock was backed up for blocks, cars crushing in from all directions in search of parking. The royal strains of "Pomp and Circumstance" soared in the distance. I got out and took off up the curving sloped lane.

By the time I reached RIMAC Field, the ceremony had already begun. I was panting and sodden, the rain disguising the sweat pouring down my face. After arguing with a security guard and a woman with a clipboard, who told me I was too late to participate—"I'm sorry, but you should have been here on time"—I forced my way past them and marched across the field toward the stage, where the chancellor was giving his speech.

I could feel the eyes of the spectators turning to look at me, could sense them smirking and nudging one another. My heart, like my head, was pounding. But I had to keep going. *My father had to see me.*

Finally the woman with the clipboard skipped up beside me. Pretending to smile for the benefit of the crowd, she made a show of escorting me helpfully to my seat.

The ceremony was long and tedious, not helped by the on-and-off precipitation. From the field, it was impossible to make out the faces in the stands, under the programs and umbrellas they held over their heads. But I didn't fret; somehow, I could sense he was there. Could feel his eyes trained on me, striking down their glacial watchfulness. A smile tugged at the corner of my mouth.

At last it was time for my row to rise. We split at the center, forming two lines, one on either side of the stage. One by one, the students were called forward, bashfully smiling and bowing their rain-slicked heads, to shake the hand of one stranger and collect their diplomas from another. Before long I was next, standing trembling at the edge of the stage.

"Grayson Matthew Hale, summa cum laude."

Stepping forward, I allowed a smiling woman to wring my hand and approached a portly white-haired man proffering a diploma encased in black leather. As he handed it to me he began to turn away, reaching behind him. I hesitated, thinking he had something else to give me, an additional token in recognition of my high honors. When he turned back to find me still standing there, reaching out for the next person's diploma, his round face screwed up in anger.

"No!" he said, waving me onward. "Not for you!"

I ripped my hand back and hurried forward. I could feel the blood rushing to my cheeks. Had anyone seen what I'd done? Had my father? I gazed up into the crowd, unable to spot him and not needing to. His humiliation thrummed through me like the thunder that broke overhead.

The moment the ceremony was over I fled the field, not even trying to find my family. I couldn't face him. Trundling down the road in the downpour, I summoned an Uber. I was drenched by the time it pulled up, and so weak I thought I might faint.

We arrived at the house half an hour later. My mother's car wasn't there—but my dad's was. How had he gotten back so fast?

As I reached the door, something on the step caused me to falter. Beside the welcome mat was a pair of shoes. My father's shoes. They were dripping wet, the upper sides coated in dirt and the soles caked in mud.

I felt something inside of me crack, and a great unleashing.

I searched the house. The kitchen, the den, and finally my parents' room. There I found him, one hand gripping the bed for balance while the other peeled a wet sock from his foot. He turned. As his gaze flicked over my sodden gown, a grave realization settled in his eyes.

I couldn't control it. Tears were already streaming down my cheeks.

"Where were you? Why didn't you—?" I broke off, unable to continue.

After a silence, he moved toward me. For one wild moment I thought he was going to hug me. My heart sank when he walked past me out of the room.

In the distance, I heard the glass slider open and close, as my father shrank back to his study.

Now the ocean of my despair flowed free, there was no restraining it. It took me in its current and filled my lungs with its brine, choking me until I ceased to fight against it. That summer, I hardly left my bed. I did not work, or read, or dream of the future. Sleep became my occupation, drink my late-night pastime. I ate only what could be ordered to the house, for after a couple weeks my mother stopped delivering meals to my room. She accused me of faking sick, called me attention-seeking, not realizing that, for perhaps the first time, the opposite was true.

I had planned to attend graduate school for English literature after a short break, but I could no longer see the point. A hundred PhDs wouldn't make my father love me. He had made it clear the day of my graduation, and every day before it, that nothing I did mattered to him in the least.

I entered a period of semi-functional melancholy. My mother couldn't throw me out and risk tainting her saintlike image, but she was not above letting me starve. And so, in order to keep the deliveries of takeout and alcohol coming, I was forced to seek employment. I took on part-time work with an online agency helping foreign students write college admissions essays, and poverty-wage copywriting jobs for local businesses connected to the family through fellowship. I didn't have to worry about awkwardness with my father, for we almost never interacted. I hardly left my bedroom, and he, his study. In the sixteen-month period following my graduation, I saw him only a handful of times.

But brief as these encounters were, I noticed a change in him.

First, there was the hiding things. One day as I was coming out of my room, I discovered him hunched down on all fours in the hallway. His back was to me, his hand reaching under a wooden floorboard he had pried up at one side. I hung back, wanting to remain unseen, for there was a hushed quality about his movements that told me this was not meant for my eyes.

After he left, I took his spot and knelt down to inspect it. How long had the floorboard been loose like this? It didn't fight me as I prized it up, creaking open to reveal a dusty hollow no bigger than a shoebox.

Inside lay a disordered stack of handwritten documents. Without lifting them out I paged through them and recognized them as my father's old sermons—his most blistering exhortations on the Adversary and the inescapability of sin. He had hidden them here, like a truth he did not want to acknowledge, but equally, like all his teachings, could not bring himself to throw away.

Things took an even stranger turn about a year after my graduation, when my mother forced me to make an appearance at her Summer Assembly, an annual backyard gathering of believers for the speaking of prayers, the grilling of processed meats, and the stuffing of checks into her cornucopia. As I played my part, circulating through the party, making small talk with the believers and deceiving them about the ruinous state of my life, I spotted my father across the deck, standing slightly stooped, facing the side of the house. As I drew nearer, I heard him muttering to himself, fast and low. Something about *"Can't be here . . . in Scotland . . ."*

I inched closer, listening hard.

"What have I done?" he was whispering. *"What have I done?"*

Before I could make sense of it, Barry Purdue clapped a hand on my father's shoulder, startling him out of his cogitation. Already three sheets to the wind on Kirkland Signature red, Barry didn't notice his minister wasn't himself and launched into a sonorous monologue about the Chargers and their rumored move to L.A.

"I'm prayin' the mayor does th'right thing," he said, slurring heavily. "Jus' give 'em what they want already! Right, Ed?"

But my father had already disappeared into the crowd.

Determined as I was not to care about my father, I put the incident out of my mind for the next three months, until I was forced to reconsider its significance.

One morning in October, I was awoken by the sound of strange voices in the driveway. Forcing myself into a sitting position, I drew back the curtain to find a police SUV parked on the street, the white door emblazoned with the official seal of the City of San Diego and its

Latin motto. *Semper Vigilans.* Two black-uniformed officers approached the house. The doorbell rang.

I had a sinking feeling. Though I'd done nothing wrong that I could remember, it seemed a foregone conclusion that they were there for me, to arrest me for the crime I must have committed; I had never been able to shake the subtle fear that I was tainted with evil. I stayed where I was, not eager to give myself up so easily. After a moment there was a knock at my bedroom door. My mother appeared and called me into the living room.

"The police are here to see us." Her calm demeanor reassured me, making me think she'd been expecting them.

The officers, when we entered, asked us to take a seat. As I did, I noticed my father wasn't there.

"Where's Dad?"

The younger officer looked to his senior, his expression wan. For a second time I felt my stomach sink.

The older officer explained that my father's body had been found at the foot of Sunset Cliffs. His head had hit a rock on the way down, a quick and painless death. "Probably an accident," they said.

I doubted that was true. On some level I had expected this my entire life. For as long as I'd known my father, I had observed a restlessness in his energy, like an animal trapped in a cage, plotting its release. The time of death was estimated to be between 6:00 and 8:00 a.m. My mother began to wail.

They took us in their SUV to identify the body. Or rather, the clothing, which he seemed to have been wearing for a week; the gray hair, greasy and unwashed; the hands, soft and gently spotted; for the face was all but unrecognizable. A grisly smash of muscle and bone, a pale glimmer of brain visible through a fissure in the skull. I suppressed the dark thought that I had always wanted to peer inside my father's mind, and now I could.

After, they brought us back to the station for routine interviews, then drove us home.

As I sat in the back of the police car, staring through the window at the city scudding by, I still had not shed a tear. I wasn't exactly sad, not in the way expected of a person who's just lost a parent. It was hard to miss someone who had never been present in the first place, who had offered so little of himself as to be almost incorporeal. And yet I felt as if my life were over. The pursuit of my father's love was the only thing I had ever lived for, the only purpose I'd ever attached to my miserable life. With him gone, and his affection lost forever, I couldn't see what justification I had to carry on.

The officer dropped us off, but I didn't go inside with my mother. Rather, diverging at the driveway, I headed around the side of the house to my father's study. The door was locked as usual. I let myself in with the key under the mat.

I paused at the threshold, a lump in my throat. Usually tidy, the room before me was in utter disarray. Books piled on every surface, papers scattered across the floor. It smelled stale and slightly rotten, like food waste left sitting for weeks.

As I stepped forward, I heard a crinkle under my foot. I had stepped on some kind of rolled-up poster. I unfurled it to discover a historic printed map—a map of Scotland. Random towns and cities circled in pen, barely legible notes scribbled in the margins.

My father's strange behavior at the Summer Assembly rushed back to me, plunging a knife of guilt between my ribs. He had seemed unhinged, driven mad by something—something to do with that country. I could have found help for him, but I'd done nothing, and now he was dead. He was dead because I wasn't there when he needed me.

I carried the map to the desk with the intention of taking a closer look, and it was then that I saw it, lying on the desktop. The handwritten letter.

My son,
By the time you read this I'll have passed from one plane of misery into the next. I've resisted the urge for as

*long as I could bear—but as you'll one day understand,
one temptation or the other was always bound to win.*

He had left a suicide note, and addressed it to me. So it was true: I
was to blame. Part of me was reluctant to read the rest, dreading what
it might say. Still, I pulled the chair around and sat, drinking the words
down my eyes.

To my relief, my father's note cast no aspersions against me. Rather,
it referenced his time as a student in Scotland, a connection I'd failed
to make to the map or his earlier muttering; after all, my father never
spoke of that time. He wrote of having been forced to make an impossible decision, which had haunted him.

*How I wish I could go back and unbind the shackles of
my life—discover in that country the part of myself I
didn't know existed, and not flee from it but welcome it
like an old friend.*

The shackles of my life. I assumed he meant his loveless marriage,
maybe even his ministerial career. According to my mother he'd orig-
inally wanted to go into academia, become a professor. I had no doubt
that, had he followed that path, he would have become one of the world's
preeminent scholars.

But something must have happened to change his course. Maybe
he got into trouble, or something happened at home—perhaps something to do with his father, whom I never met or heard him talk about.
Whatever it was, he was forced to decide between staying and going,
and chose wrong. He moved back to the States, and before long, his
life spun out of control: he got caught up in the ministry, married my
mother, fathered children. He regretted his decision, but it was too late.
He was trapped.

With time and hard work he would come close to achieving his
professorial dream: teaching at the local divinity school, publishing re-

search, becoming one of the great minds and writers of the church. But it would only ever be a pale imitation of what he could have achieved had he followed that other path. Perhaps that was why he had always been so distant, why he never took an interest in me or my meager accomplishments: I reminded him, by my very existence, of the life he did not want, the choice that had, as he wrote, stalked him to the very edge of his sanity.

It's too late for me—but there's time for you still.

Although I couldn't be sure what had happened all those years ago, one thing was clear: he wished a different life for me than the one he had chosen. But what?

I reread the letter again and again, and gradually the answer began to reveal itself. The message was subtle, but it was there. *I wish I could go back . . . but there's time for you still.* He wished for me to go . . . to Scotland.

It was all here, buried just beneath the surface: he was saying I was still young, with few attachments. I could lead the life he couldn't. Enroll at the university. Complete the highest level of study. Even become a scholar of repute. Was that why he'd addressed this letter to me and not my less intelligent brother: because only I was capable of carrying on his legacy?

All my life I'd wondered what I could do to win his approval, and now the answer was staring me in the face. I could not please him when he was alive, but if I did this—if I fulfilled my father's dream on his behalf—I would be forgiven. If not by my father, then at least by the part of me that had never felt worthy of being his son.

My path was set. By the end of the year I had applied to the University of Edinburgh. My acceptance came in the spring. I had opted to specialize in Scottish Enlightenment literature. I'd read a fair amount when I was younger—Robert Louis Stevenson, Sir Walter Scott—and considered myself a fan. There was something about it that felt as if it were made for me. The bleak view of human nature. The complex interplay between identity and religion. It was a niche in which I felt I could carve out a name for myself, a less crowded one, to be sure, than the English and American literature markets. Not only that, but my choice of subject felt right somehow—a nod to the country that had meant so much to him.

I could not have known then that, just weeks after arriving in Scotland, I would meet a mysterious stranger seeking a writer for his book. That the project would awaken my condition, threatening to destroy my well-laid plans.

As I lay on the mattress in the flat that once belonged to my father, I was struck by the similarity of our situations: here I was just a few months into my studies and, like him, I found myself faced with a decision that could determine the course of my life: press on with the book and collect my thirty-thousand-pound payday—the very money I needed to remain in Scotland—or cancel the contract and risk having to go crawling back to the States.

What was I to do? If I quit now, would I just be falling into the same trap as he had, running at the first sign of a struggle? *How I wish I could discover in that country the part of myself I didn't know existed, and not flee from it but welcome it like an old friend.* The whole point of coming here was to be the man he couldn't, to be faced with a choice and take the difficult road. To *enter by the narrow gate.*

Little though I liked it, I had my answer: I had to continue with the book.

I would never be able to live with myself if I didn't.

I could hear Asif finishing up his call in the stairwell. I rose from the bed, stood, and as I took a step forward, a floorboard wobbled beneath my foot. A coincidence surely. The wood worn loose after decades of hard labor. Still, I couldn't help thinking of the hollow under the floor in my parents' house, where my father—perhaps for years—had hidden the most potent tokens of his fear.

Had he done the same here? Could an explanation for his sudden departure from Scotland be lying under my feet at that very moment? I had to be sure.

As I depressed one end of the floorboard with my foot, the other stuck up a half centimeter above the floor. I bent down and pulled it toward me. It did not come easily like the one at home did. But millimeter by millimeter I prized it up, the wood producing a flatulent sound as it scraped the adjoining boards. At last a gap formed between the wood and the floor.

My heart sank as initially I mistook the items nestled there for refuse. A half-drunk bottle of Glenlivet, the label many decades out of date. A bag containing a small quantity of herb—I assumed marijuana. But there was something else. A book bound in a dull yellow dust jacket. Too big and specific to have found its way there by accident.

I cleared the dust off the cover, revealing the title: *Phylogenetic Systematics*. Inside, a sticker reading EDINBURGH CENTRAL LIBRARY had been stamped with due dates of checkouts past—the last one dated 10CT1976, less than two months before my father fled the country.

Adrenaline thrummed through me. This book was his, I was sure of it. But what was he doing with a biology textbook?

Then I noticed the scrap of paper tucked between the pages like a bookmark. I slid it free.

It was old and jagged-edged, a page torn out of a notebook or journal. There was writing on it, just a paragraph or two—frantic, barely legible. A close cousin to the writing on the suicide note—the work of the same author, separated by years.

Anticipation constricted my chest. At the top of the page was written a date: *November 8, 1976*. An excerpt from my father's journal? Had he kept a journal?

I read on, struggling to decipher the harried writing. I had only got through a sentence or two when Asif called out. "You still in here?"

I could hear him coming down the hall. Quickly I forced the floorboard back down into its groove, stuffed the paper in my pocket, and kicked the book under the bed just as Asif strode in.

"There you are. I've got another appointment I have to—"

"That's fine. I'm all done here."

"And what do you think?"

"I've . . . changed my mind about moving."

Asif stared. Before he could put words to the question brewing in his eyes, I hurried past him out of the flat and downstairs to the street.

Editor's Note
Exhibit I

In a warranted search of Hale's Edinburgh home, police confiscated more than three hundred documents which were retained as evidence in the murder of Liam Stewart and later turned over to me. I did not linger over these papers, which ranged from strange and macabre to outright gibberish. One document, however, stood out to me, for it closely matched the one Hale describes in the previous chapter, a journal entry he suggests may have been written by his father.

Here I present a photocopy of that document, as supporting evidence only, making no guarantees as to its origin or authenticity, or the authenticity of the narrative contained therein.

November 8, 1976

I cannot stop thinking of the previous Saturday, when I witnessed a man transform into a beast before my eyes. To look at him, one would never have believed him capable of such wickedness, such savagery.

I can still hear the screams. They echo through my mind as they once echoed through that valley. That poor hiker! What had he done to deserve his fate? And what fate do I deserve for having turned my back and run, rendered complicit by my fear?

Not that there was anything I could have done to stop it.

I ask you, what can any of us do in the face of evil but run?

Seventeen

WHEN I REACHED a safe distance from the flat, I found a quiet corner and read the rest of the journal entry. Part of me wished I hadn't.

The narrative inked upon it was brief and hysterical. In it, the author—my father, I was sure—claimed to have witnessed a terrible crime and, rather than intervene, fled in fear. I could not help feeling ashamed, even knowing I would have done the same thing. Had the incident with the hiker been what caused him to leave the country?

On the roof of the building across the road perched a winged animal. The eyes, when they turned to me, were lamp-like and yellow. For a moment the blood stilled in my veins. Returning the paper to my pocket, I took off down the street.

I did not feel much safer at home, knowing the fiends could arrive at any moment. But where could I go? It was after five; all the neighborhood cafés were closed, and a pub was out of the question. A night like that one, I'd be tempted to drink too much. Might as well put a sign on my back that read *Come and get me*.

Packing up a few things, I headed to the library. Just ten minutes' walk from my flat, it was bright and reassuringly buzzy, undergrads chatting under the fluorescent lights of the lobby and working at the tables on the mezzanine level. The partitioned study spaces on the upper floors were also well utilized, if more for socializing than their intended purpose. A screech of mirth rent the air, followed by a chorus of laughing shushes. It was strangely comforting.

I took a seat at a table near a boisterous gang, three girls and their gay friend, close enough to feel the warmth cast by their conversation. I did some grading, then some reading, taking notes as I went. It was hard to focus. I could still hear the fiends' gibbering in my head, as if they were nesting in the high shelves of the nearby stacks.

A student from my English Literature I tutorial noticed me and stopped to say hi, delivering a salvo of bright, vacuous small talk no doubt contrived to improve her grade. The floor-to-ceiling window to my right faced out onto the arboreal darkness of the Meadows. As the girl rambled about how fascinating she'd found our recent lecture, something sharp and fast-moving caught my eye: a winged shadow swooping past the glass.

When I turned back to her she had trailed off, looking hesitant and uncomfortable. I wondered if she'd seen it too but didn't dare ask.

In time my neighbors also departed. A middle-aged student took their space, but only briefly. It was getting late, after ten already. The library was starting to clear out, its former buzz diminished to a whisper. My stomach complained. I hadn't eaten anything since the Sainsbury's meal deal that morning, which felt as if it had been days ago.

I texted Ollie to see if he was home. No answer. He was probably out with his water polo buddies. Not wanting to go back to an empty flat, I left my stuff on the table and passed through the stacks to the restroom for a splash of cold water on my face.

The whole floor was deserted now, not a student or staff member in sight. As I cut through an aisle of magazines and newspapers, which stood on the shelf facing out into the aisle, I was stopped by a periodical entitled the *Edinburgh Informer*. It bore a headline about a proposal to refurbish Teviot, and I realized the paper was student-run. *Est. 1973*, proclaimed the masthead. It struck me as the kind of thing my father might have been involved in, as a columnist, or critic.

A note taped to the shelf read, *Back issues avail.—R32.*

I found the aisle at the end of the section, comprised of tall bookcases on one side and a row of stout metal filing cabinets on the other, their drawers containing thousands of magazines and newspapers. Under *E*, I located the *Edinburgh Informer*. VOL. IV, ISSUE I, AUTUMN 1976 was encased in a protective sleeve.

I removed it from the drawer. The layout was not so different from that of the recent issue. My eyes scanned the masthead through the plastic. My father's name wasn't on it, but still I slid the paper from its casing and leafed through it, interested to know what the world had been like when my father was a student.

There were the expected student complaints about fees and the administration, and an interview with the head of student housing. What surprised me was the presence of a lengthy feature on the outcome of the US presidential election, which saw Democrat Jimmy Carter narrowly defeat incumbent Gerald Ford. The writer described the occasion as "a moment of great hope, and the first step toward healing, for a country ravaged by loss and war."

Several students were quoted, and I was stunned to find my father among them.

Mhairi Gillies, a history postgraduate from Paisley, said, "I think [the US] can do better. I don't care for the president's views on integration. All that 'communities should be able to remain ethnically pure' stuff? It put me off."

Meanwhile, American undergraduate Edmund Hale, who is studying evolutionary biology, noted his approval of President Carter's plan to create a separate cabinet-level department for education.

A quotation followed, but I could not move past what I had just read. Studying *evolutionary biology*? It must have been a misprint.

And yet I was reminded of the book I had discovered in my father's flat. And the clerk in the student administration office, who had said Ratcliffe Terrace was down by the King's Buildings. *That's where the College of Science and Engineering is.*

Before I could process the possibility that my father had been a scientist, the overhead lights slammed off. The sudden darkness sent a shock through my body. But there was nothing to worry about; the library lights were on an automatic timer. I lurched forward, waving my arms around to trip the sensor.

Nothing.

I moved once more, taking a few wide steps, my hands groping the darkness haphazardly. I could barely see the shelves in front of me.

"Hello?" I called out. "I'm still in here. Hello—?"

Something *whoosh*ed behind me. I spun around and waited for the silence to break. It didn't.

"Hello?" I said again, shouting to keep the shake out of my voice. "Is anyone the—?"

Another *whoosh*. A book hit the floor behind me with a *fwap*.

Heart hammering, I backed slowly away, into the spill of ghostly light filtering in through the floor-to-ceiling window.

Whoosh.

I wheeled around as a winged shape grazed my shoulder, and a head exploded out of the darkness, scrunched and black, snapping its jaws like a rabid dog, spit flying off its lips.

With a scream, I ran. The shadows descended on me from all directions: five or six of them swooping and diving, swiping their talons and gnashing their long, needlelike teeth. I fumbled for a book on a nearby cart, swung it wildly through the air—*thwack!* Whatever I'd hit tumbled backward with a gibbering yowl. I took another hard swing—

Then stopped, squinting as my eyes adjusted to the lights that had just stuttered back on.

A library clerk stared at me, bewildered, from across the room, her arms full of volumes to be returned to the shelves. I let the book fall from my hands.

The fiends were gone. Not waiting for them to return, I crossed back to the table, snatched up my stuff, and wrestled my coat on as I tumbled down the stairs.

The lobby below was empty now, quiet as a graveyard. A lone guard gawked at me from behind the security desk.

"What happened to you?" he said with a smirk, nodding in the direction of my chest. Looking down, I perceived something I hadn't before: the shirt beneath my coat was torn and gashed, revealing my skin below. "Not been havin' a cheeky fumble in the stacks, were ye?"

"It's nothing," I snapped.

But it wasn't. A shock wave of horror crashed through me as I strode out into the night.

In all the years they had hounded me, the fiends had never touched me before. Never left so much as a mark. They weren't just back, I realized now—something was different this time.

Eighteen

THE ROADS OF the Old Town were like a writhing pit of snakes: interlocked and anarchic, twisting and coiling, driving up and plunging down. There was no grid here. No even planes. Everything existed on one of a dozen levels that slanted and curved and crossed over another, like a shadowy game of Chutes and Ladders.

Operating at the lowest level of the Old Town, the Cowgate passed under the bustle of the upper bridges like Edinburgh's own little underworld. The street was mostly empty but for a handful of pubs and clubs, thronging with the wild and unsavory: rough-looking men with indecipherable accents, teenagers puking candy-colored alcopop onto the cobblestones. Black winged fiends stalked me from the shadows, skulking along the rooftops as I searched the street for D.B.

Meet me in cowgate fri 22.00, he'd texted me earlier that week. Although I was obliged to comply, some low, unspoken part of me had protested. I didn't want to see him. Ever since that night at the library, just the thought of my employer brought a tempest of dark anxiety bearing down upon my mood. Was it the book I was worried about, or something else? And why did he want to see me so late?

Hoping at least to delay our meeting, I had texted back that I had plans with a friend, but D.B. just sent the same message again.

Meet me in cowgate fri 22.00.

He wasn't asking.

I was on time, but where was he? My eyes scanned the road as I sped along the lane. Forced to step into the street to avoid a crowd of college-age partiers, I nearly collided with a fast-moving Volkswagen, which screeched to a halt and blared its horn.

"Get oot o' the road, ye fuckin' dobber!" screamed the driver, lowering his window for the purpose. The crowd of smokers turned to laugh and casually heckle me.

"Ye dobber . . ."

"Dobber . . ."

Suddenly a fiend bolted past me, touching down on the Volkswagen's hood before bounding into the air. As the car roared off, I stood transfixed by the spectacle unfolding before me. The fiend had collided with another in midair, then was joined by a third. They tumbled in and out of the light, a black and misshapen mass. Fighting, or maybe rutting. Shrieking and gibbering in saturnalian delight, wings flapping behind them, their number growing every second as more fiends shot out of the darkness to latch on to the lumbering mass.

Before long, it had expanded into an almost human shape, as if their bodies had melded to form a new kind of a creature: a hooded figure clothed in black, with hands the color of tar, fingers ending in long, lethal points.

A trick of the light, I was sure—until the conglomeration of fiends appeared, impossibly, to put one leg in front of the other. To step over the curb.

"Get off, wouldja?" sniggered the smokers, shunting me off as I staggered back. They didn't understand, couldn't see the hooded figure as it advanced on me, hands balled into fists, boring into me with luminous, scarlet eyes.

A great light careened toward us. My head snapped in the direction of a second car as it rocketed down the lane. I averted my eyes from the glare of its headlights, and when I turned back, the approaching figure was someone else entirely: D.B., pulling the hood of his leather jacket down around his grinning face.

"Looking petrified as usual." He extended a pale hand, the nails short and perfectly round.

I couldn't seem to catch my breath. Not knowing what else to do, I took D.B.'s hand, and immediately I wanted to rip mine back. It was like I'd pressed my palm to an electric burner.

Before he let go he swung his other arm around me, steering me west along the Cowgate. He seemed to be in a good mood.

"There's a place I wanted to show ye. Hope ye don't mind."

"Wait. I don't—" I could hardly speak. The fiends were flapping after us, licking their lips with forked tongues as they threaded through the crowd—the crowd, which seemed to leer at us with unreserved disgust. It was like they could sense there was something dark and peculiar about D.B., something they didn't understand but feared and despised, and implicated me in the same sinister crime.

We passed under a sweeping archway and were swallowed by shadow, his hand sliding from my shoulder down my back. I felt it graze my backside before he pulled it away. "Just up here," he said, and walked ahead.

Here was my opportunity to run. But I hesitated, struck dumb by the building in front of me.

The converted church loomed over the street like the rotting carcass of a once-venerable tree, its slim profile squeezed between buildings on either side. It contained a tall, pointed spire and an arch above the door that once might have held a masterwork of stained glass. Now the only thing stained about the building was its stonework, which was black with the residue of the city's noxious industry. Gothic lettering glowed red above the open door to the club, drifting into focus as we approached: INFYRNO. The place was strangely familiar, like the setting of a long-forgotten nightmare.

He swept me in before I could protest.

Entering the club was like being swallowed up into the belly of a co-lossal, seven-headed beast—a red-tinted netherworld of lurching light, sweltering heat, and the raucous *thumpa thumpa* of the great animal's heart. It didn't look like the inside of a church at all. The ceilings were low and fitted with moving lamps. The decoration was minimal and modern.

The place was packed with people: men with big arms and short hair, jockeying for attention at the bar; women with big hair and short skirts, waging the same sordid battle on the dance floor. It was like I'd crash-landed on a strange and hostile planet, every part of my body screaming that I wasn't meant to be here.

"What are we doing here?" I shouted to D.B. over the riotous EDM beat. *"I thought you wanted to talk about the book."*

"We are talking about the book."

"What?"

But he had already gone, snaking his way toward the bar.

Left on my own, I felt conflicted, one part entreating me to run while the other reminded me what I stood to lose if I did.

As if by compromise I cut a path for the men's room.

It was barely quieter in there, and heinous. Paper towels and used condoms littered the floors, the urinals coated with piss and pubic hair. I crossed to the sink, before a mirror inscribed with barely legible ob-scenities and insignia. As I washed my hands, I noticed my palm with a shock, the one that had shaken D.B.'s hand.

It looked badly burned, a shining, livid red. Delicately I flexed it. Prodded it. But there was no pain.

D.B. thrust a drink in my hand the moment I emerged from the bathroom. I hesitated, then told myself not to be stupid. I'd drunk with him plenty of times before. It might even do me some good. As I took a sip, he lifted the bottom of the glass, forcing me to down it in one. A nasty concoction, several shots of hard liquor mixed with something I didn't recognize.

Taking my glass away, he nodded toward the dance floor.

I shook my head. *"I can't."*

But the drink was already working upon me; I barely put up a fight as he pulled me by the wrist into the depths of the club, even as a warning flashed lethargically across my brain. *You don't want to do this.*

A moment later, I was being jostled by a hot crush of bodies. D.B. began to sway, pulling my wrists to the music. My body felt leaden. I couldn't make it move more than inches. He peeled off his jacket, revealing a tightly fitted T-shirt underneath. A smile on his lips.

Something inside him seemed suddenly to unlatch, letting his body swing free. Raising his arms above his head, he began to undulate in time with the music, alternately rocking his shoulders and rolling his pelvis, slowly squeezing the gap between us, every gyration moving him closer to me.

I stepped back and was blocked, unable to retreat. I felt his wrists on my shoulders, his legs against mine. He was so close I could feel the heat rolling off him in waves.

Even more unnerving, I, too, was moving to the music. It was as if I were a visitor in someone else's body. I couldn't make it stop, nor could I tear my eyes from his.

A dull misgiving sounded at the back of my head; I couldn't process it. I was too foggy, my vision clouding over, my body taking pleasure in defying my mind. Inhibition deserted me. I danced with abandon. Continued to dance, for how long I can't say. Maybe minutes or hours or days. Time, like fear, was meaningless here.

After a time, I detected a change in the atmosphere of the club. The place was wild with unrestraint: men built like bulldozers barely able to stand, women rushing off to the restroom to vomit. The air was rank with the thickening scent of sex. Groups frayed as their members paired off, chests touching, tongues swirling, hands plunging into darkness. I could feel D.B.'s breath on my lips.

Jerking my head away, I spotted a skinhead in the shadows across the dance floor. A beam of light from an overhead lamp played upon his brutish face. There was a scar in his lip, the apparent souvenir of some long-ago brawl. He was leering after a woman with long dark legs. She didn't seem to notice, which concerned me. Even through the haze of my inebriation I could see there was something more than attraction in the skinhead's stare, his eyes fixed with twisted desire as she danced with someone else.

Disjointed words drifted across my mind.

Bad man . . . do bad things.

"He's here."

D.B. didn't need to lean in to speak in my ear.

"Who?" I said.

"You know. The Devil."

It reverberated through my head, a villainous refrain. *You know. The Devil. . . . You know. The Devil. . . .* Then I began to hear it differently.

You know the Devil.

Next thing I knew, D.B. was on the other side of the club, his gaze fixed on me as he whispered in the skinhead's ear. The same moving light must have caught D.B.'s eyes, for they were a blazing scarlet.

Instantly the skinhead lurched forward, bulldozing a path through the crowd. The girl's scream pierced the air as he grabbed her, then fizzled to a gurgle as—*BANG*—he slammed her against the wall, one hand crushing her throat and the other driving up her skirt.

There was instant pandemonium: people screaming, bodies leaping, bottles smashing to form weapons. The skinhead hit the floor, a rubbery triangle of flesh drooping away from his face to expose his lolling tongue. There were more screams, barely audible over the music, as several men dragged him out by the arms and legs, kicking him in the ribs as they went.

Someone was pushing into me. I thought they were trying to get past. As I turned to look at them, my body went numb.

It was D.B.

But it couldn't be. He wouldn't have had time to get back through the crowd. And yet there he was, dancing before me as if he'd never left my side: swinging his shoulders, hands in the air, his downturned face sliced open in a nasty smile.

Lifting his head, as if in slow motion, he gazed at me with eyes the color of rubies.

I struggled to breathe. The sensation rampaging through my body was unmistakable. I'd experienced it a thousand times before. The sudden feeling of emptiness in my chest, of tendrils climbing the walls of my torso and tying a vicious knot around my heart.

The sensation I'd been dreading for weeks: the one that told me the Devil was near.

I stumbled backward and fled. It couldn't be true. I was crazy to think it. But still I thrust through the crowd, clearing a path to the door. All that mattered was getting away.

I burst out into the arctic shock of the night. I wasn't wearing my jacket. I couldn't remember having taken it off. The skinhead lay on the pavement, bleeding out into the street as a crowd formed around him.

I rushed down the sidewalk, sobered by my terror.

An ambulance hurtled toward me, its high-pitched siren piercing my eardrum like a syringe: pushing in deeper the closer it got, injecting my brain with reverberating pain.

I threw a glance over my shoulder as if to scold it, then felt a chest bump mine.

"You're no' leaving?" D.B. said. "I was hoping to make a night of it."

"S-stay away from me," I stammered out.

"Have ye no' learned? Ye can't run from the Devil."

I forced my way past him and took off without looking back.

"He's here," his voice chased me down the street, "and he needs ye."

Nineteen

I T WAS AFTER 4:00 a.m. when I finally gave up trying to sleep. Slipping out of bed, I crossed the room and felt around for the gooseneck lamp on the desk. With a click it beamed, casting a stark light across the darkness of the bedroom.

I sat, feeling weak, jittery. A little nauseous. My eyes stung from lack of rest. Pulling a spiral-bound notebook toward me, I opened to the back and drew a vertical line down the center of the page, producing two imperfect columns. At the top of one I wrote *Reasons He Might Be*; at the top of the other, *Reasons He Might Not*.

This was stupid. My discomfort was easily explained. I had satanophobia, a condition that made me read demonic machinations into even the most mundane occurrence. This black, nauseating terror was just a symptom of my affliction. Sick was what I was, sick and ill-equipped. I ought to call a psychiatrist. I needed help.

And yet, rational though it was, the explanation did nothing to soothe my nerves. Did nothing to quell the thoughts and images hammering my skull with cruel insistence, telling me that I had met the Devil that night, and that any moment he would return.

And so I began to write.

Reasons He Might Be
1. Demonic shit

This one was a given. The scarlet eyes. The burning handshake. The way he was here one moment and there the next. How he seemed to materialize out of an orgy of fiends, as if he and they shared a common DNA, each one an extension of the other. I wrote none of this down, too embarrassed to admit even to myself that I believed such things were possible. But they had to be considered nonetheless.

2. He tempts people to do bad things.

I was an atheist. I didn't believe in God or the Devil or temptation or sin. But I knew what I had seen: D.B. had *made* the skinhead attack that woman.

It was like he'd been possessed. No, not possessed; possession implied infiltration, host and parasite. But that's not how the Devil worked. The horror movies had it wrong. The Adversary could only make those transgress who had it in their hearts to do so; his job was merely to unleash the evil within. My father had taught me that.

Now that I thought about it, the people in D.B.'s company seemed frequently to indulge their basest impulses. The evening we dined at the Devil's Advocate, a kid had mocked and tormented me, tossing fries at my head like a lunchroom bully. And hadn't a man thrown his girlfriend's dinner on the floor that same night? No one at the Witchery had made a scene. But it was true that the date of the woman in the red dress had stolen money out of her purse the moment she stepped away.

Everywhere D.B. went, it seemed, someone was doing something they shouldn't.

Everyone, I thought, *except for me*. I'd been in his company how many times, and the worst I'd done was lie about having read what he sent me. Why would his sphere of influence extend to everyone but me?

Maybe I was more valuable to him as a scribe than a sinner. Maybe, despite my lifelong suspicions, I was pure of heart after all.

Or maybe he'd looked inside me and found something even worse: an exceptional evil, like a fine bottle of Scotch. A thing to be saved for a special occasion.

3. Who is he?

It would've been easy to dismiss Donny Blackburn as nothing more than a deluded stranger, even a dangerously unbalanced one. And yet, after weeks in his employ, I still knew almost nothing about him.

Was Donald Blackburn really his name? What did he do to earn the money he was always throwing around? And if he was so well-to-do, why did he live in a crappy flat in Abbeyhill?

I should have been able to answer at least some of these questions by now, but each time I asked a direct question, he had said just enough to avoid seeming untrustworthy before diverting my attention to a more interesting topic. I'd looked him up online, but while there were several Donny Blackburns in Scotland—a marketing rep in Glasgow, a teenager with a peach-fuzz mustache in Crieff, a potbellied club owner in Aberdeen—none of them seemed to match with my employer. As far as I could tell, the one I called D.B. didn't seem to exist at all.

4. The book

A book to make Scotland remember the Devil. Each time we discussed the project, that was what he went back to.

I'd never understood why he was so adamant about it, or why it nettled him so much when I suggested the Devil was just a metaphor. I could only think of two types of being who would resent the Adversary's fall from power: his most loyal worshippers, and himself.

5. HE FOUND ME.

Once it occurred to me, it towered above the rest as the most per-
suasive point in favor of the impossible, the thing that seemed to make
it all make sense.

After all, he hadn't contracted just anyone to write his book. Though
many were more qualified, he had picked me. In fact, he'd made it impossible for me to refuse. Offered me the money I so desperately needed;
heaped praise on my skill and intelligence, to which I was weak; said all
the right things to keep me in, even when every part of me was saying,
Stop, go back, you don't want to do this.

All these years I had been waiting for the Devil to come back for me.
Perhaps, that night on Leith Walk, he had.

REASONS HE MIGHT NOT
1. YOU'RE PROBABLY LOSING YOUR MIND AND JUST DON'T KNOW IT YET.

Twenty

THE LIST WAS an unequivocal failure: at the end of it I still didn't know what to think, but it sharpened my fear of D.B. to a razor edge.

This discomfort multiplied tenfold by the time the morning light spilled through the bedroom window, striping my face as I lay unsleeping on the bed. I refused to look at my phone in case I found a text there, or check my email for the same reason. I never wanted to see or hear from D.B. again.

But it wasn't that simple. I still had my father's legacy to think about. The money I could find some other way; what concerned me was that, by terminating my agreement, I would be letting my father down—taking the easy way out, like he had warned me against. Running from my problems rather than facing them head-on.

But surely if he had seen what I had, he would think differently. He would condemn my employer as the Adversary in human form. He would demand no less than my total disassociation from D.B. and his book. There was no avoiding it, and to realize it was a great relief: I must never see my employer again.

That afternoon, I arrived at Sophie's Marchmont tenement flat still anxious and exhausted, but as pleased to be there as she was to see me.

Greeting me at the door, she reached up and gave me an awkward hug around the neck. "Hello."

"Hey." I patted her back until she released me.

"Come in, welcome."

Although it was just a few minutes' walk from my own place, this was my first time seeing Sophie's flat. Crossing the threshold, I was slightly knocked back. The bones of the place were not very different than mine, but the decor could hardly have been more dissimilar. Framed prints of black-and-white cityscapes hung on the walls, the plain sofa glammed up with a furry throw and pastel pillows. The air was fragrant with the smell of a fruity candle burning in the window.

"Everything all right at your place?" she asked.

"Yeah. Fine."

"I thought maybe something had—"

"Yeah," I said, remembering the plan. "Well, things aren't totally all right. Ollie and I had an argument. I just needed to get away."

"Gosh, I'm sorry." Her expression was neutral.

"And," I added, "I wanted to see you."

Her cheeks bloomed. I experienced a pang of guilt at the lie.

For several hours now, the deed had been done. My email to D.B. was short and direct, yet simple enough that, if it turned out my misgivings were nothing more than a flare-up of my condition, I wouldn't come off sounding like I'd lost my mind.

> D.B.,
>
>   I am writing to inform you that I am terminating our contract for writing services, dated September 13, 2016, effective immediately. Do not contact me again or approach me in any manner.
>
>   Grayson Hale

Next, I had opened the bottom drawer of my desk and scraped to-gether every scrap of paper connected to my employer—every photo-copy, every printout, every incomprehensible note. Stuffed them in an empty trash bag, hauled it outside, and swung it into the dumpster at the end of the road. The black lid fell with a slam, a sound of finality.

But by the time I had returned to my flat, there was already a reply waiting in my inbox. I shut my laptop and turned to my phone, which was buzzing with an incoming call from D.B. I declined it, inciting a volley of frantic texts.

> Wut this about? call me now
> We had agreemt
> Call me need 2 talk
> U took my £££ u ow me
> Dont understand wut wrong pls talk
> I need u help grayson please

He was playing mind games, pretending we didn't both know what he was. Pretending he was nothing more than a confused and desper-ate man, blindsided by a person he trusted. Or maybe he was all those things and I had gotten it wrong.

No, I thought. *Don't let him get inside your head.*

Even so, it occurred to me he'd been sending packages to my house for weeks. Were he so inclined, he knew exactly where to find me. I needed to get out, at least for the night.

As I stood in Sophie's sitting room, the phone buzzed inside my pocket, signaling the arrival of a new text. I silenced it with my hand.

"Let me give you the tour," she said.

After showing me the kitchen and bathroom and introducing me to her flatmate, Rhian, an enormously tall girl with a gummy smile, Sophie took me into her bedroom. It was neat and girly and smelled like sweet lotion. There were powder-puff pillows on the bed and a cushioned bulletin board propped up on the dresser, decorated with old photos. A family trip to Disney World. An adolescent Liam with longer hair.

I tossed my bag on the carpet. When I turned around, Sophie was smiling behind me, suddenly close. There was a pregnant pause; I sensed that she was waiting for a kiss.

"Have you eaten lunch? I'm starving."

Her face fell slightly. "Er—no. Shall I make us something?"

As we ate tuna sandwiches in the kitchen, she paused, as if debating whether to ask me the question on her mind.

"What's wrong?" I said.

"Nothing, it's just—I'm sure he had it wrong, but Liam seemed to think you were at his flat the other night."

"You mean after the Halloween party?"

"You didn't . . . follow him, did you?"

"Follow him?" My eyes crossed to my phone as it buzzed. "No, he asked me back. Did he say—?"

"It's nothing. Maybe he had too much to drink."

"He was wasted. We both were."

"That must be it, then."

She moved quickly to another subject, with the air of one who has completed a dirty job, long delayed, to her satisfaction.

~

As we settled into Sophie's full-size bed that night, she nestled into me, a hand resting on my chest. She was doe-eyed, a gentle smile on her lips. "I'm glad you're here."

"Me too."

My gaze fell to the hand on my chest, gently massaging. In that simple motion, her hunger for sex was apparent.

"I'm just so tired," I said.

There was silence but for the patter of fresh rain against the window, and the continued buzzing of my phone on the nightstand. Sophie blanched, mortified.

What could I say to make her understand? What could I say to convey the wild anxiety gnawing at the back of my head: that anything I did with her in this bed, any sin I committed, was bound to attract unwanted attention? It was insane, and I hated myself for it, and yet the fear it engendered was as potent as that of a knife pressed against my throat.

She propped herself up on her elbow, her face set.

"You're mad," I said.

"I'm fine." After a moment she added, "Are you attracted to me?"

"What?"

"Sometimes I just wonder—" She broke off and looked away, her blue eyes set too widely apart, her jaw appearing more blocky and square than ever.

"Don't be crazy—"

"Don't call me crazy, please."

My phone buzzed on the nightstand. Her gaze flicked from the device back to me.

"Who keeps texting?" she snapped.

"No one." I powered it off, catching a couple words of the message even as I tried not to look.

will find u

"Grayson—?"

"I'm attracted to you. I've just had a long day. Please, can we just go to sleep?"

She was crying now.

I wanted to be sad, I wanted to feel guilty, but the events at Infyrno had drained me of every emotion but fear. As I reached for her hand, she rolled over and switched off the light, her back to me. I found myself suppressing a sudden surge of venom. The way she pulled her hand away from mine had reminded me of my mother.

We lay together in silence for an hour before Sophie drifted off. For me, that was barely enough time for the anger to fade, for my mind to revert, as if by homeostasis, to its work of constant, churning anxiety. It replayed every moment of my day, every word I had spoken, searching for any evidence that I had sinned.

But of course I had: *I'm attracted to you.*

Why had I said it? A lie was as bad as sex. The words that told me so were forever seared into my memory: *You belong to your father the devil. When he speaketh a lie, he speaketh in his native tongue, for he is a liar and the father of lies.*

I wondered if he'd heard me. If perhaps he was already on his way, attracted by the welcome sound of his language.

⁓

I woke late the next morning. Realizing she wasn't in bed with me, I recalled my tiff with Sophie the night before.

I stumbled out into the sitting room to find her reading on the couch.

"Good morning," she said, barely looking up. "There's coffee. And cereal if you're hungry." She was working hard to pretend that she wasn't upset, yet the dullness to her energy, and the absence of her usual offers to serve me, said otherwise.

Once she had confirmed that Rhian was out, I took a seat across from her.

"Look," I sighed. "I'm sorry about last night. I really was exhausted."

"No worries."

She was going to break up with me, I knew it. What surprised me was the tremor of panic the thought sent through me. The truth was, it had nothing to do with her but Liam. If she and I broke up, especially on bad terms, he might be tempted to take her side. After all I had experienced over the past week, I couldn't bear to lose my only friend. I needed to salvage this.

"But that's not the reason I didn't want to do anything."

I had her attention now. "It's not?"

I shook my head. "There's some stuff I need to tell you."

In fact, it was she who had given me the idea the previous night, when she pulled her hand away from mine and reminded me of my mother: I blamed it all on my family.

I told her how Vera had never held me except as an act of performance, how my father's teachings had taught me to fear and despise sex, how the closest my brother ever came to hugging me was putting me in a chokehold that left stars flashing in my eyes. As I spoke, Sophie's whole demeanor changed; she sat forward in her seat, book hanging limp and forgotten in her hand. I pretended not to notice her tears.

I had never revealed to anyone this much about my upbringing, and it was satisfying in a way I hadn't anticipated. Sophie's emotion was a revelation. I guess I had always taken it for granted that my parents' indifference was a reflection of me—my awkwardness, my fractious nature, the shameful parts of me we never acknowledged. I wasn't convinced I deserved more love than they had showed me, but it was a welcome thought nevertheless. So welcome, in fact, that I was tempted to reveal even more—tell Sophie all about D.B., and my history of fear—but I held myself back. There was only so much brokenness a person could tolerate.

In the end, she confessed she was a little relieved. The steady stream of texts, she said, had weighed heavily on her mind. She'd thought I was seeing someone else.

As I was leaving, she asked if she could give me a kiss. I allowed it.

"If you're free next Saturday," she added, "you should come along to opening night of the Christmas markets. We're all going."

That meant Liam would be there. I told her that would be nice.

Editor's Note
Exhibit J

In the course of my research, I had the opportunity to speak with Nathaniel Hale, elder brother of Grayson Hale and a crucially important character in the story of his upbringing. We met via Skype on 4 September 2019. The interview had taken several weeks to schedule, owing to the interviewee's insistence that he would only participate if he was flown to Scotland at the publisher's expense. When, after several back-and-forth emails, it was agreed he would not participate in the book, he seemed to have a sudden change of heart and consented to meet virtually.

He Skyped in from his office at the insurance company where he worked—a thin man of thirty, with a long triangular jawline and watery eyes. The effect was reminiscent of a rat, which surprised me, for it was almost exactly as I had imagined him. Here I present the first part of our interview.

BARCLAY: Thank you so much for granting me this time, Mr. Hale. Or should I call you—?

HALE: Mr. Hale.

BARCLAY: Certainly. Well—

HALE: I don't really see the point of all this. I did one of these before he died and it was a waste of time.

BARCLAY: You're referring to the article published in the *Edinburgh Daily News*?

HALE: "Devil's Advocate's Brother Spills the Beans on Psycho Sibling" or whatever?

BARCLAY: I did see that. In fact, it was part of the reason for my reaching out. If it's not too painful a subject, I'd like to dive a little deeper into your childhood. What Grayson was really like, so to speak.

HALE: As long as you'll print it. Those other hacks left out half of what I said. Just cherry-picked what they wanted to fit the headline.

BARCLAY: You wouldn't call Grayson a "psycho sibling," then?

HALE: [Inaudible]

BARCLAY: Sorry, I lost you for a moment. My Wi-Fi is awful here.

HALE: I said maybe as a joke.

BARCLAY: Oh, you would?

HALE: When he was young, yeah. He was like one of those creepy kids out of a horror movie. Like, never talked but was always there. His eyes always watching you. Kind of sis—no, what's the word? Like evil.

BARCLAY: Sinister?

HALE: Sinister, yeah.

BARCLAY: In the article you mentioned he had an odd hobby.

HALE: What? No I didn't.

BARCLAY: Perhaps you were misquoted, then. The article mentioned a painting, a particularly gruesome one that Grayson enjoyed—

HALE: Oh, that. I wouldn't call that a hobby, but yeah. We had this painting of Jesus on the cross hung up in the den. Gray would just sit there and stare at it.

BARCLAY: Did he have any other—?

HALE: They left out the creepiest part though.

BARCLAY: What was that?

HALE: Jesus is pretty much naked in it. He's wearing like a scrap of fabric, barely covering his junk.

BARCLAY: Not sure I follow.

HALE: You journalists aren't very smart, are you? Think about it. It wasn't just Christ's pain he was getting off on. One time I walked into the den and I saw Gray—couldn't have been more than five or six—and he's standing right up close to it, right underneath the painting, craning his neck. Looking right up there.

BARCLAY: Up there?

HALE: You still don't get it. He was trying to see under Jesus's loincloth. *He was trying to see His fucking dick.*

Twenty-One

AFTER CLASS ON Wednesday I stopped by the bank and spoke with a man about my finances. He had left me a voicemail that morning, urging me to come in. The bank was concerned about some strange activity on my account, something about large sums of money coming in and going out.

This was easily explained. I had recently wired D.B.'s advance back to my American account in case he should make any moves to recover it now I had quit.

"Tha's all very well," said the banker, as something in the window hooked my attention. The moment I turned my head to look, three dark shapes fluttered away from the glass—fiend or fowl, I couldn't tell. "Ahm still no' certain that's what—"

"I'm pretty busy," I said, slinging my bag over my shoulder. "Thanks though."

Dark thoughts followed me through the city as I walked, wheeling and turning like winged shadows overhead.

In my eagerness to get home I tried a new shortcut and found myself on a street I didn't know, a gloomy lane of greasy chip shops, booking agents, and a boarded-up bar with the silhouette of a nude dancer. A man pushed past me without apology.

My initial burst of anger chilled when I got a fuller picture of the man. I could have sworn it was D.B. But he hadn't acknowledged me at all. Maybe I was just being paranoid.

Cautiously I continued in the same direction as the man, slowing down to maintain a safe distance. There was half a block between us by the time he wrenched open a shop door and disappeared inside.

As I passed, I noticed the shop's windows were blacked out. A sign in the door read ADULTS ONLY.

Increasing my speed, I continued down the sidewalk. A couple scummy teenagers in sweats and sneakers, no older than fifteen, swaggered down the opposite side of the street, sucking on cigarettes and cursing loudly. I put my head down and carried on. Sophie had mentioned knife crime was a big problem in Scotland.

A moment later the shop door tinkled open behind me.

The teenagers were howling with laughter now, pointing at the shop customer, who seemed to be walking behind me. "Whacha go' there?"

"Fancy a wank?" They gestured obscenely.

Even as I sped up, desperate to separate myself from the stranger, the shop customer seemed to come up behind me. A man's voice whispered in my ear.

"Look what I've got." Suddenly, there was a bag in my hand.

My fingers sprang apart; the bag and its contents clattered to the pavement. I spun around, and the shopper, D.B.—whoever it was—was gone. It was like there had never been another person there at all.

I charged down the street, my heart thumping loudly as the teenagers loped across the road toward the bag on the sidewalk, hitching up the backs of their sagging sweatpants.

Their raucous laughter faded as they discovered what lay inside.

"What the—ye fuckin' poofter!"

"Fuckin' faggot!"

"Ye better run, ye fuckin' queer!"

But it wasn't mine. I swear.

Editor's Note
Exhibit K

Text messages recovered from the phone of Liam Stewart, sent to the phone of Sophia Grant on 9 November 2016, from approximately 9:26 p.m.

LIAM STEWART

Your boyfriend's a fucking nutter, I'm fucking fuming

SOPHIA GRANT

No he's not why r u saying that?

LIAM STEWART

HE JUST SHOWED UP AT MY FUCKING FLAT AGAIN

SOPHIA GRANT

Liam what happened

What??? Why?

LIAM STEWART

Because he's fucking delusional

He just showed up started banging on the door

Soon as I opened it he started going on about some chav kids and how he thinks he's being followed and something about the guy he works for, he wasn't making any sense

SOPHIA GRANT

So he just wanted to talk?

LIAM STEWART

He still thinks we're friends . . . WE'RE NOT FRIENDS!

SOPHIA GRANT

So what did u do?

LIAM STEWART

I just let him go on for a bit and said that sounded rough and finally he fucked off home

I'm not sure how much more I can take

SOPHIA GRANT

I think ur overreacting

LIAM STEWART

He's fucking weird Soph

I want you to stay away from him

SOPHIA GRANT

I told u he's really kind

U just don't understand him

LIAM STEWART

And you do?

SOPHIA GRANT

He's not had an easy life

His family were horrible to him

LIAM STEWART

I don't care, I don't want him around

SOPHIA GRANT

What's this really about Liam

Is this like Pete again?

LIAM STEWART

Why would you say that? I told you not to fucking mention that again

SOPHIA GRANT

Alright sorry

Just trying to understand

LIAM STEWART

I just don't trust him. He's not welcome on Saturday

SOPHIA GRANT

Well I already invited him

LIAM STEWART

Fuck sake Soph

Tell him there's been change of plan and we're not going

SOPHIA GRANT

No

If he can't come then I'm not either

LIAM STEWART

> Don't be stupid, we always go to opening night
>
> Please tell me you won't bring him
>
> Sophie

SOPHIA GRANT

> I gave you my answer, I've nothing more to say

Twenty-Two

BEFORE HEADING OVER to Princes Street on Saturday night, we convened at an airy, fourth-floor flat off the Canongate with a partial view of Calton Hill. It was the home of Sophie's friends Nisha and Shaun. I was one of the last to arrive. Shaun answered the door, a slightly effeminate guy with bleached hair. His Christmas sweater was illuminated with the words GAY APPAREL. I could hear the voices of seven or eight people already laughing in the background. My stomach tightened a little.

To my relief, Sophie and Liam were among them. I went to join them and immediately got the sense I'd walked in on an uncomfortable conversation. Sophie's smile was strained. Liam barely acknowledged me before turning away.

"Everything okay?" I said to Sophie.

"All fine. Have you met Nisha?"

She whisked me away to meet the cohost, a foulmouthed philosophy graduate to whom I immediately took a liking.

As was increasingly the case these days, the conversation turned almost immediately to the outcome of the US presidential election, a topic

I tended to attract with just the sound of my voice. Everywhere I went, people were asking me if I had voted and for whom, demanding my take on Trump's surprise win. I sensed they half expected me to exalt him and were disappointed when I didn't, having only asked the question to confirm their worst fears about Americans.

It was a topic I would have preferred to avoid. My general disinterest in politics hadn't protected me from the emotional fallout and existential anxiety that Trump's win had inflicted on the majority of Americans who opposed him. After eight years of Obama, it felt as if the country had changed. There was a Black family in the White House, support for marriage equality was at an all-time high, healthcare and immigration reform had begun. The hatred and oppression that once dominated our politics seemed to be a thing of the past, those red-state deplorables relegated to an ignorant minority.

But alas, Trump's win had shattered that illusion, and with it the fragile optimism I had granted myself. Not only did ignorance still thrive, but it threatened to countermand the little progress we had made as a nation, the progress that, for a few years at least, had made people like me feel like there was hope.

Yet another reason to stay in Scotland after graduation.

There was no getting Nisha off the topic, however. As she continued to rant about the "bloated tangerine rape mogul," I allowed my attention to wander.

It fell on Liam, who kept his distance but repeatedly glanced in my direction, tying my intestines in knots with a new kind of dread. Why was he looking at me like that, like the very fact of my being here set his teeth on edge? Had I done something wrong?

"You coming to George Street after the markets?" Nisha asked. "They're switching on the Christmas lights and shooting fireworks off the castle. Bit of a clusterfuck, but it should be a good time."

"I guess so. Sure."

Returning from the kitchen, Sophie handed me a mug. It was hot, and for a second I thought she'd made me a cup of tea.

"It's a toddy," she said. "Have you never had one?" Notes of whisky, lemon, and cloves rose off the golden surface in balletic swirls, eroding my conviction not to drink. I'd managed to avoid any unwanted visitations since Wednesday and was eager to keep it that way. Still, the smell was intoxicating. Maybe one wouldn't hurt.

Naturally, one toddy led to another, and once I had started down the path of drunkenness I could not stop; it was too effective a salve for the fear and election-related despair I had carried with me all week. It appeared I was not alone in that. By the time we headed downstairs, snuggly ensconced in our coats and hats, we were all in a most festive mood—even Liam, who clapped me on the shoulder as we set off down the darkening street. My flesh prickled, remembering D.B.'s hand where Liam's now lay.

But it was only a fluke. Seeming to realize it was me he had touched, he quickly retracted his hand and shunted off.

⁓

I've never been a particular fan of the holidays. Growing up, Christmas was a time for other children to make wish lists and wait up for Santa, for other families to playact seasonal clichés like goodwill and generosity.

In the Hale residence, the true spirit of Christmas was solemn devotion. The decorations that adorned our house were for the benefit of the believers, the few presents that lay under the tree a promise of clothes and utilities. Nathaniel usually made out better than I did, but his special gifts never changed hands on Christmas morning; my mother waited for my father to return to his study after lunch before she slid Nathaniel an unwrapped Game Boy Pocket or wheeled out a Razor scooter in my favorite color, never once acknowledging that I was standing there watching.

The only thing I remember looking forward to at the holidays was the tabletop nativity scene my mother put out on the dining room sideboard, featuring wooden figurines of wise men, camels, and Joseph around the manger. They were roughly hewn and hand-painted. I could tell because the artist had botched the Baby Jesus's eyes. The irises pointed in slightly different directions, making Him look deranged. I never mentioned the imperfection to my family. Surreptitiously smirking at the cross-eyed Son of God was my own private tradition, the rare mischief I could manage without punishment.

Despite my natural disinclination to the holiday, the Christmas markets at the East Princes Street Gardens were a worthy spectacle. Lacking even an iota of traditional Scottish charm, they were Germanic in style and American in spirit. Hundreds of shoppers swarmed market stalls draped in plastic pine and Christmas lights to buy colorful facsimiles of European craftsmanship: armies of mustachioed nutcrackers, farm animals carved from tree bark, leather-bound journals embossed with Celtic symbols, gargantuan wheels of Edam and Manchego, cellophane bags of potpourri laced with cinnamon sticks and dried orange.

Sophie had her phone out as we jostled through the crowd, snapping pictures of the passing towers of handmade soap, and pyramids of marzipan in every flavor and color. As we sipped piping-hot cups of glühwein and hot plum cider, children screamed for their parents' attention from the backs of red mechanical reindeer, which bounced like a circle of horned devils to the tune of Wham!'s "Last Christmas."

Eventually we migrated to the pop-up Bothy Bar, a purpose-built chalet resembling a hipster hunting lodge. A bronze boar's head shone against a purple jacquard wall while an imitation log burner glowed in the grate underneath. The room was infernally hot in the way that Scottish rooms simply were this time of year. As we waited to order, Sophie continued to take group selfies on her phone, entreating us to squeeze in.

It felt like the whole room was watching us pose. I noticed Liam standing opposite and observing, as if not wanting to be photographed with me. Later, as we sipped our overpriced drinks, he leaned in to whisper something to Sophie, who shook her head and pulled away. He bristled, his eyes stopping briefly on mine.

Afterward we ventured back out into the night. If anything, the crowds were even thicker, a sea of heads wrapped in scarves and hoods, shuffling like a waddle of penguins through wide corridors lined with stalls.

When we reached the center of the market, the others bought tickets for the merry-go-round. I hung back, sobering up on a grilled cheese as the others mounted their chosen steeds.

The ride threw light across the ground as it began to spin, slowly at first and then faster and faster, the horses bobbing up and down on the poles in their backs. Sophie's friends looked proudly idiotic, interspersed among the toddlers and mothers. Liam rode his horse like a cowboy, arching his back with a hand gripping the pole jutting up between his legs. Shaun, on the horse behind, seemed to have eyes on him.

After a minute or two I felt a prickle on my neck, as if someone were standing too close. But when I spun around, no one was there.

"Grayson, look!"

I turned. Sophie snapped a photo on her phone as she swept past on a white stallion.

A few moments later they exited the ride. Nisha was clutching her stomach, looking nauseous. Several of us needed the toilet.

We located one by the west entrance. When I came out, the girls were still inside. It was just Shaun and me. There was an awkwardness between us, a mutual desire not to speak to each other that I could attribute to nothing in particular but did not question. I pulled out my phone, my stomach sinking as I read the notification. *Sophie Grant tagged you in 3 photos.*

Reluctantly, I opened the app.

A dark photo, which I hadn't known was being taken at the time, showed me forcing my way past a stall selling hats and scarves, my face set in an unflattering grimace.

I swiped to the next photo, a group shot in the Bothy Bar. With the eight of us crammed in together, we took up almost the entire frame.

Only a small gap in the corner of the photo was left unobstructed—just big enough to show two glowing dots in the middle distance. Behind those glaring circles of red was clearly the dim shadow of a face.

The final photo was the one Sophie had taken from the merry-go-round. Streaks of light smeared lengthwise across a crowd of waiting people. I stood among them, slightly out of focus, looking up at the camera. And there, over my shoulder, stood D.B., apparently livid, his eyes searing through the screen like scarlet fire.

"What's wrong?" Sophie had just emerged from the ladies' room to find me scanning the crowd with quiet desperation, blood throbbing through my veins, thick as sludge.

Still half drunk, I threw caution to the wind. "That man," I said, pointing to D.B. in the photo. "Do you see him?"

"Yes—"

"His eyes."

"Yes, they're red," Sophie said. "It's just the camera flash. Do you know this man?"

"He's here."

"Who is? Grayson, what's going on?"

I needed to get out of there, and it wouldn't help to whip Sophie into a panic. "Nothing," I said. "I'm not feeling well. I should go."

"But the switch-on—"

"Let him," said Liam, who had emerged from the restroom. I didn't hear Sophie's rejoinder; her words dissolved into a tumult of voices as I shouldered my way into the crowd.

At the southwest corner of the market, I escaped through a gap between the outermost stalls and strode past the entrance of the Scottish National Gallery, down a long path ending in a set of stairs leading up toward the Royal Mile.

A crowd was gathered halfway up, all eyes on the seventy-foot Christmas tree anchored on the grassy incline to the right of the stairs. It was strung with lights but they were dark, the lighting ceremony soon to begin. Winged shapes circled high overhead. I couldn't bring myself to make certain they were birds as I hurried past, thrusting so forcefully through the crowd that a woman cried out in surprise.

I was panting by the time I reached the Royal Mile, breath scraping through my windpipe like sand. The street was deserted but for a handful of tourists making last-minute purchases before the souvenir shops closed. I trundled fast down the street, checking behind and above me as I went.

My eyes lingered on the gargoyles at the tops of the buildings, peering down on me with tongues jutting from their open mouths, stone wings folded behind their backs. I could not recall having noticed them before.

The sound of footsteps drew my gaze. A dark figure was walking some distance behind me, maybe male. He kept to the shadows. I couldn't see his face—or his eyes. I quickened my pace. Kept my head down but continued to scan my surroundings, continued to check the faces of the people moving around in the rooms behind the yellow windows above.

Then something drew my eyes even farther up the building: one of the gargoyles. It seemed to have moved.

I thought it must have been a mistake—until the next one gave a shake on its perch.

I stopped, staring up at it.

Its lids parted to reveal round, jaundiced eyes.

Horrified, I stumbled back. Suddenly the fiend leapt off the edge of the building and dove down into the lane. They all did—and they were headed straight for me.

I took off across the street, disappearing down a narrow tunnel between a wine bar and a whisky shop. The close spilled out onto a claustrophobic alleyway, which split off in two directions. As I paused to get my bearings, a chorus of low gibbers echoed through the tunnel.

I bolted forward just in time to miss the fiends bursting out of the darkness, screeching and gnashing their needle-sharp teeth. They careened after me down the right-hand path, then left around the side of a building. Though fast, they were ungainly; unable to slow down in time, the fattest of them crashed into the wall and spun out wildly, rolling as it hit the ground.

I tore through the convoluted maze of alleys not knowing where I was going, taking random turns to try to lose them. I met a short staircase leading down and leapt over the steps—just about to touch down when I was hoisted back up into the air, as if by a hook snagged on my jacket. One of the fiends had me in its talons—then more than one. The ground dropped out from underneath me as their wings beat the air, the buzz of their gibbering loud in my ear. I kicked and shouted, eye level with the tops of the buildings.

A sound like ripping fabric preceded a moment of weightlessness. My stomach leapt into my throat as I fell.

I hit the ground, and let out a sharp cry of agony. I had come down on my ankle. Pain jolted through it as I clambered to my feet.

Still, I lumbered forward, just barely missing the leader of the pack as it miscalculated its dive and crunched against the ground where I had lain a moment earlier. As I lurched around a corner, I heard a loud *clang* as another fiend slammed into a black metal trash can.

The others pelted after me while I hobbled down a dark, crooked lane, along what looked like the backside of a pub. With my eyes on them, I tripped over a bag of garbage and pitched forward. Empty bottles cascaded across the alley. I swiped one and lobbed it over my shoulder, and it exploded against a fiend's claw-fisted wallop.

To my benefit, the shards caught the remaining fiends in their faces, delaying them long enough for me to scramble back to my feet and hurry around the corner.

Their gibbering started to fade. I was beginning to think I had lost them when I reached a dead end.

I cursed.

Doubling back, I was met with an advancing darkness. Slightly banged up but madder than ever, the fiends emerged from the shadows, champing vengefully at the air.

Like they had that night in the Cowgate, they began to latch on to one another. Slowly their bodies melted together and formed a new one, that of a man stalking toward me: my former employer, his face white with rage.

"I told ye not to bother running."

"What do you want?"

"To collect what I'm owed," D.B. said. "What I paid for."

I looked around for a weapon and found nothing but trash.

"Do ye still no' get it?" His eyes shone the color of blood. "You've been marked down for this since you were a baby. You were chosen."

As I stumbled back, fireworks exploded in the night sky overhead, illuminating the alley with gentle flashes of color. *BOOM-BOOM! BOOM!* D.B.'s pale face shimmered purple, then green.

"Ye want this. You've been waiting for this your whole life."

"No—"

I felt a searing pain in my right arm, as if I'd been stamped with a white-hot brand. I tore my arm out of my jacket and lifted my sleeve, revealing the flesh beneath, and the scars I'd had for as long as I could remember—different now than ever before. It was like they were alive: moving, throbbing, the usually pink flesh a deep, bloody purple.

"You're ready." D.B. removed his jacket, kicked off his shoes.

"What are you—?"

Once again fireworks pounded the sky, muting my screams at the sight of the cloven hooves protruding from the hems of his trousers.

My vision began to dim. Fear constricted my heart like a vise.

The world tipped on its side as I lost my center of balance.

The last thing I saw, before the blackness consumed me, were flashes of vibrant color across D.B.'s bare chest, and two giant horns growing out of his head.

Twenty-Three

I AWOKE ON A mattress I did not immediately recognize as my own. The duvet lay in a twisted heap on the carpet with my clothes, leaving only the top sheet, which was coming away at the corner. I lay prone and naked apart from my socks. The exposed parts of me were hard and risen with gooseflesh. I had neglected, in whatever state I'd arrived home in, to adjust the radiator.

As I rolled over, a dull pain twisted my lower abdomen. I groaned. My stomach was surprisingly tender, like I'd sustained a blow I could not now remember.

What happened last night? How did I get home? Fragments of memory surfaced like flotsam. The fiends. The alley. The burst of fireworks overhead. Then a vision of D.B. so surreal that my memories and dreams must have merged in the night, an unbroken line of fear and confusion.

Delicately I slid to the edge of the mattress and reached for my phone. There were half a dozen new messages.

U get back alright?
R u ok?
Who was that man?

Sophie.

Knowing that to ignore her would only make things worse, I tapped out a cursory response.

Sorry, just seeing this. Got back fine. Will call later.

And then what would I say?

Setting the phone aside to charge, I took a breath and lumbered to my feet, nearly buckling under my still-fragile ankle. A chill draft whistled through the crack under the window, making me shudder.

It wasn't until I stepped into my jeans that I noticed the state of the bedsheets. Horror and puzzlement mingled with shame. There was blood in them, and what was unmistakably shit.

———

Ollie was playing *FIFA* when I entered the sitting room carrying the balled-up linens. To my relief he didn't acknowledge me. I made a beeline for the washer in the kitchen. My mind churned as I stuffed the sheets in the machine. The feces I could almost accept as an embarrassing accident, but the blood? I wasn't injured, not except for the pain in my stomach. I must've been bleeding when I came in last night. Why couldn't I remember?

As I headed back to my room, I heard a murmur over the fracas of his game.

"Huh?" I said, turning to Ollie.

"What was all that about?" he repeated.

His attention remained fixed on the TV, his fingers mashing the buttons. His face was pale, tense. His eyes flicked to me, then away again.

"All what?"

His hands jerked the controller around; there was clearly something he didn't want to say.

"Ollie, what're you talking about?"

"I don't know, maybe the bloke who spent the night in your room last night?" My bewildered expression made him sneer. "Don't play dumb. I saw you come in."

"No you didn't."

But how could I know that for sure? I couldn't even remember getting home.

"You—you saw me come in with someone?"

"Friend of yours, was it?"

"Oh, him. Y-yeah." I had to play it off, had to just get through this and then figure it out. "Friend of mine. He just needed a place to crash." The TV emitted a roar of applause as a virtual man in red scored a goal.

"Sounded like you did more than crash."

Very fast, my mouth filled with saliva, the pain in my stomach displaced by a violent surge of nausea.

I rushed to the bathroom but was waylaid by my injured ankle. The first mouthful of vomit hit the lid before I could lift it.

I heard Ollie pause his game. "Were you just sick?"

I kicked the door shut behind me, then heaved into the bowl.

As I continued to purge, abhorrent images flashed behind my eyes, visions of depravity both inflicted and enjoyed—whether imaginary or drawn from some hidden pocket of memory, I didn't want to know. It felt as if my organs were trying to force themselves up through my throat. My nostrils burned and my head throbbed. I thought my skull might crack from the pressure.

When I'd finished, I didn't feel significantly better. Cleared out, yes. Practically hollow. But no less contaminated, as bloody and soiled as the sheets I had torn from my mattress.

I ran a shower. As I waited for the water to heat up, I hastily saw to the mess around the toilet with a rolled-up wad of toilet paper, then flushed it down. The room was sweaty with the smell of bile. I pulled my shirt off, trying to avoid the mirror. Still, it was hard not to notice the nail marks dug into my chest, shoulders, and back. A numb, distant feeling possessed me, like I was not looking at my own wounds but an image of someone else's. I thought vaguely, *What happened to him?*

I showered for a full thirty minutes before giving up; I could not seem to get clean. Then I snuck back into my bedroom, avoiding Ollie, who remained in the sitting room. I did not want to be seen.

As I crossed to the dresser for fresh clothes, I noticed what looked like a stack of documents on the desk.

I padded toward them. My pruney fingers spread them across the tabletop. I was getting used to things happening that couldn't be; still, the documents splayed out before me tested the boundaries of my credulity.

At the top of the pile the typewritten manuscript of *Jack and the Devil's Horn* gleamed with particular malice.

This time I would take no chances. When Ollie went into the bathroom to shower, I carried the document to the kitchen, lit the burner on the stove, and watched the fucking thing burn.

Editor's Note
Exhibit L

By October last year, I had been working on the research for this book for more than three months and had read The Memoirs and Confessions of Grayson Hale *no less than half a dozen times. Still, I felt something wasn't adding up. Though Hale writes at length about his anguished childhood, from his desperate yearning for his father's approval to his mother's callous preference for his brother, who tormented him, I couldn't help feeling that a piece of the puzzle was missing, a piece Hale had chosen to keep hidden, or perhaps, as Kathleen Prichard speculated, repressed.*

It didn't help that those who knew our author best each presented a different version of him. Nathaniel described his brother as sinister and threatening, with leanings toward sexual deviation. Conversely, to Reyna Moya-White, young Grayson was smart and kind, incapable of the kind of evil for which he was eventually—falsely, according to her—convicted.

And yet through all of this, one name kept appearing: Carlos Fernandez, Grayson's childhood friend whose parents were regulars at the Hales' home fellowship service. I made it a priority to speak to him, hoping he might shed new light on our perplexing author.

Initially hesitant to be interviewed for this book, Mr. Fernandez eventually agreed but kept his video off during our brief conversation. Here I present an excerpt of our ill-fated interview, recorded via Skype on 2 October 2019.

BARCLAY: You and Grayson were quite good friends when you were younger. Is that correct?

FERNANDEZ: We were friendly.

BARCLAY: You wouldn't say friends?

FERNANDEZ: I don't know. We saw a lot of each other, I guess. My family was at the Hales' for fellowship like twice a week. Afterward me and Grayson would play together. Sometimes he'd come over to my house, but not often.

BARCLAY: What would you play?

FERNANDEZ: Action figures. Lincoln Logs. Normal kid stuff.

BARCLAY: And what was he like back then, Grayson?

FERNANDEZ: Nice, I guess. Bit quiet. I felt bad for him.

BARCLAY: Why was that?

FERNANDEZ: Just his family . . . I don't know. They were pretty hard-core.

BARCLAY: In their faith, you mean.

FERNANDEZ: Well, yeah. All that "Adversary" stuff. It's a lot for any kid. But Vera too. Grayson's mom. She'd be really sweet to your face, but the way she talked to him when no one was around . . . I heard her a couple times. It was like she hated him.

BARCLAY: Did you ever see her get physical with him?

FERNANDEZ: I never saw her hit him, if that's what you mean.

BARCLAY: Did you notice if Grayson ever had bruises, or injuries?

FERNANDEZ: Injuries?

BARCLAY: Anything to suggest he was being abused?

FERNANDEZ: [Pause] Is this . . . sorry, I don't really—

BARCLAY: Something wrong?

FERNANDEZ: I just don't really feel comfortable talking about—

BARCLAY: Oh. No problem. We can move on if you like.

FERNANDEZ: It's just my parents are still involved in the cult.

BARCLAY: The cult?

FERNANDEZ: The church, I mean.

BARCLAY: But you call it the cult? Why?

FERNANDEZ: I don't know . . . Just from what I've read on the internet and stuff, it seems like it might be. Some of the practices they teach at the institute, they kind of mindfuck you. Make you feel like once you're in, you can never get out. But none of the believers will tell you that. To them it's just the church.

BARCLAY: This institute you mentioned. Would that be the Elected Heart Institute of Biblical Research?

FERNANDEZ: Right. That's the Bible college my parents went to. That's where they met Ed and Vera. A lot of the regulars at fellowship went there back in the day. Kind of a rest stop for people at loose ends. That's what I've heard, anyway.

BARCLAY: Speaking of regulars, I was corresponding with another family friend of the Hales' a few weeks ago, a Mrs. Moya-White.

FERNANDEZ: [Long pause]

BARCLAY: Hello? Sorry, are you there, Carlos? Have I lost you?

FERNANDEZ: I'm here. I just . . . What did she say?

BARCLAY: Quite a bit, actually. Mostly about Grayson—

FERNANDEZ: Nothing about me?

BARCLAY: Well, she did tell me a rather peculiar story about a time she was babysitting the two of you at the Hales' house.

FERNANDEZ: Maybe we should move on.

BARCLAY: It's nothing bad, I don't think. She said she found the two of you playing in the backyard behind the shed. Do you remember this?

FERNANDEZ: I really think we should—

BARCLAY: She couldn't see what you were doing but she heard Grayson whispering, "Now you go. Show me it. You have to."

FERNANDEZ: I SAID NO!

BARCLAY: Sorry?

FERNANDEZ: [No sound]

BARCLAY: Hello, Carlos? Are you there? Hello?

End of call.

Twenty-Four

THE PEAR TREE was inhumanely warm. Still, I kept my coat on to hide the wet patches under my arms and obstruct any resultant odors. He would arrive any moment. At least I hoped he would. I couldn't shake the sick, vulnerable feeling that had clung to me since the morning after the Christmas markets. I had no one to talk to, no one's company to make me feel secure from further attack. What I needed at that moment was a friend.

Even if I held back the details of what happened that night, it would be a relief just to know I wasn't alone.

But obviously something was up with Liam; I'd barely heard from him since I started dating Sophie, and Saturday night made it clear we weren't on good terms. Obviously he didn't want Sophie and me together. Maybe he held a secret flame for Sophie himself. If so, fine, he could have her. It was Jenna I wanted anyway. In any case, it was imperative that we clear the air.

Liam had said he'd meet me at eight, but it was five minutes past and still I sat alone, nursing a sweaty pint of Diet Coke. It wasn't like him to be late.

I'm here, I texted him. *Got a table inside.*

As I waited for my phone to ping, I noticed two women socializing at the next table over.

One of them did nothing but nod while her friend spoke at her without stopping, her loud, reedy voice stabbing through the sweltering air of the pub like a knife being wielded with murderous intent. Under the table by her feet lay a medium-size dog with wiry, tawny fur, a hot-pink collar throttling her neck. Despite her harness, which read *Emotional Support Animal*, the animal had a skittish demeanor that suggested discomfort with strangers.

We exchanged a look of understanding.

A server delivered dinner to the women. Underneath the table the dog sniffed the air, its nose rising as if being pulled by an invisible string.

At twelve past eight, Liam still had not responded.

You coming? I texted.

Could it be more than just Sophie? Maybe I'd done something really bad. But then why had he agreed to meet me?

I turned to the dog, as if for advice, to find one of the bar staff asking the reedy-voiced woman if he could pet it.

"Go ahead." She shrugged.

The man crouched down, his shirt riding up to reveal a lower back matted with curly ginger hair. He stuck his hand out toward the dog, letting her sniff. "Hey, doggy. Good girl."

The animal shrank back, her head facing away but her eyes trained on the man. Even from where I sat I could hear her growling—a warning sign neither her owner nor the stranger seemed to mind. The man thrust his hand toward her, ignoring her bared teeth.

Do it, I silently willed her. *Nip him.*

Suddenly, as if obeying my silent command, the dog snapped. Her teeth didn't make contact with his skin, but it was enough to make the man rip his hand away and clamber to his feet, looking shocked.

"Bad Hannah!" said her owner, landing a swift kick in the dog's ribs. She yelped and cowered, laying her paws over her snout.

My blood boiled. Even the woman's friend looked uncomfortable. I was about to say something when my phone buzzed. I looked down to read the words.

Changed my mind. Not coming. Don't contact me anymore.

I felt something inside of me splinter and explode. I couldn't hold back my anger and poured it into the message I fired back.

What the hell? What's wrong with you lately? Seriously, why are you acting this way??

The dog was growling under the table again, her ire rising in time with mine as her owner continued to agitate her with little kicks, her foot bobbing unconsciously against the dog's rib cage with every other word. The tips of the dog's fangs stuck out over her bottom jaw, her eyes fixed warningly on her owner's bare ankle. I sensed in the canine a desire to snap at her like she had the man, a desire to *punish*—one which I increasingly shared. I wanted to lash out. Wanted someone, anyone, to feel pain.

Fucking tear her leg off, I thought.

A sudden snarl preceded a high-pitched scream. The woman leapt out of her chair and fell to the floor; she couldn't stand, for the dog's teeth were a centimeter deep in her ankle, the animal's eyes bright and wild as she ripped her head back and forth as if trying to separate foot from leg.

People hurried forward as the woman screamed for help. "Grab the dog! Get it off her!" they were shouting. The end of the leash lay on the floor. I snatched it and yanked the dog back, but she could not be dissuaded, continuing to lunge at her owner, champing her jaws savagely.

"Stop it!" I shouted, and instantly the leash went slack. The dog sat. Her pink tongue lolled out of her mouth, benign.

"She just attacked!" the woman was wailing on the floor, her ankle slick with blood. "I don't know what happened, she just attacked."

"Take it outside," someone yelled. "Get that thing outside!"

I obeyed. A light tug, and the dog padded alongside me, out into the enclosed courtyard. People sat at the tables, drinking and smoking. Sensing the commotion within, they rose from their seats and staggered toward the pub door. It was only a matter of time until they came for the dog.

"Come on," I muttered.

She followed me to the street, whimpering, hanging her head. It was as if she knew she was in trouble. As if she knew what happened to dogs who attacked their owners. I felt a lump rise in my throat. It wasn't fair. It wasn't her fault. I was the one who told her to do it.

Don't be ridiculous, said a voice in my head. *You didn't cause this.*

Even so, they would come for her. I considered taking off with her, but my bag was still in the pub, my laptop inside it. I couldn't just leave. It was all I could do to unbuckle her collar and unfasten the harness, hoping she'd get the idea and make a break for it.

"Go," I commanded, as she gazed up at me. I pushed her forward by the butt. "Go!"

Finally she seemed to understand. Her head hung as she scampered across the road, her nails clattering against the cobblestones.

My heart sank as she rounded the corner of the street and was gone.

—

When I got home, Ollie was in the kitchen and wanted to talk.

"I swear to god, today I had *the best* panini I have ever—"

"Not now," I said, cutting a path to my bedroom.

He shouted after me, *"Wanker."*

As soon as the door closed behind me, I pulled my laptop out of my bag, opened a private browsing window, and searched for incidents of service dogs attacking their owners.

The proof I sought was hard to come by. I found an article about a passenger suing Delta after being mauled by an emotional support animal, and a YouTube video of a woman spitting at a Seeing Eye dog in the mall, but few examples of the kind of attack that had occurred at the Pear Tree. Nothing to reassure me that what I had witnessed was a common occurrence, an unfortunate accident that had nothing to do with me.

I wrestled again with the feeling that I was responsible, that, without speaking, I had influenced the dog to attack.

Using what, doggy hypnosis? My secret canine mind powers?

Anyway, the dog was clearly being mistreated. Abuse any animal long enough and eventually it'll bite. It was odd, though, how each time I had willed the dog to indulge its natural instincts, it had seemed to comply, like the skinhead at Infyrno when prompted by D.B.

Abandoning the first search, I tried another: *people who can make animals attack on command*. This rabbit hole was wider and deeper, filled with K-9 attack dogs, instructional articles on training your retriever to kill on command, the top ten animal attacks caught on film.

devil makes animal attack

devil makes animal attack scotland

Buried beneath multitudinous entries about Tasmanian devils and the "devil Chihuahua" that savaged a ten-year-old girl in Kilmarnock, I found a blog post entitled "Beware the Devil's Pets." It was written, coincidentally, by a reverend of the Elected Heart, who happened to live in Polbeth, not far outside the city. He maintained that some animals, among them owls, foxes, snakes, and dogs, were the familiars of Satan, that one ought not to trust them nor allow them in one's home.

> The dog is the only animal over which the Adversary has the power
> of control. All other animals are impervious to his corruption. But
> the dog being a low and unclean animal, even lower and uncleaner
> than the Adversary himself, has been known to bend to his will.

I was skeptical. My father had never mentioned a connection between dogs and the Devil. Then again, he had never quite trusted them either. He refused to let us have one. He said dogs were the creation of man, not of God, and therefore were an abomination.

I knew I ought not to read any further, that if I typed one more word I would be at it for hours, but my better judgment failed me. I fell deeper and faster into the abyss of subreddits and web forums like disembodied howls of terror, each post like a hand reaching out of the darkness to snatch my sanity away.

Sometime in the middle of the night I landed on the pages of a website called Encounters with the Demonic, which I hadn't visited since the peak of my satanophobia nearly a decade before. I remembered now why I had blocked it from my browser. It slowly ate at me, one bizarre, horrific, crudely written tale at a time.

The last thing I read, before closing the laptop with a snap, was a long thread, inactive for several months, in which a woman in South Carolina claimed to have met the Devil in the parking lot of her apartment building and invited him upstairs to have sex.

about a week later i realized the devil had gave me his power which he implanted with his seed- i could make people do bad things. Like anything i wanted, steal fight even murder. if they wanted to do it i could make them with my mind. once their was this dad pushing his baby around the walmart in greenville where i work. it wouldn't stop crying and i could see the dad getting madder and madder and i wanted the baby to shut up and in my head i was like, fucking kill that thing! and the next thing i knew he had took it out the stroller and was strangling it shaking it dead. when it was over he didn't know what happened, he was so shocked he dropped it like he just realized he was holding a bag of shit.

Twenty-Five

THE END OF term brought with it an anesthetizing frenzy of activity. For days I barely left the flat, my life a delirious barrage of grading, answering frantic student emails, working on my own end-of-term essays, and even serving as Ollie's unpaid writing tutor—this less out of the goodness of my heart than the worrying possibility that, if he flunked out, I might be forced to find market-rate accommodation (not to mention gratitude that he had never again mentioned, even in jest, the noises he'd heard coming from my bedroom the night of the Christmas markets). By revision period, I was so consumed with my escalating workload that I had managed, at least temporarily, to suppress all but my most mundane anxieties.

This was made easier by the fact that D.B. had remained conspicuously absent for weeks. Even the fiends had gone, providing a temporary stay of terror that, in addition to fueling my denial, allowed me to put a dent in the mountain of work before me.

But I was not out of the woods yet. Come the third week of December, I received a text adding one more task to my plate.

It's my birthday Friday, Rhian's throwing a party at ours, 8pm - hope you can make it. Oh and don't worry about a gift ☺

⁓

Seagulls wheeled in the sky overhead as I clomped down the flagstone sidewalk of North Bridge, my hands bundled warmly in my pockets. It was a blustery morning but unseasonably sunny, adding a layer of buoyancy to my resentment.

Waverley Mall was separate from, but adjoined, Waverley Station, the central train terminal whose tracks bifurcated the city like the fault line between two opposing worlds: to the south, the gray austerity of the Gothic Old Town; to the north, the Georgian elegance of New Town.

So close to Christmas, the mall was glutted with shoppers: middle-aged women with frosted tips and glossy nails, tourists killing time as they waited for their trains. My hackles were up before I even got through the door. There were few things I loathed more than shopping—among them, shopping for gifts, a task to which I was preternaturally ill-suited.

Whatever Sophie said to the contrary, I knew enough about women to know she would be expecting a birthday present, and I had no desire to disappoint; it seemed more than likely Liam would be there, and showing up empty-handed would only give him another reason to begrudge me.

We still hadn't been in touch. Despite the shortness of our friendship, I grieved the loss of it like a death. Liam had been the best friend I'd had for some time, maybe ever, and his absence opened a chasm in my life that no amount of busywork could fill. While out with Sophie, I had to resist the urge to flog her for information about Liam; alone, I squandered hours trawling his social media. Research Methods, which for a few weeks had become my guilty pleasure thanks to the promise of an endless stream of mordant texts from Liam, now was my biweekly torment. Each time Dr. Porter said something contemptible, or a classmate refused to stop talking, all I wanted was to catch Liam's eye—a second's acknowledgment that we were thinking the same thing. That our bond, however neglected, wasn't broken.

His refusal to even look at me hit like a wallop to the heart. Some nights I even dreamt about him. More or less the same dream every time. I would run into him somewhere, on campus or in a shop; we would acknowledge each other; and then, after a moment of awkwardness, we'd admit that we had missed each other and agree to put this all behind us. The dreams were so happy that the mere act of waking pulverized me with sadness. Then I would carry that sad feeling around with me all day, and lay down to sleep the following night hoping to be visited by the same dream again.

Unfortunately, finding Sophie the perfect gift was proving a challenge. As I wandered the mall, I became disoriented by choice. Everywhere I stopped, I'd find something that felt like Sophie's taste and suddenly experience a wave of dread as I realized that I knew absolutely nothing about her. Did she like jellies or truffles? Milk chocolate or dark? Did she wear jewelry? Did she hate the color pink? At one point I ventured into a trendy boutique but only spent a moment in the women's department, looking at cozy sweaters, frilly tops, and lacy bras, before realizing I hadn't the faintest approximation of Sophie's size or style.

As I quickly perused the men's section, my attention was drawn to a nearby couple whom I initially mistook for a man and woman. The older gentleman had close-cropped silver hair, his royal-blue polo turned up at the collar. The other was younger, with low-cut jeans, heavy stubble, and long hair falling down over his fur-lined hood.

They weren't shopping so much as making fun of the clothes, openly mocking a jacket with many zippers and pockets.

"So fucking ugly," said the younger man, his fingers entwined with the other's. "I'd rather fucking die."

His accent was American. I felt a twinge of shame.

Departing the boutique, I ultimately settled on what seemed a safe bet, a moderately expensive vanilla-scented candle. It hardly seemed worth it. Sophie had invited me to stay with her family in Kirkcaldy over Christmas; even if I knocked her birthday gift out of the park, I'd have to do it all again in a few weeks' time—not just for Sophie but the entire Clan Grant.

Already irritable, I headed up the escalator toward the Princes Street exit, joining the line behind a clot of shoppers who refused to walk up the steps.

Above me was the couple from the boutique. They were being even more revolting now, kissing obscenely, arms around each other's waists. My disgust was unprejudiced. I just didn't want to see it, least of all from them, and being forced to witness their display raised a molten hatred in my chest, an intensifying desire to see them called out for their flagrant disregard for others—to see them punished.

No sooner had I registered the desire than a stranger shoved past me up the escalator, moving fast, shouldering people out of the way to get to the couple. In an instant, the American was on the floor, shrieking as the stranger dragged him up the metal steps by his chest-length hair. *No*, I pleaded, *I didn't mean it, don't hurt him*, for there was no doubt in my mind that I had willed the attack into being just as I had forced the dog to savage its owner.

But the time for forgiveness had passed. Even as the assailant dropped his victim and sprinted toward the exit, the long-haired man screamed in pain. Onlookers emitted gasps of horror: the man's head was being yanked down toward the landing platform, his brown mane caught between the comb plate and the churning steps, which ripped his scalp away in chunks. Blood dripped from his forehead as he screamed, "PLEASE! PLEASE!"

Overcome with a sudden instinct to flee, I hastened back down the escalator, desperate to disappear into the crowd below. To separate myself from the havoc I had wrought. The shouting continued behind me as I fled back into the mall, and I wasn't sure if they meant me or the other attacker.

"Don't let him get away!"

"Someone stop him! Stop that man!"

Editor's Note
Exhibit M

Thread posted to open forum at Encounters with the Demonic, matching the description of one described by Hale in chapter twenty-four of his manuscript.

DEVIL GAVE ME HIS POWERS THROUGH HIS SEED.. AND HE GOTTA BIG C**K!!!

06-10-2016, 11:46:05 PM PST

countrychick77
Member Since: 2010
Location: greenville sc
Demonic Encounters: 27

---

onetime i met the devil in the parking lot of my apt complex and he ended up givin gme his powers. it was a couple years ago and i was just getting home from teh store. he was sitting on the hood of a car watching me as i walked by wiht my groceries, he was good looking and sexy in black suit. i told him he looked like Lucifer on that show. i invited him up to my apt and we began to fool around. he asked me if i was afraid of the Devil, i laughed and said yes. He liked that and said i should be. i felt his cock through his pants- it was *ENORMOUS* not like normal mans.

He threw me around like a doll filpped me over and ripped my skirt off my body. Stuck his cock in hot like fire, it hurt so good i screamed. there was a mirror on the back of the door and i could see his reflection as he pounded me. thats when i realized he was the Devil because he his reflection showed dark fur all over his body huge horns, his eyes were bright red as he came.

about a week later i realized the devil had gave me his power which he implanted with his seed- i could make people do bad things. Like anything i wanted, steal fight even murder. if they wanted to do it i could make them with my mind. once their was this dad pushing his baby around the

walmart in greenville where i work. it wouldn't stop crying and i could see
the dad getting madder and madder and i wanted the baby to shut up and
in my head i was like, fucking kill that thing! and the next thing i knew he
had took it out the stroller and was strangling it shaking it dead. when it
was over he didn't know what happened, he was so shocked he dropped it
like he just realized he was holding a bag of shit.

i remember the squishy little whack it made when it hit the floor, the baby
wasn't moving and there was a dent in its head like a busted soccer ball

06-10-2016, 11:51:40 PM PST

StarGirl81
Member Since: 2014
Location: Hastings, MN
Demonic Encounters: 1

OMG! That must have been terrifying! I would be scared to have that
power. Love that show by the way ☺

06-10-2016, 11:54:33 PM PST

XXxXxXxXX00
Member Since: 2015
Location: anywhere
Demonic Encounters: infinity

Fake.

06-11-2016, 12:00:20 AM PST

countrychick77
Member Since: 2010
Location: greenville sc
Demonic Encounters: 27

@StarGirl81 isn't it amazing? ☺

@XXxXxXxXX00 real actually, don't believe me then come to greenville and i'll show you

06-11-2016, 12:13:12 AM PST

> **SatanIsATop90**
> Member Since: 2013
> Location: New York, NY
> Demonic Encounters: 0.5

Literally called it

06-11-2016, 02:54:45 AM PST

> **LadyOccultist3**
> Member Since: 2014
> Location: Aberdeen, UK
> Demonic Encounters: 3

Where do I sign up haha? No but seriously though, that is crazy- hope your ok

06-11-2016, 08:56:58 AM PST

> **countrychick77**
> Member Since: 2010
> Location: greenville sc
> Demonic Encounters: 27

@SatanIsATop90 ☺

@LadyOccultist3 haha thx, best thing i ever did

06-11-2016, 10:11:03 AM PST

> **God$Homeboy**
> Member Since: 2016
> Location: Heaven
> Demonic Encounters: 0

Rot in hell demonic b*tch

06-11-2016, 12:20:01 PM PST

> **dan525**
> Member Since: 2012
> Location: buttfuck, usa
> Demonic Encounters: 1

Sure it was the Devil?... by the sound of the fur it may just have been an Iranian man...

06-11-2016, 01:00:58 PM PST

> **countrychick77**
> Member Since: 2010
> Location: greenville sc
> Demonic Encounters: 27

@God$Homeboy looking forward to it asshole

@dan525 fuck off racist

12-14-2016, 12:17:38 PM PST

> **GraysonH92**
> Member Since: 2006
> Location: San Diego, CA
> Demonic Encounters: Unsure

Late to this. How did you get rid of the powers? Think I might have them too. I can't stop hurting people. I'm so scared.

12-14-2016, 05:25:25 PM PST

> **AntwonLaVey666**
> Member Since: 2015
> Location: NYFB
> Demonic Encounters: 4

@GraysonH92 What, did you fuck the devil too? ☺

12-14-2016, 08:56:58 PM PST

countrychick77
Member Since: 2010
Location: greenville sc
Demonic Encounters: 27

@GraysonH92 still have them. no way to get rid of them. been using
mine to make extra cash... btw, offering my services to anyone in the
greenville-spartanburg area, just $500 and i'll use my powers to do
whatev u want (no killing women or rape), dm me

Twenty-Six

FIRST THE DOG, then the stranger at the mall. It couldn't be a coincidence. There was no denying it now, no getting around it. As insane as the thought was—and it was insane, frighteningly so—I couldn't shake the realization that had settled in my body like a sickness, infecting my mind with horror and revulsion: he had got to me.

The one I feared had implanted me with his vile talent—the power to make people sate their most abominable urges.

I didn't need to ask where I got it. I could feel it inside me, the part of him that D.B. had left in my body. It had been there since the night he defiled me, an acute sharpness lodged in my stomach. A seed that was just beginning to unfurl. What was it he had said to me in the alley that night? *You've been waiting for this your whole life.*

And he was right.

A painful tightness clenched my chest. It squeezed my lungs and stuttered my breathing. I was having a panic attack. Like the ones I used to have as a teenager but worse, for this time my deepest fear had come to fruition.

I needed to hear it from him. Needed to know this was real. I hoped it was, in a way, hoped this wasn't all in my head. But how could it be? People were getting hurt. I'd seen it with my own eyes. Their screams still rang in my ears—the woman in the Pear Tree, the man on the escalator. I couldn't have imagined those attacks. And that was good; it meant I wasn't going crazy. More important, it meant there must be a way to stop it.

I fumbled for my phone and texted D.B. *Need to talk ASAP*. When he didn't answer, I opened my laptop, my fingers tripping over themselves as they rushed out an email with more or less the same message.

D.B.'s replies typically came so fast they seemed automatic, but ten minutes later, twenty, there still was nothing. An hour, two hours, not the faintest flicker of acknowledgment.

I paced around my room. Used my arm to wipe the sweat that deluged my forehead. My skin was crawling, my knees shaking, my chest so tight I could barely breathe. Still nothing came.

I passed out sometime around midnight. My dreams were of Liam. We were at Teviot, fumbling awkwardly through our first real conversation in weeks. In the dream, all I wanted was for this to be over, for us to be friends again. But this time the awkwardness that hung between us clung to the air, resolute. There was something Liam didn't want to say.

"What is it?" I said. "Liam, please. What did I do?"

"What did you do?" His blue eyes swam with malice. "You work for the Devil, Grayson. *You're a heathen.*"

A sudden buzz startled me awake: a new text. I snatched up my phone. To my disappointment, the name on the screen was Sophie's.

Change of plans for tomorrow - no birthday party.
Going clubbing instead. Leith Walk, 9pm. ☺

I texted her in the morning that I was sick and wouldn't be able to make it. Behind her mask of well-wishes and understanding, she was clearly embittered. I couldn't care less. Nothing would compel me to leave the house, not now that I knew what I was harboring inside. It wasn't safe. All those squeezing, shouting people, out of control with drink and lust—anything might set me off. I was a deadly weapon, a thing to be handled with great care. Or better yet, left alone.

It was no use trying to distract myself with work. My mind was like a dozen children let out for recess: running in all directions, cacophonous, irretrievable. Ollie ordered pizza, but I said I wasn't hungry, worried what might happen if he provoked me as we sat around the table. One off-color joke could be all it took.

So instead I remained in my room, trying once again to contact D.B. I was as bad as he'd been a few weeks before, sending rapid-fire texts and messages to no avail. Through the closed door, I could hear Ollie on the phone as he emerged from his bedroom.

"*All right*, don't get your knickers in a twist. I'm leaving now, fuck." Then the welcome sound of him pulling on a jacket, an expletive-laced search for keys. At last the front door slammed shut.

Good. One less person for me to hurt.

As I stood before the open refrigerator, helping myself to Ollie's leftovers straight out of the box, I heard a noise at the back of the flat. It sounded like it was coming from Ollie's room.

The door, when I got there, was slightly ajar. I pushed it open and peered around. It was the first time I'd had a proper look inside. Even in the dim blue light of the afternoon, it was clearly trashed, the floors strewn with clothes, the surfaces piled with dishes and half-empty soda bottles. It smelled like a locker room, layered over with the sourness of old garbage. Unable to see what might have caused the disturbance, I began to back away, stopping as something shifted under the lumpy duvet.

There was someone in the bed.

My first instinct was to leave them alone. Then again, I had a right to know if there was a stranger in my home. Better than being startled later; there was no telling what I might do.

"Hello?" I murmured, knocking lightly on the door. The figure stirred, and began to roll over to face me.

But the head staring back at me from Ollie's pillow was too small to be human, too greasily black, with tiny, triangular, upturned ears. The face let out a low, gibbering giggle.

Before I could react, the duvet exploded off the bed and half a dozen fiends leapt into the air, slamming me against the hallway wall. They had me pinned. There was a smash—the sound of Ollie's bedside lamp breaking against the doorframe—then a searing pain in my hands. Sharing the shards of broken glass between them, the fiends dug out a fleshy hole in each of my palms. I was screaming. Blood spilled down my arms in hot, dripping lines.

Then ripping me forward, the fiends threw me against the opposite wall. They had me by my wrists, three on each side, smashing my palms against the wall and wielding them like bloody paintbrushes. I thought I might pass out from the pain, and then finally they released me.

I fell back on the floor, my trembling hands cupped against my chest as the fiends skittered away into the night.

Only now, peering up through bleary eyes, did I perceive the great red letters smeared across the wall—the words they had made me write in my own blood.

LEITH WALK

It took me a moment, then suddenly I understood. D.B. had received my messages. Now he was sending one back: *You know where to find me.*

Twenty-Seven

I TRAVELED ON FOOT, a shivering wreck before I even got there. It was monstrously cold, a cold so driving and merciless it seemed almost to be in league with D.B. I thought longingly of home, where before I left I had managed to scour the street name from the wall with a kitchen sponge. The paint beneath was left slightly abraded, but Ollie, if he ever noticed, would care too little to question it. I wondered if he would realize I had replaced his broken lamp with a similar, but not identical, one from my room.

As I rounded the curving glass structure of the Omni Centre, Leith Walk came into view. The name of the first club, Cafe Habana, was lit up against the black frontage in every color of the rainbow, its boisterous music buzzing through my body uninvited. As I passed it, I heard someone call my name.

"Grayson?"

It was Sophie. She was tugging down the front of her dress as she clambered out of a minicab, her lids caked and shimmering. "I thought you were ill," she exclaimed, delighted.

I muttered a low *fuck* under my breath; I'd completely forgotten she would be here.

"You should have told me you were coming." She hugged me.

"Yeah. Well. I wanted to surprise you." I hid my bandaged hands in my pockets. Sophie's tall flatmate, Rhian, who had ridden with her, joined us on the sidewalk.

"Shall we go inside?" she said. "It's bloody freezing out here."

They clomped off in their high heels toward Habana. I hesitated, and noticing this, so did Sophie. "Aren't you coming?"

I didn't have time for this.

Just a few minutes, I bargained with myself. Then I'd break away to find D.B.

The club was small and reassuringly characterless, with red walls and cheap, weathered furniture, like a ten-year-old chain restaurant blasting dance pop. A few people were gathered at the bar, mostly men in their twenties and thirties. Normal-looking, many of them, in polos and button-downs. I could almost blend in.

Liam, Nisha, and Shaun had already arrived, having commandeered an upstairs table overlooking the dance floor. When they saw us coming, Nisha and Shaun rushed over to greet the birthday girl with hugs and presents, but Liam didn't get up. He and Sophie barely looked at each other. Were they not speaking either?

With Sophie deep in conversation with the others, it was just Liam and me. After the events of the last two days, our fractured relationship was far from my mind. Still, there was no point maintaining the stalemate if it could be avoided.

I had barely taken a step toward the table, however, when Liam shrank back, shooting me a cold, forbidding look.

Casually I turned away, as if I had never intended to approach him in the first place. But it hit me like a kick to the groin, the pain radiating through my body in debilitating pulses.

Sophie's friends continued to trickle in, among them Jenna. She looked as good as ever, in a tight dress cut down over her breasts. Her nails were electric blue. I was standing by the banister, keeping a clandestine watch over the dance floor below in case D.B. should appear there, when Jenna sidled up to me, her slender forearms resting on the banister.

"No present, huh?"

"What?" I had heard her fine, but the question flustered me. It was the first time we'd ever properly spoken.

"I heard you didn't get Sophie anything for her birthday."

I threw Sophie a look over my shoulder, suddenly irritated; her laughter dulled as she caught my eye, as if intuiting the subject of our conversation. "I got her a candle. I just—forgot it."

"A candle?" She laughed. *"Nice."*

I didn't respond.

"You're not a fag, are you?" Jenna said.

"Sorry?"

"It's just every time I look over, you're either staring at Liam or those dudes down there. If you're gonna come out, at least wait until after your girlfriend's birthday."

"Did you really just say that word?" I said.

"What, *girlfriend*?"

"The f-word."

She let out another laugh, lower this time. "You mean *fag*—"

"Shut up."

She stared at me, disbelieving.

"Maybe in Maryland it's cool to be homophobic," I said. "But where I come from, it just makes you an ignorant asshole."

Her glossy lips parted in surprise. Her penciled eyebrows raised.

At last she released the banister and slid away, joining a small group that included Liam.

I could tell by the way their eyes flicked to me that she was telling them some version of what had just happened. Liam gave her a consoling squeeze. The sight of it stung. Jenna may not have been my dream girl after all, but Liam had promised not to go near her. That shouldn't change just because he and I weren't talking.

I made some effort to rejoin the festivities, but I was getting impatient. I needed to find D.B.

After a couple rounds, there was talk of moving on to a new bar. "Somewhere dancey," Sophie said. People threw in suggestions, too many of which would take us away from Leith Walk.

"What about the Silver Stag?" I interjected.

It was the only place that made sense. If D.B. wanted me to come find him, where better than the club where we had first met?

It was a popular choice; hardly anyone objected, though Jenna's eyes glinted mockingly at the fact that I had suggested it. The final decision was left to Sophie, who agreed. We downed our drinks and decamped.

The Silver Stag was just a few doors down: white-fronted with two arched windows on either side of the door, the name of the club spelled out in silver lettering above. As we approached, violet light poured out onto the sidewalk and the blaring electronic music could be heard, indeed felt, from the street, so loud it sent vibrations rumbling through my core. The night we met, D.B. had invited me inside, and the same vague feeling of discomfort that had held me back then returned to me now, despite my having been the one to recommend the place.

Inside, the club was modern, thunderous, sweltering hot, and so full of people that I had to physically push my way through. High-polished tables encircled a thronging dance floor, while a life-size chrome stag gleamed in the far corner, insensate to the Instagram dandies snapping selfies in front of it.

We ordered a round of drinks, and Sophie dragged me out to dance. My head swiveled left and right, scanning the room for D.B. as she gyrated against me. She was drunker than I had previously realized.

Though he was nowhere to be found, there was plenty to see. The clientele was different from the last place, a rarer sort: men wearing stiletto boots to match their lipstick, others displaying chiseled chests and biceps through shirts of mesh. I kept my eyes off them, not wanting to stare. They landed on Liam, who was dancing with Jenna. His hands were on her lower back, pushing her into him, their pelvises interlocked like puzzle pieces.

He caught my gaze, almost defiantly.

Sophie guzzled the dregs of her double vodka cranberry. "I need another drink," she said, her voice starting to slur. "Grays'n, would you . . . um . . ."

I spared her the indignity of completing the question; it would give me a chance to have a proper look around.

Taking her empty glass, I moved toward the bar. It was packed, dozens of people waiting ahead of me. A tall man in a tank top backed into me, assaulting my nostrils with the musky odor of his sweat-slicked body. I experienced a sharp push-and-pull behind my navel, a desire to punish and an urgency not to. *It's fine,* I told myself. *Only an accident.*

A quarter of an hour later I had still not spotted my employer but had at last managed to flag down the bartender. She was petite and masculine, her tattooed scalp shaved on one side. She smiled as she saw me. "Haven't seen you here in a while."

"Sorry?" The music was so loud I thought I must have misheard.

"Where've you been?"

"I've never been here before."

"Aye, good one." She gave a little laugh.

"I haven't."

Her smile faltered. She only now seemed to realize I wasn't joking, and looked uncomfortable. "Okay . . . what can I get you?" She quickly returned a wave to someone behind me, apparently another one of her so-called regulars.

In the mirror behind the bar, I glimpsed the person before he disappeared into the crowd. D.B. had entered the building.

Five minutes later, as I forced my way back to the dance floor holding two drinks above my head, my eyes searched for him.

Sophie was waving to me unsteadily. "Grays'n, over here!"

She accepted her cocktail with overstated thanks, wrapping an arm around my neck so violently that her drink splashed back on my shirt. "Oh no . . . sorry . . ."

There was no time to be annoyed. I headed off, having spotted D.B. by the stag. But he was gone by the time I got there.

He was by the bar, chatting with a meathead with a thick, veiny neck. For the second time I forced my way over to him, but once again, in the instant I took my eyes off him, he seemed to dematerialize. I barely caught a glimpse of him slithering through the crowd.

Deserting all sense of reserve, I forced my way after him. "Donny," I called, ignoring the jeers and protests of the jostled bystanders. He was so close I could almost touch him. "Donny, wait!"

Thrusting my way through a thick copse of drag queens, one of whom rewarded me with a violent shove, I staggered forward.

What I saw next stopped me like a punch to the chest, forcing a grunt of brute surprise from my diaphragm.

I felt as if I were falling from a great height: I experienced a sickening, weightless feeling, an unthinking moment of rapid descent, and finally the sensation of exploding against solid earth. Except my pain did not stop at the moment of impact; it seemed to intensify with every passing second, as if my body had punched through the planetary crust and was tunneling down through countless layers of sediment, every second bringing a more unbearable heat, a more exquisite suffering.

I lost control of my body; it belonged now to a part of me I did not recognize as my own. I could merely watch on as it thrust my body forward and laid my hands on Liam's shoulders, tearing him back so that his lips detached from Jenna's and he twisted around to hear me scream, "WHAT THE FUCK! WHAT THE FUCK ARE YOU DOING, YOU PROMISED—"

"Get away from me!" he roared, thrusting me back. "What're ye on aboot?"

"YOU SAID YOU WOULDN'T—YOU PROMISED—"

"Promised what? I've barely even spoken to ye, ye fucking psycho!"

Barely spoken? What was he talking about? I could feel it twitching inside of me, the desire to punish, to make him pay for his lie. To order the crowd to dogpile on him, tear him apart. I held the command in my mind like a finger on a trigger.

"Liam, don't," Sophie said, pushing her way to the front of the crowd that was forming around us. "Please."

"No. I've had fucking enough of this! He's fucking mental." He took my shirt roughly in his fists, his knuckles dug into the skin of my chest, his face monstrous with rage. "Stop following me around. Stop writing on my Facebook. *We're not friends,* d'ye hear me? We've *never* been friends."

Tears stung my eyes, unbidden. Why was he saying this? It wasn't true. Had our friendship meant nothing?

"Make him remember," said a voice in my ear—D.B.'s voice. I could feel his hands on my shoulders, not quite solid, but there. *"Make them all remember."*

"No," I protested. But there was only so long I could resist. I needed to get out before something happened that I couldn't take back.

Shrugging the thought of D.B.'s hands from my shoulders, I fled toward the door, past Sophie as she clung to me, weeping, mascara and eyeshadow streaking her cheeks. Past the mocking, laughing, piteous faces of the crowd. I was halfway to the door when I felt my whole body jerk backward. Over my shoulder I saw that a pair of fiends had besieged me, tearing at my clothes as they fought to drag me back into the club.

"Get off of me," I spat, railing against them with all my might, conscious of the bystanders, Sophie, Jenna, Liam, gasping, muttering, laughing—but of course they couldn't see my captors; I must have appeared to have been clawing and swinging at the air. Tears spilled down my cheeks as I fought and scrabbled. This couldn't be happening, not now—I couldn't take it anymore.

"Do it now," D.B. whispered. *"Make them pay."*

"I can't . . ."

"*Make them remember.*"

"NO!"

As I ripped myself free, my built-up momentum sent me hurtling forward. The crowd jumped out of the way, clearing a path. The sight of me talking to myself and fighting off invisible phantoms had darkened their expressions. I was no longer a joke to these people. I was something frightening. Something dangerous.

A splash of hateful cold hit my face as I burst out of the club and into the night. A siren wailed in the distance. I set off at a run.

Twenty-Eight

"YOU'VE USED THE wrong 'there' here. And this, this doesn't make any sense."

Two days after Sophie's birthday disaster, I found myself in Ollie's bedroom for the second time, seated before his final essay on Russian foreign policy. For some reason I thought he was following along with my critiques, embarrassed into silent submission. This delusion was corrected when, upon hearing a laugh behind me, I turned to find him lying back on the bed, watching a video on his phone.

"What are you doing? I'm not writing this for you."

"Oh just fix it," he said, "fucking hell."

As my flatmate continued to splutter on the bed, Sophie's name flashed up on my phone, which lay on the desktop beside a stack of dirty dishes.

It was the first I'd heard from her since Friday. *She must be done hating me for ruining her birthday.* Maybe she wasn't; maybe she was finishing with me for good. Part of me wished she would. I might have done it myself if I weren't so ashamed. It was hard to imagine I'd ever be able to look at her without thinking of Liam, and the things he had said in front of all those people. Things I still couldn't quite believe. *We're not friends. We've* never *been friends.*

Was he just trying to hurt me, or was it true? Had I gotten it all wrong, interpreted our furtive glances and texts as exchanges between like-minded companions, while the whole time he'd been wishing I would leave him alone? When I looked back at our messages—which I had, obsessively, since that night, desperate for proof that I wasn't deluded—it didn't seem possible. More than half the time, it was Liam who had contacted *me*. And the things he wrote—not all the time but now and again—it was like we were better than friends.

The phone buzzed again, this time displaying an unknown number.

Curious, I reached for the device, realizing, as I unlocked it, that Sophie had included me in a group text.

> Has anyone heard from Liam? Haven't been able to reach him since the silver stag and his flatmate says he hasn't been home. Family hasn't heard from him either, i'm worried ☹

Someone had replied that they too were struggling to reach him. Several more chimed in to say the same. As the messages continued to roll in, the truth of the matter came to light: Liam Stewart had not been seen for thirty-six hours.

As soon as the realization sank in, I was bombarded with intrusive thoughts. Liam hit by a car. Liam kidnapped. Liam's body lying in a ditch.

I needed to find him. Needed to know that he was okay.

Although I knew it was probably pointless, I texted him. No answer. Nor did he pick up when I called.

Then something else occurred to me, a thought even worse than the possibility that Liam might be missing or hurt.

"What're you doing?" Ollie said, propped up on one elbow as I paced around the room.

"Shut up," I snapped. "I need to think."

I could not expunge the terrifying thought chewing at the back of my mind like a cancer. I could not deny the possibility that I was more than just an innocent bystander.

The thought grew louder in my head with every second that passed: *I did it. It's because of me that Liam's disappeared.*

And yet, it didn't add up. Every time I'd hurt someone before, it was because I'd lost control, because I'd had it in my heart to punish. It was true that I wanted to get back at Liam that night. After the ways he'd embarrassed and betrayed me, of course I had. But I held myself back. I got out of there before anyone got hurt. Whatever happened to Liam must have happened after he left the club. I could not fairly hold myself accountable for every possible calamity that might have befallen a drunk twenty-three-year-old in the middle of the night.

Do you even remember where you went after the club? said a voice in my head.

Sure I did. I was starving and had stopped at some seedy little takeout place selling pizza and kebabs. After that I walked home, and must have fallen in the street. When I woke the next day, my clothes had been damp, the hems of my jeans covered in mud.

You don't remember?

It occurred to me now that I couldn't. I hadn't thought about it before—I was too upset about what had happened at the club—but there was a gap in my memory. One moment I was ordering a kebab, the next I was waking up in bed the following morning. I must've been drunker than I realized. But blackout drunk?

I couldn't answer. I couldn't answer any of these questions. And yet they kept coming, each more frightening than the last.

Where did you go?

What happened that night?

What did you do to Liam?

Editor's Note
Exhibit N

Second of three-part interview with Nathaniel Hale, elder brother of Grayson Hale, recorded via Skype 4 September 2019.

BARCLAY: Would you say your relationship [with Grayson] was quite combative?

HALE: Combative?

BARCLAY: I mean, did you fight a lot?

HALE: Well, yeah. All brothers fight.

BARCLAY: Sure.

HALE: And sometimes he acted up. He deserved what he got.

BARCLAY: Which was what, exactly?

HALE: You're gonna make me say it?

BARCLAY: You would hit him.

HALE: Let's just say I'd rough him up when I needed to.

BARCLAY: Did he ever come away with bruises? Marks?

HALE: Well that's the idea, isn't it?

BARCLAY: Anything worse than that?

HALE: I don't remember. It was a long time ago.

BARCLAY: How did your mother feel about your fighting?

HALE: How did she feel?

BARCLAY: Did she break the two of you up? Yell? Send you to your rooms?

HALE: Not exactly.

BARCLAY: Did she ever . . . ?

HALE: Just say it.

BARCLAY: Did she ever instruct you to hurt your brother?

HALE: [Laughs] I mean, she never told me to.

BARCLAY: But she was aware?

HALE: Say again? You broke up.

BARCLAY: She knew you were hurting Grayson and she never stopped you. Is that what you're saying?

HALE: You make it sound bad, but it wasn't like that. I told you, all brothers fight. Anyway, it was only when he really deserved it. When he needed to be punished.

BARCLAY: Punished.

HALE: Like when he threw a huge tantrum and gave my mom a black eye. Or when she'd tell me about something sick he did. Something perverted he drew, or said.

BARCLAY: So she confided in you. She'd tell you when he needed to be punished.

HALE: Not directly.

BARCLAY: But she'd indicate. Give you a sign.

HALE: I was her little warrior. That's what she used to call me.

BARCLAY: You sound proud of that.

HALE: I was. I am.

BARCLAY: What did you feel you were at war against?

HALE: Not what. Who.

BARCLAY: The Adversary.

HALE: With everything that's come out about Gray since, it looks like I was right.

BARCLAY: What about then? What's the worst thing he ever did?

HALE: You'll have to ask Carlos Fernandez about that.

BARCLAY: Tell me about Carlos.

HALE: Paola and Esteban's son. He and Gray were best friends until Gray tried to make him—well, you'll have to ask Carlos.

BARCLAY: This incident, you saw it happen?

HALE: I was inside. Carlos came and told me about it though, right after it happened. He was scared. Asked me not to tell anyone, but—

BARCLAY: You told your mom.

HALE: I had to. Fellowship was our life. Our livelihood. And Grayson was taking boys behind the garden shed and—well. Just ask Carlos.

BARCLAY: Did you punish him for it?

HALE: He got his comeuppance. Never did it again either, not that Carlos went anywhere near him after that.

BARCLAY: And your mother, how did she react?

HALE: She said it was the last straw. She kicked him out of Bible study lessons. Said he was a lost cause, that he'd just spread his evil to me. She finally realized what he was.

BARCLAY: Which was?

HALE: You tell me. You're the one writing a book on him.

BARCLAY: Speaking of your mother—

HALE: What about her?

BARCLAY: I just wanted to say, I'm sorry for your loss. It must be so difficult for you, having lost your whole family. First your father, then your mother, and now—

HALE: She was the only family I ever had. And he murdered her.

BARCLAY: Who did?

HALE: Who the fuck are we talking about?

BARCLAY: You mean Grayson? You're saying Grayson murdered your mother?

Twenty-Nine

INHERENT IN THE bustle of Waverley Station was a threat. Travelers shuffling in endless lines toward the ticket counter. Sipping peppermint lattes as they sat waiting for their trains. Flooding the concourse in a distracted scrum as they crossed and swerved and stood gazing up at the departures boards. They filled every corner of the station, their eyes flicking lazily across my face, infusing my body with fresh dread and forcing me to break their gaze before the inevitable moment of recognition.

It was stupid, really, this fear of being recognized. These people didn't know who I was.

After all, it was only my name they had seen in the papers.

⁓

The Scotsman had been the first to report Liam's disappearance. The article appeared online less than twenty-four hours after Sophie's group text, the details scant but disconcerting.

Vanished just before midnight on Friday evening . . . girlfriend Jenna Mankowitz taken in for questioning Monday afternoon . . . had been celebrating a friend's birthday at the Silver Stag on Leith Walk . . . last seen leaving Palmyra Pizza on South Bridge . . .

Reading that, I paused. Palmyra Pizza. The name was familiar. Was that the restaurant I'd stopped at on the way back to my flat?

The following morning, unable to sleep, I'd bundled up and ventured out into the cool hush of twilight, meeting the newsagent as he opened his shop. Disturbing as the online article had been, it was the morning broadsheet I wanted to see. I had it in my head that, if the story had made it into print, then I would know it was actually real, that Liam truly was missing. That this wasn't all just some terrible misunderstanding, some cruel joke being had at my expense. My heart raced as the newsagent turned the key in the lock, lifted the security gate, and finally held the door open for me to enter.

"Newspaper?" I said without greeting. He ambled behind the counter, broke the binding on a fresh stack of papers, and tossed one on the counter before me.

There it was. Not quite the story of the day but notable nonetheless, the opening lines of the article scrunched into a corner of the front page.

EDINBURGH UNIVERSITY STUDENT MISSING
FOLLOWING SCENE IN CLUB

My stomach sank. The online article hadn't said anything about a scene. Had someone told the press about my blowout with Liam?

Paying my one pound seventy-five, I absconded with the paper, resisting the temptation to look until I was back in the flat.

Once I was inside, with the door locked behind me, I spread the paper out on the desk. Much of the article was as it had appeared online. I skimmed over those sections, my eyes stopping as they met with new content.

. . . the missing student's girlfriend, Jenna Mankowitz, 22, was taken in for questioning Monday afternoon but released later that evening.

In an exclusive interview with *The Scotsman*, Mankowitz alleged that Stewart had been involved in an altercation with a classmate at the Silver Stag earlier that evening.

The student, identified as Grayson Hale from California, United States, is alleged to have accosted Stewart, apparently over his relationship with Mankowitz.

According to Mankowitz, Hale suffered what she described as a "psychotic episode" shortly before fleeing the club.

"He just went crazy. It was really scary."

Mankowitz claims that she and Stewart left the Silver Stag together shortly thereafter and visited Palmyra Pizza on South Bridge, where Hale allegedly appeared.

"I turned around and there he was, sitting at one of the tables. He was eating a kebab, just watching us. He had this look on his face, just, like, completely blank, but it was obvious he followed us there. I was like, 'Liam, let's go,' and he was just like, 'You go. I need to handle this.' He said he'd text me later."

Mankowitz claims that she witnessed Stewart and Hale exiting Palmyra Pizza together and walking south along South Bridge.

"That's the last time I saw him." Mankowitz added, "He never texted."

I threw the paper aside. "Fucking bitch," I spat. Jenna was lying. Lying to get back at me for insulting her at Cafe Habana. Sure, I'd gone to the restaurant, but I hadn't *followed* them. If she and Liam were there at the same time, that was news to me, and Liam and I certainly hadn't left together.

How can you be so sure?

After all, I could hardly remember anything from that night. The restaurant, yes, but not how I'd gotten there. Anyway, I left the club before Liam and Jenna. If it was true that I'd shown up to the restaurant after them, then I couldn't have gone straight there. There must be another gap in my memory.

I was left with more questions than answers, but one thing was clear: whether or not she was telling the truth, Jenna had painted a target on my back. According to this article, I was the last person to have seen Liam in days. The police were probably already on their way.

Suddenly eager to get out of the city, I threw together a bag and called an Uber. I admit the impulse was completely irrational; were the police inclined to track me down, they were unlikely to be greatly waylaid by my sudden disappearance. I might buy myself a couple days at best. But I wasn't operating from a place of logic. Piloted by pure, raw fear, I left the flat, not even bothering to tell Ollie I was going, and headed straight to Waverley Station.

As I fed my orange ticket into the slot, the gate swung open to admit me. My train was already at the platform. I hurried forward, lugging a small duffel at my side. My ticket read *Inverness*, but I'd get off before then. Somewhere remote, where they wouldn't think to look. I'd check into a bed-and-breakfast. Perhaps stay through Christmas, if I managed to avoid them that long. I was meant to spend the holiday with Sophie's family, but there was no chance of that now. How would she react when she saw the news? Would she think I had done it? That I was dangerous, some kind of lunatic killer?

How do you know you're not?

The train car was stuffy and hot. I sat, throwing my bag on the open seat beside me. Folding my arms over my chest, I gazed through the window. Liam's face smiled back at me from the front page of the newspaper a man sat reading on the platform. I recognized the photo as one of Liam's old profile pictures. Even in black and white, his cheeks were visibly sun-kissed, his eyes bright and kind. My friend. My best and only.

In that moment I would have traded anything—even my freedom—just to know he was okay.

But part of me already knew that day would never come. D.B. had made sure of that. It was comforting to remember that it was he, not I, who had caused this. I was merely a tool at his disposal—to what end, I didn't know.

Make them remember. Make them remember the Devil.

As I waited for the train to depart, I noticed a large Black man seated across the aisle. He had close-cropped silver hair and was dressed for a day at the office. A pair of spectacles sat low on his nose as he read from a very small book, gold lettering stamped across its gray-blue cover.

I had only ever seen one like it.

Eventually the man closed the book and got to his feet, leaving the hardcover on the seat as he collected his belongings from the overhead rack. While pulling on his jacket and wrapping a scarf around his neck, he seemed to forget about the book. It remained lying on the seat as he proceeded toward the exit.

Once I was certain he wasn't coming back, I scooted out into the aisle and hoisted my duffel bag over my head, appearing to take advantage of the free space in the overhead rack while surreptitiously stealing a glance at the book.

It lay facedown, the title obscured.

As I reached down to grab it, a voice rang out over the loudspeaker, female and polite.

"This announcement is for the passenger named Grayson Hale. Grayson Hale, will you please collect your belongings and exit the train? Your presence is requested on the platform."

My eyes moved to the window. A pair of officers stood waiting on the platform.

Thirty

AFTER THE OFFICERS arrested me they took me back to St. Leonard's Police Station, coincidentally located just a few blocks from Liam's flat, and put me in a holding cell. They offered me a call, but I refused it. The only person I could think to contact was Ollie, and I couldn't see how it would help me to be laughed at right now. I did accept the offer of legal assistance, however, and spoke briefly with a government-issue solicitor on the phone. When I hung up, I realized I had retained not one word of his advice.

I sat in that cell for hours, my body seeming to eat itself with anxiety and discomfort. They would want to know what happened the night Liam disappeared. What would I tell them? It would be reckless, surely, to admit I couldn't remember, but perhaps equally reckless to lie. The only safe option was to avoid questioning. To escape custody, if only for a bit. Concentrating my mind on the male officer who'd put me in the cell, I attempted to exert my influence on him, willed him to appear at my door and set me free.

But when he finally slid his key into the lock, it was clear he had no intention of abetting my escape. "Come on," he said. "Time for a wee chat."

He escorted me, hands cuffed behind my back, into a small room with a table and chairs. My solicitor, a suited man in his forties, was already there. I took the seat beside him. On the other side of the table sat the detective inspector. She was older, with short spiked hair dyed mahogany and a broad accent. She introduced herself as Yvonne.

"Now, ah have a few questions," she said reassuringly, like a nurse preparing a patient for a shot. "We're just collecting information, so please just answer as best ye can, all right?"

"All right."

"First," she began, "when's the last time ye spoke to Liam Stewart?"

"I wish to remain silent," I said.

Yvonne paused, her eyes flicking from me to my solicitor, then back again. Clearly this was not the answer she expected.

"Next question," said my solicitor.

Yvonne proceeded. "After ye left the Silver Stag on the evening of the sixteenth of December, where did ye go?"

"I wish to remain silent," I repeated.

The inspector sighed. She tried, in an almost motherly way, to advise me against holding my tongue, how bad it would look when this went to trial.

"On what evidence would this ever go to trial?" quipped my solicitor. "You've not got a shred of physical evidence."

Acting as if he had not spoken, Yvonne reached a hand across the table to me, a gesture of compassion. "Ye dinnae want the jury to think ye're hiding something, do ye?"

"No," I admitted.

"Well then—"

"I wish to remain silent."

The solicitor caught my eye with an approving nod. In fact, he seemed so unfazed by my silence that I wondered if it had been his advice that I not speak.

In any case, he was right about the lack of evidence. I had consumed enough BBC crime dramas to know they could only hold me for twenty-

four hours, then either had to charge me or let me go. It was a calculated risk, but without a body, it was unlikely they'd be able to justify
a charge. As far as anyone knew, Liam had run off to ride elephants in
the circus.

At the conclusion of the interview, I was returned to my cell. There
I spent the night, restive and overheated. As I tossed and turned, doubt
crept in. Had I done the right thing by refusing to talk? Was the inspector right that I had just made myself look suspicious to the jury who
would eventually be appointed to decide my fate?

In the end, my strategy seemed to pay off. By noon the next day an
officer had appeared outside my cell, saying I was free to go. They gave
me back my things, and I was released without charge.

My relief, however immense, was short-lived. As I trekked home
from the police station, I concluded that my position remained perilous.
Although I'd dodged a bullet, nothing about my future felt secure. Liam
remained missing, whether dead or alive I didn't know. The specter of
his reappearance, in either condition, loomed over me even as I longed
for his safe return.

And yet perhaps the greatest threat was the one that roiled inside of
me: this dangerous affliction, which I could neither expel nor control.

Was that what D.B. had wanted for me? To lose control? To hurt
someone? Is that what he meant by "make them remember the Devil"?
And what did any of this have to do with the book?

When I got back to the flat, tired and on edge, Ollie was once again
playing FIFA in the sitting room. True to form, he hadn't even noticed
I'd been missing for more than twenty-four hours.

I retreated to my bedroom. I tossed my duffel on the bed and, as
if the police might have followed me home, shut my bedroom door
against their prying eyes.

From my unzipped bag, I removed the object that had been playing
on my mind the whole journey home, little though I wanted to see it.

Indeed, I had been actively avoiding the folktale for the better part
of three months, remembering the effect it had had on me when my

father gifted it to me on my thirteenth birthday. With its grayish-blue cover and velvet-soft pages, this could have been the very same copy. It projected a malign character, more like a person than paper and ink. Perhaps that was why it kept presenting itself to me.

Perhaps someone, and I could guess who, was trying to send me a message.

Perhaps it was time I listened.

Editor's Note
Exhibit O

Here I present the complete text of Jack and the Devil's Horn by Ned Duhamel, a copy of which was found among the personal effects of Grayson Hale
subsequent to his death at HMP Edinburgh. Provenance unknown.

A long time ago, long before your time or your father's,
there lived a young man named Jack who was traveling
across the hills and glens of Scotland. It is not known where
or for what purpose young Jack was traveling, only that,
each day, he walked miles and miles, along a solitary path
leading straight. Most days Jack did not encounter a single
soul on his travels. It was an arduous journey, to be sure.

One day, as he walked, Jack felt himself becoming hungry, but his path was an isolated one, with nowhere for
miles to stop and sate his hunger. He'd had not a crumb
of food for days. Eventually the trail led him to the opening of a great forest. The tall trees cast a pall over Jack as
he followed the path into the wood, winding through the
cracked trunks and dense undergrowth. Soon the forest
darkened further still, a spray of silver stars pinpricking
a violet sky through the branches gently swaying above.

Nearby was a small clearing, and there Jack decided to
set up camp for the night. He gathered some kindling and
built a fire, which crackled and spat and waved its warmth
over him. But it did not satisfy the aching of his belly,
which was so great that Jack was beginning to worry. What
would happen if he found nothing to eat? Already he felt
himself fading away, becoming smaller. He must eat soon,
or he would perish.

Then suddenly, as he sat warming his hands over the fire, Jack heard the snap of a twig behind him. From the shadows emerged a dark stranger, dressed in black from head to toe, with a cloak so long that it rustled the leaves on the ground and covered his feet. The fire fluttered its illumination over the face of the man, causing his eyes to glow faintly red.

Jack said, "Who are you? Where have you come from?"

"Oh, never mind where I come from," said the stranger. "I've been watching you all day and you seem very hungry."

"I am," said Jack. "I've been walking for days without a bite to eat."

"But I have food," replied the stranger. "Lots of it." And with a snap of his fingers there appeared in his hands a great platter of delicious meat and drink: steaming-hot pies, roast fowl, fresh bread and cheeses, goblets of red wine and lager.

A cold wind blew through the trees. Jack shuddered.

"No normal man could produce such a feast from air," he said. "Who are you?"

The stranger said, "Never mind who I am. You're hungry and I am here with food. Would you rather know who I am or how it tastes?"

Jack knew his answer; the savory aroma of the meats and pies danced on the wind and made his mouth water. He asked the stranger, "What's your price? I have some money."

The stranger said, "I ask not a farthing, and I would take none from you. I haven't any need for currency of that sort. The meal carries a different price. For all the food you see here I ask that you complete a task of my choosing. Complete the task and this food will fill your belly for weeks; fail to do so and you will starve."

"I'll do anything," Jack said. "Anything you ask!"

The stranger said, "So I thought," with a smile. "Your task is simple. Not far from here, just a few miles through those trees, is a village. Take this here horn . . ." And suddenly the platter vanished from his hands, and there appeared a horn like off the head of a goat. "Take this here horn and walk to the edge of that village, and blow into the horn so that every person in the village may hear. Then you shall have a banquet fit for a king."

"For what purpose do you make this request?" asked Jack. "What have you to gain from making the whole village hear the call of your horn?"

"What difference does it make what I shall gain?" said the stranger. "Does the offer not tempt you?"

"It does," said Jack.

"Well, then come over here and take my horn," said the stranger.

Jack did as he was told. He took the horn in his hands. It was large, extraordinarily heavy, and smooth to the touch. He imagined the tremendous noise it would make when he sounded it through the village. "Do you accept my challenge?" asked the stranger.

"I do," Jack said.

"Go then," ordered the stranger. And Jack trekked off through the trees.

As he walked and walked and no village appeared, it occurred to Jack that the stranger may have taken him for a fool, that he was only wandering deeper and deeper into a darkness from which he would never return. But his mysterious acquaintance had spoken no word of a lie. The village swam into being like a dream. Pausing at the edge of the community, Jack brought the point of the horn to his lips, drew a deep breath—and found he could not exhale.

This was due not to a failure of the young man's lungs, but a hesitation of his will. After all, it was the dead of night. The windows of the village's houses were all dark. Not a soul stirred that he could see, for the villagers were all asleep in their beds. If Jack blew the horn now, he would wake every one of them, and they would run out of their houses, every man, woman, and child, waving their fists in anger for the disturbance he had wreaked. Jack could not stand to be the cause of so much unrest, no matter what he stood to gain from it.

And yet he remained very hungry. In fact, he was more ravenous now than ever before. The smells of the succulent meats and hearty cheeses lingered in his nostrils and whispered ideas in his ear. At last, Jack turned on his heel and marched back toward the campsite with deceit in his heart.

Finally he arrived with the horn in tow. And as soon as he saw the stranger waiting for him, Jack donned a triumphant smile and lied better than the Devil himself.

"I've done it!" he said. "I've blown the horn, and every person in the village did hear!"

"You did!" remarked the stranger. "Wonderful news. Although it is strange. I do not recall hearing the call of the horn myself. Did you blow it very hard?"

"As hard as could be," Jack lied. "I blew the horn, and every person in the village did hear, and they chased me in anger for waking them but I escaped back into the woods. You must have been too far off for the horn's sweet sound to reach your ears."

"Sweet sound, you say?" repeated the stranger, with a glint in his eye. "Very well."

Unlike Jack, the stranger was true to his word. He presented once again a banquet fit for a king, which Jack took unto himself and instantly began to devour.

It was more delicious a feast than he had ever tasted before. The pies were still steaming hot as he champed them, the lager still cold as it frothed down his throat. Soon he'd put away the entire platter of food, leaving only a few bones and scraps. Setting the platter aside, he looked up to thank the benevolent stranger who'd filled his belly, but the man in black was nowhere to be found, receded into the darkness like a shadow. Jack was unconcerned. The food and drink had made him drowsy. Curling up in front of the fire, which was his blanket for the night, he instantly drifted off to sleep.

Jack was awakened early the next morning, and not by the chill that had crept in over the ashes of the burnt-out fire. No, Jack was awakened by a most peculiar feeling: a terrible hunger like he had never felt before in his life. The sensation as much shocked as pained him. After all, how could Jack be hungry? He had eaten enough the night before to keep him full for weeks, and yet he felt as if he had not eaten for that long!

He wondered, could it all have been a dream? The tall dark stranger, the horn, the feast: Could it all have been a fantasy invented by his own mind? But how could it? On the ground beside him lay the platter of scraps and bones. It must have been real! But so too was Jack's appetite; it tore at him from the inside out, like a savage animal trapped within. He had nothing to do but pack up his things and carry on down the path, in search of something else to satisfy his body's ravening want.

Eventually he came upon a burn, and by the burn was a man sitting on the bank and washing his hands in the flowing water. The man had a red beard and a little dog, which ran around barking and wagging his tail as Jack approached.

"Hello there," Jack called out to the man, but the man returned neither his greeting nor his smile. And so Jack made to depart from the man, until he noticed the man's bag had fallen over in the grass, revealing its contents of more than a dozen rabbits, freshly killed and ready for skinning. Jack was no lover of rabbit, but his stomach had no such oppositions. Turning back, he said, "Excuse me, sir, but where did you get your rabbits? I'm very hungry myself and I could do with some fresh meat."

The man said, "These here? Ach, I cacht them. I'm a hunter, and I catch my own rabbits, wi' the help of Angus o' course." This he said with a look at his frisking, yipping dog.

Jack said, "That's a good dog you've got there, to catch all those rabbits. I wonder if you would be kind enough to spare one or two? I'm very hungry, you see, and I haven't any food, nor a clever dog to fetch my supper. What say you? Could you spare a rabbit or two?"

The hunter said, "No, laddie, I cannae gie ye one o' these rabbits. These rabbits are for to feed mysel' and Angus tonight. Ye'll have to find your supper elsewhere." And he returned to washing himself in the burn as if to say, I've had enough of talking, now away with you!

But Jack persisted. "I do not mean to take your dinner," he said. "It's just that I am certain I shall starve if I do not soon eat. Please could you spare me just one rabbit? I have money, if payment is what you're after. Please, could you find it in your heart to spare even one?"

The hunter snapped, "I told ye already, these rabbits are fer Angus and me and no one else. If ye're hungry for rabbit, then go and catch one yersel'."

The hunter turned his back on Jack, and in turn, it was like Jack was possessed by Auld Clootie himself. Rage such as he'd never experienced before overtook him. He rushed up behind the man and thrust his head down into the stream and did not let it back up even when the hunter flailed and splashed, and Angus the dog flapped and yapped around him. Jack kept the man's head submerged under the icy water until finally the hunter's body slackened. The hunter rolled over, his body as lifeless as his rabbits.

His rage having swiftly abated, Jack cried out in horror for what he had done. He had never hurt a person before in his life, and now he had killed! The thought made him sick with regret, and he released the limp body into the burn, watching the water carry it gently away while Angus the dog followed after, yelping for his master to return.

But though Jack's rage had vanished, his hunger had not, and now he had all the hunter's rabbits to himself. He took them, and roasted them over a fire, and ate every last one.

When he was done, his belly moaned as if he had not eaten a bite.

Jack could not fathom it—twelve rabbits and still he was hungry—but he wasted no time guessing and continued on down the trail in search of something more to eat.

Eventually the trail wound its way out of the forest and led him past a small cottage on a grassy hill. In the front of the cottage Jack saw a wee girl of two, who sang a little song while she picked bluebells from the grass. She was a bonnie girl, with white-gold hair that fell down in silky ringlets. A woman several years older than Jack, who must have been the girl's mother, came out of the cottage and called out, "Hen, your supper's almost—oh!" That's when she saw Jack on the path and said, "What's a young lad like yersel' doing traveling all alone on this path? We dinnae see many travelers out this way."

Jack said, "Why, I'm just looking for something to eat. I'm very hungry, you see, and I haven't any food."

The mother said, "Say nae more, son. Come on in and have yersel' a bite to eat. We've got more than enough to share."

Jack thanked the woman, and came into the cottage, and introduced himself to the mother and her two bairns: the little girl he had seen picking bluebells in the grass, and her older brother, who was no more than five. Jack took a seat at the table and got to talking to the family, who were very kind and warm and full of laughter and asked if he had anywhere to lodge for the night. Jack admitted he did not.

"Then ye'll kip here tonight," said the children's mother. Jack found she would not take no for an answer. He was very grateful to her, but not as grateful as he was hungry. Fortunately, she had cooked up one of his favorite dishes: lamb-and-potato stew, with a loaf of warm bread.

"It looks delicious!" Jack said, and so it tasted. He ate down his entire bowl, and his whole portion of bread, before anybody else was even half done.

"Why, ye must be very hungry indeed!" said the mother, and ladled Jack a second helping of stew. He ate this down too, as quick as the first. And though he should have been full, the stew, like the rabbit, did not satisfy him a bit. He felt hungrier now than he had all day.

The mother said, "Well, that's all the stew and bread there is. I'm afraid ye're gonnae have to wait till breakfast for anything more."

"Please," Jack said, "isn't there anything else I can eat? I'm ravenous still. Please, can you cook me something else?"

"I'm sorry," said the mother, "but ye've had enough already. Gluttony is the work of the Deil, and he isnae welcome at my table. I'm sorry, son, but ye'll no' get one more bite to eat from me th' nicht."

For the second time Jack was afflicted with a sudden, uncontrollable rage. He snatched up the knife the mother had used to slice the bread and drove it down into her breast. Her eyes sparkled wide, and she dropped to the floor, and Jack took up the knife and plunged it again and again into her bosom, painting the walls of the cottage with her blood. The woman's daughter screamed. Her son wept as he assailed Jack with his hands and his feet. Twisting around, Jack applied the blade swiftly to the boy's throat. Finally, he silenced the girl.

His hands still clenched her white throat when, with a tremor of despair, he came back to himself and realized what an unforgivable thing he had done. It was too much to bear, and he wanted it gone: every trace of his evil act.

Tears poured down his face as, half a mile down the path, he turned back to watch the cottage burn.

But what could Jack do but carry on?

He had traveled no more than three or four miles before he came upon a village, not unlike the one he had visited with the horn. It looked to be a good size, with plenty of provisions for a traveler like himself. Jack spotted an inn and decided to go there, hoping to find lodging for the night. He entered the establishment and the old innkeeper greeted him heartily, even though it was obvious he was foreign. Jack informed the old man that it was lodging he was after. "O' course, laddie," the innkeeper said, and then he shouted out for his daughter.

In hurried this bonnie lassie. Jack looked at the old innkeeper's daughter, and she was the most beautiful lassie he had ever laid eyes on. The moment Jack saw her he knew there was something special about the girl; he knew in an instant he must make her his wife.

The innkeeper told his daughter, "This young lad'll be lodging wi' us th' nicht. Be a good lass and show him to his . . ."

But Jack did not hear another word, for he had bolted out of the pub. He could not stay there, could not stay in the village at all. Not for a night or a single moment longer.

He was hungry, hungrier now than ever before. His stomach felt like it was eating itself with teeth like silver daggers. All the food in the village, he felt sure, would not be enough to sate this hunger, and when it was not, he would lose control. He would end them all—even the love of his heart.

And so he rushed out of the village, into a field, and paced back and forth in a frenzy. He thought, What do I do? Will I never cease to be plagued by this accursed hunger? Why, I'd sell my soul to the Devil just to be cured!

And that is when the stranger reappeared before him, tall and dark and dressed in black from head to toe. Jack saw him and said, "Stranger! Please, I need your help!"

The stranger said, "What ails you, my friend?" But it was as if he already knew; the stranger did not appear at all surprised as Jack told him about the hunger, how it had driven him again and again to madness.

"Well, of course," replied the stranger. "You did not blow the horn. You brought this upon yourself, Jack, with your dishonesty."

Jack apologized for the lie, and for failing to carry out the stranger's wishes. "It's just that one blast of the horn would have woken the whole village," he said.

"Then you should have woken them," said the stranger, "and nourished yourself."

Jack said, "I'm sorry. I beg you, just take this hunger away. Make it stop before I hurt anyone else."

The stranger said, "I'll end your hunger—again, if you complete a task of my choosing."

"I'll do anything," Jack said. "Anything you ask!"

And in the stranger's hands appeared, once more, a horn like off the head of a goat. "You want me to blow it," Jack said, "and make everyone in the village hear its sound? I'll do it. Give it here, I'll do it!"

The stranger said, "That was a fair price to pay to satisfy your natural hunger; to sate this accursed famine, you must do even more. You must blow into this horn, and make everyone in Scotland hear its call."

Jack believed it was impossible. Still, what had he to lose by trying? And so he took the horn in his hands and he brought it to his lips and, where before he had faltered, now he sucked up the sky, and with all the strength of his pain, and his love for the old innkeeper's daughter, and his desperation to finally be free, he blew.

The sound was as colossal as it was terrible, as loud as thunder and shrill as terror itself. Piercing the firmament like a flaming arrow, it engulfed whatever it touched in agony and destruction. Jack's ears poured, leaving a bloody smear on his hand when he wiped them. But he had done it. Every man, woman, and child in the land had heard the sound of the horn.

And once again the stranger kept his promise, producing a simple loaf of bread, which he held out to Jack. "One bite of this bread and your hunger will flee," he said, "and once again you'll crave food like a normal man."

Jack took the loaf, and champed down on it. It was the most delicious bread he had ever tasted. Instantly the hunger disappeared from his body—and that is when Jack heard the screams.

At that precise moment every person in the village, every person in Scotland, rushed out of their homes, howling in terror.

"The Deil! I heard him! I heard his call!"

"The Deil, back in our beautiful land!"

"God save us from Black Donald, returned to Scotland!"

And suddenly the stranger was gone.

Rushing back into the village, Jack found his bride-to-be shrieking and spluttering upon the ground, blood coursing from her ears and tears streaming down her face. He tried to comfort her, but she was inconsolable.

He asked her, "What is it? What's wrong?"

And looking up into his eye, she wailed, "I'm feart—feart what I might do with the Deil returned!"

Jack said, "Don't be afraid. Just eat this."

And he gave her what remained of the enchanted bread.

She devoured the loaf, and the moment she swallowed down the first bite, her sobs subsided and the tears stilled in her eyes. She looked around at the other villagers, including her father, who remained imprisoned by the spell of the horn. The man could not be helped.

Jack said, "We must go. We must leave this place."

His love nodded and he helped her to her feet. And forsaking the fear that gripped the country in its black, taloned fist, Jack and his love set off down the path, foot by foot, hand in hand.

And that is the end of my story.

Thirty-One

READING THE FOLKTALE for a second time was different. The earthshaking, incapacitating fear I'd experienced at thirteen was like a memory from a past life. This time, I experienced only a sickening sense of clarity.

Jack's story bore an extraordinary likeness to my own. For all our differences, we both had been beguiled by the Devil, signed away our soul for an earthly pittance, only to be left with an unholy curse that wrought destruction wherever we went.

But there was a difference between us that gave me hope. Jack had managed to escape it. Prostrating himself before the Devil, he had made Scotland hear his master's call, and only then was he released from their bargain.

He did it by making Scotland remember the Devil.

That was it: to end the curse, I had to do as D.B. had instructed from the beginning.

But how? Jack at least had a magical horn. All D.B. had ever given me was a hack job of an introduction and a few scraps of so-called research. A collection of random, sinister documents meant to be magicked into—

The book.

Had the book been the answer all along? Was that why he'd looked so furious the night of the Christmas markets, why he'd beset me with this loathsome curse—because he was furious with me for pulling out of the deal? Was the curse my punishment, like Jack's hunger was his, for failing to keep my side of the bargain?

It all fit. The book was my Devil's horn. The instrument by which I would awaken the nation to his presence and finally be free of this curse.

And yet, writing a book was a great deal more complex than sounding a horn. It would have to be exceptional just to get published, let alone have any kind of impact on the country as a whole. Not just enlightening, but accessible too, and entertaining. A chart-topping success.

Or did it?

I dug out our contract, needing to be certain of the wording.

This Contract Agreement for Writing Services ("Agreement") is effective as of 13 September 2016, and entered into by and between Grayson Hale ("G.H.") and Donald Blackburn ("D.B."), for the development and delivery of one original manuscript of literary nonfiction . . .

According to this document, all I needed was to produce a manuscript.

That I could do.

At the very least I had to try. If not for my sake, then the sake of the people I might hurt if I didn't. If not for my sake, then for Liam's.

No more procrastinating. No more shrinking away in fear.

It was time to make Scotland remember the Devil.

Thirty-Two

I STARTED IMMEDIATELY.

First was research.

I raided the library. Pulled together as much source material as they would let me leave with. Books on Scottish history, novels, journal articles, archived newspapers, anything that could attest to the country's obsession with the demonic. Read all day and into the night, continuously collecting my half-formed thoughts into a sprawling, twenty-page document of bullet points stretched out to rambling paragraphs. Pulled out the most cogent insights among them and grouped them into broad categories: the impact of Calvinism, the witch hunts, English oppression, popular occulture. Plastered my bedroom walls with huge swaths of paper, turning them black with marker scratch—an outline of sorts, which became increasingly frenzied the longer I worked at it, with endless crossings-out and insertions and notes scribbled in the margins, and yet somehow more lucid, every day a little closer to coherence. The glossy black handwriting glittered in the moonlight, alive with the promise of genuine discovery.

Christmas Day came and went. New Year's Eve passed almost without notice. With Ollie gone home for the holidays, the flat was silent, free from distractions. I hardly left except to visit the library and replenish my stock of soda. Meals could be ordered in. It was better that way; at least at home, on my own, nothing could bait me into losing control.

At the end of two weeks, I was nowhere near done reading and thinking and outlining, but at least I had something to work with. A compass pointing me in the direction of a book.

Leaving the introduction for last, I dove straight into the body of the text, and drowned in an ocean of insecurity. I questioned my eloquence, my understanding of key concepts. I doubted the strength of my arguments. Was it an exaggeration to say that for many Scots the English government had become the new Satan? Was my evidence, a letter written by a high-ranking member of the Jacobite army calling King George II "a demon of royal blood" and "the enemy of God," enough to carry the weight of my argument? I kept thinking of my father, reading the words back through his eyes, and experiencing his disappointment as if it were my own. Some days my self-doubt was so all-consuming I struggled to drag myself out of bed before three in the afternoon. Even then, I barely managed to keep the document open in front of me, cycling repeatedly through email, Facebook, the news. Checking for nonexistent updates about Liam, though police had begun searching for his body. On my worst day I managed less than a hundred words.

Is it any wonder the fiends returned? Could I blame them for swarming the windows, for filling the flat with their odious gibbering? They came bearing a message I needed to hear: D.B. saw my dithering, and he wasn't impressed. *Keep this up and he will come for you.*

How could I be so careless with my winter break, so wasteful of my one opportunity to make significant progress on the book without the constant interruption of classes and work? In just over a week the new semester would start. I would be forced back into the society of my classmates, my lecturers, one-on-ones with Fiona—and as long as the book remained unfinished, I was a liability to myself and others.

Casting aside my inhibitions, I recommitted myself to the book.

Morning and night, I did nothing but write. Most days the words came easily; others, it was like pushing a boulder uphill. But still I pounded away at the keys, refusing to be distracted by anything—insecurity, mental exhaustion. Some days I even forgot to eat, holding my cravings at bay with endless cans of Diet Coke. They formed a growing mountain of silver on the carpet and bore me aloft on a fizzing high of chemical sweetness and caffeine, as if my body had internalized the buzz of the fiends and sent it shooting back and forth between my brain, heart, and fingertips.

I spoke to no one. Not even Sophie, who had been in touch several times, clearly distraught about Liam's disappearance and disturbed by the rumors of my involvement, saying things like "I can't cope" and "I really need to speak with you." I didn't have time to be dragged into her misery. I had wasted too much time already.

But I made up for it now. Once I hit my stride, I was writing upward of three thousand words per day, the minimum needed to appease my employer. Less than that, and something bad would happen. I believed this without question, as incontrovertible as gravity.

Classes started up again mid-January, as did my TA appointment. I managed to tear myself away from writing for a few hours to attend a few classes and muddle through a tutorial for English Literature II. In the end, it didn't matter that I hadn't done any of the reading, for all anyone seemed to be talking about was me. Their whispers followed me from class to class and swirled around the lecture hall. *Isn't that that guy? Which guy? The American who was last seen with that missing student, Liam something? I read he was arrested but they didn't have enough evidence to hold him.* Hardly anyone showed up to the tutorial, and those who did seemed to do so on a dare. Five minutes in, a male student stuck his hand in the air and said, "I just found out my mate was texting my girlfriend behind my back. Any advice for how to make him disappear?"

Until now, the university had done right by me; their public statement on Liam's disappearance took a neutral stance as far as I was concerned, affirming that I was a student in good standing and would remain so until more significant evidence of wrongdoing came to light. But now they were receiving complaints, not just from students but parents too, threatening to stop tuition payments unless I was removed. I was summoned to meet with the head of the English department and, when I didn't show up, she called to deliver the news that although my enrollment wasn't affected, my teaching assistance was no longer required.

It would be a hit to my finances but otherwise a stroke of luck. Just a week into the semester, it was already clear I couldn't maintain my output on the book while also researching and writing a separate thesis, passing two classes, and maintaining my university employment. I would have liked to defer my place altogether and focus on the book, but that was out of the question; full-time enrollment was the only thing keeping me in the country. So in addition to leaving the TA job, I scaled back my attendance to the bare minimum and formally changed my research topic.

Fiona, when I next met with her, loved the new title of my thesis: *A History of Fear: The Devil in Scottish Culture and Literature.*

With that, I was just about able to meet my daily goal. Three thousand words a day, about a chapter a week. Much of it garbage, sure—but not all. Now and again I read back a passage so cleverly worded, so original in its conjecture, that I couldn't help but fire it off to D.B.

For the first time in a long time, I felt good, even as my life began to crumble around me: Sophie became increasingly desperate, and I received increasingly dire messages from my lecturers, threatening to fail me if I didn't start showing up to class. My PhD aspirations were in jeopardy, but I couldn't think about that now. I just needed to keep going, needed to rid myself of this curse. Two hundred pages written. The first draft half done. In another few months I'd be free of my employer, and twenty thousand pounds richer. The end of my torment was in sight.

D.B. didn't immediately respond to the bits and pieces I sent him, but I could tell, by the fiends' mellowed attitude, that he was pleased. They huddled languorously on the windowsill, their gibbering like a contented purr. I could practically hear him in my ear, whispering praise.

That's it, son . . . you're almost there.

Editor's Note
Exhibits P, Q, and R

Excerpt of my interview with Fiona Wood, professor of Scottish literature at the University of Edinburgh and Grayson Hale's academic supervisor, recorded in person at her office on Buccleuch Place, 11 June 2019.

WOOD: It was all going fine until second term. Suddenly he [Hale] seemed a different person.

BARCLAY: Different how?

WOOD: He became quite hostile. Even in email. *I'm extremely busy, I need your answer today*—that sort of thing. And his appearance . . . it was shocking. We had a supervision meeting end of January and when he came into my office I almost didn't recognize him. I was aghast, and blurted out something silly. "Wow, you look well." Something like that. But if I'm being honest, he looked quite ill. His eyes were sunken, his skin was sallow, and he'd lost just an *incredible* amount of weight.

BARCLAY: How much?

WOOD: Two stone maybe? Mind you, it had only been about a month since I'd seen him.

BARCLAY: Did you ask him about it?

WOOD: Didn't have the chance. He wouldn't even sit, just shut the door and started talking about wanting to change his research topic. Pacing around, quite frenetic. He wanted to write about the Devil. The Devil in Scotland.

BARCLAY: Had he ever mentioned the subject before?

WOOD: Never.

BARCLAY: That must've come as quite a surprise, then.

WOOD: It's fairly common for students to change their research topics, but rarely that dramatically, or so late in the academic year. I was more concerned than anything. Thought the stress might be getting to him. I admitted it wasn't a topic I knew much about, so I wasn't sure I'd be much help to him. He said I'd never been much help to him anyway.

BARCLAY: Gosh.

WOOD: It was the way he said it, really. Quite vicious. [Sobbing] He seemed to really hate me.

BARCLAY: Oh dear. I think I have a tissue.

WOOD: Thank you. Sorry, I'm being silly.

BARCLAY: Not at all. That must've been quite frightening.

WOOD: I was a bit speechless to say that least.

BARCLAY: But you agreed, didn't you? To the change in topic?

WOOD: I didn't feel I had any choice.

BARCLAY: Of course you didn't.

WOOD: He left straightaway after that. Didn't even say goodbye.

Incident report filed by Patrick Hay, library assistant at the University of Edinburgh, on 6 February 2017.

UNIVERSITY OF EDINBURGH
Incident Report Form

EMPLOYEE DETAILS

REPORT FILED BY   *Patrick Hay*

EMPLOYEE ID   ▮▮▮▮▮

DEPARTMENT   *Library Services*

PHONE/EMAIL   ▮▮▮▮▮

DESCRIPTION OF INCIDENT

Location: *Front Desk, Main Library (30 George Square, Edinburgh EH8 9LJ)*

Date: *5 Feb. 2017*

Time: 11:15 PM

Police Notified:

[X] No

[ ] Yes

INCIDENT DETAILS:

CAUCASIAN male student, midtwenties, North American, approached library desk with numerous books. Upon scanning ID card, I informed student he had nearly reached checkout limit and could only take away two more. Student became abusive, shouting profanity and demanding his ID back. While lunging across desk to retrieve his ID, student inadvertently knocked computer monitor to the floor and broke it (student info lost in the process). Security was called. Student managed to wrestle back his ID and ran, removing the books illegally from library before security could arrive. Last seen heading west toward George Square.

HR NOTES (PLEASE LEAVE BLANK)

Incident details confirmed by on-site security staff. CCTV footage unavailable due to ongoing issues with main library camera system, as reported to security director on 22/12/16.

Testimony of Sophia Grant in the trial of Grayson Hale, continued.

HIGH COURT OF JUSTICIARY
HM Advocate v. Hale [2017]
Transcript of Proceedings

ADVOCATE DEPUTE: Was there ever a time when you had cause to doubt the accused's mental stability?

GRANT: Once. After Liam went missing.

ADVOCATE DEPUTE: Please elaborate if you would.

GRANT: Everyone was saying Grayson was responsible, that he had *done* something to Liam. I didn't want to believe it, but after hearing what Jenna said . . . I kept trying to contact him, Grayson, but he wouldn't answer. I went to his flat and when I got there the door was unlocked. I let myself in. He was in his bedroom and . . .

ADVOCATE DEPUTE: What did you see, Ms. Grant?

GRANT: The first thing was the mess. Rubbish all over the floor. Clothes and takeaway containers and hundreds and hundreds of cans.

ADVOCATE DEPUTE: Cans?

GRANT: Fizzy drink. Diet Coke, all of them.

ADVOCATE DEPUTE: Was the accused's bedroom always like this in your experience?

GRANT: No. No, not at all. He wasn't himself. I could see that straightaway. He didn't even acknowledge me when I came in. Just sat hunched over his desk, typing fast. I thought maybe he was trying to meet an essay deadline. But then I noticed the walls. They were covered in all sorts. Posters and papers, pages torn out of books, strange images.

ADVOCATE DEPUTE: What kinds of images?

GRANT: Drawings of pentagrams. Devils. Photographs of naked women on altars, bleeding from their throats. Terrible things. I was so frightened I, well, I started to get upset. I even gave him a shake, but it was like he was in some sort of trance. He just shrugged me off. Eyes glazed. His fingers flying across the keyboard. It looked like he'd been at it for days, maybe longer. I could tell he hadn't showered. He had lost so much weight. And the words on the screen . . . I was quite surprised, reading them. I don't remember the specifics, but it was academic writing, like an essay. I said, "Grayson, what's going on? What are you writing?" Then I realized he was murmuring.

ADVOCATE DEPUTE: Murmuring?

GRANT: Very quietly. I had to lean in to hear him.

ADVOCATE DEPUTE: What was he saying?

GRANT: *"He's here. Make them remember. Make them remember."* I said, "Who's here? Make who remember?" It was like I had set something off inside him. His voice got louder. He stood up, stiff as a board. Shouting now. Screaming. *"Make them remember! Make them remember! Never again forget the Devil!"* He rushed at me, and I screamed, and all of a sudden he stopped dead. His head was tilted, angled toward the window. There was a strange smile on his face.

ADVOCATE DEPUTE: Strange?

GRANT: Like a child, but disturbed. He was whispering now. "Do you hear it? The gibbering, do you hear it?" I couldn't hear a thing. He said, "I never used to like it. But it's not so bad, really, is it?"

Thirty-Three

I WAS ON NINETY-SEVEN thousand words, chapter five of six, when a growing din from the sitting room intruded upon my concentration. It flooded in under the door like a rising tide, a sloshing roar of voices and laughter and music. Ollie hadn't mentioned a party. Then again, we'd hardly spoken since he got back from London. I'd been so consumed with the book, and almost immediately he had gone out of town again, traveling with his water polo team. How long had he been away? A couple days, a month? Even now, the weeks streak together in my mind, a dreamy brushstroke of intense, writerly focus.

I felt my jaw tighten in irritation as I typed. It wasn't just the noise that bothered me, but the fact that I hadn't been invited to join. I would have refused, but still I felt bruised and neglected. Every drunken cry and screech of laughter a reminder that I had been excluded, that I was not wanted. That even in my home, I did not belong.

More than I wanted peace, I wanted their happiness to stop. I wanted to take their smiles and their laughter and reduce them to ash.

I pushed back from the desk and burst into the sitting room—then halted, reeling at what I saw. Of the two dozen strangers desecrating my flat, at least half were men wearing next to nothing, their matching Speedos straining to contain their masculinity. I used my hand to shield my eyes from the unwelcome sight.

Spotting me through the crowd, Ollie sent up a cry. He too was nearly nude, his stomach soft and smooth, a trail of light hair spilling down his navel, toward a coarser undergrowth peeking out of the top of his swimwear. He was shouting at me, something about his water polo tournament—apparently they had won—but a low-down sensation of panic compelled me to retreat. Hurrying back into my bedroom, I slammed the door behind me and locked it.

Bang bang bang. I could hear Ollie's voice through the door.

"Come on, Grayson. Come have a drink."

"Leave me alone," I shouted.

A drawer crashed open behind me. I recoiled as a winged ball of black burst out of the desk. Another appeared from under the bed, and two more entered through the window, one holding it open so that its friend could crawl through.

Within seconds a dozen fiends had encircled me. They hissed and champed as their wings beat the air. But there was something different about them tonight, a subtle change in their disposition. Rather than threatening, they seemed indignant on my behalf, like they had come to assist me—and were awaiting my direction.

Bang bang bang.

"I said fuck off!"

But one fiend seemed to have a different idea. Breaking ranks, he streaked toward the door and scrabbled at the knob, struggling, with his long-taloned hands, to unlock it.

"No!" I lurched forward, too late. The door swung open just long enough for Ollie to stagger in, nearly falling to the floor, before the fiend slammed it shut behind him.

"You need to get out—" I began. But no sooner had he regained his balance than he was pulling me toward the party.

"Come on. One drink." He slung an arm around my shoulder. I could feel the heat of his body pushing in through my clothing.

I shoved him off me. "No!"

Ollie stopped.

The next thing I knew, his lips were on mine, his tongue drilling into my mouth.

I thrust him back. *"What are you doing?"* I bellowed.

Almost instantly terror displaced my fury. Interpreting my reaction as a command, the fiends swarmed him like a murder of crows besetting a worm. Their thin tails whipped the air as they tore at him, Ollie thrashing against them, his screams barely audible over the deafening music.

"GET OFF ME—NO," he pleaded, as they yanked him into the air by his leg—then swung him into the wall with a heavy thud, sending a cloud of notes and papers swirling.

"Get back!" I shouted.

I rushed forward, the fiends skittering away with bowed heads.

Ollie's ribs were deeply bruised. A raised mass swelled around his eye, bleeding. He looked like he'd lost a barroom brawl; his attackers' talons had left few cuts.

As I approached him, he shuddered, whimpering. "Please. No—"

"I'm not gonna hurt you."

"No more," he added breathlessly. "Just leave me alone."

———

Ollie's teammates had no trouble believing that their offensive center had spontaneously passed out cold on my bedroom floor but refused to accept this as adequate justification for putting an early end to their celebration. Only by threatening to have them removed by police did I manage to get them all out before the ambulance arrived.

The paramedics required a different story, which Ollie, lying unconscious on the floor, was in no state to contradict. I told them there was a party, and some guy took this girl into my bedroom. Apparently it was a girl Ollie liked, for he barged in and picked a fight with the guy. By the time I found him, I said, Ollie was like this and the couple had gone. The lie seemed to pass muster; they didn't ask any questions.

I followed the paramedics as far as the curb, declining their offer of a seat in the ambulance. I needed to get back to work on the book, and anyway, something told me I didn't want to be there when Ollie woke up.

Thirty-Four

T HE DISTANT SOUND of banging woke me the next morning.

I sat up in bed, the memory of the previous night resurfacing like a bout of acid reflux. As the banging continued, I was filled with dread. It was day. Ollie must have regained consciousness by now and told the hospital what had happened. Or at least some version of it. Not even he would be stupid enough to admit he'd been attacked by demons.

I answered the door, relieved not to find the police there. Instead it was a woman. She was not yet thirty but had the air of a matriarch, her hair pulled back in a sleek ponytail, a designer satchel slung over her shoulder.

"Can I help you?" I said.

"I'm Victoria. Ollie's sister?" she added impatiently, as if nothing could be more obvious. "I'm here to grab some of his things."

Without waiting for a response, she strode past me into the flat, halting as she impaled a Foster's can with her stiletto. I hadn't had a chance to clean the place up.

"Jesus," she spat, dislodging the can with disgust.

"You came from London?" I said.

"We all did. The rest of my family are at the hospital."

"How's he doing?"

She tutted. "You have a nerve asking that."

Why shouldn't I care how Ollie was? Had he said something?

"Hello?" she said. "Where's his room?"

"Last door on the left."

As she disappeared down the hall, I was tempted to follow her. My mind crackled with anxious questions. What had Ollie said about his injuries? Had he blamed me? Instead I grabbed a trash bag from the kitchen and began to fill it with detritus. It was nearly full when Victoria reemerged from her brother's bedroom, lugging two rolling suitcases toward the door.

"We're taking Ollie back to London. You should probably start looking for someplace else to live." She paused with a hand on the doorknob, her expression taut with repressed anger. "I just want you to know, if my father wasn't seeking reelection next year, you'd already be in jail. Lucky for you, it's in neither of our interests for this to make headlines. Apparently assault doesn't test well."

"Assault?"

"My brother may be scared of you," she said, "but I'm not. Touch him again and I promise you'll live to regret it."

"But I didn't. What did he—?"

She swung the cases into the hall, and slammed the door shut behind her.

As I stood there, my mind working to make sense of her parting words, I felt a throbbing pain in my right hand.

I grabbed it, and it smarted. That's when I saw it. How hadn't I noticed it before? The knuckles were bruised and swollen. Dried blood was caked in the creases of my fist, and the pain. It radiated up my arm, as if it had held itself back for eight hours and now was making up for lost time. The incident with the fiends must have spiked my adrenaline; I hadn't been aware of my body, unable to feel the effects until now.

I attacked Ollie. Nearly killed him with my bare hands. It was the only thing that made sense, and not just because of my hand. It was the only thing that explained why Ollie told his sister I had attacked him. Why, the previous night, his body had showed no cuts, only bruises and broken bones. The fiends had had nothing to do with it; I had imagined the whole thing.

Of course, the fiends had always been figments of my imagination. At least, that's what I told myself after my satanophobia went into remission, that they had only ever been a by-product of my condition. But since they had returned, something was different. It was like they were real in a way they never had been before, imbued with new power. They had torn my clothes, hoisted me up over the Old Town.

If I had imagined their attack on Ollie, how could I trust anything had been real? What other brutality had I enacted and projected onto a delusion of fiends?

More important, why?

Because the Devil was putting visions in my head, or because my head was conjuring visions of the Devil?

⁓

Not knowing where else to channel my fear, I returned to work on the book. My progress was slow, my mind unfocused. A thought kept nagging at me. Like an itch, it grew more intense the longer I left it.

I couldn't stop thinking about D.B.

Though I'd sent him three or four excerpts of the manuscript, I hadn't yet heard a word from him, not outside the veiled messages I had gleaned from the behavior of the fiends. Not even a text to acknowledge he'd received them.

Now I thought about it, how long had it been since we'd spoken? The last I recalled seeing him was at the Silver Stag—by my count, nine weeks before. Fourteen since the night of the Christmas markets.

Had it really been that long? How could so much time have passed without my notice? It was reckless, in a way. I had given everything to the book for weeks. Devoted endless hours, spurned relationships, nearly gotten myself thrown out of university for nonattendance. How could I have risked so much for this manuscript when more than three months had passed since I had heard from its commissioner?

Although I should have welcomed it, D.B.'s disappearance from my life felt ominous given all that had transpired since our last meeting—especially Liam's disappearance, the circumstances of which seemed to implicate me in a series of events that were absent from my memory. For months I had clung to the knowledge that, if it had been my doing, at least I had the Devil to blame, that it was under his influence I had acted. As such, D.B.'s absence felt less like a boon than an indictment against everything I had believed for months to be true.

Though I should have known better by this point, I grabbed my phone and rushed out a text.

DB, what's going on? Haven't heard from you in months. Please respond.

Even worse than not receiving a message back was the one that appeared on the screen a moment later, in red.

Not Delivered.

Writing it off as a fluke, I copied and pasted the message, sent it again, and waited. The message repeated itself.

Not Delivered.

My heart was beating uncomfortably fast. Tapping D.B.'s name at the top of the screen, I pressed the phone icon and held the receiver to my ear. It cut off abruptly after the first ring.

"The other person has cleared," answered a robotic female voice. Then the line went dead.

The other person has cleared? What did that even mean? A quick Google search confirmed my first guess: this was the British version of *I'm sorry, the number you have dialed is no longer in service.*

But why would D.B. change his number? Hadn't he hired me, paid me, hounded me for months to write his book? Why would he now be trying to avoid me?

Maybe, like the fiends, he never existed at all.

No. The fiends were different; only I had ever been able to see them, even as a teenager. But D.B. was real. I had evidence he existed—documents, photos, messages going back months. I just needed to hear from him. Needed to know the deal was still on. Needed to know that this wasn't all—

Just in your head?

No, I protested. Of course it wasn't in my head.

It couldn't be. If I'd imagined D.B. like I had imagined the fiends, that would mean—it didn't matter what. Because unlike the fiends, D.B. was real. I needed to find him, that was all.

I needed to find him now.

Thirty-Five

P AST THE END of the Royal Mile and the palace, hugging the curving green edge of Holyrood Park, Abbeyhill did not stand up to the beauty that surrounded it. Its streets of run-down flats were crowded with dumpsters and hatchbacks, a street corner tagged with graffiti. Fine for a working family or student, but it always seemed strange to me that D.B., with all his resources, would choose this area to call home.

With a little searching I managed to locate the shabby beige block of flats where we had ended our walk from the Witchery.

Beside the locked front door, a steel panel of call buttons contained only numbers. I was about to start trying buttons at random when suddenly the door swung inward. I stepped aside, allowing a woman to pass. Rosacea burned her cheeks and nose a livid red, only partially obscured by the bushy mane of hair that fell around her face.

We acknowledged each other with thin smiles. But as I moved toward the door closing behind her, she stopped as if to block my passage.

"Can I help you?" Even as she spoke, she did not look directly at me, angling her head down toward the pavement.

The door clicked shut.

"Sorry, I'm looking for someone. He lives in this building but I'm not sure—"

"Pradeep?"

"Um. No. His name's D.B. I mean Donny—"

"Pradeep's the only man what lives here. The rest is lasses."

"Right," I said. "Maybe you've seen my friend. He's about thirty. Dark hair." I felt silly saying it: "Wears a lot of black?"

"Sorry."

Fearing that if I lingered any longer the woman might call the police, I thanked her for her help and retreated from the building, heading back up toward the Old Town.

So D.B. didn't live there. That didn't prove anything. He'd never exactly said he did, and as I had already determined, it was unlikely to begin with.

Still, my desire to find him was starting to burn. If not him, then at least some sign of him: the smallest reassurance to quiet the apprehensions caterwauling in my head like the siren of the firetruck that could be heard in the distance. It flew past the end of the lane with a short burst of unpleasant sound, reminding me of the ambulance that screamed down the Cowgate the night the skinhead was attacked.

Infyrno was just one street over from the Royal Mile, not far from where I was headed anyway. Would the club be open at this hour? Would anyone who works there know D.B.?

Determined to try, I made my way in that direction, feeling displaced as I reached the Cowgate some fifteen minutes later. Had I been seeing things that night, or was the street completely different in the daylight? Instead of seedy bars and leering strangers, I found an attractive, pitched lane filled with chain hotels and trendy watering holes closed until late afternoon. Passing under the archway of South Bridge, I emerged before a tall sandstone building that looked like an office, followed by a pebble-dash one occupied by a youth hostel.

I stopped, my eyes lashing back and forth along the street. This is where Infyrno had been—just after the archway. But the converted church wasn't there. It was like it had fizzled into the atmosphere and the buildings on either side had sidled over to fill the available space.

How does a building just *fucking disappear*?

You imagined it. You imagined it, just like you imagined him.

But I hadn't imagined him. The evidence was on my phone. As if to prove it to myself, I opened the text I had sent him that morning and scrolled up to find messages going back to September.

Writing going well. At 70,000 words. Another excerpt coming soon.

Just sent you an excerpt. Let me know if I'm on the right track.

Need to talk ASAP.

Okay, plans canceled. I'll be there.

Sorry, have plans with a friend that night. Rain check?

Sure, that works. See you then.

That would be great. Looking forward to it.

They were all . . . from me.

Where were his replies? There'd been dozens of them. All the angry texts he'd sent after I quit the project. His demands that I meet him on the Cowgate, at the Witchery, the Devil's Advocate. All gone.

I told you: you imagined it all. There never was anyone named D.B.

If there was no D.B., then how did I explain the money sitting in my account right now? He had paid me an advance, a thousand pounds on signing, then a further nine. How could I have simply *imagined* ten thousand pounds that I'd been living off of for months?

But you haven't been living off it. You had it wired to your American account weeks ago.

Then it should still be there.

I pulled up my US mobile banking app and punched in my details. A circle of dots appeared on the screen before my information loaded, delivering an impossible result: the account was nearly as empty as I had left it in August.

But I was certain that I had ordered a transfer. I remembered because I'd had to go into the bank to do it. Surely they would have kept a record of it?

Heading back the way I'd come, I eventually turned up a side street, and from there managed to find my way to the upper streets of the Old Town. The Royal Bank of Scotland branch on Nicolson, where I'd made the transfer, was just a few blocks away.

On a Saturday morning the bank was busy. I waited nearly a quarter of an hour before the teller, a girl no older than nineteen, greeted me from behind the glass window.

"Thanks for your patience. How can I—?"

"Can you confirm that a wire for ten thousand pounds was made from my account?" I said, sliding my debit card and ID into the tray.

"Of course, sir," she said, appearing not to register my rudeness. "Do you know the transaction date by any chance?"

"November something. I'm not sure."

"No problem. Let me just take a look here."

I waited, my hands jittering against the counter. My whole body thrummed with nervous energy. She was taking forever.

"How's it coming?" I said.

"Sorry. Computer's running a little slowly today, stupid thing."

Finally, she managed to get my details on-screen.

"Sorry, sir," she said, brow furrowed as she looked at my account. "I can't see any record of a wire transfer. Do you have a confirmation number? You would have received one when the transfer was made."

"Not anymore," I snapped.

She continued to search my account history, looking tense. After a moment, something changed in her expression.

"Ten thousand pounds, you said it was?"

"You found it?"

"Not a wire transfer, but I do see that two cash withdrawals totaling ten thousand pounds were made from your account around that time. One for a thousand pounds on the thirteenth of September, and another for nine thousand pounds on the tenth of October."

"Cash?"

"From an RBS branch. This one, in fact. And—that's odd. It appears those same amounts were deposited back into the account shortly after. One thousand on the fifteenth of September and nine thousand on the eleventh of October."

"You're saying I took the money out—then deposited it again?"

She hesitated, perhaps afraid I might snap at her again. "That's what it looks like. Sorry, sir," she added sympathetically. "S'there anything else I can—?"

"The Devil's Advocate."

"Pardon?"

"Tell me if you see a charge for the Devil's Advocate. In September."

"The Devil's Advocate," she repeated under her breath, already working on it.

"And another for the Witchery, in November."

"Here, the Devil's Advocate," said the teller. "Fifty-nine pounds forty, on the thirteenth of September."

The day I met D.B. for dinner. *I paid for the meal myself.*

"And on the tenth of October," she continued, "one hundred and eleven pounds and eighty pence at the Witchery by the Castle."

"One hundred elev—*fuck.*"

"There's one other thing as well. Seems a bit strange, but it might not be anything."

"What is it?" I wasn't sure how much more I could handle.

"On the eleventh of November. Twelve pounds at—it's just numbers and letters. You might want to put this into your phone: S-L-V-S-T-E-H-1-3-A-A."

I had her read it out to me again as I punched the numbers into Google. The realization hit me half a second before the proof appeared on my screen: on the night of November eleventh, D.B. hadn't thrust a drink in my hand at Infyrno; I had bought my own, at the Silver Stag.

"Sir?"

But how? Sophie's birthday was the first time I'd been inside, and that wasn't until mid-December. Or had I misremembered that too?

Haven't seen you here in a while, the bartender had said.

"Sir? Are you all right?" The voice of the teller became smaller as I lurched toward the exit. "Sir?"

I burst through the door, nearly sending a man leaping back into on-coming traffic. I needed to get home. There lay my only hope. The last shred of evidence I had in defense of my sanity. The final strand of sense keeping my life from blowing apart.

Arriving back at the flat ten minutes later, I headed straight to the bedroom, straight across to the desk. I paused, my hand poised on the bottom drawer, begging it not to be empty, and yanked it back.

Relief and amazement flooded through me. The drawer was full of documents. Hundreds of them. News clippings, printouts, a torn-out sheet of notebook paper, all covered in D.B.'s spiky handwritten—

No.

D.B.'s notes. They had vanished.

I checked every page. Not so much as a squiggle. D.B.'s longhand introduction reduced to a blank, jagged-edged scrap.

As far as anyone could tell, I had assembled these documents myself and mailed them to my own address.

I was in the process of opening my bank details again, this time to check for postal charges, when something at the bottom of the drawer caught my eye. A small corner of yellow poking out from underneath the mess of papers.

A Post-it. The one I had found months ago in one of D.B.'s mailings. But unlike the rest of these documents, his writing still lay upon it. At least I had thought it was his.

dbismyname
DevInScot2016

Upon first discovering the note, I had questioned whether it was meant for me. It looked like a login—the login, I had assumed, to D.B.'s personal email.

Immediately I opened my laptop and navigated to Gmail. Logging out of my account, I clicked the empty text box and typed *dbismyname @gmail.com*, then tabbed down to the box below and added the supposed password.

I hit return.

An inbox filled the screen. An inbox containing less than twenty messages, all of them unread.

All of them from me.

I guided my cursor to the left-hand panel. It moved lethargically across the screen, as if mired. Burdened by the weight of my encroaching doom.

Finally, the cursor hovered over the word *Sent*.

As I clicked, an expanse of white filled the screen, sprawling and barren as a tundra, oblivious to the chaos it had just screamed into my life.

The folder was empty.

Not one message had been sent from this account.

All those emails I'd received from D.B. were just the same as those texts and those dinners: I had imagined them all. Donald Blackburn did not exist. The Devil wasn't real.

The longer I sat with that thought, the more life as I knew it seemed to unravel, like a favored sweater, comfortable and well-worn, stripped down to a pile of disordered yarn.

If I was not possessed of the Devil's powers of influence, then everything I believed about the last few months had been a lie. The fiends had not attacked Ollie; I had. A faceless stranger had not attacked the man at Waverley Mall; I had. The Devil had not caused Liam's disappearance; I had done that too, and wiped the memory from my consciousness to avoid the pain of having to face the truth—that my best friend was gone because I had hurt him.

Or had our friendship been invented too, an added layer to the all-consuming delusion? That would explain his outburst that night at the Silver Stag. *I've barely even spoken to ye, ye fucking psycho!* It would explain, too, why Liam in the flesh and the Liam I knew by text were almost like separate people. Why, for weeks before he disappeared, he had avoided me, distrust and dislike written in plain English on his face. We had never been friends. I had imagined his confidence like I had imagined D.B. Every text, every look, every small way he made me feel seen: every bit of him I had come to admire was a lie.

It all fit.

I was sick. Dangerously sick. I had hurt people. Likely even killed. And if I did not get help, I would do it again.

But how could I, with Liam still missing? A psychologist might be able to help me manage my delusions, but if I told them any of what I now knew—that I'd been unknowingly hurting people for months, possessed of a violence I could not control—they would be obliged to turn that information over to the authorities. They would know that I was involved in Liam's disappearance. I'd be arrested, tried for murder, a plea of insanity my only hope of freedom.

No—I couldn't say a word. I had to pretend none of this had ever happened. I ought to move home—no, not right away. It would look like I was running. I had to finish my degree first. Yes, then I could go back to the States, get a job somewhere. Claw back some semblance of the banal existence that I once took for granted.

But first, I had to erase D.B. from my personal history. Eliminate any scrap of evidence that I had ever been ill.

That same day, I deactivated the email I once thought of as D.B.'s. Deleted our one-sided text conversations from my phone. Removed all evidence of the book from my walls and my desk, making a plan, as I did so, to set them alight and scatter their ashes from the top of Arthur's Seat. Already I could imagine the weightless feeling I would have as the powdery remnants dispersed into the atmosphere, carrying my troubles away on the wind.

But a minor disruption cut my reverie short. As I removed a handful of documents from the drawer, something slid out from them and hit the floor.

Upon closer inspection, I realized it was a photograph. One of the several Polaroids of himself that D.B. had mailed me some months back—coincidentally, the one of my employer on Arthur's Seat, beside a younger, brown-haired stranger. *Edinburgh*, read the inscription beneath the image.

It took a second for the significance of the photo to sink in.

It was unchanged from the time I had received it. Unlike the handwriting that had disappeared from his documents, the image of D.B. remained intact. There he was, smiling up at me in full color: photographic evidence that at some point in time my employer had existed.

What did this mean? How could he be present in this photo when everything else seemed to suggest he had existed only in my mind?

That was not all.

As I continued to stare at the photo, it was not D.B.'s face that drew my eye, but that of the brown-haired stranger.

I brought the photo closer, staring hard in sick disbelief.

The man was my age, maybe a couple years older, yet his bearing was that of one who had not experienced much life. Reticently he gazed at the camera, head bowed, shoulders piked, hands buried in the pockets of his Sherpa-lined jacket.

I remembered thinking, the first time I saw the photo, that he was familiar to me somehow.

Now I realized why: I knew him. Or an older version of him, at least.

The man in the photo was my father.

Thirty-Six

I T DIDN'T SEEM possible. My father knew D.B.? My father, Edmund Hale, an ordained reverend of the Elected Heart, was once friends with the man I strongly suspected of being the Devil?

But that would mean D.B. was real, and had been in Edinburgh in the 1970s. If this photograph was to be trusted, he hadn't aged a day in more than thirty years.

I felt as if I were trapped in a never-ending collision, thrown from the seat of one vehicle only to be hit by another. Just hours ago I had come around to the idea that D.B. was a product of my fractured psyche, and now here was ostensible proof that he not only existed, but that his existence did not conform to the rules that bound all living things.

The uncertainty of it was maddening, especially as the threat of my arrest loomed ever nearer. Although two months had passed since the story first broke, the public interest in Liam's disappearance had barely abated. Every few days seemed to bring a new search, a fresh assurance that the police were "exploring all possible lines of inquiry," each new development adding a block of ice to the cold soup of anxiety that sloshed around my vital organs. It felt like the worst would come at any moment: they would find his body and charge me with his murder, and this time I would have no hope of escape. No procedural loophole to ensure my freedom. My fate was all but sealed.

I thought about packing up and flying back to the States, finding someplace to lie low for a while. At the very least it would buy me some time. While I was there perhaps I could dig up more information on my father's time in Scotland.

Then it hit me.

Crossing to the nightstand, I confirmed that it was still there, that it was real. I was not disappointed. The scrap of paper I had extracted from the floorboards of my father's old flat on Ratcliffe Terrace. The journal entry whose date matched the time period my father had lived there, bearing handwriting so very like his.

It was true, then: he had kept a written journal of his time in Edinburgh. If he met the Devil in Scotland, would he have mentioned it in his journal? Could this torn-out narrative, of having witnessed a terrible crime, have anything to do with D.B.?

What were the chances he had kept his old journals? He'd never mentioned them, but that wasn't necessarily out of character. What would have been out of character was for him to have thrown them away; he never got rid of any of his writing. The journals were probably moldering in a box at this very moment, waiting to be exhumed. My money-grubbing mother would want to publish them as soon as the dust settled on his casket, flog them to the believers for whatever she could get.

Maybe that was the answer to everything: the journals. If I could just get my hands on them, I would be one step closer to knowing the truth, maybe even to proving that D.B. was real and I wasn't a murderer. Either they would save me or they would be my undoing.

In any case, I needed to go home.

⌒

It wasn't until the plane pulled back from the gate that I finally breathed a sigh of relief. By now, I was so accustomed to bad luck that I half expected to be stopped at check-in, my passport marked with an order to prevent me from leaving the country. To my surprise, the immigration officer had scanned my passport without a second's pause, handing it back with an extra stamp and a perfunctory "Enjoy your flight."

The hazy light of afternoon pressed in through the porthole window as we taxied. I could feel its cold breath on my face as I stared out, my mind drifting to Dad.

I might have denied it, but for the first time I was glad he was dead. It was a relief that he'd never know all the ways I had ashamed him.

I had come to this country to honor his memory by finishing what he'd started all those years ago. But rather than carrying on his legacy, I had undermined it, falling prey to the one being he had dedicated his life to fighting. In trying to become the man my father never could, I ended up becoming the son he never would have wanted.

For all the turmoil I had found here, my heart broke to be leaving the country, not because I would miss it, but because I had never felt closer to him.

Unzipping the bag at my feet, I rummaged through the inside pocket for the Polaroid of Edmund and D.B. on Arthur's Seat, gazing at it without removing it from the bag. It was the only vestige of my employer I had kept. In my defense, it was the only photo of my father I had.

Though I had seen the photo a hundred times already, I was struck by the strangeness of Edmund's expression. Despite his uncertain stance, a smile played on his lips. A small, twisted repression of joy, as bright as a mirror reflecting the sun. I had not seen him look that happy my entire life. How long had it been before he discovered his friend's true identity?

I thought again of the impossible choice my father had been forced to make, the one he had regretted the rest of his life. I wondered now if that decision had anything to do with D.B. Was that why he had abandoned his studies and moved home? Was he the reason my father had ended his life?

I've resisted the urge for as long as I could bear—but as you'll one day understand, one temptation or the other was always bound to win.

One *temptation* or the other, he had said. Had he been trying to tell me something?

"Sorry, sir," said a passing flight attendant, "could you just pop your bag under the seat for takeoff, please?"

I closed the bag and shoved it away.

Once she had continued down the aisle, I snuck out my phone and brought up the news. It was the last chance I'd have to check the headlines before liftoff.

Reassured by the absence of any new developments, I put the phone in airplane mode, returned it to my pocket, and leaned my head against the headrest in a poor imitation of relaxation. The news I had been dreading would not break for another two hours. For now, secure in the knowledge that I was heading to safety, I closed my eyes and slept.

Editor's Note
Exhibit S

I still remember the day they found him. It was a freezing morning in February, and I was in the kitchen, still in my pajamas, my boyfriend already gone to work. We were out of coffee so I had to settle for tea. The kettle was just starting to boil when my phone began to ring. The name on the screen belonged to a close friend, a lifestyle reporter for a local newspaper, who had heard a rumor around the office she thought I ought to know.

The moment I hung up, I threw on some clothes and departed for Holyrood Park without a drop of caffeine in my veins.

The result was the following article, written by myself, published online in The Scotsman, *21 February 2017, and in the following morning's print edition.*

BODY FOUND IN ST. MARGARET'S LOCH

An unidentified body was pulled from St. Margaret's Loch Tuesday morning with the assistance of the Borders Water Rescue Team.

Members of the rescue team were called in by police after local birdwatcher Chadwick Thompson spotted the body while walking the loch, near the base of Arthur's Seat in Holyrood Park.

"I was tracking a family of white-winged scoter when I saw a commotion," Thompson said. "A flock of cygnets were flapping and squawking, all gathered in the same spot. In all the years I've been coming here, I've never seen anything like it."

According to Thompson, the birds could be seen pecking at an unidentified shape on the water, which he described as "quite large and hairy."

"I thought maybe it was a fox or a cat," Thompson said.

After scaring the birds off by throwing a stick, the witness claims to have had a look through his binoculars. "That's when I saw the head and shoulders—it was a person."

Shazia Nour, press officer for Lothian and Borders Police, confirmed that crime scene investigators found unspecified signs of struggle on the body. In light of these findings, a murder inquiry has been opened.

According to Nour, police believe the body to be that of missing Edinburgh University student Liam Stewart, 23, who has not been seen since December. Prior to Tuesday's events, no traces of the missing student had been found despite extensive searches of the city.

"Liam Stewart's family has been contacted to help identify the body," Nour said. "Regardless of the outcome, we are deeply saddened by the senseless act of violence inflicted on a member of our community, and we will do everything in our power to ensure that the person responsible is brought to justice."

A classmate of Stewart's, Grayson Hale, was arrested in connection with Stewart's disappearance in December, but was released without charge. Nour declined to comment on whether Hale was still a suspect, saying only, "We are exploring all possible lines of inquiry."

Thirty-Seven

THE ARRIVALS CURB outside San Diego International Airport was teeming as I emerged into the slanted, golden light of late afternoon. The sun hung low over a horizon flecked with waving palm trees in silhouette, the breeze warm and salty.

Hundreds of travelers, clad in T-shirts and flip-flops, rifled through their bags and flagged down passing cars, gabbing and laughing and complaining as they waited. I'd become unconsciously accustomed to British voices; these American ones tweaked my ear like a strain of forgotten music. There was something both comforting and oddly threatening in the sound. Every one of them, I was convinced, was talking about me.

But they couldn't have heard the news. I had only just seen the story myself: a body found in St. Margaret's Loch. Liam's body, I had no doubt, and once the family identified him as their son, the police would be after me.

I had no time to waste, but nor could I go straight to my mother's house. I didn't want her to know I was in town; she would only make things difficult if she did.

I checked into the Ramada by the harbor and slept for twelve hours, waking early the next morning, well rested but starving. After availing myself of the continental breakfast, I called an Uber to the hotel.

It was a typical San Diego morning, crisp and overcast, the marine layer not yet burned off to reveal the fullness of the sun. My mother's house was just over the hill. After a short journey, the driver dropped me in front of it, its cream-colored frontage and sky-blue shutters all but hidden behind the voluminous foliage of the carob tree that stood sentinel in the yard, its branches fat and overgrown.

As expected, Vera's car was not in the driveway. On a Wednesday she would be at her bookkeeping job until at least after lunch—plenty of time to grab what I needed.

Once the driver pulled away, I approached the house. The door was locked, but I still had my house key. As I turned it in the lock, the dead bolt slid free, and the door opened onto the cozy living room where my father had once conducted his teachings and, since his death, a weekly rotation of special guests had attempted to fill his shoes—ministers brought in from out of town for fifty bucks a pop, and believers brave enough to try their hand at sermonizing. I wasn't sure which was the greater insult.

Beyond the front room, the house had an empty, neglected feeling. My mother seemed to have relinquished her standards of cleanliness. The kitchen counters were discolored with splotches of dried food, the sink uncharacteristically full. Unlike Nathaniel's, my old bedroom had been converted into a guest room, one choked with boxes and bins of holiday decorations, stinking of the soiled litter tray beneath the desk. The new addition, an overfed tabby with different-colored eyes, lounged on a pile of folded clothes on a chair in my mother's room, exposing its belly suggestively in my direction.

I guessed, by the state of the house, my mother had taken on extra hours at work, perhaps gotten a second job. I'd never stopped to consider that my father's death had put a strain on her finances. The prospect heartened me.

In the dining room, I headed through the glass slider into the backyard, which, like the front, had gone untended for some time. The door that led to the study was locked and coated in dust. Lifting the mat, I collected the key from underneath it and let myself in.

The windowless room beyond the threshold was, as it had always been, like the interior of a faded office building. As I flipped the switch, fluorescent lights buzzed over a thin blue carpet crowded with dated furniture. A threadbare pullout. A hulking desk, the dark wood veneer chipping off at the edges. Several mismatched bookcases, their contents relegated to a pile of cardboard boxes.

Still, it was far from the place I remembered. Gone was the aura of scholarly mystery that had enveloped it, the sense of standing outside a stronghold of intellectual discovery. Reduced to a few bits of old furniture and empty shelves, it bore the melancholy stench of an institution. A prison. Whatever knowledge had been born between these skeletal walls, it was nothing compared to the pain they had concealed.

Parrots screeched in the trees outside, as if in lament.

Not sure where to start, I selected a box at random and disentangled the flaps. It was filled with junk. Papers, office supplies, abandoned drafts of essays and sermons. Several boxes of books contained mostly theological texts, pedagogical manuals, and four decades' worth of the Elected Heart Press's stultifying output. Another held my father's many honors and plaques, including the Cyril Lagrand Award for Pastoral Excellence 2006.

I closed the box and shoved it away, continuing to search for something that looked like a journal.

At the bottom of the pile I discovered a box unlike the rest. While the others bore mundane, handwritten words such as BOOKS, DONATE, TRASH, this one contained a more baffling label.

DESTROY.

Intrigued, I excavated the box and pulled it away from the others.

As I got down on the floor and opened it, I initially experienced a feeling of anticlimax. This box appeared no different than the others, containing the same tangle of books, papers, and old sermons.

Digging through, I found an old photo album, pausing to take it in hand and flip open its faded, brown-leather cover. Inside were several photographs from a bygone era. Four young men drinking beer in someone's apartment. Coeds posing in bathing suits in front of a lake. Among them was my father, barely twenty years old, with thick sideburns and wild, curly hair, his serious face set apart from the others' easy smiles.

As I turned the page again, my hand stilled, and a cold feeling unfurled in my stomach.

How could it be here when it still lay in the pocket of my bag, back at the hotel? The Polaroid from Arthur's Seat. Eagerly I continued to flip through the album in search of more photos of them together, but there were none.

Returning to the box, I rifled through papers, shook out books. Searching for more evidence, something, *anything*, to answer the questions crackling in my head like burning wood. Had my father known D.B.'s true identity? Had they met by coincidence or had D.B. sought him out? Why, standing beside him, did my father look so happy?

As I overturned the box, a small notebook slid out onto the carpet, bound in green suede. I opened it, letting the pages fan out. Hope rose like a fountain in my chest. The pages were covered with cramped handwriting, each entry preceded by a date.

October 18, 1975

I feel as if I am disintegrating. Every day I remain in this town, in the company of these small, narrow people, I feel another part of me calve, like ice falling away from a glacier. I feel myself becoming smaller by the day, weaker. Something inside of me rattles, pleading. It longs for freedom as I do. This country is slowly poisoning us. We must get out.

It was a journal. My father's journal.

Doing the math in my head, he would've been about twenty-four when he wrote this. Probably still living in Arizona, where he grew up.

As I flipped through the book, my eyes raced from entry to entry, lingering just long enough to follow the thread of events.

April 27, 1976

> *I have accepted a place at the University of Edinburgh. I begin in the fall. Finally I shall be free from the burning manacles of this desert. Father will rage when I tell him. He still believes my place is in the church. But I shall not follow blindly in his footsteps as he did my grandfather's. When will he accept that I do not share his delusional view of the universe, that I worship at the altar of science and reason? Reverend Edmund Hale—I can hardly restrain my laughter at the thought of it. He doesn't know yet I shall be studying Darwin's teachings, that one day soon there will be a scientist in the family.*

So the *Edinburgh Informer* was right. He *had* been studying evolutionary biology. I read on.

May 1, 1976

> *I told Father about my coming emigration, and he reacted even worse than I had expected. Surprisingly, he was more incensed by my choice of country than my sacrilegious program. I was dumbfounded. He had never mentioned any such aversion to Scotland before, which I believe runs through our veins to some minor degree. When pressed for an explanation, all he would answer was, "The Devil. The Devil's in Scotland." I must admit it gave me a chill, as Satan's name always has, despite my superior reason. When I asserted that I would not be held captive by his backwoods fanaticism, Father erupted with such a fury as I have never witnessed in him before. "Disobey me," he raged, "and you shall never step foot under my roof again! I shall not allow you to invite evil into my home, not after all I've done to escape it!" What does he mean by that?*
>
> *It saddens me to know I am so expendable to him. Does he not realize how deeply I have revered him, how everything I have done in*

my life has been in pursuit of his pride and admiration? Still, however it pains me, if he should force me to choose between the pursuit of knowledge and his love, I shall not hesitate to follow the path of wisdom.

August 20, 1976

I have lived one week in Great Britain, and already I long for home. The books and films lie. They pretend as if our countries were brothers, two variations of the same species. How quickly one realizes it is a farce. There is very little here that the American eye does not recognize, and yet nothing at all that is truly familiar—a million insignificant points of differentiation that add up to a feeling of total alienation. It tugs downwards on the soul, pulling me under, away from the familiar world dancing above. Shall I ever surface?

August 30, 1976

With the start of classes my homesickness has thankfully abated. Every day this strange place feels more like home, and I, more like the person I longed to become. Who that person is I am not yet sure, but I feel closer than ever to finding out. Here I am unshackled, liberated by anonymity. It is as if a door has opened in my mind, revealing a part of me I did not know was there. I stand upon the threshold, peering into the darkness. What lies beyond, I feel I shall soon find out.

After this I noticed a change in my father's writing, a growing unease.

September 8, 1976

What is wrong with me? Perhaps I am drinking too much coffee. Lately I have been on edge in the worst way possible—unable to shake the feeling that I am being followed.

Nearly every day for the last week I have seen what I believe to be the same man. He has dark hair, smirking features, and never seems

to wear anything but black. He appears to me wherever I go—leaving
Hume Tower, in the Meadows at night, in the aisles of the corner shop.
His eyes linger on mine, as if he is working out a problem in his head.
Sometimes he is gone before I can take a second look, and other times I
sense him behind me, following me home.

A dark figure lingers on the street at this very moment, looking up
at my window. I am certain it is him.

September 17, 1976

I saw him again, the mercurial man who has dogged me for weeks,
and this time I confronted him. I even know his name.

It happened at the Central Library. I was there picking up a copy
of Hennig's Phylogenetic Systematics, which I had been holding on
reserve. There was a line at the desk when I arrived. As I stood waiting
to be served, my eyes were drawn to a far set of shelves. I was certain
I had spotted him, my pursuer, attired as usual in black, restocking
books from a cart. But when I looked again, it was a young woman I
saw, in a thick sweater of mauve.

The librarian called me forward. Somewhat ill at ease, I received
my book and quickly made to leave.

So quickly, in fact, that I neglected to look where I was going and
collided with the stranger who blocked my path.

"Sorry," I muttered, and tried to get around him, until I realized
that it was my pursuer himself.

Though I was at a loss for words, the man before me was uncharacteristically full of them. He apologized, as if it were he who had collided
with me, then seemed to notice my book. "Is that Hennig?" he said.
"The English translation, I'm guessing, unless you're fluent in Ger-
man." He followed this with a few words in that language, a question I
didn't understand. It was rather impressive.

I noticed his eyes. Like a winter night sprayed with stars of gold.

The shock and wonder of it all took the edge off my ire. So I answered his question about the book, and asked how he knew it. He an-

swered drolly that, as a student of Western cultures, he was well-read in a great number of seminal fictions.

He followed me toward the exit and we conversed for some minutes outside. What astounded me was how easily it came. I should not be doing this, I found myself thinking. This man has been following me. He could be dangerous, a madman for all I knew. And yet it was like I had happened upon an old friend. I could not repress the flow of words from my lips, or the glowing feeling in my chest, of having at last met an equal.

He suggested we take our conversation to a café across the road. Although I was tempted, this felt like a step too far. I refused him.

"Another time," he said.

"Perhaps."

Before I left, I asked his name.

"Dougal Blair," he said. "But you can call me D.B."

What followed were approximately twenty more entries, spanning two months, describing my father's burgeoning acquaintanceship with the man who called himself D.B. My knees stiff from kneeling, I sat back on the carpet and read voraciously.

Initially, the young men's connection seemed to be an intellectual one. D.B. was knowledgeable across many subjects: the humanities, theology, even the biological sciences, of which he nevertheless was a skeptic. He engaged my father in lengthy debates about the theory of evolution and its inability to reconcile the notion of adaptation with the immutability of the human condition: how, as a result of natural selection, the body of man was constantly changing, and yet the appetites and desperations that drove him—hunger, sexual desire, violence, social acceptance—kept him in a state of arrested development. How despite the vortex of societal change that swirled around us, we carried our fathers' burdens as if they were our own, even when they did not fit the present moment. How they imprisoned us from birth until we drew our last breath.

In the unchangingness of fear and longing, D.B. said, that was where God and the Devil lived.

Although my father harbored reservations about his new acquaintance, he was willing to accept on faith D.B.'s strenuous assurances that he had never intentionally stalked him, and that any such encounters had been purely accidental.

And so they became constant companions. The pair hardly seemed to go anywhere outside each other's company. D.B. would find my father on campus and accompany him to biology lectures, whispering cutting critiques and counterarguments in his ear the whole time. By the time the lecture was over, my father was less certain of his knowledge than he had been going in. They took frequent excursions, from the peaks of Arthur's Seat to the valleys of Glencoe, and passed the nights either carousing or embroiled in a state of fierce argumentation.

Whereas our earlier intercourse was detached and intellectual, now it is something else entirely, an almost physical interlocking of minds, so intense that our exertions frequently go on until sunrise, leaving me panting and drenched in sweat.

At the same time, I observed a further change in my father's writing that unsettled me. The more fervid his friendship with D.B. became, the more details my father held back. For example, he might report that they had a disagreement that led to several days' silence, yet neglect to mention what it was they had quarreled about. On another occasion, D.B. and my father were purportedly taking a ramble through the Pentland Hills "when, as we stopped to catch our breath, my companion perpetrated such a vile act on another hiker that I took off running and did not stop until I had reached the road." My father never clarified what the vile act had been, nor did he ever mention it again. I was not surprised to find the next entry had been torn from the book. And it was not the only one.

I sensed in his writing a strengthening undercurrent of disquiet that cast a pall over his pages. Even the handwriting grew more frantic, the style increasingly erratic.

November 15, 1976

More and more, he compels me to do things . . . unspeakable things . . . things I once would have regarded as reprehensible, the work of heathens and sinners, but now—egad, what's happened to me? There is something inside me, something black and ravenous, I can feel it . . . a dark hunger that demands feeding. For although I should decry his requests with revulsion, I find myself overcome with a raging red desire to give in, so fierce I can scarcely hold myself back. "Do it," my companion whispers, ready to assist me in the blackest of deeds, assuring me there's nothing wrong in it. Besides, no one need know . . . our little secret.

I feel myself bending to his silver tongue. Another few days and I fear I may snap. He would like that, I am certain. But why?

It occurs to me that I don't know my companion at all. He hardly ever speaks about his past or his future. Who is this man, I wonder . . . if he is a man. I have seen him do things that defy explanation. Each time I have convinced myself that my senses are faulty. After all, I am a man of science. I do not believe in such things as phantoms, or fiends . . . what was it my father said about this place? The Devil's in Scotland . . . Now I recall them, the words spin round and round in my head . . . I mustn't think such a thing of my companion, even in private. He may hear . . . for sometimes it is like he knows my thoughts.

My father was right. I should never have come here. The soil of this country is rich with evil . . . it nourishes the dark hunger that nests inside me . . . I feel it wanting to blossom . . . to burst . . .

I need to get out.

And with that, the entries stopped. Every page that followed had been torn from the journal, leaving a thick, jagged fringe at the end of the book.

I dug through the box and its contents, searching for the missing pages, searching for another notebook that picked up where this one left off.

But there weren't any. The memoirs and confessions of Edmund Hale had come to an unceremonious end.

The only thing I found was a corner of paper poking out from beneath the bottom flap of the box. Deflated, yet curious nonetheless, I tugged at it.

It snagged on the box as it came free, leaving a long tear through the back page, the last of more than a dozen. The document looked old, musty, and yellowed, typewritten in square, uneven lettering.

Turning the front pages over, I apprehended the title stamped across the top of the manuscript, as if by the strikers of an old typewriter, and felt my stomach give a lurch.

```
            JACK AND THE DEVIL'S HORN
                 by Ned Duhamel
```

It was not just the same story my father had given me for my thirteenth birthday; it appeared to be the original manuscript.

This one was not yet perfected, the word "reason" struck out and replaced with "purpose," "forest" spelled with an extra _r_. I flipped the document, observing a set of handwritten scribbles on the back, in what was undeniably my father's writing.

My eyes followed them down the page, trying to make sense of them.

Edmund Hale

~~_Date Hemund_~~ _too obvious_
~~_Dan_~~
~~_Dunn_~~
~~_Len Mend_~~
~~_Lane (or Elan?)_~~ _Hem_

~~Lane Elan Had~~
~~Adele Han~~
(?) Dunham
~~Edel Dunham~~
~~Dean Duhmel~~
Duhamel
~~End~~
~~Den~~
Ned

<u>Ned Duhamel</u>

It was an anagram. Of Edmund Hale.

My father had written the folktale himself.

Written it, then presumably had it printed and bound to give me on my thirteenth birthday—the only gift I had ever received from him. But why? This story had terrorized me. Together with my brother's own cruel fictions, it had kindled the phobia that would dominate my life for years.

What was it he had said that night? *You're a young man now. Soon you'll face new temptations. You'll have questions. The answers are in that book.*

I should hope you understand it.

Finally, it made sense. My father had known the Adversary would come for me, like the Adversary had come for him all those years ago. He had given me the book as a warning, a cautionary tale against submitting to the temptations D.B. would throw at me.

But if that were true, then why was the book necessary at all? Didn't the Bible say enough on the subject? James 4:7: "Resist the Devil and he will flee from you." Peter 5:8: "Be alert and of sober mind. Your enemy the Devil prowls around like a roaring lion looking for someone to devour." The folktale must have contained some other message, but what? After all the sermons he had delivered, all the prayers he had bestowed, all the exhortations he had foisted upon me, what did my father need me to know that he could not speak from his own mouth?

I checked the time; it was after one. My mother would be home any minute.

Hastily I repacked my father's box, preparing to take it with me. As I snatched up the album, a stray photograph slipped out and landed faceup.

I reached down, pausing as I saw it properly, recognizing the setting at once. Sunset Cliffs, deep afternoon. A male figure stood against a purple-orange sunset, an ocean breeze pushing his hair back as he regarded the camera. The face darkened by shadow, but I had no doubt whose it was.

Followed me from the hills and glens of Scotland . . . stalked me to the very edge of my sanity.

My father may have gotten away, but had he truly escaped?

Editor's Note
Exhibits T and U

Third and final part of my interview with Nathaniel Hale, elder brother of Grayson Hale, recorded via Skype, 4 September 2019.

BARCLAY: Are you saying Grayson killed your mother?

HALE: What, you think it was a coincidence? You think she just *happened* to be knifed in her bed the few days Grayson was home from Scotland?

BARCLAY: How did you know he came home? Did he contact you?

HALE: I saw him. You don't know? He didn't write that in his little story?

BARCLAY: No, actually.

HALE: Well, I did. Coming out of my mom's place. I was bringing her lunch. She wasn't home yet, so I pulled into the drive, and I see Gray sneaking out the side door. I was like, "What are you doing here? I thought you were in the UK." Then I notice he has this box under his arm. I'm like, "What are you taking?" I try to grab it and he doesn't want to let go. The box sort of tears at the side and all this stuff falls out—my dad's stuff—and Gray gets down on his knees to put it all back. I bend down and pick up a photo. It's of a guy at Sunset Cliffs and I'm like, "Who the fuck's this?" Gray says it's no one, and the way he says it, all fast like that, I can tell he's full of shit. He's found something out about Dad, I know it. Something he doesn't want Mom and me to know about and now he's trying to get rid of the evidence. I go for the box again and he puts his hand out to stop me. "Wait!" he says. "I'll tell you. But I need to be sure first." He says he needs to go to Sunset Cliffs.

BARCLAY: Why?

HALE: I just remember him saying, "He's there. If it's true, I'll find him there."

BARCLAY: The man in the photo.

HALE: I guess so.

BARCLAY: And he did go. That night. That part's in the manuscript.

HALE: I know. I took him.

BARCLAY: Did you? Why?

HALE: I always knew there was something not right about Dad. Something Mom wouldn't say. But I'd never been able to prove it. If there was someone there who could, I wanted to talk to him myself.

BARCLAY: So take me through what happened that night.

HALE: We got there right as the sun was going down. Parking was ridiculous, so Gray made me drop him at the curb while I looked for a spot. By the time I found one, he'd already taken off down this dirt path. It runs all the way down the cliff. I follow him, call out for him to slow down, but he won't. I'm trying to catch up with him but he's so far ahead. It gets dark really fast and I can't even see him anymore. But I keep going, keep walking. Five minutes, maybe ten. Then finally the path breaks off and leads to an open area, a dirt lot with a few cars. Most people probably don't even know it's there. I didn't. I thought maybe Gray was meeting someone there, that he'd gotten in one of the cars.

BARCLAY: So what did you do?

HALE: So I started going car to car, looking for him. The first one was empty, so I keep going. I can hear rustling in the bushes, which kind of freaks me out. There's this big Toyota pickup, big four-seater, you know. As I get up to it, I can see people moving around in the back and I get this bad feeling. Something tells me to stay away from that truck. So I step back but I'm not looking where I'm going. I sort of stumble back into another car. I turn around, and in the back seat . . . the windows are fogged up, but I can see something moving, and I can hear this sort of . . . [hitting table, *THUMP THUMP THUMP*].

BARCLAY: You mean . . . ?

HALE: Then a hand smears the window. I look away, but I can't unsee it.

BARCLAY: Unsee what?

HALE: Men. Both of them. All of them, actually. In the cars. In the scrub . . . fuck, some of them weren't even being quiet about it. Then it hits me. It all makes sense, you know?

BARCLAY: What does?

HALE: Why he always came to look at the waves even though he didn't surf. Why he never let us get out of the car.

BARCLAY: You think your father was going there to meet men?

HALE: I always knew there was something off about him. Him and my brother both. Mom always said they were cut from the same cloth.

BARCLAY: Where was Grayson at this point?

HALE: I don't know. I didn't see him. I took off running and didn't look back.

Article published in The Scotsman *on 24 February 2017, three days after Grayson Hale arrived in San Diego, written by myself.*

POLICE CONFIRM IDENTITY OF EDINBURGH LOCH BODY

Police have confirmed the identity of the man whose body was found by specialist search volunteers in an Edinburgh loch earlier this week.

The deceased has been identified as 23-year-old Liam Stewart of Kirkcaldy, the Edinburgh University postgraduate student who has been missing since December.

Borders Water Rescue Team members located the body in St. Margaret's Loch in Holyrood Park on Tuesday.

The deceased's father, Paul Stewart, wrote in a statement on Facebook: "We are devastated to now know what we have suspected to be true for the last two months—that our beautiful son Liam was taken from us. Our hearts are broken, not just for ourselves but for the countless lives Liam touched in his short time on this earth. We are deeply grateful for all the police and volunteers who tirelessly worked to bring our son back home."

Stewart's positive identification follows a preliminary

postmortem report, published Wednesday, which found that the body had been submerged underwater for nearly two months.

Noting that liquid was found in the lungs, the medical examiner's report concluded that the victim had been strangled unconscious, but was not yet dead, when his body was dumped in the loch.

It was furthermore noted that stones were discovered in the pockets, mouth, and pushed down into the throat canal.

These weights, along with the weeds entwining the legs and waist, are believed to have kept the body floating near the bottom of the loch for several weeks until decomposition caused it to distend and float to the surface.

The procurator fiscal registered the death as suspicious late Monday, and a murder inquiry has been opened.

Stewart's classmate, 25-year-old Grayson Hale, was arrested in connection with Stewart's disappearance in December, but was released without charge.

Shazia Nour, press officer for Lothian and Borders Police, said Thursday: "We have not eliminated any suspects in the investigation."

Nour added: "If you have any information related to the death of Liam Stewart, however small, we urge you to please come forward."

Thirty-Eight

ONCE THEY IDENTIFIED the body, it was all just a steep downhill slide to the bottom. On Saturday, a warrant was issued for my arrest, and before the weekend was out *The Scotsman* was already reporting that police had traced me back to San Diego and were requesting my extradition.

Based on what I knew about that process, I wasn't immediately concerned. Criminal deportation proceedings could take years. By the time the State Department had signed off on the application and the presiding judge had given his blessing, I could have gotten an apartment, started a career, begun a whole new life.

But what would be the point? Tempting as it was to postpone the inevitable, nothing could keep the storm of my reckoning from coming. Whether today or in five years, the police would get their signatures and approvals. I would be shipped back to Scotland like a piece of cattle, face trial for Liam's murder, and, I had no doubt, be convicted. After the terror and uncertainty that had dominated that last four months of my life, there was something appealing about fast-tracking my fate. At least then I could be sure of it. Even the grim monotony of life in prison would be a welcome reprieve from five more years of anxiety and despair.

Still, I am certain I would have stayed were it not for Sunset Cliffs.

The evening after I raided my father's study, I hitched a ride to the seaside bluffs where my father had frequently walked. For years, I believed this spot had been nothing more to him than a favorable vantage point for looking at the surf. A spot, perhaps, where he could escape the travails of his life and, for a brief moment, be at peace. But my opinion changed when I found that photo among his personal effects, the one that showed D.B. standing at the edge of the cliff. Here was proof that my father continued to be hounded by his companion long after he fled back to the States—for decades, perhaps until his dying day, locked in an endless push and pull of temptation and fear, wanting to be free of him and yet, as suggested by the existence of the photo, unable to deny his summons to the Cliffs.

The one place, I hoped, I might find D.B.

It was already dark when I got there, the sky a deepening smear of indigo and blue. I set out along the path, lined on the left side with a high wall of sage scrub and open, on the right, to the vastness of the sea. The path was all but deserted, bearing the last few sightseers back to their cars.

As I followed it, my knees began to shake. Why? What had I to be nervous about? That I might find D.B. waiting for me at the end of the cliff, or that I might find nothing at all? Find that I had it all wrong. That once again this was all in my head.

Eventually a figure appeared on the path. It was so dark now that he was little more than a shadow, but I could see his head turn to face me as I stopped, and just as I had known the man in the photo was D.B., so I recognized my employer now.

After a moment, he turned and continued down the path.

"Wait," I called out quietly, and hurried to follow.

He led me down a fork in the path to a small clearing. A dirt road snaked away from it, no doubt leading back to the street.

He disappeared inside one of the vehicles parked there. Again I followed, swinging open the passenger door and climbing into the back. It felt safer that way, with D.B. in front. Although I couldn't see him fully, the eyes in the rearview mirror were unmistakable.

"What do you want?" he said. His accent was different, altered by his surroundings. He could almost have been a local.

For months I had pursued him. Now he was here in front of me, I was at a loss for words. "What do I want?"

"You followed me. You must want something."

The only thing I could think to say was: "I want to know why."

"Why what?" D.B. said.

"Why me? Why my dad? You knew him, didn't you?"

"You could say that."

He hadn't answered my question. "Well?"

"You know perfectly well why."

An icy recognition engulfed my body. It was true. I had always known there was something corrupt in me, something malignant, my body fertile soil for an evil seed. But my father too?

Turning his own question back on him, I asked, "What do you want?"

"I think you know that too."

I gazed out the window. The bushes were moving. The wind must have picked up.

"To make them remember."

He feigned confusion, toying with me now. "Remember?"

My eyes met his in the mirror.

"To make them remember the Devil."

"Right." He grinned. "Exactly."

"I'm almost done with the book—" I began, but he cut me off.

"Book? You think I brought you here to talk about a book?"

I faltered, not understanding. If all this wasn't about the book, then what?

There was something about the gleaming eyes in the mirror that told me I had missed something. I had been deceived.

"You don't care about the book. It's never been about that."

As I said it, it all started to make sense. What happened at the Silver Stag, what happened to Liam—it was all part of a larger plan. He had wanted me to kill him—Liam Stewart, so perfect, so handsome, whose disappearance would command the attention of the nation. He *wanted* me to be caught, so that when they asked why I had done it, I could tell them: the Devil had made me, for he was alive and well.

"You just wanted to use me."

D.B. grinned.

A terrible anger swelled within me, tinged with sorrow. I had been taken for a fool, and Liam, my best friend, was dead because of it. We had been tools of the Devil, nothing more. Pawns upon the grandmaster's chessboard. I could feel his hands bearing down upon me even now, compelling me toward an unwanted climax.

I had to go back. Tell all of Scotland what he had made me do. Only then would I finally be free.

I pushed open the door to get out. "Hold on," D.B. said. I jerked my head around, the scowl tight across my face.

"Sorry about your father," he said. "He was one of my favorites."

I hopped down from the truck, and fled.

Thirty-Nine

P ERHAPS I HAD been flattering myself to expect I would be arrested the moment I touched down in Scotland—to imagine that the police, whose every waking moment had been spent tracking my movements, would somehow be alerted to my imminent arrival and dispatch a squad of uniformed officers to meet me at the gate.

I emerged from the jet bridge with nothing but the terminal to greet me. I had been in San Diego eight days, but it was as if barely an hour had passed. Not sure what else to do, I collected my bag and joined the line for customs.

It was only as the immigration officer scanned my passport that anyone seemed to take notice of me. She did a double take at the alert that must have appeared on her screen and, with a polite smile, asked me to step aside.

A security guard was already on his way over.

They held me at the airport for half an hour before the police showed up. Then they arrested me and took me back to the station. By the time we arrived it was after midnight. I had been awake for more than twenty-four hours and was suffering from exhaustion bordering on delirium. I remember babbling to the arresting officer that I needed to speak to Yvette—no, Yvonne—to which he replied that the police, not I, would determine whom I spoke to and when.

At the station, they put me in a holding cell for barely long enough to nod off before forcing me out again, groggy and insecure about not having showered, and led me to the same small room where I had been questioned before.

Yvonne was already there, looking somewhat disheveled as she made a cup of tea. I found myself apologizing for getting her out of bed.

"Dinnae be silly. Have ye had yer call?" She seemed to think I might want my solicitor present.

"It's fine. Let's just get this over with."

Sitting across from me, she smiled in a sad way that told me she wasn't looking forward to this. "Why'd ye come back?"

"I had to."

"Had tae?"

I shrugged. "It's the right thing to do."

"Ye know what ah'm gonnae ask ye, don't ye?"

"If I killed Liam Stewart?"

She nodded.

"The Devil made me do it."

She faltered, her eyes darting to the mirror that I expected concealed an audience.

"Say again?"

I told her the truth. The whole truth, at least as I understood it—from the night I had met the Devil on Leith Walk, to the night he had compelled me to kill Liam Stewart.

Had I been more lucid, I might have held back some unnecessary details, or at least done a better job of not making my story sound so utterly ludicrous. Even as I noticed Yvonne's expression starting to change, the puzzlement fading to concern and finally to dismay, I couldn't stop myself talking, digging deeper and deeper into my woeful tale, knowing D.B. would have it no other way.

The next day I was reunited with the same solicitor who had represented me during my previous interview. I learned his name was Myles.

Understandably, he was furious that I had said what I had. Had he not been ordered by the court to represent me, I'm certain he would have resigned on the spot. "We're trying to fight our way to the top of a mountain with no kit, no food, and no water," he said, "and you've just taken us to the very bottom. You've made this all a lot harder on yourself. Especially given—" There was something he couldn't bring himself to say.

"What?"

He released a steadying sigh and said, "A woman by the name of Vera Hale was found dead in her San Diego home on Tuesday. Multiple knife wounds to the chest. The police date the murder between the twenty-sixth and twenty-seventh of February—the day before you returned to Scotland. Am I correct in guessing that this woman is your mother?"

"She—she's dead?"

"Did you see her at any point during your visit?"

In fact, I had. But not by my choice. Nathaniel had told her where I was staying. The night before I returned to Scotland, she showed up at my door, asking to speak to me. A family of tourists lingered in the hallway. Not wanting to be overheard, I let her in.

"What do you want?" I said.

When she turned to me, I saw she looked older than I remembered, and very thin. Neither the lovely version of herself nor the cruel one; this Vera was withered, a moldering husk. "I'm glad you came back."

"Why?"

"You found his things, didn't you? His journals?" She circled the small room. My eyes flicked unconsciously to the box under the desk. "Do you still idolize him now you know what he was?"

"It doesn't change anything," I said.

"Of course it doesn't." She drew back the curtains with an emaciated hand, revealing a view of the parking lot below, the marina just visible across the street. "I felt the same way about my father, even when he let me suffer."

I was surprised; my mother rarely spoke of her past. "Suffer?"

"I suppose you might as well know. Your grandfather was a butcher named Frank Critchley. Your grandmother Helen was a vituperative drunk whose only purpose in life was to torment me. The state of my clothes, the dirt under my fingernails—every part of my appearance was a dagger to be plunged and twisted with relish."

"Such cruelty," I muttered ironically.

Vera explained that she was eight years old when her mother began to cast daily aspersions against her purity. Barely eleven, in the flush of her first womanly blood, when Helen accused her of seducing her own father, of slipping into his bed and climbing on top of him in the middle of the night while Helen lay passed out in the living room.

Vera never spoke back. She moved around her mother like a piece of furniture, accepting her mutterings like the creaking and groaning of the house. But at this, she could hardly suppress her tears of hate and disgust. And so it became her mother's favorite slur. Hardly a week passed without some reference to the fictional tryst. The drink shredded Helen's mind to ribbons, and by the time Vera was a teenager, Helen had convinced herself the lie was true. She would fly at her husband, screaming, punctuating her vitriol with ring-clad raps round his head. *You fucked her, didn't you, you son of a bitch? You fuck her every night. You lick her cunt and make her come, you sick fuck.*

"The night my dad sank his best butchering knife into my mother's hand, pinning it to the wall through a needlepoint sampler, was the night I packed a bag and left. I was seventeen."

For a while Vera stayed with her father's brother in Petoskey, but when he demanded she fuck him as payment for lodging, she was forced to move on again.

She was nineteen and living in a squalid studio in Grand Rapids, desperate for work, when she answered a vague ad in the newspaper. The

man on the other end of the line didn't have a job to offer, but a calling
of a different kind.

The next morning, two missionaries from the Church of the Elected
Heart came to her apartment and told her she was very special. " 'The
Almighty Lord our God has chosen you for a very important task.' "
This was, of course, to spread His true Word, of which the Elected Heart
alone was the rightful custodian. They had books and pamphlets. They
had answers to every question my mother asked and many she didn't.
They had a plan for her, which was more than she had for herself at the
best of times. Within a week she had sold nearly everything she owned,
packed up what remained in a single rolling suitcase, and boarded a bus
headed to the Elected Heart Institute of Biblical Research.

"I was a good student," she said. "Pre-seminary. I didn't know what
I'd do after. Maybe teach in a Sunday school. I'd always loved kids."

I scoffed but didn't interrupt.

"In my second year, I met your father. He was older, a TA in my
Advanced Old Testament Analysis class. He was handsome, intelligent.
Tortured in a way I thought I understood. For most people, he was too
intense. Too devout, even in that environment. But I revered him. The
rigor of his principles, his searing detestation of immorality and vice.
Revered the secret thoughts that flashed in his eyes, though I couldn't
pry them out of him and didn't try." My mother wasn't like the other
girls, who needed constant chatter and reassurance from their men; she
thrived in the silence that bound them. Theirs was a courtship beyond
words, a union more vital than love.

The same week she received her degree, they married. The ceremony
took place at the local courthouse. Witnesses were provided for a fee.

Many of their friends were moving west, so they decided to follow.
Vera helped my father start his own ministry. They had Nathaniel, and
all seemed well.

"But then Edmund grew restless. We had just bought the house
when he wanted to move again. He even mentioned going abroad. With
an infant and a growing business, I told him it was impossible. He be-

came distant, retreated into the study he had altered to make inaccessible from the house. I began to see men going in and out."

D.B. in various forms, I presumed. I resisted the temptation to show her the photo from Sunset Cliffs.

"I could feel the demons closing in around us. He had invited the Adversary into our house. From what I could tell, they were well acquainted. I realized I had made a terrible mistake; my husband was not the man I had thought. If he committed his life to Christ, it was only as an act of rebellion against his true nature, a feeble attempt to contain the evil inside him. By the time I realized what I'd married, it was too late. I had made a promise to God, and where would I go even if I could leave? In the name of the Lord, I vowed to stay. To change my husband if I could. And then we had you, and the moment I held you in my arms, I knew you were the same. Just as unnatural as the way you were conceived. Just as *wicked*."

"Shut up!" I shouted.

"We tried to help you. Do you remember? Nathaniel and I, we tried to force the evil out of you. But you couldn't be helped. You were too far gone. And now look at you. On the run from the law. A *murderer*."

"SHUT UP!" I exploded. But as she approached me, my body cowered back in fear, as if conditioned to expect violence.

"I'm glad," she whispered, her thin lips tweaked in a menacing grin. "I'm glad everyone knows what you are. Now I can finally say aloud what I've been thinking all these years: You are no son of mine. You're a monster, you were born a monster—and I've never loved you."

I felt my mouth go dry; I couldn't speak.

"If there is anything you want from the house," she had said, "come get it. After tonight, I never want to see or hear from you again."

But as I explained to Myles, I hadn't gone to the house that night. Not that I could remember. Then again, I'd done plenty that I didn't recall.

"There's no physical evidence linking you to the crime," he said. "They never found the murder weapon. It just—well, it just doesn't look good. Hopefully the Scottish media doesn't get wind of this, or it could be very bad for you indeed."

Forty

MYLES AND I continued to meet often in the run-up to the trial. I was scheduled to appear in court in a couple weeks' time. At the initial hearing, he explained, we would state our intention to plead guilty or not guilty before the trial date was set. He was adamant we should enter a plea of not guilty by insanity, a strategy I opposed.

"Unfortunately you haven't got much choice," he said. "It's a mental disorder plea or you're looking at a life sentence, and public opinion is pushing hard for the latter. I mean, haven't you seen the papers?" I hadn't, of course, and the police had taken my phone when I was arrested. I'd had no way of knowing what was happening on the outside for weeks.

"They found out about my mom," I speculated.

"Worse. Your confession leaked. Everyone knows what you told the police about the Devil, all that 'make them remember' stuff. The whole country is terrified of you. They're calling you the Devil's Advocate."

The Devil's Advocate. It rang a bell, and not just as the name of a restaurant off the Royal Mile. One of the officers had called me that while letting me out for my daily walk. I thought I'd misheard him. The accents on some of these people were unreal.

"Lucky for you, the whole thing may be a blessing in disguise," Myles said. "The press are making you out to be a crazed lunatic. It gives credence to our case that you're mentally ill, that you weren't in possession of your reason at the time of Liam's death. A mental disorder plea can work, but you'll need to undergo evaluation. We'll need a formal diagnosis and an expert witness—"

"I'm not doing that."

Whatever he might have been thinking, Myles held my gaze with a practiced impassivity. "Can I ask why not?"

"Because I don't have a mental disorder. What I told the police, it's true. I know you don't believe me. That's okay. But it's true."

"I'm not here to tell you what you should or shouldn't believe, but as your solicitor—"

"I get it. I'm not stupid."

"I know you're not. Which is why I'm shocked you'd even consider—"

"We enter a plea of not guilty. No special defense."

"But you've *already confessed*—"

"I said I couldn't remember killing him," I corrected him. "The onus is on the prosecution to prove I actually did it. Beyond a reasonable doubt, isn't that right?"

"Yes but—"

"And as far as we know, there was no DNA found on Liam's body. No physical evidence."

"There wouldn't be. Not after that long underwater."

"Then we can make a case."

Myles was clenching his jaw so hard, I thought his teeth might break. "You understand I strongly advise against this."

"I do."

"And that we're likely to lose. Almost certain. Especially once the prosecution finds out your mother was murdered in cold blood not two miles from your hotel."

"If it's your reputation you're worried about, I'll make sure everyone knows you warned me against it. Just please, do what you can."

Although Myles agreed to honor my request, he departed in a slightly frosty mood, and I didn't hear from him again until the day before the hearing, when he called to tell me what to expect and to try to convince me once again to change my mind. I didn't begrudge him.

After all, he was right. We could make a strong case for mental illness. It might be the only chance I had to secure my freedom. But there was only one kind of freedom that mattered to me anymore. Frightened as I was of being convicted, I would rather spend the rest of my life in prison having placated the Devil than walk free with him still by my side for having dismissed him as a disturbance of the mind.

⌒

The initial hearing, held at the Edinburgh High Court, was brief. A bailiff led me into the courtroom where I stood handcuffed before the judge, an elderly man with ruddy jowls who wore a gown and wig. Myles was already there, also begowned. He offered barely a smile as I entered, which gave me pause.

But despite my worry that he might go rogue, he acted as directed. "The accused intends to plead not guilty," he announced to the judge.

A few minutes later it was over.

My trial was scheduled to begin on the twentieth of June. Myles's request for a bail order had been denied, so I was moved to the local prison, where I would remain in remand until the start of trial.

Despite its modern front building, the innards of HMP Edinburgh were bleak and institutional, riven with high, windowless halls of cells heaped on cells, the ancient walls flaking off their skins of pale yellow and cream. At the very least, I was not forced to share.

In the months to come, Myles would visit me every week or two to talk through our defense strategy and share news of what was happening in the press. The public interest seemed to be growing by the day. Classmates I had hardly spoken to were being quoted in the tabloids. Religious leaders wrote competing op-eds for *The Herald*, debating whether my claims bore the hallmarks of demonic possession.

Soon they began to dig into my past. The *Edinburgh Daily News* came out with a laughable interview with Nathaniel that painted me as some sort of horror-movie demon child. *The Scotsman* published a long exposé on my upbringing in the Elected Heart, which they described as "Westboro Baptist Church meets the Manson Family," and my father's suicide, which was presented as proof of a family history of mental illness.

It wasn't long until they dredged up the news about my mother. HOLY HALE—DEVIL'S ADVOCATE SUSPECTED IN BRUTAL MURDER OF SAINT MOTHER, read the headline of the paper Myles brought to our strategy session. This, despite no evidence of my wrongdoing having been found nor any charges brought against me. One particularly distasteful tabloid made a meal of the fact that my mother had been stabbed eighteen times.

> Eighteen is the product of six times three, or the sum of three sixes. 666 is widely regarded as Satan's number, making it all the more likely that whoever committed the crime had ties to the occult.

At least the attention seemed to please D.B. That he hadn't surfaced since my return to Scotland struck me as a sign that he was content with how things were progressing. After all, hadn't this been his plan all along? To instigate a media circus, to ensure all the papers were shouting his name. KILLER CONFESSES, SAYS DEVIL MADE HIM DO IT . . . AMERICAN KILLER CLAIMS SATAN IN SCOTLAND. I was his Jack: blowing into the Devil's horn, making it heard across the land, sending the whole country into fits of terror with the sound of it.

It might cost me my freedom, but, I thought, at least it would all be over soon.

Forty-One

I AWOKE ON THE twentieth of June to the sound of scratching at the window. A low, furtive sound, like the *psst* of a friend in the back row of social studies.

I lifted my head, looking up toward the small square of light at the top of the wall. Though I'd barely slept, my vision was dull and bleary, barely able to distinguish a black shape rapping on the glass outside. I rubbed my eyes, but whatever had been there fluttered away out of sight. A crow, like the ones that circled the exercise yard? Or a messenger, come to tell me that *he* would be watching?

If D.B. was in attendance at my trial, I didn't see him. Not in the mob of paparazzi waiting outside the High Court, the clerks and advocates seated around the central tables, or the members of the jury along the far wall. Not even among the spectators and journalists that crowded the back benches, pulsing with fear and revulsion as I entered the courtroom in cuffs.

As the bailiff led me in, a couple I was certain were Liam's parents locked eyes with me from the front row, their hands clasped in mutual support. It was not just the physical features that gave them away—the pronounced jawline that father had passed to son, the straight short nose that Liam had inherited from his mother—but the damaged quality that shone through their hatred. I wanted to tell them that I understood. That perhaps save for them, no one had cared more for their son.

"Call the diet of Her Majesty's Advocate against Grayson Hale," began the clerk of court. "Are you Grayson Hale?" she addressed me.

"I am."

She instructed me to sit. Bailiffs stood flanking me. I had hoped to have Myles at my side; with him seated with the other advocates at the wells, I felt acutely exposed.

The clerk of court read the indictment. No opening statements were made before the prosecution called its first witness.

The advocate depute, who represented the prosecution, did not cut a very intimidating figure. He was a short, simpering man whose obese neck did not match the rest of his body, which was merely fat. The powdery white wig that perched upon his head gave him the impotent look of eighteenth-century nobility, and the hem of his black gown, several inches too long, rustled along the floor in his wake. Nevertheless, he proved quite a talented jurist, wielding his witnesses like an artist with a brush—each one a different daub of paint on his palette, each question a delicate brushstroke on the canvas of the jury's minds.

The picture he painted was dark and compelling, but not at all what I had expected. I was ready, of course, to be drawn as violent and unpredictable, and to begin with I was.

Fiona was the first to take the witness box, narrating my transformation from a polite if overly serious student to a wild-eyed thug.

"He asked for permission to change his research topic," she said, beginning to tear up, "and, well, I barely had a chance to respond when suddenly he began *hurling abuse*."

Next an employee of the university library testified that I lashed out at him over a few books, an incident I could not recall in the least; and Jenna was trotted out to give her biased account of the night Liam disappeared, embellishing my "violent outburst" at the Silver Stag, as the advocate depute put it, with veins throbbing in my head and spit flying from my mouth.

"I was just so scared. I thought he was going to kill us!"

I would have been happy to do so now.

Still, this was no more than I had anticipated, and I nurtured a flame of hope that the jury would have reason to question my guilt. After all, demonstrating my volatility, even rage, was not the same as proving I had committed murder.

It was on the next bit of testimony, however, that the prosecution's case seemed to pivot.

"The prosecution calls Ms. Sophia Grant to the witness box."

The preceding months had not been kind to Sophie. She approached the bench, fifteen pounds heavier than she'd been in December, drained of the bubbly energy that once animated her. Though appearing to resist the urge, she eventually caught my eye, squeezing out a thin, almost involuntary smile that I took as a reassuring sign.

Once his witness had been sworn in, the advocate depute began by establishing the details of our relationship. How we met, how long we had been acquainted, what I had been like, to begin with. Then he embarked on a new and puzzling trajectory.

"You maintained a romantic relationship with the accused for how long?" he asked.

"Two months approximately," Sophie said.

"And during these two months, did you and the accused engage in intimate relations?"

By the look on her face, which had frozen, mouth agape, Sophie was every bit as shocked by the question as I was. I directed my outrage at my solicitor, who, as he caught my eye, just shook his head. His meaning was clear: *Not now.*

"Sometimes," answered Sophie finally.

Not put off by the witness's obvious discomfort, the advocate depute said, "How many times, if you had to guess? Ten? Twelve?"

"Em . . ."

She glanced at me nervously, as if seeking permission to answer. "Just once that I recall."

"Only once?"

"He . . ." She glanced at me again. "He wasn't often in the mood."

Well of course I wasn't. Who would be, I thought, when they were being pursued by the Devil, when even the slightest sin could draw him to their location like a moth to the flame?

"And on this sole occasion when the accused *was* in the mood," continued the advocate depute, pacing before the witness box with his hands behind his back, "was it he who initiated the intimacy or yourself?"

"I did."

"You're saying the accused never indicated a desire for sex, except at your suggestion?"

"That's correct."

"And on this occasion, did the accused seem, shall we say, eager?"

Now she seemed to be avoiding my eye. "He was quite . . . nervous to begin with. Trembling almost. He struggled to get . . . em . . . Then once we got going, he wasn't able to . . . Sorry, I'm not sure—"

"That's fine, Ms. Grant. You've answered my question. Thank you."

I was livid, as much with Myles for allowing this gross invasion of privacy as with the advocate depute for perpetrating it. The prosecution was trying to humiliate me. What other explanation could there be, when the line of questioning was so blatantly irrelevant to the case at hand? What possible argument could they be trying to make?

Next the advocate depute questioned Sophie about my relationship with Liam, which did not seem significantly less distressing to her. Under oath, she was forced to admit what, I learned, she had taken pains to conceal from me for months: Liam had never viewed me as a friend. He had advocated for my exclusion from their group, stating on multiple occasions that I was "obsessed with him."

Again, this much I was prepared for; even I had deduced that our so-called friendship had largely existed inside my head, an illusion concocted by D.B. to serve as a powder keg for my rage when Liam's eventual "betrayal" came to light. Far more disturbing was Sophie's testimony that on more than one occasion I may have appeared outside Liam's home uninvited, and that the day we went up Arthur's Seat, we had not done so as a pair. It was not he who had left me behind, she attested, but I who had stalked him to the top of the hill.

These revelations struck me with concussive force, leaving me weak and confused. None of this was as I remembered it. But it was well documented that my perception was not to be trusted. Besides, what reason did Sophie have to lie? Some of it even made a disquieting kind of sense. It was one thing for Liam to abandon me on Arthur's Seat, but another that I couldn't even recall having made plans to meet him there in the first place.

Sophie's examination went on for hours, far longer than any before or after. She was weak from standing by the time she stepped down. And yet, for most of the time, the prosecution's central argument remained a mystery to me, each carefully calculated question hinting at a deeper significance that I couldn't quite piece together—not until the advocate depute asked his final question.

"Ms. Grant," he said. "Please, if you would, allow me to summarize. It is a matter of agreement that on the night of the sixteenth of December, the accused accompanied you and Mr. Stewart to a nightclub called the Silver Stag, which the accused recommended himself and which is a known LGBT establishment. After he found Mr. Stewart and Ms. Mankowitz locked in a romantic embrace, the accused became enraged. He screamed and raged that Mr. Stewart had betrayed him, then seemed to experience what has been described as a sort of 'psychotic fit.' Mr. Stewart was last seen walking with the accused down South Bridge later that night, after which he disappeared, only to be found, months later, submerged to his death in St. Margaret's Loch."

"Get on with it, Advocate Depute," chided the judge.

"Indeed. Now, Ms. Grant, given these facts and your own observations of the accused, from his lack of interest in intimate relations with yourself to his alleged obsession with the deceased, do you believe the accused was secretly in love with Liam Stewart and that it was because of this unspoken homosexual desire that—"

The rest of the advocate depute's question was drowned out by the murmurs of the audience, Myles's objection, and the judge's severe admonition.

"Let us not devolve into gossip, Advocate Depute. You know better than that."

"Apologies, Your Lordship." He bowed his head deferentially, but his point had been made.

Finally it made sense. In the absence of any physical evidence or a single witness to the crime, the prosecution was running a smear campaign against me: a feeble attempt to convince the jury I was some kind of repressed homosexual, who, upon discovering Liam in the arms of a woman, had flown into a murderous rage. The suggestion was so utterly ridiculous that I had to stop myself laughing, instead emitting a stifled grunt that earned me a sharp look from my advocate.

But why shouldn't I laugh? It was absurd. To accuse me of wanting anything other than Liam's friendship was not just a lie, but so egregiously transparent that I couldn't believe for a second that it posed a legitimate threat to my freedom.

However, the prosecution's examination was not yet over. Thanking Sophie for her time, the advocate depute invited her to return to her seat and turned to face the court.

"As its last witness, the prosecution calls Oliver Fillmore to the witness box."

The sight of my former flatmate lumbering down the aisle had a darkening effect on my mood. It was the first time I'd laid eyes on him since the night of that disastrous house party and, judging by the scar at the corner of his eye, the incident had left an indelible mark.

"Oath or affirmation?" said the judge, as Ollie stood inside the witness box.

"Oath." With the New Testament held like an alien artifact in his upraised hand, he repeated, "I swear by Almighty God that the evidence I shall give shall be the truth, the whole truth, and nothing but the truth."

"Mr. Fillmore," began the advocate depute, ambling as usual about the court. "I believe you were, until recently, a student at Edinburgh University. Is that correct?"

"Yes."

"What subject were you reading?"

"International relations."

The advocate depute nodded. "Very impressive. Do you recognize the accused?"

"Obviously. He was my flatmate."

Ollie shot me a look laced with malice.

"So you, better than anyone," said the prosecutor, "know what the accused was like behind closed doors. What he got up to when no one was watching."

"I suppose."

"According to your written statement, you left the flat in Lauriston Gardens in February, just one month into the academic term. An odd time to move house, is it not?"

"I didn't have a choice," Ollie said. "He put me in hospital. My family had to bring me back to London, nurse me back to health."

I had to resist rolling my eyes. Still, the advocate depute feigned shock. "Put you in hospital?"

"That's right." Ollie stood a little straighter behind the podium. "It was the night of February seventeenth. I had some people at the flat. A party to celebrate our win against St. Andrews in the water polo final, our first in years." It was clear from the practiced quality of his storytelling that he'd rehearsed this. If not with the prosecution, then perhaps a member of his father's personal PR team. "Some of us were still in our Speedos," he continued. "Grayson liked that." His eyes pierced me like a poison dart. "I noticed him staring. But I'd had a few drinks, you know, to celebrate, and Grayson saw his chance. He forced me into his bedroom. He shut the door and stuck his tongue down my throat. Then he just went mental, like, *literally* mental. He threw me against the wall and started kicking me, punching me. I blacked out. Next thing I knew, I woke up in hospital with a fractured eye socket and three broken ribs."

"I'm so terribly sorry, Mr. Fillmore. That must have been incredibly traumatic."

For a second Ollie looked so miserable that I actually pitied him.

His voice was small, a child's. "Cheers."

"Did you report the incident to police?"

"No, I . . ." He faltered. No doubt the truth, that his father had forbade him in order to avoid a scandal, was off-limits. "I was too scared. That if Grayson found out, he'd come find me."

"Was this the first time the accused had ever demonstrated proclivities suggesting a same-sex attraction?"

Ollie scoffed. "No way."

"No?"

"There was another time, last year," Ollie said, his lingering stare starting to make me uncomfortable. "I was up late playing *FIFA* and Grayson came in, and he had this guy with him. Blotto, both of them. Apparently they'd been to the Christmas markets. I didn't recognize the other guy. At least not then. They went back to Grayson's room, which I thought was weird."

"Weird? Why?"

"Just, because. You don't bring guys into your room unless you're . . . you know."

"Go on."

"I went back to playing my game," Ollie continued, "but I stopped it again, listening. I could—well, I didn't want to. But I could *hear* them."

"Hear them?"

"Fu—" He broke off. "Having it off."

A whisper of shock rippled through the back benches. "You're certain of this?" said the advocate depute.

"Positive."

"You said you didn't recognize the other man when you first saw him."

"Not then. But I did later, after I got out of hospital. I was stuck in bed for days. All I could do was watch telly. That's where I saw him, the guy Grayson brought back."

"On TV?"

"On the news."

"Who was that man, Mr. Fillmore?"

Ollie's eyes flicked to me, and this time they contained something more than hatred. I detected, too, a shimmer of fear.

"That guy they pulled out of the loch. That Liam."

Forty-Two

THE TRIAL WAS as good as over by the time Ollie stepped down from the witness box. Though Myles wouldn't admit it, it was written in the language of his body: the rigid slouch of his torso, the tightness in his jaw. I sensed an anger too, mixed in with the defeat. A desire to say, *I told you this would happen. Now look what you've done.*

Perhaps he was right. Still, I didn't feel I could take all the blame. After all, it was Ollie who had lied. It wasn't true that Liam had come back to my flat after the Christmas markets; that was D.B. And it was D.B., too, who had taken me unawares.

How do you know? When you woke up, you couldn't remember a thing.

Even so. Liam and me? It was impossible—as much for his part as for mine. Liam was a sportsman, a bloke's bloke. The picture of masculinity. No, Ollie was just trying to get back at me by bolstering the prosecution's case, making me out to be some sort of discarded former lover, hell-bent on revenge.

I slept uneasily that night, tossing and turning for hours, before the chattering of my mind melted into a fever of dark and brutal dreams. I remember flashes of them now. Visions of chasing Liam through Holyrood Park at night. His blue eyes staring up at me, bulging with terror, as my hands throttled the milky softness of his neck. Dragging his body through the mud into the loch. The indifferent way the water swallowed him down, shimmering blackly under the moon.

The moment I woke, I rolled over and spat a mouthful of vomit on the floor. I'd had enough nightmares to know that these were something else. I didn't want to find out what.

The taste of bile still stung my throat two hours later as I took my place before the judge and the clerk of court reopened proceedings. Even though the jury's verdict was all but certain, we still had our rebuttal to get through before the end.

Myles did what he could, but it was clear his heart was no longer in it. Without a solid alibi to lean on, the best he could do was call Ollie's testimony into question, establishing, on cross-examination, that he had been drinking the night he saw me come in with Liam and therefore his testimony could not be relied upon.

Even my own stint in the witness box, following a two-day recess for the weekend, added little value to my defense. This was partly my own doing. Myles had advised me to keep off the subject of D.B. "Answer the questions I ask you. *Only* what I ask you. You've got nothing to be gained by going into details, particularly about—all that. You'll just make yourself look mentally unstable." A reasonable request, and the least I could grant my solicitor after tying his hands. But under the septic glare of the courtroom lights, I felt beholden to my affirmation: to speak the truth, the whole truth, and nothing but the truth. For although I couldn't see him in the crowd, D.B. would be watching, measuring my performance against his exacting standards. I could almost hear his voice in my head. *Make Scotland remember the Devil.*

So when Myles asked how I knew Liam Stewart, I didn't stop at "He was my classmate."

"I thought he was my friend," I continued. "But I was wrong about that. That was just an illusion the Devil put in my—"

"Thank you, Grayson."

Myles fixed me with a look like a clout at the back of my head.

After a moment, he hazarded another question. "Grayson, were you at any point in love with Liam Stewart?"

"No," I said, bristling at the suggestion.

"Did you ever engage in sexual or romantic relations with Mr. Stewart?"

"No."

"And did Liam Stewart at any point visit your home at Forty-Two Lauriston Gardens?"

"Never."

"So when Oliver Fillmore says he saw Liam Stewart enter your flat, and that he heard you and Liam engaging in sexual relations inside your bedroom . . ."

"It's a lie," I said, suddenly angry.

"I see—"

"It wasn't Liam who fucked me; it was the Devil."

The hysteria that tore through the courtroom was matched only by the fury in my solicitor's eyes.

He took a very long pause before continuing, and in that pause I sensed a shift in his bearing, like a guardian relinquishing his duty of care. Myles had never thought we could win, but here now was the moment he gave up trying. Although he finished his examination, never departing from the questions we had discussed in our strategy sessions, he did nothing to manage my responses, allowing me to tell my story to the fullest extent the judge would allow.

The prosecution declined to cross-examine me. I suppose I had already given them everything they needed.

On the seventh day of trial, the jury returned the verdict we all had been waiting for. The word, as it echoed through the courtroom, filled me with relief. At last it was over. The dread. The despair. The fear that one day the evil that lived inside me would be my undoing. Twenty-five years' worth of angst snuffed out in a second. The question of a lifetime, finally answered.

"On the charge of murder, the jury finds Grayson Hale guilty."

Best of all, D.B. had gotten what he wanted. His name would be writ large across every newspaper in Scotland, trumpeted across the airwaves, streamed direct to every television. They would hear it, every last one of them. And they would weep to know he was back.

I wished he were there. After all these months, he still hadn't presented himself, not since that night at Sunset Cliffs. I would have liked to see his reaction to the verdict, to at last hear him say, *It is done now. Good job.*

As the bailiffs escorted me from the courtroom, which resounded with the restrained jubilation of the crowd, he appeared: seated at the back of the court in his fine black suit, tracking my progress across the room with hooded eyes.

Within a second, the delighted surprise had been snatched from my heart, the air around me turned frigid and still. For unlike the people all around him, who wept and hugged and praised God, my employer was not rejoicing.

I had never seen him more displeased.

Forty-Three

THE SENTENCING, WHICH took place a week later, was largely a formality. Under Scots law, the automatic penalty for murder is life imprisonment. It is further mandated that each such sentence include a "punishment part," the length of time a convict must serve before being eligible for a supervised release. Myles had reassured me that the longest punishment part ever given in Scotland was thirty-seven years. At a paltry thirty-one, mine meant that, with good behavior, I could be out before my sixtieth birthday.

Like a wave breaking at the base of a cliff, this knowledge washed over me.

For the time being HMP Edinburgh would remain my home, but I was moved to a new cell, in the segregation unit.

"Segregation?" I said to the officer who came to collect me.

"Aye. Ye'll prob'ly know it as solitary."

The room was basic and institutional, white walls and metal fixtures—but a small TV, a steady supply of books from the unit library, and regular visits with Kathy, the mental health counselor, prevented me from missing the company of others. I was adjusting admirably, even Kathy said so—until D.B. began to appear.

He was different this time. More a shadow than a man. A formless wraith, whispering from the darkness that lay just beyond the reach of my lamp.

It was constant, the whispering. Working upon me every hour of the day. So constant that sometimes I forgot it was there. His words slid into bed with me as I tried to sleep . . . infiltrated the pages of my book as I attempted to read. They were the food on my lunch tray, filling me up with their evil. The hand under my sheets, jerking my cock.

They told me to do things . . . bad things.

They told me to hurt people.

Like a tuneful song, they stuck in my head; I found myself repeating them without realizing I was doing it. They piloted my body, such that it was no longer my own. One day in the exercise yard, I stabbed a man—ballpoint pen to the throat. Though I don't remember it happening, there were witnesses . . . CCTV . . . it's lucky I wasn't killed—or unlucky maybe.

Sixteen months I've been in this cell, and still he won't stop coming . . . won't stop whispering . . . I don't care what Myles says, they'll never let me out now—not after everything he's put me up to. My hands still tremble with the memory of the day I awoke on the floor in a pool of my blood, bits of my arm still stuck in my teeth and every inch of the walls covered in the same crusted words, upways and longways, in letters big and small, again and again and again . . . *HIS NAME IS DB HIS NAME IS DB HIS NAME IS DB HIS NAME IS DB.* Why does he haunt me? Didn't I do what he asked? I came back when I could have stayed . . . told the truth when I could have lied . . . refused to deny him when I could have been free.

He ought to face me like a man, but he won't come. Merely whispers. Sometimes I talk back to the darkness. "What do you want from me? What will it take?"

He says, *What I've always wanted . . . to make them remember . . .*

"But I DID," I plead. "I DID!"

You lie . . .

I cast my mind back to that day—a lifetime ago, it seems—as we strolled along the Canongate, talking about fear. *You're just the kind of writer I need*, he said. *The very person to make Scotland remember the Devil.*

That's what he had paid you for, remember? A writing job. What were the words in the contract? *One original manuscript of literary nonfiction.* Long ago I had decided the book was a lie . . . a shiny deception created to entrap me in his web of sin—but what if I was wrong? After all, a BOOK was what he had talked about for months—and the only thing I hadn't yet given him . . . but how could he expect me to write it where I was now, with no RESOURCES, no NOTES, no PRIMARY TEXTS??

Maybe he doesn't want that kind of book . . .

Literary nonfiction—that could be ANYTHING! A biography, a collection of essays, a personal history . . .

MY personal history???

There would be an appetite for it, surely, now the whole country knew my name. They'd want to hear MY side of the story, they'd want to know my SECRETS . . . They'd line up for hours to get their hands on a copy—thousands of people, maybe MILLIONS! It would dominate the bestseller list for weeks . . . whole WEBSITES and PODCASTS devoted to its dissection . . . It would spread across the internet like a raging FIRE . . . the one from my dreams, reducing the world to ash . . . Not a single person would be able to escape it . . .

But of course, that's what he wanted . . . what he always had wanted. YES, how could I be so STUPID?! Not a boring old research project, no—an autobiography, a SHOCKING TELL-ALL. *The Memoirs and Confessions of Grayson Hale*—this, the very book you hold in your hands . . . it has all led up to this—your eyes on these words, at this very moment. Yes, his whispers tell me so . . . I can feel him in the room with me even as I commit these words to paper . . . reading over my shoulder—his breath warm at my ear, egging me on—

TELL them, he whispers . . . *TELL them everything!!*

MAKE THEM, every one of them, REMEMBER THE DEVIL.

Editor's Note
Exhibit V

News posting from the Scottish Prison Service website on 24 January 2019.

Death in Custody

Grayson Hale, 25, a prisoner at HMP Edinburgh, has died. He was convicted at Edinburgh High Court on 28 June 2017. Police Scotland have been advised and the matter reported to the procurator fiscal. A fatal accident inquiry will be held in due course.

Afterword

AND SO IT goes without saying, our author never did see his book published. Just two weeks shy of his twenty-sixth birthday, Grayson Matthew Hale was discovered hanged in his cell. The unidentified lacerations marking his body, as it was laid to rest in an unmarked grave at Saughton Cemetery, in Edinburgh, were heralded as the ultimate testament to the singularity of his life and the mystery of his death.

Although we may never know for sure what occurred that night, what remains of Hale's correspondence may provide some insight into his final anguish. Letters found among his personal possessions reveal that, in the three months preceding his demise, he contacted at least six publishers and more than two dozen literary agents in an attempt to secure a deal to publish his memoir. The offer was rejected by all who returned his letters, and likely many more who did not. As one agent, who has asked to remain anonymous, wrote:

> Although I agree that your manuscript would generate sufficient public interest to merit its publication, I am afraid that you will be hard-pressed to find a publisher amenable to giving a convicted killer

a platform to profit off the death of an innocent victim—less out of respect for the deceased, you understand, than for fear of incurring lasting damage to their public image.

Hale's psychiatric file further suggests that this disappointment may have driven him to suicide. Case notes authored by Kathleen Prichard, mental health counselor at HMP Edinburgh, show that Hale became extremely distressed after failing to find a publisher for his book, triggering what she referred to as "a rapid deterioration of his mental integrity." In a report filed just days before Hale's body was found, she observed:

Patient's physical demeanor virtually unrecognizable. Hardly ceased rocking in his chair or muttering under his breath for duration of session. Did not seem to acknowledge my presence at all. From what could be gleaned from mutterings, patient continues to suffer from delusion that if his book is not published, the Devil will never depart from him, nor cease to compel him to commit wicked acts against himself or others. Patient complained too of a persistent "gibbering" that was audible only to him.

Given Hale's heightened state of psychosis, Prichard recommended that he be placed on immediate suicide watch, but due to unspecified administrative delays, he was not scheduled to be moved into twenty-four-hour care until three days later—by which time Hale was already dead.

When I received Hale's case files from the National Records of Scotland following my successful appeal to the information commissioner, it was his manuscript I was most eager to read. Like many, I had spent the last two and a half years consumed with the mystery of the Devil's Advocate, and it had turned my life upside down. My career had ground to a halt, my health deteriorated, and my relationship fallen apart, all because of that lingering question: Was Grayson Hale simply insane, or had he really been recruited by the Devil to kill? At last I had it in my hands, the one document that might be able to shed light on the enigma that was the Devil's Advocate. But to my surprise, it was Ms. Prichard's reports that ultimately I found far more illuminating, for their incisive insight into the troubled workings of our author's mind, and confirmation of the past trauma I long had suspected.

In a report filed on 10 April 2018, Prichard documented that after months of therapy, Hale experienced a breakthrough, gaining access to long-repressed memories of having been abused by his brother, Nathaniel, often at the behest of their mother. The abuse typically occurred after the youngest Hale engaged in so-called acts of depravity such as carnal thoughts, sexual arousal, and masturbation. The abuse, Prichard noted—and as we well know—ranged from physical to psychological, including hitting, kicking, restraint lasting hours, and repeated assertions that the Devil would come if said "depravity" did not stop. The case notes continue:

> As a result of this abuse, patient learned to conflate sexual desire with evil and even the demonic. It was likely this conflation that led patient to develop Devil-related phobia and hallucinations during early adolescence, a peak age for sexual self-discovery. It has been well documented that sexual repression, particularly among men, can lead to extreme aggression and even violence in adulthood. It is therefore reasonable to conclude that patient's history of abuse, coupled with a restrictive upbringing fueled by religious fanaticism, may have resulted in later psychosis and homicidal tendencies.
>
> Furthermore, although patient identifies as heterosexual, the erotic nature of his demonic delusions (e.g., that he met the Devil at an LGBT establishment, and that the Devil penetrated him without his knowledge and "implanted him with his seed") strongly suggests that patient's repression is, and always has been, both homosexual in nature and largely unconscious.

Ms. Prichard, the only known mental health professional to have evaluated Hale, appears to confirm that he was deeply disturbed, his visions of the Devil nothing more than a disorder of the mind born from abuse and long-standing repression.

This made sense to me, especially after receiving an unexpected email from Carlos Fernandez, Hale's erstwhile friend, the day after our explosive initial interview. I'm deeply grateful to Mr. Fernandez for bravely allowing me to transcribe that message below, for its importance to Hale's story cannot be overstated.

Hey Daniella,

Sorry for what happened yesterday. I shouldn't have hung up on you like that. I hope you can accept my apology.

I've never spoken about what happened between Grayson and me behind the shed, and when you asked me about it I just kind of freaked out. But I think it's important you know what happened.

As you said, Reyna was watching me and Grayson at the Hales' place that day. Ed and Vera were attending a conference for the cult. The three of us were hanging out in the house, drawing or coloring or something. When Reyna left to go to the bathroom Grayson asked me to accompany him outside. He said there was something behind the shed he wanted to show me.

When we got back there I was confused because there was nothing there but some old lumber.

Then Grayson asked if I wanted to see his penis.

I said no but he insisted, and afterward he wanted me to show him mine back. Although I didn't want to, I did it to make him stop asking.

When Reyna showed up, Grayson made it seem like we were just playing pretend with invisible guns. She believed him.

After it happened I was really freaked out and ashamed, and ended up telling Nathaniel. He said Grayson wouldn't get in trouble, but the next time I came for fellowship, there was a cast on Grayson's arm and he wouldn't look at me. His mom was telling people he fell off the monkey bars at recess, but I knew that was a lie. We went to the same school. Grayson didn't like to play outside. Usually he stayed in and helped the teacher.

I still don't want to comment on what might've been happening behind closed doors, but I think you can connect the dots. I've always felt guilty for telling on Grayson, but I know I shouldn't.

Sorry again and I hope this helps you make sense of his story. For the record, I think he was a good kid. It couldn't have been easy growing up in that environment, especially . . . well, I think you get it.

Carlos

Between this illuminating testimony and Ms. Prichard's previous assessment, I was prepared to close the book on the mystery of the Devil's Advocate.

For twenty-five years Grayson Hale lived in fear, less of the Devil than of himself. Suppressing his most essential human need bought him a few years, but by the time he moved to Scotland in the summer of 2016, cracks were already beginning to show. His mind, left mangled by his family's abuse, invented the character of Donald Blackburn as an expression of his repressed homosexual longing.

Then he met Liam Stewart, a man like no other, beautiful and kind and brilliant to boot, and our author committed a fatal flaw: he fell in love. Desperate to reconcile his infatuation with his heteronormative self-view, he deceived himself that they had been friends for months, and that his fondness for Stewart was nothing more than platonic.

But Liam, too, was fighting a secret battle against his own desire. Anonymous sources close to the Stewart family report that Liam, although outwardly supportive of LGBT rights and marriage equality, had long denied his own bisexual tendencies out of fear of repercussions from his father, Livingston FC manager Paul Stewart, for whose son a strict adherence to normative notions of masculinity was not negotiable.

"Liam was never allowed to express himself," said a family friend. "Like when he was really young, he wanted to do gymnastics. He always talked about it, but his father wouldn't let him because he said it was a girl's sport. Made him do football instead, for years. Liam didn't even enjoy it. He just did it to please his dad."

The strictures of machismo plagued Stewart into early adulthood. Edinburgh resident Peter Callahan, who claims to have engaged in a months-long affair with Stewart during their first year of undergraduate studies, alleges that, after Liam's father found out about the relationship, Stewart summarily cut all ties with Callahan and denied the relationship had ever occurred.

It is a pattern Stewart seemed keen not to repeat. Made uncomfortable by Hale's unsubtle affections, possibly because he returned them, Stewart asked Sophia Grant to exclude Hale from their friend group. She refused, however, and one night, after a few glasses of mulled wine at the Christmas markets, he and Grayson made a mistake that would change the course of their lives: they went back to Hale's flat and made love.

Whilst Hale reconciled the encounter as an act of demoniac rape, Stewart, frightened by what they had done, spurned Hale as he had Callahan, claiming, among friends, that Hale was "obsessed with him." He even hid the affair from Grant, despite her being aware and accepting of his sexuality, perhaps because she was dating Hale herself and would have been devastated to learn her best friend had betrayed her.

The emotional fallout from Stewart's rejection appears to have triggered an escalation of Hale's aggression. He began to lash out at strangers, even attacked a same-sex couple at Waverley Mall, deluding himself that the Devil had conferred on him, through insemination, his power to control the actions of others.

Unbeknownst to Grayson, it was his own actions that were beyond his control. At the time when he most needed help, he shut himself away, building up rage and hurt over Liam's rejection. When finally came the night of Sophie's birthday, the night he discovered his former lover in the arms of another, he suffered a mental break from which he would never recover. He murdered Liam Stewart. Some speculate one murder led to another, when, months later, Vera Hale was slaughtered in her sleep less than two miles from the hotel where her younger son was staying, just hours after she allegedly visited his room and disowned him for being "wicked" and "unnatural." Convinced he would be haunted by "the Devil" forever, that his shameful desire would "never depart from him, nor cease to compel him to commit wicked acts against himself or others," he ultimately, tragically, took his own life.

Perhaps it is no coincidence that the man Grayson admired above all others, his own father, had met the same desperate end. It's impossible to know for certain whether Edmund Hale was a closeted homosexual, but it makes one wonder about the note he left his son before he died. "How I wish I could go back and unbind the shackles of my life—discover in [Scotland] the part of myself I didn't know existed, and not flee from it but welcome it like an old friend. It's too late for me—but there's time for you still."

Time for Grayson to do what, I wonder: resist the Devil that was waiting for him in Scotland? Or step into the fire, like Edmund himself never could?

Although on the face of things Hale's psychosis is hard to dispute, I must admit that certain elements of his narrative continue to trouble me, making me question whether there isn't more to his story than Ms. Prichard's interpretation allows.

For one: Edmund Hale's diaries. Grayson describes, in his manuscript, a green-suede journal in which his father described meeting a stranger who bears a striking resemblance to Donald Blackburn. The day Grayson returned to Scotland, he must have had this journal on his person, for upon his death it was found secreted in his living quarters, along with a battered, hardcover copy of *Jack and the Devil's Horn*. How these items found their way inside Grayson's cell is unclear. However, prison records show that, after he died, they were returned to his next of kin, his brother, Nathaniel.

The older Hale son was kind enough to share a copy of this diary with me last year. Frankly, I didn't know what to expect to find in its pages, and was shocked to discover they were exactly as Grayson had represented. If his father's personal writings are to be believed, Edmund Hale too met a man with the initials D.B. while studying in Edinburgh in the 1970s, a man whose coercive and allegedly violent behavior brings Grayson's employer instantly to mind.

A coincidence?

Perhaps.

Still, it is enough to stoke the embers of my unease.

That, and the unanswered question of what person, creature, or spirit may have attacked Hale the night he died, tearing his clothing and leaving his body marred with wounds like "claw marks from a small, three-fingered animal." Given what we now know about Hale's so-called hallucinations, it is hard to read that description and not think instantly of fiends. There too remains the question of the triad of scars on Hale's arm: evidence of the Devil's mark, I ask myself, or that Hale may have been the victim of familial abuse before he even learned to speak?

Here I find myself at the end of this book, surrounded by reams of research and evidentiary documents, and still Hale's story doesn't fully add up. In my foreword to this manuscript, I posed a question to you, reader. I asked: What is this strange memoir? An imaginative fiction? A first-person account of one man's descent into madness? Or worse, a warning sent straight from the depths of hell?

To you I say now, I still am not sure.

But in the end, the nature of Hale's manuscript matters little. Whether fact or fiction, his story is fit for purpose: it reminds us all that the Devil lives on in Scotland, in the darkness that bides within the human soul. That no matter how decent we flatter ourselves to be, we are each capable of an evil that our minds may not even be able to fathom.

Indeed, the Devil is alive, in you—and in me.

You would do well never again to forget it.

—D.B.

Acknowledgments

These few brief words are unequal to the gratitude I feel for all who made this book possible with their time, talent, and support. To my incredible agent, Maria Whelan, I am so grateful to call you my friend as well as my representative. Thank you for loving and believing in this book, for seeing its potential more clearly than I ever could, and for being a joy to work with every day.

To my brilliant editor, Loan Le, thank you for your editorial insight, your tireless dedication, and your deeply twisted taste in fiction. You may have a passion for horror stories, but working with you is anything but. Thanks also to those who worked behind the scenes at Atria Books to bring my nightmare of a novel to worrying fruition: Libby McGuire, Lindsay Sagnette, Dana Trocker, Nicole Bond, David Brown, Dayna Johnson, Paige Lytle, Iris Chen, Kathleen Rizzo, Erica Ferguson, Dana Sloan, Elizabeth Hitti, Claire Sullivan, and James Iacobelli.

I am indebted to the friends who read early versions of *A History of Fear* and whose support, both then and long before this novel existed, kept me going through years of uncertainty: Melissa Wells, Alex Stephenson, and especially Maya Lim, the best critique partner I could ask for, whose thoughtful feedback was instrumental in helping me discover, after years of solitary toil, what this book was meant to be.

I am deeply appreciative of the authors both contemporary and classic whose works paved the way for this book in one way or another. Among them are Scottish novelist James Hogg, whose 1824 masterpiece *The Private Memoirs and Confessions of a Justified Sinner* inspired not only this book but my enduring fascination with Scottish demonic fiction; Scottish storyteller Duncan Williamson and editor Linda Williamson, whose collection *Jack and the Devil's Purse: Scottish Traveller Tales* provided the model for my own "Jack and the Devil's Horn"; and Dr. Michelle D. Brock, whose excellent book *Satan and the Scots: The Devil in Post-Reformation Scotland, c.1560–1700* was a lifesaving resource as I attempted, along with my protagonist Grayson, to envision what D.B.'s mysterious book might look like. Any inaccuracies are my own.

Of course, this book would not exist were it not for the city of Edinburgh, the University of Edinburgh, and the faculty, administrators, and students who inspired, challenged, and supported me every day I was there. Thank you all.

To my parents, Mary and Bryan, who have supported my writing journey in their own meaningful ways, you have my never-ending love and appreciation.

And finally, to my funny, handsome British husband, Adam, who never begrudged the endless hours I spent at my desk instead of by his side, who never tired of reading drafts or being asked, "How would a British person say this?"—and most of all, who never tired of me—thank you. I love you always.

About the Author

Luke Dumas was born and raised in San Diego, California, and received his master's degree in creative writing from the University of Edinburgh. His work has appeared in *Hobart*, *Last Exit*, and the queer anthology *The Whole Alphabet: The Light and the Dark*, among other publications. *A History of Fear* is his debut novel.